the POISON of POLYGAMY

China and the West in the Modern World

William Christie, Series Editor

The China and the West in the Modern World series publishes original, peer-reviewed research on cultural, diplomatic, and trade relations between China and the West from the accession of the Manchu Qing dynasty in 1644 to the present. The series brings into play different national and disciplinary perspectives to achieve a more thorough and cross-culturally nuanced understanding of the political, economic, and cultural background to the negotiations and realignments currently underway between China and Western nations.

The Poison of Polygamy
Wong Shee Ping, translated by Ely Finch

小說會社
多妻毒

the POISON *of* POLYGAMY

A SOCIAL NOVEL

Wong Shee Ping

Translated by Ely Finch

SYDNEY UNIVERSITY PRESS

First published by Sydney University Press
Translation and translator's introduction © Ely Finch 2019
Historical introduction © Mei-fen Kuo and Michael Williams 2019
© Sydney University Press 2019

Sydney University Press
Fisher Library F03
University of Sydney NSW 2006
Australia
sup.info@sydney.edu.au
sydneyuniversitypress.com.au

 A catalogue record for this book is
available from the National Library
of Australia

ISBN 9781743326022 paperback

Book design by Duncan Blachford, Typography Studio
Maps by Peter Johnson

The creators gratefully acknowledge the support of the Victorian Government and
Public Record Office Victoria for making this project possible.

The creators gratefully acknowledge the role of the Chinese Australian Historical
Society and its consultant historian Michael Williams in initiating this project.

Contents

LIST OF FIGURES   VII

WONG SHEE PING 黃樹屏   I
    Michael Williams

WHY IS POLYGAMY POISONOUS? AN HISTORICAL CONTEXT   II
    Mei-fen Kuo and Michael Williams

TRANSLATOR'S INTRODUCTION   37
    Ely Finch

THE POISON OF POLYGAMY   79

ACKNOWLEDGEMENTS   401

APPENDICES
    I: CHARACTER NAMES AND CONNOTATIONS   407
    II: THE ROMANISATIONS USED IN THE TRANSLATION
    AND THE FOOTNOTES   415
    III: BUSINESS NAMES   419
    IV: THE NEWSPAPER BUSINESS AND CHINESE AUSTRALIANS   423
      Mei-fen Kuo
    V: PLACE NAMES   435

MAPS   441

ABOUT THE CONTRIBUTORS   445

List of Figures

Figure 1: The author Wong Shee Ping in about 1915.   VIII

Figure 2: Performance of a drama written by Wong Shee Ping, Melbourne, 1920–22.   4

Figure 3: Wong Shee Ping in about 1920.   7

Figure 4: A dinner fork from Melbourne's Pekin Cafe.   9

Figure 5: Street scenes from an 1899 newspaper feature on the Chinese community of Little Bourke Street, Melbourne.   17

Figure 6: Melbourne's See Yup Society Temple.   21

Figure 7: The Woah Hawp Canton gold mine at Ballarat.   23

Figure 8: Chinese Nationalist Party convention, Melbourne, December 1921.   30

Figure 9: Preface to "醉古堂劍掃"   51

Figure 10: Advertisement for the new novel *World of Robbers* by the author of *The Poison of Polygamy*.   60

Figure 11: The foreword to the first instalment of *The Detective's Shadow, Chinese Republic News*, 21 June 1919.   62

Figure 12: The "Social Lens" illustration that accompanied each instalment of the novel.   68

Figure 13: The masthead of the *Chinese Times*.   427

Map I: Empires (the latter half of the 19th century).   441

Map II: The See Yip Region in the timeframe of the novel.   442

Map III: Melbourne's Chinese precinct.   443

Figure 1: The author Wong Shee Ping in about 1915, in a studio portrait taken at the Burlington Studios, 294 Bourke Street, Melbourne. (Kuo Min Tang Society of Melbourne)

Wong Shee Ping 黃樹屏

Michael Williams

The Poison of Polygamy's 1909–1910 serialisation in the *Chinese Times* was published without its author being named, a not unusual circumstance for the times. However, references discovered in other stories published in this and another newspaper make it clear that the author is Wong Shee Ping (黃樹屏), also known as Wong Yau Kung (黃右公/黃又公).[1] Beginning with that name a picture of the author has now gradually evolved that includes not only elements of his life before and after the novel's publication, his Christian ministry, political affiliations and additional literary efforts, but also the fact that descendants via his Australian-born daughter, Bonnie Ping, live in Australia today.

Wong Shee Ping was in his thirties when he wrote *The Poison of Polygamy*, having been born in Kaiping County (開平) in the 1870s.[2]

---

1   See the Translator's Introduction, footnote 8, for a more detailed explanation. Shee Ping was his original name, and Yau Kung was adopted as his pen or courtesy name.

2   Also known as Hoi Ping or Hoy Ping. His exact year of birth is uncertain. In his 1919 Chinese Nationalist Party membership record, his date of birth is 1875 (Sydney KMT Archives, Records of membership [Melbourne, Perth, Broome, NZ and Hamilton], 1916–1924, 523-01-0152-108); in his January 1923 marriage certificate it is 1878 (State of Victoria, Certificate Marriage, No. 946, 31 January 1923); and in his December 1923 CEDT it is 1871 (National Archives of Australia, ST84/1, 1923/358/31-40).

Kaiping had long been one of the primary districts in southern China from which people travelled throughout the Pacific and so it is not surprising that even before he left home Wong Shee Ping had been trained as a Christian preacher as well as in traditional Chinese culture.[3] That Wong Shee Ping would go to Melbourne was no coincidence either, as his father was a shareholder in Sun Goon Shing & Co. at 198 Little Bourke Street, Melbourne and his brother Wong Shee Fan (黃樹藩) later became its manager.[4] This brother was also part owner of the Pekin Cafe and was so immersed in the Australian ethos that at one time he was sued for unpaid overtime by a unionist waiter.[5] Wong Shee Ping himself was originally appointed a compositor for the *Chinese Times* before joining the editorial team with Lew Goot Chee in 1910.[6]

Wong Shee Ping's Australian connections were, therefore, well established by the time he arrived in Melbourne. More than this, it can be seen that it was his family's stories that inspired and shaped the plot and characters of the novel. Not only had his father been a gold miner but, like Ching Nam in *The Poison of Polygamy* (who had the same name), he owned a mine in Ballarat and employed European miners to work it for him.[7] Even more closely connected, an incident in the novel involving a girl reflects a case prominently covered by Melbourne's English-language press that took place on premises associated with Wong Shee Ping's father's business

---

3   Yong, *The New Gold Mountain*, p. 129. Wong Shee Ping was trained in China as a preacher: see A. W. Stephenson, *A Hundred Years: A Statement of the Development and Accomplishments of Churches of Christ in Australia* (Melbourne: Stone-Campbell Books, 1946), p. 67, available online at http://digitalcommons.acu.edu/crs_books/398

4   *Chinese Times*, 19 February 1902, p. 1 and *Chinese Times*, 21 November 1914, p. 2.

5   *Age*, 6 December 1912, p. 13.

6   *Chinese Australian Herald*, 22 October 1910, p. 2. Lew Goot Chee arrived in Australia in 1908; *Critic*, 15 April 1908, p. 25.

7   *Ballarat Star*, 28 July 1883, p. 4.

interests.[8] Regarding the factual basis for other characters and plot incidents we can only speculate. But that Wong Shee Ping was not only thoroughly aware of Chinese-Australian history but also intimately connected with it there can be no doubt. Thus Wong Shee Ping arrived in Melbourne as a young educated man well versed in the literary traditions of China and keen to engage with the modern world, to which he was anxious China should belong. For a man of Wong Shee Ping's background, the modernisation of China meant foremost the removal of the non-Han Manchu rulers of the Qing dynasty and their replacement with a modern republican form of government.[9] He was therefore involved from an early stage with those who later established the Kuomintang (KMT) or Nationalist Party, which governed or aspired to govern mainland China from 1912 until 1949. But for Wong Shee Ping China's modernisation also meant reform of its culture, a reform that involved religion and education. These were for him interlinking concepts, believing as he did that Christianity was the only doctrine that could save China and the Chinese.[10] To this end Wong Shee Ping was a leading Christian pastor, a writer of novels (and at least two plays), as well as a newspaper editor, and in his later life a republican government official.

Wong Shee Ping rose to the position of editor of the *Chinese Times* after Lew Goot Chee moved in 1914 to the United States. Such a position was heavily political and in 1918 Wong Shee Ping was elected Chinese-language Secretary (中文書記) of the new 奧洲華僑維持禁例會, "Maintenance Association of Australian Chinese Against the Prohibitory Regulations", an association founded to resist the White

---

8   *Weekly Times*, 18 August 1888, p. 11 and *Ballarat Star*, 26 January 1882, p. 4.
9   See *Chinese Times*, 26 June 1909, p. 9 and 11 October 1911, p. 13, for examples of speeches by Wong Shee Ping on these themes.
10   *Chinese Times*, 13 November 1920, p. 5 in an open letter to his fellow party (KMT) members.

Figure 2: Performance of a drama written by Wong Shee Ping, who is seated front and centre in suit and bow tie. Temperance Hall, Russell Street, Melbourne, 1920–22. (Kuo Min Tang Society of Melbourne)

Australia Policy and in particular to re-institute permission for Chinese wives to come to Australia.[11] Wong also found himself criticised by his political opponents, who used the rival *Tung Wah Times* newspaper to do so. In 1919 he was described as being "silver-tongued"[12]—though not, it appears, in English; in 1921 he needed an interpreter to be interviewed by a Perth English-language newspaper after more than a decade in Australia.[13] The *Tung Wah Times* also insinuated that Wong was formerly an opium addict. While this may be a piece of scandal from a political rival, it could also hint that the strong condemnation of opium usage found in the novel was inspired by an ex-addict's abhorrence.[14]

Wong moved to Sydney and served, from June 1919 to late 1920, as acting editor of the *Chinese Republic News*.[15] At the same time he was very active in Australia's Christian communities and in the early 1920s was appointed by the Federal Foreign Mission Committee of the Churches of Christ Conference (外國總傳道會) to travel and preach on behalf of the church in South Australia and Western Australia.[16] At one point he resigned as editor to pursue this pastoral work.[17] Despite this change of occupation, on these pastoral visits Wong also helped to establish branches of the Chinese Nationalist Party in Adelaide and Perth.[18] His political efforts were not limited to

---

11 *Chinese Republic News*, 9 November 1918, p. 7 and 24 August 1918, p. 6.
12 *Tung Wah Times*, 20 December 1919, p. 8 and again criticised 14 February 1920, p. 8.
13 *Call*, 1 July 1921, p. 1.
14 *Tung Wah Times*, 20 March 1924, p. 7.
15 *Chinese Republic News*, 21 June 1919, p. 6 and 12 December 1919, p. 6; *Chinese Times*, 20 November 1920, p. 5.
16 *Chinese Republic News*, 13 November 1920, p. 6; *Call* (Perth), 1 July 1921, p. 1; *Daily News* (Perth), 9 April 1921, p. 5.
17 *Chinese Republic News*, 10 July 1920, p. 6.
18 See Mei-fen Kuo and Judith Brett, *Unlocking the History of the Australasian Kuo Min Tang 1911–2013* (Melbourne: Australian Scholarly Publishing, 2013, and *Chinese Republic News*, 6 November 1920, p. 6, for his itinerary.

giving speeches, and in 1921 he and other leading party members in Australia sought and secured—in a move very much in line with the views on women expressed in the novel—the approval of the party's leader, Dr Sun Yat-sen, to exempt female members from membership fees and to open committee membership to women. Finally, among all this political and proselytising activity, he also found time to write plays, which were performed in Sydney and Melbourne in connection with Chinese Nationalist Party conventions held in 1920 and 1921.[19]

When the *Chinese Times* was re-launched, this time in Sydney in 1922, Wong was again its editor.[20] The following year he married Ellen Louisa (Cissie) Sam, and a daughter, Maude Florence (Bonnie) was born very soon after.[21] Both the wedding and birth occurred in Melbourne, and Bonnie would go on to marry and raise children of her own without knowing more than the vaguest details of her father.[22] This was because within a year of his marriage Wong Shee Ping had left Australia, never to return.[23]

His Australian ties were not cut entirely, however, and in 1924 he was representing Australasian KMT branches as an official delegate to the inaugural National Congress of the Chinese Nationalist Party in Canton. Following the convention, he was appointed by Dr Sun Yat-sen as one of the executive members of the party's first Central Propaganda Committee. His editing work also continued, and soon after this political appointment Wong became involved with the *Hong Kong Morning Post* (香港

19   *Chinese Times*, 4 February 1922, p. 5; *Chinese Australian Herald*, 1 May 1920, p. 2; *Chinese Republic News*, 10 July 1920, p. 6.
20   *Sun*, 27 August 1922, p. 2.
21   Births, Deaths and Marriages, Victoria online index. The Sams were a Tasmanian Irish-Chinese family.
22   Correspondence with Mar family members, July 2018.
23   *Chinese Republic News*, 5 January 1924, p. 6.

Figure 3: Wong Shee Ping in about 1920. (Photograph courtesy of the author's family)

晨報). From 1929 to 1931 Wong was an executive member of the Overseas Chinese Affairs Commission of China's government.[24] In the middle of the 1920s Wong Shee Ping also held a number of positions as "County Head" in Guangdong Province while continuing to be attacked by his enemies in Sydney's *Tung Wah Times*.[25] However, by the end of the decade, and looking considerably more gaunt in a final 1929 image, there is no further mention of Wong Shee Ping—or Wong Yau Kung—in the English or Chinese press in Australia. His ultimate fate remains a mystery. A great deal more detail could be provided concerning Wong Shee Ping, his life in Australia and perhaps with further research, also about his life (or at least his death) after years in China. Here it is sufficient to emphasise that it is to this member of the Chinese diaspora of the beginning of the twentieth century, a man bridging both traditional Chinese and modern culture just as the empire of China was transforming into a republic, that we owe the dramatic, political and moral Chinese-Australian tale that is *The Poison of Polygamy*.

*

As interesting as the original story of *The Poison of Polygamy* is, and as exciting as its re-publication over 100 years later in bilingual form, the discovery of Wong Shee Ping's continuing Australian connection is also not without its fascination. The keen investigations of Ely Finch and Mei-fen Kuo proved that the originally anonymous author of the novel was in fact Wong Shee Ping, who

---

24   See a letter from Wong to the Central Committee of the KMT in 1924, Archive of KMT in Taipei, '漢 7959'. *List of Officials of the Government of the Republic of China, 1925–49* (國民政府官職年表 *Guominzhengfu Guanzhi Nianbiao*) (Beijing: Chunghwa Publishing, 1995), p. 283.

25   *Chinese Republic News*, 7 February 1925, p. 6; *Tung Wah Times*, 21 March 1925, p. 5; *Chinese Republic News*, 12 December 1925, p. 8.

Figure 4: A dinner fork from Melbourne's Pekin Cafe. The cafe was next door to the *Chinese Times* on Russell Street and part owned by the author's brother Wong Shee Fan. (Photograph courtesy of the author's family)

was also known as Wong Yau Kung.[26] As was often the case with Chinese names in an anglophone environment, the Wong family name was replaced with his given name, so that he became Mr Shee Ping, and even Pastor Shee Ping.

Knowing this allowed further Trove searching by Ely Finch, who discovered that a Bonnie Shee Ping of Essendon in Melbourne had married a Raymond Honman Mar of Sydney in 1954.[27] This led to confirmation via the birth and marriage records that "Joseph Wong Shee Ping" had married "Louise Ellen Sam" in 1923 and that Bonnie Shee Ping was the daughter of our author.[28] But were there any further descendants? Mar is a fairly common family name and name-by-name inquiry through the telephone book was a daunting prospect.[29] A chance stab at tracing Raymond Honman Mar's middle name, as it is less common, turned up a link. "Honman", despite its possibly Chinese look, is in fact British in origin. However, the "false" Honman who had been contacted kindly pointed out a Commonwealth Gazette entry of 1981 that had not previously been seen. In this Bonnie and Raymond Mar are mentioned as certified tax agents, and

---

26   See the Translator's Introduction.
27   *Argus*, 24 June 1954, p. 8.
28   State of Victoria, Certificate of Marriage, No. 946, 31 January 1923.
29   There were at least forty-five Mars in New South Wales alone.

most decisively for the research, that they then lived in Ryde.[30] This allowed for a quick check as to the number of people named Mar in the Sydney suburb of Ryde, which revealed a mere four. A call to the first on this list found one of four sons of Bonnie and Raymond, who confirmed that the descendants of Wong Shee Ping in Australia were numerous and were delighted to discover a long-lost grandfather. A delight only tinged with sorrow that their mother Bonnie had not lived to learn more of the father she never knew.

---

30   Commonwealth Gazette, 1981, p. 74, and correspondence with Louise Honman, June 2018.

Why Is Polygamy Poisonous?
An Historical Context

Mei-fen Kuo and Michael Williams

The Poison of Polygamy now ranks as the first novel of Chinese Australia, leap frogging by more than half a century all previous contenders. But this serialised novel, which first appeared in Melbourne's *Chinese Times* in 1909, is much more than the novelty of its ranking. It is a remarkable imaginative glimpse into the world of the Chinese diaspora, of the historical Chinese-Australian experience, of late-Qing revolutionary beliefs, of Chinese literary culture, and perhaps most rarely, of the role and feelings of the women of the diaspora. *The Poison of Polygamy* is also a dramatic, fast-paced story intended to excite as well as educate its readers, readers now extended to those of English by this meticulous yet highly accessible translation.[1]

---

1   The many much shorter pieces of literature appearing in Australia's Chinese-language media since the 1890s are well documented in Haizhi Luo's "Towards a Modern Diasporic Literary Tradition: The Evolution of Australian Chinese Language Fiction from 1894 to 1912" (Masters thesis, University of New South Wales, 2017). Luo has also suggested that the first Australian Chinese-language novel to appear after this novel was Huynh Huy's *Red Shadow* (苦海情鴛), published in 1985 (Brian Castro's *Birds of Passage*, 1983, being of course in English). See also Zhong Huang and Wenche Ommundsen, "Poison, Polygamy and Postcolonial Politics: The First Chinese Australian Novel", *Journal of Postcolonial Writing* 52, no. 5 (2016): pp. 533–44. For an explanation of what is meant by "Literary" Chinese, see the Translator's Introduction.

The Poison of Polygamy was originally serialised in Melbourne's *Chinese Times* newspaper, in roughly weekly instalments, from June 1909 to December 1910.[2] The story is a morality tale that follows the highs and lows in the life of anti-hero Wong Sheung Hong, his wife, and the many characters he comes in contact with, during time spent in southern China, in south-eastern Australia and en route between the two. The novel offers a dramatic and detailed account of Wong's humble beginnings, his not always moral efforts, and his eventual rise in prosperity in Australia before a return to his long-suffering wife in his home village.

This novel grants us a rare window into nineteenth-century Australia from the perspective of Chinese Australia, along with valuable insights into the emotional lives of gold seekers and the wider social concerns of Chinese Australians at the time of writing. It is also to be valued for offering a Chinese perspective on the experience of migration more broadly, and on the consequences of migration for families and communities. The novel, moreover, touches on a range of subjects that continue to resonate today, including Chinese nationalism, political and social thinking, race relations, women's rights, the challenges of migration, marriage, religion, modernisation, and the value of kinship and brotherhood (or mateship) to Chinese immigrants in Australia.

The novel is also rich in historical and literary allusions that go deep into China's cultural past. Fortunately the translator's detailed footnotes and introduction provide many interesting and learned explanations that make this an enjoyable and enlightening prospect. Readers will discover the origins of the Chinese word for money, many colourful euphemisms ("hibiscus paste" for opium; "little star" for concubine), and much more. And these explanations relate not only to Chinese culture. For example, in

---

2   For an account of the role of the Chinese-language press in Australia at this time, see Appendix IV.

Australian culture, where in accounts of Chinese-Australian history the phrase "Gold Mountain" is ubiquitous as the name given to Australia by Chinese gold miners and those who came after them seeking their fortune.[3] Here it is wonderfully described as "a fanciful pidgin-English calque that has taken on something of a life of its own". If *The Poison of Polygamy* helps to dispel the idea that Chinese diggers sought out an exotic "Gold Mountain", while those from Europe simply went to the goldfields, much "othering" that still passes for Australian history would be avoided.[4]

The author, Wong Shee Ping, lived in Melbourne, then Australia's capital, shortly after its 1901 Federation, among a Chinese community not yet decimated by the White Australia Policy (described in the novel as "the harsh regulations of today"), and abounding in older members who had originally arrived in Victoria from their south China See Yup villages seeking their fortunes during the gold rushes of the 1850s and 1860s.[5] It is in this earlier period that the story begins. Thus the author was writing historical fiction, though claiming his story to be based on "vaguely lingering memory", and in fact appearing to use some of his own family history as material.[6] Despite this historical grounding, like any fiction, the work contains some errors and anachronisms and to fully appreciate the novel not only a few corrections but also

3   "Gold Mountain" is used abundantly and unreflectively by both Chinese and non-Chinese historians and authors, ranging from the classic *The New Gold Mountain: The Chinese in Australia, 1901–1921* by Yong Ching Fatt (Richmond, S.A.: Raphael Arts, 1977) to the most recent novel, *New Gold Mountain: My Australian Story* by Christopher W. Cheng (Lindfield, N.S.W.: Scholastic Press, 2011).

4   See for example the translation simply as "goldfield" by the prominent Melbourne merchant Louis Ah Mouy, *Herald*, 2 July 1884, p. 3.

5   For an explanation of See Yup and the districts of origin see Appendix V.

6   For Wong Shee Ping's family see the biographical note.

some historical context to the Chinese diaspora in Australia, including its political and modernist aspirations, is necessary.

THE CHINESE DIASPORA[7]

Most of the characters who appear in *The Poison of Polygamy*, as well as the author himself, are Chinese-Australians and also part of the Chinese diaspora. During the nineteenth century millions of Chinese people, mainly men, travelled to South-East Asia and around the Pacific, most with the intention of earning money to support families in their villages and returning home. Though, as our author states, "tastes are many and varied", and many also "stayed on". This was a pattern long established and one intensified by the establishment of Hong Kong as a British-controlled port, with the significance of Hong Kong well illustrated in the novel, giving as it did those of the nearby Pearl River Delta districts easy access to European shipping, and hence to the Californian and Australian goldfields.[8] Two to three million Chinese people are estimated to have crossed the seas over the period from 1847 to 1882, to South-East Asia, the Americas and Oceania.[9] These are people who added to a Chinese diaspora that interacted with modern

---

7   The term "Chinese diaspora" is itself problematic and was very much evolving at the time our author was writing. Chinese diaspora and its sister term "overseas Chinese" (*huaqiao*) are useful shorthands, though those appearing in the novel might have referred to themselves simply as "travellers". The best discussion of the general history of these terms is by Wang Gungwu, "South China perspectives on overseas Chinese", *Australian Journal of Chinese Affairs* 13 (1984): pp. 69–84.

8   See Map I.

9   For a general overview of the evolution of the Chinese diaspora as it relates to the Pacific, Australia and North America, see Elizabeth Sinn, *Pacific Crossing: California Gold, Chinese Migration, and the Making of Hong Kong* (Hong Kong: Hong Kong University Press, 2015), and Michael Williams, *Returning Home with Glory: Chinese Villagers around the Pacific, 1849 to 1949* (Hong Kong: Hong Kong University Press, 2018).

trends in places such as Australia and North America and helped to contribute new ideas to China itself.[10]

After 1850, Chinese arrivals in Australia travelled initially to the Victorian goldfield districts, particularly Bendigo and Ballarat—featured in the novel—where their numbers peaked at around 40,000.[11] In the novel this number is inflated to "over a hundred thousand", a constant returning and replacing of people making accurate numbers difficult. Arguments over numbers are the stuff of history and it is the charm and value of this novel that it helps bring an individuality and humanness to what are too often mere numbers. Nearly all were men, intending to earn money to support their families in the village, just as the main character of the novel Wong Sheung Hong does. While they came from a relative handful of districts, they also often spoke dialects or languages incomprehensible to one another.[12] Ties of kinship and connections based on these districts of origin were of great importance and often determined business relationships as well as where people travelled, and this is clearly central to the

---

10   See Shelly Chan, *Diaspora's Homeland: Modern China in the Age of Global Migration* (Durham, NC: Duke University Press, 2018) for an analysis of this aspect of the Chinese diaspora.

11   C.F. Yong, *The New Gold Mountain: The Chinese in Australia, 1901–1921* (Richmond, SA: Raphael Arts, 1977) remains one of the best histories on this. Gold was discovered in Victoria in 1851 and according to one account, Louis Ah Mouy, a native of See Yup, reputedly sent a letter to his family sharing news of the discoveries, and by 1854 more than 3,000 of his fellow See Yup people were on the goldfields. Chinese official statistics estimate that 10,000 Chinese left for Australasia during the 1801–1850 period, which increased to 60,000 between 1851 and 1875. See also Sheng Fei, "Environmental Experiences of Chinese People in the Mid-Nineteenth Century Australian Gold Rushes", *Global Environment* 7/8 (2011), p. 111, republished by the Environment & Society Portal, Multimedia Library at https://bit.ly/2FcN99a

12   For an explanation of See Yup and the districts of origin see Appendix V, Map II, and the Translator's Introduction.

plot. As Wang Sing-wu noted, these early Chinese-Australian migrant movements relied on a "credit-ticket" system. The majority of the Chinese labourers on the Victorian goldfields in the 1850s were free but nevertheless indebted labourers who, as does the protagonist in the novel, purchased their ship tickets from firms in Hong Kong with the support of family or friends.[13] These tickets were issued under unwritten contracts supported by an arrangement between the migrants' local connections and an international network of Chinese firms located in Hong Kong, Australia and other destinations, such as the "Kwong Wing Goldfield Agency" of the novel.[14]

Before the end of the nineteenth century gold mining greatly lessened in significance and many occupations, ranging from scrub cutting and storekeeping to tobacco farming and furniture making, took their place as sources of livelihood for Chinese people in Australia. It is just such a transition by many of the characters in the novel, from gold miners to businessmen of various kinds, that is an essential feature of the plot. Such economic mobility helped create increasingly urban Chinese-Australian communities that also featured wealthy international merchants, newspapers, many Christian converts, and an increasing interest in the political and social fortunes of the then Chinese Empire. This was an empire (老大帝國 "the big old empire" as the author disparagingly expresses it), ruled by the Manchus of the Qing dynasty, a distinct people from the Han Chinese who are the

---

13   See Sophie Loy-Wilson, "Coolie Alibis: Seizing Gold from Chinese Miners in New South Wales", *International Labor and Working Class History* 91 (2017), pp. 28–45, for an account of the origin of the myth of Chinese miners as unfree, "coolies" or indentured.

14   Sing-wu Wang, *The Organization of Chinese Emigration: With Special Reference to Chinese Immigration to Australia* (San Francisco: Chinese Materials Center, 1978), pp. 112–18; see p. 112 for written contracts "given up" due to British regulations. The credit-ticket arrangements continued long after the gold rushes and are the basis of some people's migration even today.

Figure 5: Street scenes from an 1899 newspaper feature on the Chinese community of Little Bourke Street, Melbourne. From the *Leader*, 11 February 1899. (State Library of Victoria)

novel's main characters, and who blame many of China's problems on the "foreignness" of these rulers.[15]

This broad background brings us to two considerations, awareness of which assists in understanding the novel as an historical
source. The first is the minutiae of family and individual life lived
between Australia and China, specifically in the villages of the See
Yup districts and Melbourne, in the late nineteenth and early
twentieth centuries. The second is the political and moral agenda of
the author Wong Shee Ping in writing *The Poison of Polygamy* at all
and the manner in which he chose to do so.

THE CHINESE-AUSTRALIAN EXPERIENCE

The Poison of Polygamy gives us a vivid picture of life for poorer people in a south China village at the turn of the twentieth century:
from cutting cooking fuel to village gossip, from bandits to the
exercise of "domestic law". The novel also gives us a depiction of
people who are able to connect to the goldfields of Victoria via relatives already travelled, and of agencies set up in Hong Kong to
facilitate this movement, as well as the journey itself. This is a picture that historians have documented well, though largely via
outsiders, usually Europeans, with much reliance on official
records.[16] This is a history, therefore, that has been less forthcoming
about the emotional and psychological problems encountered with

15 The rulers of the Qing dynasty were Manchu people from beyond the great
wall of China, to the north, who invaded China in the 1640s and overthrew
the previous Ming dynasty. The Manchu Qing dynasty collapsed in 1911 and
with it China's imperial form of government.

16 For Australia see Yong, *The New Gold Mountain*, and Williams, *Returning
Home with Glory*. For those from similar Pearl River Delta districts travelling
to North America, see Madeline Hsu, *Dreaming of Gold, Dreaming of Home:
Transnationalism and Migration between the United States and South China,
1882–1943* (Redwood City, Calif.: Stanford University Press, 2000).

the separation of families, or the role of women left without husbands in traditional village society.[17] The novel's reflections on women and gender issues thus deserve particular attention, while the Chinese origin and the imaginative element make the novel a unique and valuable addition to our more prosaic sources. Vivid details abound: a "sick pan" as a required purchase before boarding ship; the adoption of "Western" habits such as hand shaking; the use and abuse of opium; the anxious waiting of the wife—"married widowhood"—in the village for news and remittances; Hong Kong accommodation employees fawning on returnees they had looked down upon when they left for the goldfields; the importance of mateship, and of co-operation according to one's district of origin. Much that has only been inferred by historians is here laid out in full view by an author who mixed and talked with people who had done similar, including his own father and other relatives, and who in fact had done similar himself.

An important feature of overseas Chinese (*huaqiao*) history is the gradual rise in family prosperity as people left and returned, adding wives, children and more prestigious houses as the years and the remittances went by. This pattern is clearly illuminated in the actions and progression of the various characters, even as life takes a tragic turn for one of them.[18] Public co-operation and contributions to village and community causes are also a notable element in the history of the Chinese diaspora, and the novel provides us with an outstanding historical example in the building

17   An outstanding exception, regarding the women of the more northerly province of Fujian, is Huifen Shen, *China's Left-Behind Wives: Families of Migrants from Fujian to Southeast Asia, 1930s–1950s* (Singapore: NUS Press, 2012).

18   For a detailed analysis of the *huaqiao* lifestyle, see Williams, *Returning Home with Glory*.

of Melbourne's See Yup Temple, a still thriving institution in that city today.[19] For Wong Shee Ping, with his modernising (and Christian) outlook (explained below), this was an ambiguous achievement, "constrained by the old mindset of several decades ago", but one we feel, as a See Yup native himself, he was nevertheless proud of.

The Chinese-Australian experience is often seen in stereotypes, such as when its history is cast merely in terms of racism. While this element is indisputable, it by no means constitutes the entirety of the story. For the author of *The Poison of Polygamy*, racism ("different races are wont to mistrust one another" is how he mildly puts it at one point), at least in so far as Europeans perpetrated it, was not his chief concern. In fact, European Australians feature hardly at all—once as a rescuer—instead we are given a picture of a relatively self-contained Chinese community with generally satisfactory relations with the wider society. Though a hint this is not always the case is perhaps seen in a concern for "our respectability as Chinese people". Similarly, with regard to gold mining, which remains perhaps the single most prominent stereotype of Chinese people in Australian history, with its myths of round mining shafts, constant re-working of old tailings and rioting white miners.[20] In the novel we see no riots, a new mine worked in co-operation with European miners, and a range of other occupations, such as horticulture, storekeeping and furniture making.[21] In fact the author's father was manager

---

19   See Figure 6.

20   For an excellent study of the basic lack of divergence among miners, Chinese or otherwise, as well as less stereotypical reasons for why, when they did diverge, see Barry McGowan, "The Economics and Organisation of Chinese Mining in Colonial Australia", *Australian Economic History Review* 45 (2005), pp. 119–38. See also *Leader*, 18 June 1910, p. 36 for a gold mine abandoned by Chinese miners then re-worked by Europeans.

21   For the mine see *Ballarat Star*, 28 July 1883, p. 4.

Figure 6: Melbourne's See Yup Society Temple near Albert Park. The novel describes its founders "extraordinary vision" and the "grand, tall and spacious" temple. (W.W. Lindt / State Library of Victoria)

and second largest shareholder of the Woah Hawp Canton Quartz Mining Company, a large-scale mining venture which employed both Chinese and European labour.[22] This is all part of the ChineseAustralian experience of the period that has been well documented academically but is yet to penetrate the popular imagination.[23]

Despite Wong Shee Ping's drawing on his own family history, some anachronisms and errors do appear in what is after all a

22 *Ballarat Star*, 26 January 1882, p. 4, and 28 July 1883, p. 4.

23 For a recent example of this kind of nuanced history see Peter Gibson, "Australia's Bankrupt Chinese Furniture Manufacturers, 1880–1930", *Australian Economic History Review* 58 (2018), pp. 87–107, where bankruptcies, such as occur in the novel, are explained for reasons other than racial discrimination. See also the list of suggested reading at the end of this introduction.

fictional account. Some of these inaccuracies are small, such as the first ship's passage via Port Darwin, which would not become a regular port on the journey from Hong Kong until closer to the time in which the author himself was writing. Others are amusing, such as the beast that attacks and kills a number of people in the Victorian bush: it seems to be a geographically challenged and very tiger-like Tasmanian tiger. Other weaknesses are more significant, such as the treatment of the walk from Robe in South Australia to the Victorian goldfields, which shows ample evidence of embellishment on a number of levels. The historical fact of Chinese gold seekers arriving via the South Australian port of Guichen Bay or Robe (in order to avoid a £10 poll tax levied only on Chinese people enacted by the colony of Victoria in 1855), is wonderfully employed in the plot.[24] It does however greatly exaggerate the rate of death en route, and breaks into lyrical poetry in commemorating the walk for posterity. Indeed, the limited poetry found in the novel is used largely to commemorate the trek from Robe to the goldfields. This is an interesting feature, as while dramatisation for effect is understandable in a work of fiction, this is perhaps also evidence of mythologising on the part of the Chinese community (or author) of a period of undoubted hardship and discrimination now a distant memory for most.[25] Most significantly, the author does not use the hardship of the walk he describes to decry the discrimination against Chinese people that

---

24 While a thorough academic study of the Robe trek seems lacking, a well researched if unselective account full of local detail is to be found in Fiona Ritchie, *Guichen Bay to Canton Lead: The Chinese Trek to Gold* (Robe, SA: District Council of Robe, 2004).

25 A memory recently re-enacted by Chinese Australians and memorialised at Guichen Bay. See "Robe to Riches: A Chinese Pilgrim Route", *The Spirit of Things*, ABC Radio National, 11 June 2017, https://ab.co/2DMwiby

Figure 7: The Woah Hawp Canton gold mine at Ballarat. (Fraser / State Library of Victoria)

obliged the alternative route, but rather employs it to attack "the authoritarian government of a foreign race" (the Manchus) whose rule of China is the reason Chinese people "must today seek our living in foreign countries".[26]

Of note too is the racist (and inaccurate) account of an attack by Aboriginal people with their "eyes ugly" and non-existent arrows (Aboriginal Australians did not use bows and arrows, poisoned or otherwise). Again, the desire to mythologise the hardships of the past may explain some of this account, but the highly racist representation can also be seen to be consistent with the social Darwinist strain of nationalist ideology circulating at this time in China and among Chinese nationalists abroad.[27] Some have suggested that the novel's treatment of Aboriginal people reflects the racial hierarchies of White Australia.[28] The racist depiction contrasts, however, with other Chinese sympathies for native peoples at this time. Certainly in their more prosaic non-fiction writings many early twentieth-century Chinese journalists and community leaders depicted Indigenous Australians as the owners of their native land, and circulated tracts critical of their dispossession.[29] Additionally, recent historical research into relations between Indigenous communities and Chinese arrivals in Northern and Western Australia at the time

26   The political agenda of the novel is discussed in greater detail below.
27   See for example James Pusey, *China and Social Darwinism* (Cambridge, Mass.: Harvard University Press, 1983); Frank Dikotter, *The Discourse of Race in Modern China*, revised edition (Oxford: Oxford University Press, 2015).
28   "However, in its eagerness to portray the decadence of imperial China, *The Poison of Polygamy* perpetuates many of the stereotypes circulating in the white community". Zhong Huang and Wenche Ommundsen, "Poison, Polygamy and Postcolonial Politics: The First Chinese Australian Novel", *Journal of Postcolonial Writing* 52, no. 5 (2016), p. 543.
29   For example, *Chinese Australian Herald*, 1 December, 3 December and 8 December 1900, p. 5. The *Chinese Times* circulated an influential revolutionary book by Chen Tianhua (陳天華), which not only attacked Western colonialism and imperialism in China, but also racism toward overseas Chinese and the ill-treatment of indigenous peoples in European colonial territories. In his

of both the novel's action and writing indicates widespread and friendly interactions, and in many cases vocational partnerships.[30]

One of the most significant features of Chinese-Australian community life over the period in question was the absence of women and families in Australia and their location in the villages of southern China. Wong Sheung Hong's wife, Ma, is depicted as one of these left-behind women. Her lot is to do such work as "collect firewood by day and spin and weave by night", despite her bound feet, while awaiting the intermittent arrival of letters and remittances from her husband in Australia. The scene when Ma's husband returns after six years is particularly evocative of the conflicting emotions this lifestyle, often so dryly recounted by historians, would have generated in life. Ma is depicted as faithful but illiterate and hence dependent on relatives or "a local scholar" to read the letters she receives from her husband during his absence. Such letters home were important for maintaining emotional ties across divided families, while the remittances became essential for maintaining family life and lifestyle.[31] Both were eagerly awaited in the villages.

---

influential book *Menghuitou* (猛回頭 "*Sudden Awakening*"), published in 1903 in Japan, Chen was especially critical of British colonists' near-elimination of Aboriginal people in Australia.

30 For example, Julia Martínez, "Plural Australia: Aboriginal and Asian Labour in Tropical White Australia, Darwin, 1911–1940", PhD thesis, University of Wollongong, 2000; Victoria Haskins, "'The privilege of employing natives': The Quan Sing Affair and Chinese-Aboriginal Employment in Western Australia, 1889–1930", *Aboriginal History* 35 (2011): pp. 145–60; Pate Stephenson, *The Outsiders Within: Telling Australia's Indigenous-Asian Story* (Sydney: University of New South Wales Press, 2007); Cathie May, *Topsawyers: The Chinese in Cairns 1870–1920*, (Townsville, Qld: James Cook University Press, 1984).

31 僑批 *qiaopi*, 金信 *jinxin* and 銀信 *yinxin* are Chinese expressions for "remittance letters", the letters sent with money by Chinese living overseas in the nineteenth and early twentieth century. For a brief history of the Chinese-Australian remittance trade in the nineteenth century see Mei-fen Kuo, "Jinxin (金信), the Remittance Trade and Enterprising Chinese Australians, 1850–1916"

The fact of most women remaining in the villages implies few Chinese women in Australia. Non-Chinese women—"swollen-breasted slender-waisted Western Venuses"—are mentioned to emphasise the unlikelihood of interracial relationships that were in reality not so unlikely.[32] A minor character provides us with a soliloquy on the virtues or otherwise of all types of women by class and race, mixed or otherwise, that provides us with the not uncommon view of the frustrated male in search of a house slave, or a woman "refined and virtuous", as the character expresses it. Despite the rarity of Chinese women leaving the village, we are treated to a veritable "women's army" in Melbourne confronting the main character at one stage of the story. Any large number of women does not match with known figures for Chinese women in Australia at the time, and so this would again seem a case of artistic licence in order to provide a level of dramatic pressure that the plot requires at this point.

THE MORAL AND POLITICAL AGENDA

As interesting as the plot is for readers and the confirmations are for historians, the main intention of Wong Shee Ping was in fact political and moral. Or in his own vivid style, the intention was "that it might act as a Zen shout and bat-thwack about the heads of my fellows residing in foreign lands". So why did he choose to write a novel? The genre of the social novel first appeared in the fiction magazine 新小說 New Fiction, launched by intellectual

---

in Gregor Benton, Hong Liu and Huimei Zhang (eds), *The Qiaopi Trade and Transnational Networks in the Chinese Diaspora* (New York: Routledge, 2018), pp. 160–78.

32   See for example Kate Bagnall, "Rewriting the History of Chinese Families in Nineteenth-Century Australia", *Australian Historical Studies* 42, no. 1 (March 2011), pp. 62–77.

and political leader Liang Qichao (梁啟超) in 1902. This magazine introduced a range of fiction genres, including political, historical, scientific, diplomatic, social, and detective fiction.[33] *The Poison of Polygamy* sprouted in Australia from this literary movement, which aimed not just to tell a story about the world but to change it. Literature of this type carried strong moralising overtones and imagined its readership as new citizens in need of enlightenment on the social and political issues of the day.[34]

Wong Shee Ping's use of a social novel for revolutionary purposes was not therefore unusual. But why was polygamy poisonous? Although set in the Australian goldrush era, the tone and themes of *The Poison of Polygamy* reflect developments and events underway at the time of writing in the early twentieth century. The author was an editor of a pro-revolutionary newspaper whose sponsors believed not only in the need to overthrow the ruling Qing dynasty, but to reform Chinese culture and traditions. This was in order that a modern China, as opposed to a China Wong Shee Ping at one point describes as a "semi-civilised country", might take its place in the modern world. This was a place from which China could protect members of the Chinese diaspora being discriminated against, it was believed, as the result of a traditional China's weaknesses.

At a time when Australia was undergoing a rapid transition from a collection of imperial colonies into a federated commonwealth, the Chinese immigrant community was witnessing social

---

33   See Pingyuan Chen, *Xiaoshuo shi: Lilun yu shijian* (小說史:理論與實踐 *The History of Fiction: Theory and Practice*) (Beijing: Beijing University Press, 2010), pp. 1–22. For more on Chinese language newspapers in Australia, see Appendix IV. The Translator's Introduction discusses this topic from a different angle.

34   See Xiaobing Tang, *Chinese Modern: The Heroic and the Quotidian* (Durham, NC: Duke University Press, 2000), p. 13.

transformations of its own, in China, in the home villages, and elsewhere in the Chinese diaspora. Politically, the Chinese community was engaged with the implications of federation in Australia and the growth of nationalist movements in China.[35] Culturally, it was moving with the times, and this included Christianity, with many, especially among the merchant class, converting to its various sects.[36] There are many condemnations in the novel of superstition and Buddhist or Taoist practices, even when those in fear of their life begin to pray to their chosen deities, but there is nothing overtly Christian, unless it is the deliberate use of the term 罪惡 "wickedness".[37] The author's focus on gender and family relations is closely allied to his nationalist agenda of seeking to create a modern social identity for Chinese Australians in the first decade of the twentieth century. Polygamy as a feature of old culture was thus a prime target, as are many other aspects of traditional culture criticised in the novel. These aspects range from superstitions and the lack of education for women to foot binding and of course the lack of female equality.

Political conflicts within the Chinese diaspora in the late nineteenth and early twentieth centuries revolved around the question of whether the Manchu Qing state should be reformed—the position of constitutional monarchists—or overthrown and replaced with a republican form of government—the position of revolutionary nationalists led by Sun Yat-sen among others.[38]

---

35   For a detailed look at this involvement see John Fitzgerald, *Big White Lie: Chinese Australians in White Australia* (Sydney: UNSW Press, 2007).

36   For a detailed look at this merchant class see Mei-fen Kuo, *Making Chinese Australia: Urban Elites, Newspapers and the Formation of Chinese Australian Identity, 1892–1912* (Clayton, Vic.: Monash University Publishing, 2013).

37   See *The Poison of Polygamy*, footnote 369, on the possible Christian allusion here. On Wong Shee Ping's Christianity, see the biographical note.

38   For politics within the Chinese-Australian community see Fitzgerald, *Big White Lie* and Kuo, *Making Chinese Australia*.

Wong Shee Ping was often a target of harsh criticism from rival reformist newspaper the *Tung Wah News* of Sydney as part of these differences.[39] It is worth remembering, however, that while the revolutionaries of the Kuomintang (Nationalist Party), of which our author was a strong supporter, were ultimately successful, there were other challenging viewpoints. There were those for example who would not have tried to make China so "Westernised", let alone wish to see it Christianised. In fact a strong intellectual movement attempted to make Confucianism a rival to Christian pretensions.[40]

Despite this contentious background, *The Poison of Polygamy* is not overtly political. Instead Wong Shee Ping adopts a social approach with underlying political implications. He depicts, for example, the wife Ma as both harshly treated by her husband and a victim of traditional thought. Critiques of this kind were not uncommon in China and around the Chinese diaspora at the time the author was writing. However, the other women characters of the novel are by no means as put-upon, and manage to get their own way in modern Australia despite traditional restrictions. As one such female character expresses it to another: "Living in prosperity in a land where women's rights are especially strong, you would have the freedom to act as you please." Ideas about confining women to the home and family came in for regular criticism in Chinese-Australian newspapers of the period, whose editors no longer held fast to the

---

39 For more on this see Wong Shee Ping biographical note, and Appendix IV: The Newspaper Business and Chinese Australians.

40 See for example, from our author's own newspaper, "The Suitability of Confucianism as a Religion Today", *Chinese Times*, 31 October 1908, p. 2, and for a study on this question, "Confucius from Afar" in Shelly Chan, *Diaspora's Homeland: Modern China in the Age of Global Migration* (Durham, N.C.: Duke University Press, 2018), pp. 75–106, concerning the efforts of Lim Boon Keng at Amoy University in the 1920s.

Figure 8: Chinese Nationalist Party convention and celebration of the completion of the party building pictured, through the addition of a façade designed by Walter Burley Griffin. Melbourne, December 1921. (Kuo Min Tang Society of Melbourne)

traditional restrictions imposed on women and urged Chinese men who valued freedom, education, advancement and equality to allow women the same opportunities as themselves.[41]

Progressive Chinese-Australian journalists sympathised with the plight of Chinese women like the novel's Ma, and actively promoted the practice of monogamy to break down discrimination against women embedded in traditional beliefs.[42] Articles return time and again to criticising traditional values and manners that demean the place of women, including the practice of foot-binding, the primacy of sons, and unequal educational opportunities for women. Our author speaks of the need for "a women's revolutionary army to beat the bell of freedom", and depicts polygamy in particular as a form of immoral behaviour that runs counter to natural feeling, a definitive argument against it being delivered to the main character as he weds his second wife, an argument he fails—to his ultimate regret—to understand.

After 1908 and under the new direction of editor Lew Goot Chee, the *Chinese Times* expanded its literary supplements and shifted to a populist, colloquial approach suited to its mission of popular education. The paper also adopted a folk-oriented style, and published a range of humorous satires. The aim was to distinguish the newspaper from the rival reformist faction's and expose more readers to the ideas of the Chinese revolutionaries.[43]

---

41 For example, *Chinese Times*, 23 March 1904, supplement.

42 For example, the *Chinese Times* published news of a white Australian girl's tragic suicide as a result of her Chinese lover being unable to marry her on account of his already having a wife in China. This story emphasised the importance of monogamy and the risks of violating it (see *Chinese Times*, 23 September 1903, p. 3). Similarly, the *Tung Wah Times* declared, in 1904, that as monogamy was the norm for all modern civil societies, China could never modernise unless it were to enforce the law of monogamy. See *Tung Wah Times*, 24 December 1904, supplement.

43 *Chinese Times*, 25 September, pp. 9–10 and 18 December 1909, p. 9.

As a political reformer and newspaperman, Wong Shee Ping probably did not consider himself a novelist, though he did begin to write at least one other novel.[44] In the main he wrote about politics, reform and his other great preoccupation, Christianity. Thus the novel does show evidence of hasty, unplanned writing (perhaps week by week as it was serialised), with some new characters clumsily introduced seemingly to make a new political point regardless of the plot, and some loose ends left unresolved.

The publication of the novel coincided with an expansion of grassroots support for the Chinese revolution in Melbourne, which can be credited in large part to the concerted efforts of the *Chinese Times* from 1908. The Melbourne revolutionaries had made connections with the Revolutionary Alliance (同盟會) through the editor of the *Hong Kong China Daily*, Feng Chien-hua.[45] The Young China League (少年中國會), the first Chinese-Australian revolutionary organisation to support Sun Yat-sen, was launched on 23 January 1911 at the Temperance Hall in Melbourne, in collaboration with the *Chinese Times*, the offices of which were diagonally opposite it on Russell Street. When the revolution broke out in China in October 1911, the Young China League became the headquarters for supporters of the Chinese republican revolution throughout Australia. This marked the beginning of the Chinese Nationalist Party of Australasia—the Kuomintang. The author of the novel, Wong Shee Ping, was a leading figure in its development.

---

44   See the Translator's Introduction, p. 60.
45   See Feng Ziyou (馮自由), *Huaqiao geming kaiguo shi* (華僑革命開國史 *The Contribution of Overseas Chinese to the Revolution and Founding of the Country*) (Taipei: Commercial Press, 1953), p. 119.

CONCLUSION

Research into Australian history has begun to tell the story of Chinese Australia beyond the stereotypes of racism, victimhood and hard-working gold miners. *The Poison of Polygamy* tells this story in a literary form and told it over a century ago, when the presence of a strong Chinese community in Australia was well known and before the demands of a White Australia sought to erase it both physically and from history itself. Unfortunately the successes of academic history in rediscovering this story have yet to penetrate the popular imagination to any great degree and Chinese-Australian history thus often remains a vague impression of hard done by, largely faceless, victims of white domination. It can be confidently expected that this re-publication of the first novel of the Chinese-Australian experience in both the original language and in this outstandingly erudite and readable English version will do what more academic efforts have so far failed to. Namely, to reveal something of the motivations, the individual and family struggles and the scope of exertions that went into this fundamental component of Australian history which can broadly be described as "Chinese". Racism, white aggression and gold mining all played an undeniable and significant role, but this inadequate view needs to be seen in the context of family, dialect/language, individuals and even politics and "the big old empire", if a properly nuanced and complete history of Australia is to become part of the popular as well as wider academic understanding.

The author, the novel, the newspaper, and the many readers who enjoyed *The Poison of Polygamy* when it first appeared in print all merit a place in the social, political and literary history of contemporary Australia. This is a place long denied not simply because the novel was written in Chinese but also because it was written in Literary Chinese, a form of writing that has now all but disappeared.[46] A new generation of English readers of *The Poison of Polygamy* are extremely fortunate in being able to relish this Australian story, one that all Australians can now enjoy and treasure, both those with and without Chinese ancestry.

SUGGESTED FURTHER READING

A fully comprehensive general history of Chinese Australia has yet to be written, especially one that takes in the geographic diversity, or the significance of continuing connections with the south China villages. Nevertheless for those wishing to go beyond the incomplete view of faceless, hard-working, yet victimised gold miners and market gardeners, the following is a summary of the best representative work to date.

Bagnall, Kate. "Rewriting the History of Chinese Families in Nineteenth-Century Australia", *Australian Historical Studies* 42, no. 1 (March 2011), pp. 62–77. [On women]

Benton, Gregor. "Australia", in *Chinese Migrants and Internationalism: Forgotten Histories, 1917–1945,* pp. 72–91. London: Routledge, 2007. [On radicalism]

Fitzgerald, John. *Big White Lie: Chinese Australians in White Australia.* Sydney: UNSW Press, 2007. [On politics]

Fong, Natalie. "The Significance of the Northern Territory in the Formulation of 'White Australia' Policies, 1880–1901", *Australian Historical Studies* 49, no. 4 (2018), pp. 527–45. [On the North]

Gibson, Peter. "Australia's Bankrupt Chinese Furniture Manufacturers, 1880–1930", *Australian Economic History Review* 58 (2018), pp. 87–107. [On business]

---

46   See the Translator's Introduction, p. 50, for a detailed explanation of this.

Kuo, Mei-fen. *Making Chinese Australia: Urban Elites, Newspapers and the Formation of Chinese Australian Identity, 1892–1912*. Clayton, Vic.: Monash University Publishing 2013. [On merchants]

Loy-Wilson, Sophie. "Coolie Alibis: Seizing Gold from Chinese Miners in New South Wales", *International Labor and Working Class History* 91 (2017), pp. 28–45. [On coolie myths]

May, Cathie. *Topsawyers: The Chinese in Cairns 1870–1920*. Townsville, Qld: James Cook University Press, 1984. [On North Queensland]

McGowan, Barry. "The Economics and Organisation of Chinese Mining in Colonial Australia", *Australian Economic History Review* 45 (2005), pp. 119–138. [On miners]

Sheng Fei. "Environmental Experiences of Chinese People in the Mid-Nineteenth Century Australian Gold Rushes". *Global Environment* 7/8 (2011), p. 111. [On the environment]

Williams, Michael. *Returning Home with Glory: Chinese Villagers around the Pacific, 1849 to 1949*. Hong Kong: Hong Kong University Press, 2018. [On the villages]

Yong, C.F. *The New Gold Mountain: The Chinese in Australia, 1901–1921*. Richmond, S.A.: Raphael Arts, 1977. [A classic]

Translator's Introduction

Ely Finch

It was in July 2015 that I agreed to undertake the translation of *The Poison of Polygamy*, because it seemed to be such a unique and important work. Gratifyingly, as my familiarity with this surprising novel grew, so too did the strength of that initial impression.

As a work of literature, the novel admittedly has its deficiencies, and is far from deserving of a place in the Chinese literary cannon. Nonetheless, it has many other claims to distinction. It is Australia's earliest-identified Chinese novel, i.e. the first written in Chinese, and the first about the Chinese-Australian experience. Indeed, not only the first, but the only one for the best part of a century. It may also be the earliest novel of the Chinese-diaspora experience, and the earliest Chinese-language novel to have been written anywhere in the West.

The novel's story and the story of its story is also significant. It concerns the history of the Chinese diaspora in Australia, and was written by a member of that diaspora for his fellows. Set in both imperial China and the Australian colony of Victoria, against the goldrush backdrop of the Victorian era, and written from an individual and Chinese perspective, the novel provides a rare window onto that world's everyday life, albeit a window that presents a distorted view.

It is also a work preoccupied with the social and political issues of its own time, that of early Federation Australia and late-Qing China. Its author was one of the revolutionaries who were soon to succeed in overthrowing the Qing, China's last imperial dynasty, and who then attempted, unsuccessfully, to establish the Republic of China along similar lines to Western nation states. They were people who made a significant contribution to China's modern history, and whose social and ideological legacy forms part of the makeup of the Chinese world today.

The translation, despite its undoubted deficiencies, may also have some claims to distinction. Relatively few individual works of fiction written in Classical Chinese (or what is more technically termed Literary Chinese) have been translated into English: so far as I can establish, this would appear to be the largest, and perhaps the only actual novel.[1] The approach taken to the translation has been both rigorous and ambitious. The sense and allusions of the original have, so far as practicable, been translated without resort

---

1   Literary Chinese and vernacular Chinese often appear in combination in works of Chinese fiction. When this is the case, it is the extent to which they are combined that is the essential factor in the determination of a work's classification. Such works as 紅樓夢 *The Dream of the Red Chamber*, 西遊記 *Journey to the West* and 好逑傳 *The Fortunate Union* are considered to be written in premodern vernacular Chinese, though all contain a Literary Chinese element. 三國志通俗演義 *The Romance of the Three Kingdoms* is a rare example of a novel that is considered to be written in an even mixture of Literary and vernacular Chinese. Like the longest Literary Chinese novel, an untranslated eighteenth-century work entitled 蟫史 *"A Silverfish History"*, *The Poison of Polygamy* contains some vernacular language. For more on Literary Chinese and vernacular Chinese, and the proportions and varieties of each in *The Poison of Polygamy*, see the sections of this introduction entitled "Chinese and the Novel's Language" and "The Novel".

to overt domestication—such as the replacement of unfamiliar Chinese literary allusions and ideas with Western ones. Explanatory footnotes have been used as a means of assisting readers to bridge a cultural and literary gulf. This annotated approach aims at illuminating the original, and providing the background necessary for a more nuanced appreciation of the novel and the Chinese world to which it belonged. It also aims at opening the original up to the broadest possible range of interpretations, and avoiding the misleading impression of quaintness and oddity that, through want of explanation and attention to subtleties, is so often a corollary to translations from Literary Chinese. It should, however, be perfectly possible for readers to enjoy the book on one level without referring to footnotes. Another key objective of the translation has been the faithful reflection of the style, feeling and poetic value of the original's language. Finally, the publication of translated and original text in parallel is uncommon, and will hopefully not only add to the translation's transparency and accessibility for bilingual readers, but to its usefulness as a potential resource for academic and language-learning purposes.

My intent below is to lay out, under the heading "Key Points for Readers", a variety of information that readers may find helpful to note before approaching the text. I shall then attempt simple overviews—for present or future reference—of the type of Chinese in which the novel is written, the approach that has been taken to its translation, and matters of literary relevance. This will, I hope, in combination with the historical introduction, furnish a unique publication with some much-needed context, and point readers in the direction of topics that warrant further consideration and investigation.

KEY POINTS FOR READERS

Character Names

From the characters of Chaucer's *The Pilgrim's Progress*, to the protagonist's work-horse steed in Cervantes's *Don Quixote*, to Dickens's Ebenezer Scrooge and Fleming's James Bond, to common political hack Jim Hacker and deranged scientist Dr Strangelove, character names in the West have always been far more than arbitrary designations. Chinese character names, from those of high literature to folk ballads, are no different. Indeed, the practice of imbuing character names with heightened significance started early in Chinese literature, which had, for example, a character name that was the equivalent of Agatha Christie's U.N. Owen by around the year 100 (憑虛公子).[2] The author of *The Poison of Polygamy* was writing in this tradition, and his character names reflect deliberate choices on his part. Some are not very far from the caricature-like names of characters like Mr Stone the Mason and Miss Pill the Doctor's Daughter in the Victorian card game of Happy Families; others have subtler and more complex associations, the interpretation of which involves a greater degree of subjectivity.

The approach taken in this translation has been to give phonetic renderings of character names, in preference to the fraught alternative of inventing English names with similar connotations. Because this approach reduces the names to sounds, some informed speculation on the associations of a selection, including those of all the principal

---

2   Like the "U.N. Owen" of Christie's *And Then There Were None*, this character name is code for "unknown": the first character 憑, which can be taken to represent the surname, means "to be based on", and the second character 虛, which can be taken to represent the given name, means "emptiness" or "nothing"; the final two characters, 公子, form a title, which might be translated as "sir". (The literary source of this name is the 漢 Han-dynasty work 西京賦 "*A Lyrical Depiction of the Western Capital*" by 張衡 *Chang Hêng*).

characters, is given in Appendix I. This appendix also contains guidance on the names' approximate pronunciations in standard modern Cantonese. My advice for those readers who would prefer not to attempt these pronunciations is to refer to the characters by way of their initials. This approach may make it easier to remember the names, reducing the potential for confusion.

Business Names
For those readers interested in everything business-related, or in the real history the novel draws on, Appendix III contains a list of all the novel's business names, along with their noted locations, guidance on pronunciation, the numbers of the instalments in which they feature by name, and speculation on the identity of the actual businesses that their names appear to be word plays on.

The Novel's Geography
The geography of the novel is real and will no doubt be of interest to many readers. With this in mind, maps are provided for ease of reference at the end of the book, with the identifiable place names marked on them. For information on these place names, see Appendix V, immediate to the maps.

The Chinese and English Text
The novel was originally published in fifty-three serialised instalments in Melbourne's *Chinese Times* newspaper. I have transcribed the Chinese text from the images of the newspaper that are freely available on the National Library of Australia's Trove website, making reference where they were unclear to the original copies, which are held in the collection of the State Library of Victoria. The text of the transcription, like that of the original, is in traditional characters—the newspapers well and truly predate the introduction of the nominally simplified characters now current in mainland China, Singapore and Malaysia.

An attempt has been made in transcription, for the sake of added flavour, to reflect the variant forms of the characters that appear in the newspaper, e.g. when "番", the vulgar form (俗體) of the character "番", appears, it is given as such. This has, however, not always proven possible, due to the unavailability of many variant forms in electronic character sets.

A rectangular frame around a character indicates that it was significantly mutilated or almost or entirely missing in the newspaper, but has been reconstructed, with a reasonable degree of certainty, on the basis of such things as context and comparison to other characters. In the small number of cases where the identity of these misprinted characters could not be determined, they are represented in the transcription by the Chinese symbol for a missing character, a square box (□).

Notes on character determinations and other textural issues are given in the form of a critical apparatus, which accompanies the Chinese text and is written in Literary Chinese. These Chinese footnotes also contain the odd comment or explanation of possible relevance to the reader of the original text.

The direction in which the Chinese text flows has been changed. In the *Chinese Times*, the novel's text runs downwards, the vertical lines moving across the page from right to left. This is the traditional format, and the reason why the newspaper's spine, like those of traditional Chinese books, is on the opposite side to English book spines. The change was made because the parallel format of this publication, in which English is the dominant language, would have required readers of the Chinese to turn pages in an unnatural direction. The Chinese therefore runs in the same direction as the English, as it is nowadays often written. (Chinese text is more amenable to such changes. Indeed, the approach taken here has a precedent in eighteenth- and nineteenth-century parallel-text translations from Chinese to Manchu, in which the directionality of Chinese was subordinated to that of Manchu, which flows downwards but from left to right.)

The original serialised version of the novel contained no chapter divisions, and, so as to avoid the imposition of any particular reading, none have been introduced. Instead, the serialised structure has been reflected by means of parenthesised markers, which contain the number of the instalment they follow and the date of its publication. However, in view of the fact that the current publication is not serialised, the newspaper's section headings and the pre-instalment reappearances of the novel's title and subtitle have been removed. For the same reason, the one instance of the phrase 仍未完, literally "continues; not the end" at the end of Part 3—which finishes mid-sentence—and the fifty-one instances of the phrase 未完 "not the end" or "incomplete", which accompanies all the other parts except the last, have also been removed.

Square brackets in the English text correspond to misprints or errors in the source text where the determination of the original sense is speculative. The translations given between the brackets are therefore contingent upon the accuracy of those determinations. Where the sense of a missing or mutilated character could not be determined, it is represented in translation by three asterisks.

While Literary Chinese text naturally resolves itself into clauses, sentences and paragraphs, which were recognised concepts, punctuation and paragraph breaks were traditionally optional. In the newspaper, only the preface, a letter, and the poems are spaced as independent blocks of text; and only a limited range of punctuation marks is employed. This reflects the norms of Chinese writing at the time. The approach taken in translation has been to follow the norms of English writing, through the introduction of paragraph breaks, punctuation, capitalisation and italicisation, the delineation of authorial comments independent of the story's text, and what for English is the very necessary introduction of spaces between words, which are rare in Chinese and do not feature in the original text. I am not disposed to view these changes as improvements. They are intended to highlight what is implicit in the original, and to reflect its style relative to its cultural context. And in some respects, their addition still fails to compensate for all that is implicit in the original. For example, sentence-final particles in the Chinese, which can be regarded as a form of written intonation (or "classical emojis"), convey far more about a speaker's tone of voice than English's limited range of punctuation marks.[3]

Quoted Speech

Quoted speech in Classical or Literary Chinese generally works differently to quoted speech in the written form of a spoken language, such as Mandarin, Cantonese or English. It tells the reader a speaker's meaning, but not through the words the speaker would naturally use to express that meaning. This is a foreign concept for most English readers, because English does not have a written language that is distinct from speech.

3　In English, changes in pitch reflect a speaker's intonation. Chinese languages are tonal, which means that changes in pitch can alter the meaning of words. There is therefore less room in Chinese languages for intonation. To compensate, a range of sounds are used at the end of utterances. These sentence-final particles fulfil the same function as intonation, and come with the added advantage that they are easily written down. In general, the more tones a Chinese language employs, the less room it has for intonation, and the greater the number of its sentence-final particles; hence their numerousness in Cantonese relative to Mandarin. Literary Chinese also employs numerous sentence-final particles. For example, in the novel, the final character in the rhetorical question 奚望生爲 "How could I hope for life?" indicates what might be termed an in-point-of-fact tone of voice, whereas the final character in the sentence 汝等瘋耶 "Are you all deranged?" turns it into question with a suggestive and rhetorical overtone. Likewise, the sentence-final particles 乎, 哉, 也, 矣, 焉 and 歟 each serve to indicate different overtones to questions that appear in the novel, which in English might only be indicated by means of intonation. Sentence-final particles are used with other sentence types too, and sometimes appear in combination.

An English-speaking television viewer might accept the unreality of an impossibly short telephone conversation, recognising that it is a necessary conceit, preferable to the potential tedium of realistic portrayal. Similarly, a theatre-goer might accept the unreality of a performer speaking in song or poetry, recognising that it is a conceit that might produce a hyperreal unreality, which allows a character to express themselves more powerfully and clearly than would be possible in natural speech. Quotation in Literary Chinese works along these lines. It enables meaning to be conveyed in a succinct and hyperreal form, giving the reader the sense that they are hearing a heart or mind speaking, or that a character has been transformed into a master of language whose every turn of phrase is eloquent. (This does not mean that as a mode of expression it is devoid of the linguistic colour that might indicate such things as the social background or personality of the speaker, because it is possible for this colour to be conveyed in other ways.) The reader of Literary Chinese naturally accepts this conceit, just as English speakers accept the conceits of television and theatre. The translation that follows may not always succeed in disguising the resultant unnaturalness of quoted speech. Readers may therefore need to remind themselves that Literary Chinese between quotation marks generally represents a speaker's meaning, not verbatim speech.

Phraseology which Gives the Impression of Crudeness

Another difference between Literary Chinese prose and prose in a spoken language relates to its potential for conciseness and directness that does not come at the expense of elegance. One of the reasons for this, apart from the compactness of its grammatical structure, is that writers of Literary Chinese do not always have to rely on the employment of a higher register, and more complex grammatical constructions, in order to achieve sophistication. The situation is somewhat like the one that pertains between archaic and modern English. Archaic exclamations like "lo" and "alas" are generally considered elegant, but modern exclamations like "hah" and "damn" are not, and are consequently avoided in formal or elegant writing, in a way that their archaic equivalents may not be. The vocabulary of Literary Chinese has the higher status of an archaic register. Its writers can therefore write tersely and directly without fear of sounding crude or gauche. Unfortunately, it is not always possible to achieve the same effect in close translation. Readers should therefore adopt a sympathetic standpoint and bear in mind that phraseology which gives the impression of crudeness in translation may sometimes reflect the very opposite in the original.

Romanisation

Appendix II summarises the approach taken to romanisation in the text and the footnotes. This is a complex subject. Chinese characters are somewhat similar to universal symbols, and do not therefore have fixed pronunciations. For example, the Arabic numeral "3" has the same significance in English, German, Italian and French, but is pronounced differently in those languages, as "three", *drei*, *tre* and *trois* respectively. Likewise, the Chinese character "口", which means "mouth", shares a similar significance in Mandarin, Cantonese, the See Yip language and Teochew, but is pronounced differently in them, as *kŏu*, *háu*, *hɔu* and *kháu* respectively. A choice must therefore be made as to which pronunciation to give a Chinese character when transliterating it into English, and what spelling to use. E.g. Does one render the Chinese surname 陳 as Teochew "Dang" or See Yip "Chin"? Does one spell the Mandarin pronunciation of the classical name 季子 according to the Wade-Giles transliteration system, as *Chi Tzŭ*, or the Pinyin system, as *Jìzǐ*? Appendix II answers such questions.

CHINESE AND THE NOVEL'S LANGUAGE

The Poison of Polygamy is written in a particular style of Chinese. To say this is, however, to be so vague as to fail even to answer the question of what language or languages the novel is written in. The following is an attempt to explain why, and to provide a clearer characterisation of the novel's language.

Chinese Spoken Languages

From a linguistic perspective, Chinese is not one language, but a language family. A language family that is made up of many spoken languages, and the independent written language of Literary Chinese, which is addressed further down. These spoken languages are not mutually intelligible, do not belong to the same language continuums, and also have their own sometimes highly divergent dialects, just like English has Cockney and Glaswegian. Linguists have been pointing this out for well over 150 years, but people are surprisingly still confused about the status of these spoken languages. Cultural and political issues are one reason, but the continued use of the misnomer "dialect" to describe them may also be an important factor. This is something that has been perpetuated by linguists who recognise the term's inaccuracy, but have felt obliged to bow to established usage. I shall only use the word "dialect" in this introduction and the translation in reference to real dialects.

The table overleaf highlights the sorts of differences in grammar, vocabulary, and pronunciation that exist between Chinese languages. It shows how the simple sentence "Give him one more" is constructed in three Chinese languages: Mandarin, Cantonese and Teochew. In Cantonese, for example, one says the equivalent of "give more a/an him", whereas in Mandarin one says "give him more one a/an". The table also shows the Chinese characters for each of the words, and inspection will reveal that these often differ; in fact the Teochew example contains no characters in common with the others. These differences point to the fact that the words are not cognate, i.e. not related. A very crude rendering of the pronunciations is also given, which should be enough to indicate just how unalike the sentences sound.

ENGLISH	give	him	one	more	
MANDARIN	給 give *gay*	他 him *tar*	多 more *dwor*	一 one *ee*	箇 an *ger*
CANTONESE	畀 give *bay*	多 more *dor*	箇 an *goh*	渠 him *koe*	
TEOCHEW	分 give *boong*	伊 him *ee*	加 more *gair*	介 an *gai*	
DANISH	giv	ham	en/et	mere	

The differences in grammar, vocabulary, and pronunciation are thus comparable to those that divide languages like English and Danish, or French and Italian. Indeed, the Danish equivalent of the sentence that is included at the bottom of the table is much closer to the English than these examples are to each other.

The unique and unitive nature of Chinese characters has a lot to do with why Chinese is so often mistaken for a single language. Chinese characters are a sort of written etymology, representing senses not sounds. Had the Germanic languages also developed a character-based script, the sentence in the previous table would be indistinguishable in written form between Danish and English, because all the words are cognate, i.e. they are the Danish and English versions of the same words.[4]

Vernacular Writing

All Chinese spoken languages can be written in Chinese characters. This style of writing is called vernacular writing. Literate speakers of one Chinese language, however, may not understand vernacular writing in another, because the characters and grammar might be unfamiliar, and the senses of the known characters might differ. The situation is similar to that faced by monolingual speakers of English who attempt to make sense of Spanish or French writing. Some simple words might already be familiar; others might be recognisable by virtue of their similarity to English words, but could turn out to be what are termed false friends, or to have divergent senses despite being related; others might be utterly unrecognisable.

Today, vernacular writing in standard Mandarin is the most common written language amongst speakers of all Chinese languages. Many have acquired it purely as a written language, never learning how to pronounce the characters in any language but their own, i.e. they learn the grammar and vocabulary, but use their own language to read the characters aloud.

Literary Chinese

While *The Poison of Polygamy* contains the odd word or phrase in vernacular writing, it is predominantly written in another language, one that does not accord with any Chinese spoken language. This language is properly called Literary Chinese. It is so named because

---

4   This statement hinges on the theory that the Danish indefinite articles evolved from the source of the English numeral one, or vice versa.

it was the dominant language of Chinese literature. But Literary Chinese (with a capital L) should not be mistaken to mean Chinese that is literary: literature can be written in vernacular Chinese too, and Literary Chinese, as the universal written language of the Chinese world until very recently, was often used for decidedly unliterary purposes. Literary Chinese is simply the name of an independent written language.

Literary Chinese is a language that has played a similar role through much of Asia to that played by Latin in Europe, in that it was a universal written language used between speakers of different spoken languages. It also developed out of Classical Chinese, as later forms of Latin developed out of Classical Latin. (Technically, Literary Chinese encompasses the ancient Classical Chinese, which forms the basis of its grammar and vocabulary.) However, the analogy to Latin only goes so far. Latin can only be read aloud in Latin. Literary Chinese can be read aloud in all Chinese languages, and even in unrelated languages like Japanese, Korean, and Vietnamese. This is something it has in common with mathematical notation, which can likewise be read aloud in different languages as if it were a part of them.

The specimen of Literary Chinese text shown in Figure 9 might make for a good illustration. It was written in Japan, by a Japanese speaker, for Japanese readers. However, people conversant in Literary Chinese can read it with ease, whether or not they know a word of Japanese. To the reader of Literary Chinese, it is just as clear as the mathematical equation beside it would be to any modern-day mathematician. Like the equation, it can be read aloud in different languages, and it is not possible to tell which language its writer spoke. Unlike the equation, though, it is written in logograms not ideograms, i.e. its symbols represent words with all their complex nuances. All of this makes Literary Chinese a truly amazing written language, and a very different thing to the written forms of spoken languages that are familiar to most English speakers.

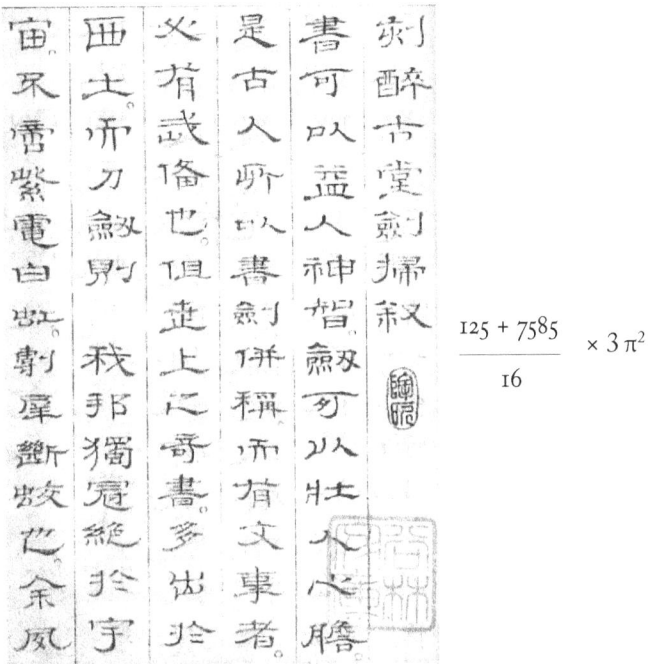

$$\frac{125 + 7585}{16} \times 3\pi^2$$

Figure 9: Preface to "醉古堂劍掃" (National Institute of Japanese Literature, CC BY SA 4.0, DOI 10.20730/200013472)

These singular qualities meant that Literary Chinese formed a written continuum between distinct spoken languages, and this naturally conferred great advantages. Furthermore, in addition to its ability to transcend linguistic, national and cultural boundaries, or what might be considered boundaries of place, Literary Chinese also transcended time in a striking way. While not immune to change or untouched by literary fashions and movements, Literary Chinese has remained relatively stable over the millennia, to the extent that it is possible to read something written in it and not be able to tell whether it was written yesterday, 600 years ago, or 1600 years ago. Thousands of years' worth of accumulated literature is thus readily accessible to those conversant in Literary Chinese.

This circumstance has had a great influence on its writers, and is reflected in the almost ever-present allusion to history and literature that characterises their literary productions.

Literary Chinese was still the language of Chinese literature and general communication when *The Poison of Polygamy* was published in the early 1900s. Apart from the occasional piece of vernacular writing, in the form of folk songs for example, the news, editorials, advertisements, readers' letters and other content in Melbourne's *Chinese Times* was all in Literary Chinese. Nowadays, though, Mandarin being the dominant written language amongst Chinese speakers, knowledge of Literary Chinese is much poorer. Many Chinese speakers today would therefore have difficulty reading *The Poison of Polygamy*, even though it is a work of popular fiction.

The Novel's Chinese

Apart from the occasional ornate flourish characteristic of a higher style, *The Poison of Polygamy* is written in simple Literary Chinese, into which is introduced the odd word or phrase of vernacular language. The vernacular content is not confined to a single spoken language, and, since it goes to the question of the novel's literary influences, is discussed below, under the heading "The Novel".

THE TRANSLATION

Translation, even between closely related languages, is rarely a simple matter of sequential replacement, in which one language's words are exchanged, in the order in which they appear, for natural equivalents in another.

To begin with, the sequential approach might alter the sense completely, on account of the invisible influence of grammar. In some languages, for example, "the grass eats the cow" means "the cow eats the grass". Usually the change in meaning is more subtle, but attempts at preserving the original word order (the syntax) often result in distortions of emphasis and flow. So it becomes necessary to rearrange the original order of the words and phrases according to the target language's grammar, in order to reflect the actual grammatical structure of the original, i.e. the actual relationships between the words and phrases.

There is then the issue that words which are natural one-to-one equivalents are rare. There might in fact be no word with a sense remotely close to the one in question. Alternatively, there might be any number of partial equivalents, by virtue of differences in semantic scope or grammar, e.g. depending on the context, Chinese 羊 could be sheep or goat(s), and English "rice" could be 稻 the rice plant, 米 uncooked rice or 飯 cooked rice; the same is true for verbs, conjunctions and other classes of words. Semantically close equivalents might exist, but introduce undesirable consequences. The unrepetitive Cantonese sentence "我哋晚清陣時 邊有夜瞓晏起 翻學遲到之理" translates as the awkwardly repetitive "There wasn't any question of us sleeping late, rising late and arriving late for school in the late Qing (dynasty)". This example is also based on differences in semantic scope—four words in Cantonese that describe different types of lateness—but there are many other possibilities. A translation that is a close match for a word's central sense might carry very different overtones, introduce or reduce ambiguity, destroy a rhetorical play, or fail to convey an important idiomatic sense. Do the pickled peppers in "Peter Piper picked a peck of pickled peppers" matter? Is it more important that the translation be a tongue twister than that any of the original words be preserved? Do the individual senses of the words "I beg your pardon" matter so much as the function of the phrase? Does the alliteration in *Charlie and the Chocolate Factory*, *A Christmas Carol* and *Peter Pan* matter? Would "*John and the Chocolate Factory*", "*A Christmas Song*" and "*George Pan*" sound as good? Would Blake's "Tyger Tyger, burning bright, In the forests of the night" still sound wonderful without the alliteration, metre and rhyme? Should archaisms, colloquialisms and rare words be translated as such? The list goes on.

Then there is that elusive quality upon which language so often depends. It is the reason when we hear a situation described as a "witch's brew" that we know the speaker means an utter hotch-potch, rather than something poisonous. It is often central to humour. It is a quality which one thinker of the Enlightenment era alluded to when he observed that languages are "formed on the particular notions and manners of a people, without knowing which, we cannot know the language. We may know the direct sig-nification of single words; but by these no beauty of expression, no sally of genius, no wit is conveyed to the mind. All this must be by allusion to other ideas."[5]

These things and more mean that translation is always imper-fect, that it is an art of compromise, a balancing act in which the translator must decide what aspects of an original are to be sacri-ficed so that others can be preserved. The translator's aims have a critical role to play in these decisions.

My overarching aim in this translation, to explain by way of a culinary analogy, has been to produce an English equivalent to a Chinese dish, one that looks and tastes the same, but is formed from English ingredients, combined by means of the techniques of the English kitchen. I have tried to avoid the simplistic direct approach, the one that swaps shiitakes for English field mush-rooms, soy sauce for Worcestershire, etc., mirroring the original but in doing so producing something unpalatable and utterly unalike. I have also tried to avoid the domesticating approach, the

5   These are the words of the Corsican leader General Paoli, as recorded in
     James Boswell's *The Life of Samuel Johnson* (London: Encyclopedia
     Britannica, 1952), p. 166.

one which caters for Western tastes, and serves up a dish that bears little similarity to the original.

This is to say that my ambition has been to convey both the sense and flavour of the original, or in more specific terms: the various layers of literal and implied meaning; a sense of the rhetoric in which that meaning is expressed; and the style, spirit and idiom of the original. The approach has involved close attention to detail, and the considered treatment of nuances—denotational, connotational, implicational, idiomatic, pragmatic, rhetorical, discursive, argumentational, stylistic, etc.

It has been a process of continual compromise, in which I have prioritised the preservation of one aspect of the source text over another on a case by case basis, in light of various considerations, prime amongst which have been the requirements of a number of intended audiences.

The first and foremost of these audiences has been historians, since it is historians who instigated and have supported the whole project. Of paramount importance for them has been the reflection of the exact meaning of the text and the insights it gives into the author's thinking. In other words, what the great translation theorist of the Scottish Enlightenment, Alexander Fraser Tytler, posited as the first of his three general rules for translation: that "a translation should give a complete transcript of the ideas of the original work".[6] Adherence to this principle has necessitated many compromises on rhetoric and style, and a more labourious approach. In some instances, it has meant hours spent fashioning the best possible translation for a single word, a level of intellectual engagement I considered necessary if the translation was to prove serviceable for the purposes of analysis.

---

6   Alexander Fraser Tytler, *Essay on the Principles of Translation* (1791) (Edinburgh: A. Constable & Co., 1813).

The second intended audience has been the general reader, in consideration of whose requirements I have endeavoured to make the translation not less readable than the original would have been for its audience.

I recognised at an early stage that the text, being written in good but not terribly challenging Literary Chinese, and in a common style, coupled with the approach I was taking to the translation, the convenience of the parallel-text format and the exciting nature of the story, might combine to make for a finished book that would be useful as a resource in language learning and teaching. The presence of the odd word or two of vernacular language did not concern me, since vernacular language has always been combined with Literary Chinese, and readers need to develop the ability to recognise it. The third intended audience has therefore been language learners.

The merit of the translation for language learners' purposes, as I see it, is its closeness and the manner in which it emphasises grammatical and semantic nuances. There are two sets of semantic nuances reflected in translation that I should like to highlight. The first relates to synonyms. Languages are filled with synonyms, and the ability to recognise the subtleties that divide them is central to the attainment of linguistic competence. To quote Mark Twain, "The difference between the *almost right* word and the *right* word is really a large matter—'tis the difference between the lightning-bug [firefly] and the lightning." Where possible, the translation attempts to reflect these subtleties, which should distinguish it from many examples of translation from Literary Chinese, and old vernacular Chinese, for which this is not a focus.

The other nuance relates to Westernisation, or rather its absence. Westernisation has had a huge impact on the Chinese language. Words have been redefined, independent of the natural process of linguistic development. What is an apple today might have been an orange yesterday. The translation attempts to reflect the senses words had in the author's day. This should make for a point of difference from some modern translations of Literary Chinese that are coloured by readings based on standard Mandarin, English, and unreliable bilingual dictionaries. The desire to reflect language and its nuances faithfully also extends to the footnotes, in which my own translations of such things as book titles and quotations from classical literature are often given in preference to pre-existing ones.

The needs of a few other audiences have been considered as well, not least amongst which have been those with an interest in Australian writing in languages other than English, and literary critics, who I can only hope will be understanding of the translator's limitations and the project's challenges.

Lastly, my own aims have played a role in my decisions. Chief amongst these has been the desire to avoid the unreflective quaintness, peculiarity and alienness that characterises so much translation from Literary Chinese: to show it as it is, a language just as human as English. The footnotes, which compensate to a degree for what is lost in translation and strive to familiarise the reader with the unfamiliar, are designed to dispel some of this strangeness. The desire to introduce readers to China's linguistic and literary landscape has also played a role.

Another aspect of my approach has been the considered reflection of the source text's rhetoric, especially its rhetorical figures. Rhetorical figures are those little tricks of wording that make phrases memorable and powerful, such as the aforementioned alliteration and metre. The English names for the various figures are generally taken from Greek, "anadiplosis" and "antanaclasis" for example, which, like alliteration and metre, are common to both Literary Chinese and English. Literary Chinese and English, though, being about as far removed from each other as it is possible for two languages to be, do not share all their rhetorical figures, and those they do share do not always function in the same ways, which is of course to be expected of languages that lack the same classes of words and fundamental grammar. This said, rhetorical figures, and rhetoric more broadly, are essential to fine writing in both languages. How and whether or not rhetoric is reflected in translation can accordingly have a significant effect on the impression a translation gives. See *The Poison of Polygamy*, footnote 230, for an illustration of my approach.

Kumarajiva, a celebrated translator of the fourth and fifth centuries, bemoaned that in translations from Sanskrit to Chinese "the literariness and ornament is lost, such that, while the gross sense is achieved, the result is so far removed in literary style as to be like a serving of pre-chewed rice, which not only lacks the flavour but induces biliousness too."[7] As a person who likes to savour language, and who comes to translation as a lover of Chinese literature, I must admit to occasionally sharing these visceral sentiments when reading examples of translation from Literary Chinese to English. One aim of this translation has been the avoidance of such defects, which, at their worst, manifest in what can only be described as pidgin-English translation. This can result when a translator, presented with rhetoric that is not amenable to direct translation, fails to consider the rhetorical purpose of an author's wording. I have endeavoured not to lose sight of our author's rhetorical purpose, and to adopt the closest techniques of English rhetoric in translation, in order to achieve the same effects.

A more detailed description of the challenges of translation from Literary Chinese and of my translation strategies cannot be accommodated within the limited scope of a translator's introduction. The general comments above touch only on the surface of these matters, but should give at least some insight.

---

7   The original line is "改梵為秦失其藻蔚雖得大意殊隔文體有似嚼飯與人非徒失味乃令嘔噦也" and appears in the 高僧傳 (卷第二), which was compiled in the first half of the sixth century and is accessible via the Chinese Text Project website (https://ctext.org).

THE NOVEL

Like much of the writing in the *Chinese Times*, *The Poison of Polygamy*'s instalments were not accompanied by any form of attribution. Historian Mei-fen Kuo and I suspected the author to be one of the newspaper's editors, a certain Wong Yau Kung (黃右公).[8] After a two-year search and the unearthing of much circumstantial evidence, I had resigned myself to the unenviable task of supporting this claim by means of a work of comparative stylometric analysis. My last-minute discovery of an advertisement on page 7 of the 30 June 1917 edition of the *Chinese Times* (see Figure 10) obviated the need for all of this, because it provided the verification we and other researchers had been seeking.[9]

Roughly translated, it reads:

---

8   A.K.A. (Joseph) Wong Shee Ping. Shee Ping would seem to have been his Chinese given name, and to have been adopted as his English surname, a not uncommon occurrence, owing to the fact that given names follow surnames in Chinese and are thus readily mistaken for them. In characters, the given name Shee Ping appears to have been 樹屏 (a match for his brother's name Shee Fan 樹藩), later simplified to the homophonous 樹平, which is used in connection with his activities as a Christian pastor. Yau Kung, which was written as 又公 and 右公 in Chinese, is the name he went under as a journalist and republican. Note that the same name has been romanised in such modern histories as C.F. Yong's *The New Gold Mountain: The Chinese in Australia, 1901–1921*, Mei-fen Kuo's *Making Chinese Australia: Urban Elites, Newspapers and the Formation of Chinese Australian Identity, 1982–1912*, Mei-fen Kuo and Judith Brett's *Unlocking the History of The Australasian Kuo Min Tang, 1911–2013,* and John Fitzgerald's *Big White Lie: Chinese Australians in White Australia* as "Yue-kung", "Yue-kong" and "Yung-kung".

9   Like the original instalments of *The Poison of Polygamy*, this advertisement can be viewed on the National Library of Australia's Trove website.

Figure 10: Advertisement for the new novel *World of Robbers* by the author of *The Poison of Polygamy*, from the *Chinese Times*, 30 June 1917. (State Library of Victoria)

TAKE NOTE, TAKE NOTE: THE RELEASE OF A NEW NOVEL.

Expert novelist Kong-ha Yee-long,[10] who previously wrote a book which has long enjoyed the approbation of society, *The Poison of Polygamy*, is now writing[11] a new detective novel named *World of Robbers*, for publication by instalment in the *Chinese Times*.[12]

---

10   Kong-ha Yee-long is a *nom de plume* which appeared to be a wordplay on Wong Yau Kung's name, it being formed from a place-name associated with his surname (江夏) and an expression synonymous with one of the given names he went under (二郎 Yee-long "second/different fellow" = 又公 Yau-kung "additional/other gent"). This proved to be the case.

11   "… is now writing" could also be translated as "has now written", because the aspect of the verb "to write" is not indicated in the Chinese.

12   This reincarnation of the *Chinese Times* was known in Chinese as the 平報, which might be translated as "*The Democrat*". This translation is made in consideration of the declaration, on the newspaper's front page, that its

The book describes how a wealthy Hoi Yip businessman[13] is kidnapped by bandits and how his son, who is studying in the Americas and rushes home on hearing the news, sets out in person to detect the bandits' hideout and save his father. His various methods compare favourably with those of the great detectives of Europe and America, and the descriptions within of the havoc wreaked by Lung,[14] the brutishness of the bandits, and the corruption of society will surely be of great benefit to people's hearts and minds, and the state of the world. The ingeniousness of its structure and the classical elegance of its diction will thus be little more than ancillaries.

The first instalment of the advertised novel, 強盜世界 "*World of Robbers*", made its appearance on page 5 of the same edition. Soon afterwards, the *Chinese Times* closed.

We knew that the publication of *World of Robbers* had been recommenced some two years later in Sydney's 民國報 *Chinese Republic News*, wherein, appearing under the revised title 偵探之影 "*The Detective's Shadow*", it was clearly attributed to the newly appointed editor-in-chief, Wong Yau Kung. The *Chinese Times*'s confirmation that both novels were the work of the same author thus confirmed Wong Yau Kung's authorship of *The Poison of Polygamy*. A biography of the author—a revolutionary firebrand and Christian preacher, and an important figure in Federation Australia's Chinese community—is provided separately to this introduction.

---

central objective is to 闡明平民政治原理 "elucidate the principles of democracy", which appears to have been intended to clarify the title's sense: see page 1 of the 20 December 1919 edition of the *Chinese Times*.

13 A businessman from the city now known in Mandarin as *Táishān*, in Cantonese as *Tòihsāan*, and in its local vernacular as *Hoi San* (臺山).

14 Presumably republican-era general Lung Chi Kwang (龍濟光). ("Lung" should be pronounced *loong*.)

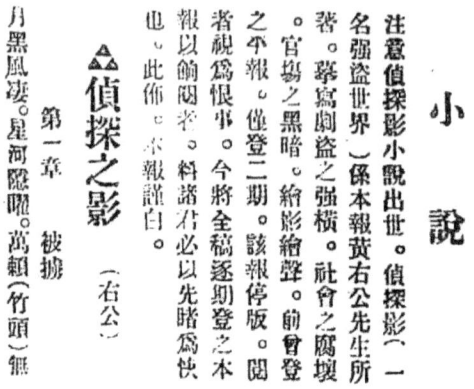

Figure 11: The foreword to the first instalment of *The Detective's Shadow*, *Chinese Republic News*, 21 June 1919. (State Library of New South Wales)

Like the advertisement in the *Chinese Times*, the advertisement that appeared with the *Chinese Republic News*'s first instalment of *World of Robbers*, which was published 21 June 1919 and is shown in Figure 11, also provides some interesting insights into how *The Poison of Polygamy* was viewed.

The following is a rough translation:

NOVEL

Take note: Release of the novel *The Detective's Shadow*.

    The Detective's Shadow (A.K.A *World of Robbers*) is the work of this newspaper's Wong Yau Kung, and vividly[15] depicts the brutishness of hardened bandits, the rottenness of society, and the black state of officialdom. It was previously carried in the *Chinese Times*, but the newspaper ceased publication after just two instalments, which readers viewed as a matter of regret.

---

15   It is perhaps worth highlighting that the Chinese expression translated here as "vividly" (繪影繪聲) implies the vivid description of both images and sounds, which is characteristic of the author's style.

The full manuscript will now be carried, by instalment, in this newspaper for the entertainment of its readers.[16] We expect, gentle readers, that each of you will be eager to see it first.

The Chinese Republic News.

THE DETECTIVE'S SHADOW (Yau Kung)

Chapter One: Kidnapped.

A literary phenomenon took place in the final years of the Qing dynasty (from around 1900), and *The Poison of Polygamy* was part of it. Reformers and revolutionists had recognised the socially transformative power of fiction, in consequence of which the Chinese world had been flooded with literature intended to expose social ills and moral horrors, awaken readers, and rouse them to action. The modernist literary critic Lu Hsün (魯迅), in his book 中國小說史略 *A Brief History of Chinese Fiction*,[17] which was published in 1930, labelled it 譴責小說 "censorious fiction".[18] He described it therein, in an epitome that is today generally considered to have been just, as 命意在於匡世似與諷刺小說同倫而辭氣浮露筆無藏鋒甚且過甚其辭以合時人嗜好則其度量技術之相去亦遠矣 "purposed for the correction of the world, and seemingly a counterpart of the satire, yet unveiled in tone, unrestrained in execution, and given, in conformity with contemporary prejudices, to be overly severe, such that the divide within between technique and magnanimity of spirit is great."

---

16 Despite this statement, the full manuscript was not carried: only the first sixteen instalments.

17 Lu Hsün (*Lǔ Xùn*) was an outspoken exponent of vernacular writing and a savage critic of Literary Chinese; nevertheless, he chose to write his *Brief History of Chinese Fiction*, which is in fact a large work, entirely in Literary Chinese, citing brevity as his justification.

18 In the English translation of the book, published in 1959, the same term is rendered as the risqué-sounding "novels of exposure". I introduce here and below, in inverted commas, my own translations.

Censorious fiction and its social context reflected each other. The late Qing was a period of transition and transformation. Decades of foreign aggression and encroachment, and consequent humiliation and internal turmoil, had given rise to powerful social and political reformist and revolutionary movements, to which Westernisation, industrialisation and nationalism were central. Subject to suppression within Manchu China, the voices of these movements rang out loudest in foreign-controlled havens. These included Hong Kong, Shanghai, and various overseas outposts of Chinese civilisation, such as Japan, Singapore and Australia.

Advances in printing technology had provided the means, spawning newspapers, magazines and books that catered to a public eager for open and reliable sources of news, and Western knowledge and ideas. Reading was more popular than it had ever been. Translations of Western literature, often very heavily modified, flowed from the presses, as did new native works of nonfiction on all manner of subjects, as well as censorious fiction, for which entertainment value was understood to be key to success. This was a period of literary innovation and experimentation.

An anonymous Cambridge-educated Chinese writer detailed these momentous happenings in a 1908 edition of the *Contemporary Review*:

> First and foremost among these changes [taking place in China] came the development of the Press [...] Before the Chino-Japanese War[19] two daily papers were published in Shanghai [...] They had some resemblance to a newspaper, but they were badly written and worse printed. There was a

---

19   1894–95.

weak and timorous leading article—the editor dared not say anything beyond what was metaphorical—and the news was more or less local and hardly worth reading. Their readers were consequently very few. In my native town, where there were sixty thousand people (out of whom at least three thousand could read), only one copy of the *Sin-pao*[20] was to be found. The privileged reader of this solitary copy was, of course, an exceptionally well-read man. I remember well, when the war with Japan was going on, how people used to flock to his residence for news, and how they expressed their indignation and disbelief when a defeat on our side was announced. The paper was sent to him weekly, and often arrived at its destination after a delay of three or four weeks, although we were within a night's journey of Shanghai, where it was published. The fact is, there was not a single Government post-office in my town then, and the papers were delivered by a merchant's agent, who not only read them first, but circulated them among his friends and relations before finally putting them into the hands of the original subscriber. To-day, what a contrast! In the same town two hundred copies of the above-mentioned paper are sold, besides many other journals.

The number of newspapers has increased with amazing rapidity within the last decade. In Peking, where no newspapers existed before 1902, there are now ten; and—most surprising of all—one of these is edited by a woman. In all the large provincial towns—even in such a one as Tai-yuan-foo in Shan-se, which is situated so far from the coast that until recently the difficulty of communication has been extreme—local papers are published. It is at Shanghai, however, that these palpitators of public opinion abound. Under the

---

20   A.K.A. the 申報 *Shun Pao* or *Shanghai News*.

protection of the settlement, they are free from interference by the officials, and, taking this advantage, the editor's attitude has become easy and bold. The result of this is that not only is the increase in numbers great, but the improvements which some of these papers have undergone within a short period is amazing. Take, for example, the *Chong-wai-tse-pao* (the *Universal Gazette*), which was founded about 1898, under a management that was shocking in the extreme. Five years ago it had only four pages, but now it has twelve. It has special correspondents all over China, and all the news is sent by wire. Important news is printed in large type and neatly arranged in order of the provinces. The leading articles are very outspoken and bold. They are probably of very little literary value, but this is arranged expressly for the purpose of widening its circulation among the less-educated classes. Foreign news is not neglected. Though it has no special correspondents in Europe, it has one in Japan, and voluntary contributions from our students in Europe (which are plentiful) are eagerly sought after and carefully chosen.

No less well-organized is the *Tse-pao* (the *Eastern Times*). In fact, as far as internal politics are concerned, no newspapers in Europe or in Japan are so well informed. Its managers spare neither pains nor expense to "fish out" those secrets which the Government wishes to keep, and their achievements toward this end are a continuous history of remarkable "scoops." [...] Then, besides politics, many interesting topics are discussed. Serial and short stories are published: some of them are translations of well-known works in English or French, but more frequently we find in them satires written in a form calculated to expose the rottenness of the existing Government and Legislature.

Parallel with the improvements in newspapers runs the increase in the number of books and periodicals. All sorts of monthly and fortnightly reviews have literally sprung into existence, and new books come out by the score every month, most of them being translations of works on politics, history, philosophy, laws, science, and arts. In the periodicals party spirit sometimes runs very high, and two papers of different parties—for instance, the *Min-pao* (the *People*), which is conducted by Dr. Sun Yat Sen, the well-known revolutionary leader, and the *Sin-min-chung-pao* (the *New People*), the organ of Mr. K'wang Yu Wei,[21] the great reformer—will often engage in a hot debate over questions of burning importance.[22]

This essay contains the odd inaccuracy, but paints a representative picture overall, and makes many pertinent observations, some not included in the above extracts. *The Poison of Polygamy* was a product of the new newspapers it refers to, which, along with the literary periodicals, had ushered in an age of instalment fiction. Interestingly, the writers of this fiction were often candid about their political and social aims and motivations, and detailed them and their literary theories and analyses in revealing articles that were published alongside. The author of *The Poison of Polygamy* was clearly influenced by these theorists.

One of the best-known literary magazines, the 中外小說林 "*Miscellany of Chinese and Foreign Fiction*", carried an essay in 1907 that makes a number of statements relevant to our novel. The first is that 小說 ... 如顯微鏡增其眼光 "Fiction ..., like a microscope's

---

21 "K'wang" appears to contain an erroneous W. The individual in question is K'ang Yu Wei (康有為).

22 "Social Transformation in China", *Contemporary Review*, December 1908, quoted in Rossiter Johnson, ed., *The Great Events by Famous Historians*, vol. XX, *The Awakening of China (a.d. 1905)* (1914) (New York: The National Alumni, 1919), but unattributed in the latter.

Figure 12: The "Social Lens" illustration that accompanied each instalment of the novel. (State Library of Victoria)

lens, enhances vision." The trope of literature functioning as a 鏡 "mirror", "looking glass" or "lens", which enhances a viewer or reader's capacity for (in)sight, is a common one in Chinese, and might be contrasted with the English trope of "shining a light". Connected with this idea is the illustration of the schoolboy in Western dress holding a large lens over the word 社會 "society" in the section heading 社會鏡 "Social Lens" that precedes many of the novel's instalments. Another idea advanced in the essay is that histories are not as good as novels on history, since the former induce somnolence, and the latter excitement.

These periodicals also theorised on and promoted writing within a range of literary genres inspired by Western fiction. Genre names generally constituted the works' subtitles. They included 偵探小說 "detective fiction/novel", 冒險小說 "adventure fiction/novel", 航海小說 "navigation fiction/novel", 寓言小說 "allegorical fiction/novel", and 歷史小說 "historical fiction/novel". *The Poison of Polygamy*'s subtitle, 社會小說 "A Social Novel", was the name of one such genre.[23]

In fact, one of the four most celebrated works of censorious fiction, a novel entitled 二十年目睹之怪現狀 *Bizarre Happenings Witnessed over Two Decades*, was published under the same subtitle

---

23   The same expression can also be translated as "social fiction".

when it first appeared, in 1903, as a work of instalment fiction in the earliest fiction periodical, 新小說 "*New Fiction*".[24]

I have translated the name of this genre (社會小說) as "social novel", in preference to the equally feasible "novel on society", because it would appear to have been intended as a match for the Western genre of that name. Evidence of this is provided by such things as the incomplete novel 上海之秘密 "*The Mysteries of Shanghai*", which was an imitation of a Western social novel, Eugène Sue's *The Mysteries of Paris*, that was presented as a 社會小說 "social novel" when published in 1906 in 月月小說 *The All-Story Monthly* (a Shanghai literary magazine edited by the author of the abovementioned *Bizarre Happenings Witnessed over Two Decades*).[25]

One thing that distinguishes *The Poison of Polygamy* from most works of censorious fiction is that it is written in Literary Chinese. This is not to say that it is the only example, or even the only example within the social-fiction genre.[26] However, the anti-Literary Chinese vernacular-writing movement was active when *The Poison of Polygamy* was written, and had been for some time. 裘廷梁 Ch'iu T'ing-liang, a member of the movement's vanguard, had declared over a decade earlier, in an influential essay advocating the abolition of Literary Chinese, that:

---

24   "*New Fiction*" had been established in Yokohama in 1902 by the protégé of the aforenamed "great-reformer" K'ang Yu-wei, 梁啟超 Liang Ch'i-ch'ao. A year later it relocated to Shanghai.

25   There was an awareness of what the Western social novel was: works such as *Uncle Tom's Cabin* (黑奴籲天錄) and *Les Misérables* (慘社會) had been translated into Chinese. However, these translations were heavily manipulated and differed in character to the originals.

26   One other example of a work of Literary Chinese censorious fiction written within the social-fiction genre is 黃伯耀 "Wong Pak Yiu's" 煙海回瀾 "*The Sea of Fog's Turning Tide*", which was published in Hong Kong's 中外小說林 "*Miscellany of Chinese and Foreign Fiction*" in 1908. It is, however, only a short story.

愚天下之具莫文言若智天下之具莫白話若[27]

"There is no appurtenance which addles the world so much as literary language, and none which enlightens it so much as vernacular speech."

Ironically, Ch'iu was expressing himself in Literary Chinese.

Many other exponents at the time, seemingly influenced by Western assessments of the backwardness of the Chinese written language, spoke in similarly excoriating terms, while advocating the same modernisations as our author, and not infrequently continuing to write in Literary Chinese.

The vernacular-writing movement had reached the Pearl River Delta: newspapers and works of fiction were being printed in Cantonese. Our author also composed vernacular fiction for the *Chinese Times*.[28] Nevertheless, he chose to write *The Poison of Polygamy* in Literary Chinese. The advertisement stressing the classical elegance of his diction suggests that it might have appealed to his audience. This said, his Literary Chinese was not strictly pure.

While Chinese-language authors can opt to write in either pure Literary Chinese or pure vernacular Chinese, they can also combine the two to varying degrees. This combination was not unusual: many Literary Chinese works of fiction made some use of the vernacular. Even today, various Literary Chinese words and expressions are often employed in Mandarin vernacular writing, to which they lend a sense of formality and elegance. Conversely, in the *Chinese Times*, vernacular expressions were often mixed into the predominant Literary Chinese, adding colloquial flavour and a sense of simplicity and familiarity.

---

27   裘廷梁, "論白話為維新之本" (1898) quoted in 烏國平, 黃淋, "中國文論選: 近代卷" (下) (南京: 江蘇文藝出版社, 1996).

28   又公, "牛女談情", the *Chinese Times*, 4 September 1909, p. 9.

The author and most readers of the *Chinese Times* were speakers of the See Yip language (四邑話), whose homeland is the See Yip region (also known as See Yup, Sze Yup, and *Sìyì*) southwest of Canton (or *Guǎngzhōu*), from which most of Australia, the USA and Canada's early Chinese gold seekers and settlers came. (Hence its old byname of 小世界語 "The Little World Language".) While largely incomprehensible to the average Cantonese speaker, it is nevertheless a sister language to Cantonese, and shares a fair proportion of its vocabulary with it.[29]

In the author's day, a very special written admixture had particular currency in the Pearl River Delta, i.e. within the vicinity of Canton. Known as 三及第文 "tripartite writing", it was a medley of three things: Literary Chinese; a regional Chinese vernacular; and the written form of one or more of several historic or current national languages (these national languages were linguae francae based on the vernaculars of the various central and northern Chinese capitals).[30] *The Poison of Polygamy* shows the influence of

---

29 The following address is that of an online dictionary of the See Yip language's Taishan dialect, which is a rare and convenient resource on the language, and a useful form of comparison with Cantonese and Mandarin: http://www.stephen-li.com/TaishaneseVocabulary/Taishanese.html

30 The primary and literal sense of the term 三及第 "tripartite" is "the three who attained the grade", meaning, to put it in sporting language, the gold, silver and bronze medallists in the highest of China's civil examinations, the palace examination: preeminent scholars known respectively in Chinese by the titles 狀元, 榜眼 and 探花. This collective term for the top three scholars in a palace examination later developed into an elegant epithet, e.g. in botanical and culinary names, for things that are characterised by a medley of three elements. The humorous Cantonese expressions "三及第粥" and "三及第飯" for congee and rice respectively that is burnt underneath, cooked in the middle, and uncooked on top are well-known examples of the use of the term today. (Note that these expressions can also be applied to properly cooked rice and congee dishes that contain a mixture of three additional ingredients.)

tripartite writing, both through the type of vernacular language it employs, and the way in which it is employed.

Some examples of local vernacular language in the novel are quite overt:

- 眼瞓病 "Sleep Sickness", which is used throughout as the protagonist's nickname. (The second character is now more commonly written 瞓.)
- The expression used for "roots" in Part 10's 植物之根蕸 "the roots of the vegetation". The first character of this set vernacular expression is a standard word for root; the second is a colloquiallism, which refers especially to a thick fibrous type of root, as can be produced by grasses.
- Part 29's 有等 "some". (The second character is now more commonly written 啲.)
- Part 38's 懵丁 "bleary-eyed dolt".
- Part 43's 好心咯 "How good of you!"
- Part 53's 笠 "loose-woven basket" in the expression 豚笠 "pig basket" (this is a distinct sense to that of "pig pen", which the same expression has in other vernaculars).

Other usages are concealed within the Literary Chinese. This was a common trick, which involves the use of a word that has the same or similar senses in both Literary Chinese and the vernacular of the author and audience. Readers unfamiliar with the vernacular are liable to overlook these usages, but they are not lost on its speakers. Examples include:

- Part 25's 偏益儂耶 "that it would have been for my benefit alone?" in which the use of the character 益 "advantage" as a transitive verb is standard in Cantonese and the See Yip language, but could be taken for an example of Literary Chinese anthimeria.[31]

- What is both the Literary Chinese and the See Yip word for 食 "eat", which appears throughout the novel, even replacing, in Part 31, the Mandarin equivalent 吃 in a Mandarin idiom. The word also has the extended sense of "to smoke" in Cantonese and the See Yip language, and appears in that sense with reference to opium in Part 48.
- The word 藥鐺 "medicine pot" in Part 48, which is both the Literary Chinese name of an ancient style of three-legged vessel for the decoction of medicines, and the standard Cantonese and See Yip term for a medicine pot, typically one without legs.

The second vernacular element in modern tripartite writing is typically the lingua franca of Mandarin, one form or another of which has been the national spoken language of China's Ming, Qing, Republican and Communist states, i.e. the national spoken language of China since the fourteenth century. However, older tripartite writing also drew on the national spoken language of the Song dynasty, which was not Mandarin, though it bore some similarity to it. The earlier national vernacular was particularly familiar to China's literati, because a celebrated form of poetry called 詞 "tune poetry" made great use of it. Part 43's use of 箇處 in the sense of "here" provides one clear example of the use of this early national vernacular in the novel, and points to the influence of an older style of tripartite writing.

---

31 Anthimeria is the use of one part of speech for another, like Shakespeare's use of the noun "elbow" as a verb, which happens to have stuck, thus spawning a new word, "to elbow", the use of which no longer counts as anthimeria.

This hybrid style of writing had—and still has—its proponents and detractors. One distinct advantage it offered its authors was the ability to produce all manner of different effects through the adept exploitation of its numerous registers. The author of *The Poison of Polygamy* demonstrates a strong ability in this regard.

Tripartite and censorious fiction are far from the author's only literary influences. I should like to highlight two in particular that I suspect to have been important stylistic influences. The first is the renowned collection of Literary Chinese stories entitled 聊齋志異 *Strange Tales from a Chinese Studio*,[32] which dates from around the turn of the eighteenth century. The second is the productions of a contemporary literary school, later labelled the 鴛鴦蝴蝶派 "Lovey-dovey School" or the 禮拜六派 "Saturday School" by its realist critics, which are characterised by ornate prose (lots of parallel couplets) and sentimentality.

So far as intellectual influences are concerned, the author's assertive brand of Christianity cannot be overlooked. It perhaps finds expression in the novel's criticisms of polygamy, foot binding, folk religion, opium smoking, and authoritarianism. Confucianism, referenced through frequent allusions to Confucian literature, was clearly another intellectual influence, and suggests that the author might have trained for the imperial examinations. Whether or not there was a connection between his Christianity and his scholarly background is difficult to say. Christian missionaries were, however, responsible for the introduction of the modern newspaper and involved in the growth of censorious fiction. They are also noted to have employed men of letters schooled for the imperial examinations as writers.[33]

---

32   Also known by such names as *Strange Stories from a Chinese Studio* and *Liaozhai Zhiyi*.

33   See Patrick Hanan, "The Missionary Novels of Nineteenth-Century China", *Harvard Journal of Asiatic Studies* 60, no. 2 (December 2000), pp. 413–43.

Huang and Ommundsen, in their 2016 paper "Poison, Polygamy and Postcolonial Politics: The First Chinese Australian Novel", observe that the *The Poison of Polygamy*'s plot development was carefully devised to suit the instalment format.[34] Regular small climaxes and twists in the story line would seem to support this observation. Certain flaws, however, such as awkward backtracking and the unexplained disappearance of some minor characters (e.g. Tsiu Hei's daughters and Kam Ngau's wife Lee), suggest that the novelist was writing the story as it was being published. Something else which supports this speculation is the appearance of a hunter's dog in Part 14 and an imposing pair of mastiffs at a market garden in Part 16. This would appear to be associated with an editorial written a week before, for which our author was seemingly responsible. It concerns a visit to the 斐李寧頓農務博覽會 "Flemington Agricultural Exposition", which contemporary English-language newspapers confirm to have been Melbourne's long-running Royal Agricultural Show at the Flemington showgrounds. The writer was evidently highly impressed with the dogs on show there, and devoted some time to their description, commenting particularly on their usefulness in agriculture.

All told, *The Poison of Polygamy* measures a shade under 32,000 Chinese characters in length, which equates to a shade over 40,000 words in translation,[35] or around the length of a

---

34   Zhong Huang and Wenche Ommundsen, "Poison, Polygamy and Postcolonial Politics: The First Chinese Australian Novel", *Journal of Post Colonial Writing* 52, no. 5 (2016), pp. 533–44.

35   These figures are based on electronic character counts of the fully transcribed and translated text. At one-and-a-quarter English words per Chinese character, the translation falls well within the ratio of two words per character that is relatively standard for Literary Chinese-to-English translation.

novella or short novel. Whether it is best termed a novella or a novel is debatable. But the movement back and forward between China and Australia and the associated changes in character focus, when considered in light of overall length, plot complexity, and the variety of themes and subjects, tend to my mind toward distinguishing it as a short novel. This appears to be the view of the academics who have written papers that concern *The Poison of Polygamy*, e.g. the aforenamed Huang and Ommundsen, and Haizhi Luo, whose 2017 master's thesis, entitled "Towards a Modern Diasporic Literary Tradition: The Evolution of Australian Chinese Language Fiction from 1894 to 1912" (UNSW), is the first overview of early Australian Chinese-language fiction.

The elements of the story seem to suggest that the novel's timeframe stretches from the 1850s through to the 1880s. We are told how many new years Sheung Hong and Ma have passed as a married couple before he leaves for Australia, and how many years the sojourns in Australia last. The suggestion is that it is winter when Sheung Hong first arrives in Australia. Kam Ngau's name suggests that he was born in the Chinese year that began in early 1865 and ended in early 1866. The list goes on, and everything appears to tally, with one exception: the reference in Part 4 to the Hakka Punti War and the Taiping Rebellion; but these might have been inserted anachronistically simply to reinforce the direness of the conditions described.

There is much more within the novel that could be discussed: the rake's progress at its heart, the character types, the convention of the doomed protagonist in the fiction of the period, the writer's creative metaphors, such as "Mr Sleep Sickness" for the Chinese man who is slow to "awaken", how the author was influenced intellectually and stylistically by the classical models of Confucian literature, and the story's nonfictional elements are but a few examples. The above is a brief foray into this broad literary landscape. The intention, like that of *The Poison of Polygamy*, is to shine a light and pique the interest of readers, who I hope will carry on with this rewarding activity of shared analysis, interpretation and discovery.

REFERENCES

Boswell, James. *The Life of Samuel Johnson*. London: Encyclopedia Britannica, 1952.

Chang, Kang-i Sun and Stephen Owen (eds). *The Cambridge History of Chinese Literature* (2 volumes). Cambridge: Cambridge University Press, 2010.

France, Peter (ed.). *The Oxford Guide to Literature in English Translation*. Oxford: Oxford University Press, 2001.

France, Peter and Kenneth Haynes (eds). *The Oxford History of Literary Translation in English, Volume 4: 1790–1900*. Oxford: Oxford University Press, 2006.

Hanan, Patrick. "The Missionary Novels of Nineteenth-Century China," *Harvard Journal of Asiatic Studies* 60, no. 2 (December 2000), pp. 413–43.

Heine, Bernd and Tania Kuteva. *World Lexicon of Grammaticalization*. Cambridge: Cambridge University Press, 2002.

Johnson, Rossiter (ed.). *The Great Events by Famous Historians, Vol. XX: The Awakening of China* (1914). Second edition. New York: The National Alumni, 1919.

Kuo, Mei-fen. *Making Chinese Australia: Urban Elites, Newspapers and the Formation of Chinese-Australian Identity, 1892–1912*. Clayton, Vic.: Monash University Press, 2013.

Luo, Haizhi. "Towards a Modern Diasporic Literary Tradition: The Evolution of Australian Chinese Language Fiction from 1894 to 1912." Masters thesis, University of New South Wales, 2017.

Norde, Muriel. "'So odd an article in Danish': A Reply to Van de Velde", *Language Science* 30 (2018), pp. 1–14.

Tytler, Alexander Fraser. *Essay on the Principles of Translation* (1791). Edinburgh: A. Constable & Co., 1813.

Yvan, Daniel and Shih-Lung Lo. "'Mystères urbains' en France, 'Mystères urbains' en Chine: des perspectives incomparable?", in *Les Mystères urbains au XIXe siècle: Circulations, transferts, appropriations* (2015), ed. Dominique Kalifa and Marie-Ève Thérenty, http://www.medias19.org/index.php?id=17039

Zhong Huang and Wenche Ommundsen. "Poison, Polygamy and Postcolonial Politics: The First Chinese Australian Novel", *Journal of Post Colonial Writing* 52, no. 5 (2016), pp. 533–44.

王尹姿:〈趣味／道德／覺世:《月月小說》研究〉, 碩士論文, 臺北: 國立政治大學, 2009年。

王瓊玲:〈屠紳「蟬史」初探〉,《世界新聞傳播學院人文學報》, 1995年7月。

阿英:《晚清小說史》,臺灣商務印書館, 1996年。

林瑞明:《晚清譴責小說的歷史意義》, 國立臺大出版中心, 1980年。

黃伯耀、黃世仲:《中外小說林》, 夏菲爾國際出版有限公司, 2000年。

裘廷梁:〈論白話為維新之本〉收入王運熙主編, 烏國平、黃霖編著《中國文論選: 近代卷(下)》, 南京: 江蘇文藝出版社, 1996年。

寧稼雨:《中國文言小說總目提要》, 齊魯書社, 1996年。

魯迅:《中國小說史略》, 上海古籍出版社, 1998年。

歐陽健:《晚清小說簡史》, 秀威資訊, 2015年。

釋慧皎:《高僧傳》, 卷2, 中國哲學書電子化計劃網站, https://ctext.org/library.pl?if=gb&res=91024, 頁126–127。

The Poison of Polygamy

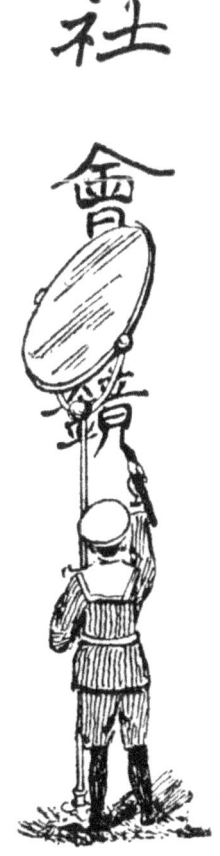

Monogamy is the most perfect of systems, but China is a country of polygamy,[1] *and consequently of gloomy boudoirs and extinguished happiness. The collapse of whole families is often heard of, and time and again bedchamber changes are the cause. In lament of this, I have chosen from village events the saddest and most tragic, in order to hold a lens to society. From beginning to end, my knowledge of these events is most clear, and I recount them truthfully, without resort to fictional means, save, for consideration's sake, slight changes to names.*

For those who have been long resident here, the story's first half should still be a vaguely lingering memory, which the act of reading will call to mind. As to the second half, its conclusions are filled with content of such interest as should give cause for sadness, sighs, surprise, and fear. Yet while the story's events are, alas, no more than neighbourhood trivia, in the interests of morality, they may serve as a clarion call, and perhaps wake some from that sweet concubinary dream.

---

1   The book's title could be more technically translated as "The Poison of Polygyny", polygyny having the specific sense of marriage between one husband and multiple wives, as opposed to polyandry, which involves one wife and multiple husbands. Polygamy is the coverall term, and one more familiar to English speakers, in consideration of which it is given here. It

世界一夫一妻之制　最爲完善　中國爲一夫多妻之國　致
令香閨愁暗　幸福消滅　往往因床第[1]之變　而傾覆一家
者　時有所聞　僕哀憫之　爰舉鄉間極慘極悲之事　爲社
會之鏡鑒焉　斯事之始末　僕最爲明晰　照實詳述　並無
寓託　但名字稍爲變易　以存厚道也　此事前半幅料久客
此間者　猶隱現於腦海　觸目自能記憶　後半幅其結果儘
有趣味[2]　令人可悲可嘆可驚可懼也　嗟夫　事雖里巷瑣
聞　然有關風化　可作暮鼓晨鐘　或能警其衾裯之酣夢乎

1　此字等，原作「第」，而當作「第」。第者，床之竹席。讀若姊妹之姊。
　　與「第」字形似而易混。今皆改正。後不贅注。
2　此處本無空格。疑當有之。今擬補。

should also be noted that under Chinese law polygamy had only a very
limited existence. A concubine was not considered to be a wife, and as such
monogamy was held to be the dominant practice. The author adopts a
different standpoint, viewing concubines as being tantamount to wives,
which they were, but for their lower status and lesser legal entitlements.

Wong Sheung Hong was a native of Pak Hang,[2] Llin Nen,[3] Kwang Tung.[4] He had a thin sallow face, lightly whiskered cheeks, a sharp-tipped nose, and a muddled way of speaking, and one could tell him at a glance to be a treacherous and cunning type. His addiction to opium being strong, he often shut his eyelids, as if sleeping though not, which habit had earned him the nickname Sleep Sickness. He was a barely literate man, without any fixed vocation, who, while cruelly greedy by nature, had not a penny to his name. He had taken as a wife the daughter of a Mr Ma. While of middling looks, Ma[5] had a faithful and gentle disposition, and had taken to the love of her marriage bed as a fish to water. She was, moreover, of a kindly temperament, being on good terms with her fellow villagers, and quarrels between her and her sisters-in-law being unheard of. Time soon flowed on, her youthfulness slipping away in its stream, and all of a sudden three years had passed. Yet within her quarters, the sound of a son or daughter at play was not to be heard.

At that time, Sheung Hong had a mother of over sixty years, aged and decrepit, and dependent on others. Ma, despite her impoverished circumstances, did her level best to care for her, and

---

2   百行 "Pak Hang" (roughly pronounced *bark hung*) would appear to be an invented name and possibly a play on the real place name 德行 c°. "Tak Hang" (see Appendix II for the key to the symbols used with romanisations), which was one of s. Llin Nen's six 都 "subdistricts" (for Llin Nen, see next footnote). A literal translation of the name might be "Every Character", from which the expression's sense of "people of all different characters and levels of morality" should be evident. In §52, however, the same name is written slightly differently, and this sense is no longer apparent. Tak Hang "subdistrict" covered a large area in the north of the district of Llin Nen.

3   新寧 s. Llin Nen, which is roughly pronounced *thin nen*, is the native pronunciation of one of the See Yip region's four districts. It was also known as Sinning, Sun Ning, etc. Today it is known under its new name of 臺山 c^M. Tòih-sāan in Cantonese, m^M. *Táishān* in Mandarin, and s. Hoisan in its native vernacular. "Llin Nen" reflects the spelling used by missionary

黃尚康。隸籍廣東。新寧縣。百行鄉人。面黃而瘦。腮部微
有髯鬚。準頭尖削。言談吞吐。一望而知為陰險狡詐者。然
烟癖甚深。常似睡非睡。閉其眼簾。故又混名眼睏病[3]。其人
粗識之無。執無專業。性雖貪酷。而家復赤貧。娶馬氏女為
妻。馬氏貌雖中姿。而秉性貞靜。結褵以來。床第之愛。如
魚得水。兼且心性和靄。鄉鄰親睦。妯娌之間。不聞勃谿。
無何歲月如流。韶光逝水。倏忽三年。而閨闈之內。璋瓦之
聲。寂然無聞。惟時尚康有母。年逾花甲。老邁龍鍾。舉動
需人。馬氏雖處此貧苦之境。猶竭意奉養。

3   「眼睏」為粵語習用語，意即「昏昏欲睡」。其睏字之粵音讀若「訓」，故
     俗作「瞓」。見廣東人民出版社西曆千九百九十七年付梓，麥耘、譚步雲
     編著《實用廣州話分類詞典》之〈眼訓(睏)〉條，及同頁諸條，暨臺山話
     詞彙網站www.stephen-li.com/TaishaneseVocabulary/Taishanese.html等。

Alexander Don in his 1882 description of its city's vernacular, which was
entitled *The Llin-nen Variation of Cantonese*.

4   廣東 Kwang Tung was and is the Chinese province that neighbours Hong
     Kong. Canton being its capital city, it was also known in English as "Canton
     Province". (In the common sphere, English speakers often used the word
     "Canton" for both the city and the province; however, authorities generally
     considered the latter to be an inappropriate usage, presumably because it was
     a contraction that introduced ambiguity.)

5   In Chinese, married women can be referred to by either their maiden or
     married surnames, there being different titles for each purpose. Sheung
     Hong's wife is referred to here and throughout the book by means of her
     maiden name and the title appropriate to it. However, while "Ms" is now
     available in English, its use in translation would be anachronous, and so,
     while a title is used in the Chinese, none is given here.

to humour and please her, waiting on her constantly, her unmitigated filial devotion and her genial countenance being sources for both respect and lamentation. One day, Hong's[6] mother met with illness.[7] She ceased at once to eat or drink, developed a blazing temperature, and sank into a deep and dazed slumber, punctuated by outbursts of delirium. Panicked and worried, Ma nursed her as best she could.

Sadly, the women of China—being both uneducated and limited in their thinking by backward provincial customs— still hold to the superstitions concerning spirits and ghosts.[8]

Ma, witnessing the gravity of her mother-in-law's sickness, was anxious to save her, but was inwardly panicked and pressed for lack of a decent strategy. So she engaged witches and witch doctors, and the three maids and six matrons,[9] who overran the house. There were those who propitiated; those who administered medicines; and there were those who, with a lamp rush dipped in oil, burned their head, face, body and limbs and whose moaning was unbearable to the ear. Pasted upon the doors were spells and talismanic inscriptions; and piled within the curtained rooms[10] were mock offerings and joss-paper.

---

6   The name "Sheung Hong" is here abbreviated to "Hong", and the same is occasionally done with other disyllabic names later in the book. In light of the difficulty that many English readers have recognising and remembering Chinese names, such abbreviations have not been reflected in translation, with the exception of the present example, for the reason given in the following footnote.

7   The second syllable of Sheung Hong's name, i.e. Hong, means "health(y)". The phrase 康母遘疾 "Hong's mother met with illness" therefore has the double meaning of "the healthy mother met with illness". Unfortunately it is not possible to reflect all such little rhetorical flourishes in translation.

8   "Spirits" and "ghosts" are less-than-ideal translations for what are tutelary (guardian) and malign spirits respectively (the two being reversible depending on one's relationship with the dead).

承顏悅色。侍事無間。其一片純孝之性質。和順之儀容。令
人可敬可憫。一日康母遘疾。飲食頓輟。熱度炎蒸。沉沉昏
睡。時發譫語。馬氏驚惶失措。盡心看護。可惜中國之婦
女。並無教育。又爲鄉愚陋習所囿。於鬼神一道猶爲迷信。
斯時馬氏目擊家姑病危。急欲施救。而中情惶遽。又苦無善
策。於是延請男巫女覡。三姑六婆。奔走滿室。有禱禳者。
有施藥者。有以燈草點油。炙其頭面與肢體。而呻吟之聲。
耳不忍聞者。粘貼門戶之上。則咒書符籙。堆積庭帷之中。
則紙馬冥錢。

---

9   The 三姑 "three maids" are generally considered to be 尼姑 "Buddhist nuns",
道姑 "Taoist nuns", and 卦姑 "diviners", and the 六婆 "six matrons/older
women", 牙婆 "women brokers", 媒婆 "matchmakers", 師婆 "witches", 虔婆
"madams", meaning women who manage prostitutes or non-prostitute
"geisha"/courtesans, 藥婆 "women medicine sellers or women doctors", and
穩婆 "midwives". Traditionally, women of these vocations did not enjoy high
social standing, and thus the expression "the three maids and six matrons"
often carries derogatory overtones. Note: the phrase is used here in a general
sense not inclusive of all the aforementioned trades.

10   The women's quarters or Sheung Hong's mother's room(s).

In the space of a few days, dowry, clothes and ornaments were all pawned away, but contrary to expectation it was to no avail, the sickness instead increasing in severity.

Alas that these most precious of assets should be invested in the most useless of places. Throughout China, those beset by illness generally die at the hands of shamans and village physicians: what could be more lamentable. However, in a semi-civilised country where even men think as such, at what fault was Ma? In her sincere filial devotion, Ma instead thought this to be the naturally honourable course—but enough digression.

At that time Ma could do nothing else but keep a bedside watch, and quietly sob. Suddenly she heard the shuffling footsteps of someone approaching smugly from outside.[11] It was Sheung Hong. He berated his wife: "What's going on? The sun's below the eaves, and you've still not fired the stove to cook."

His wife responded reproachfully, "Your mother is gravely ill, her life hanging in the balance, and I her daughter-in-law am miserable to the core, with no time for food or drink. Yet you, her own son, pay no attention whatsoever. How can you be so heartless?"

"It's a common thing for an old person to be ill," replied Sheung Hong. "Why must you make such a frightening fuss over it?"

---

11   The second phrase in this sentence 施施從外來者, translated in this context as "someone approaching smugly from outside", is a quotation from *Mencius* (a seminal text of Confucianism that records the words and deeds of a Confucian philosopher of China's Warring States period named Mencius). It appears in a parable about a man who brags to his wife and concubine about going out each day to feast with high officials, but whom they discover actually spends his time doing such things as scavenging leftover offerings from cemeteries. The lesson at the end is that, from the perspective of the greater man, the methods by which the vast majority of men seek their fortune are enough to make their wives and concubines so ashamed as to gather together to weep.

不數日間盡將贓奩衣飾。典質一空。誰料依然罔效。而病勢
反加增。嗟夫。以此最重之資財。投之最無用之地位。舉中
國一般之罹病者。盡死於神巫村醫之手中。可哀孰甚乎。然
半開之國。男子尚然。於馬氏夫何尤哉。在馬氏孝心懇摯。
反以爲此義所當然也。閒話休題。是時馬氏無法可施。惟有
守護床頭。嚶嚶啜泣而已。忽聞履聲纝綷[4]。施施從外來者。
尚康也。罵其婦曰。日落屋簷。猶未炊爨。爲何者。婦詰責
之曰。汝母病勢沉危。命在旦夕。妾爲媳婦中心慘戚。豈遑
飲食耶。君乃人子。反慢不措意。何無心肝乃爾。康曰。老
人疾病。乃是常情。何必故作此態以嚇人。

4　原文作「察率」，並注曰：「絲旁」。「察率」蓋即「蔡辛」之誤。今據
　　正爲「纝綷」。按，「纝綷」一語罕見，或爲「綷纝」之倒文。字書云：
　　綷纝，紈素聲也；纝綷，猶綷纝。

Ma knew he was being unreasonable. Revealing her face sincere and sorrowful, and with tears running, she said, "Mother-in-law's sickness is truly cause for worry. And while she is but Mother-in-law to me, she is Mother to you. Without medical treatment, what would you do if misfortune struck? (§1, 5/6/1909)[12] Over the last few days, you have been away and uninvolved with things at home. For Mother-in-Law in her illness, I have had the gods besought and treatments administered. I have exhausted every avenue, except for engaging a doctor from the town. If you know of any of marvellous skill, why not hire him to come and make an examination?"

Sheung Hong narrowed his eyes to think for a moment. Then he said, "There is a well known doctor in the Pak Sha market-place,[13] Ng Shau Sai,[14] who says he can bring the dead back to life. People seeking treatment flock daily to his door. If we could get him to examine her, I should reckon the two sprites[15] would have nowhere to escape to. Would only that we had some square-holed friends."[16]

"Don't worry," said Ma. "I still have a set of new cotton-padded clothes, which I was keeping to stave off the winter cold. Go quickly and pawn them to make up the cost of treatment."

Sheung Hong took the clothing to the pawnbroker's and received six dimes[17] for it. He then went and entreated Ng Shau Sai to come to his home to perform a pulse examination.

---

12   Throughout, the number of the instalment and its original date of publica-
      tion are indicated in parentheses at the end of each instalment.
13   白沙 c°. "Pak Sha" (Mᴹ. *Báishā*) is a town located roughly twenty kilometers
      to the west of s. Llin Nen or current-day Mᴹ. *Táishān* and eighteen
      kilometers southwest of the modern city of c°. Hoi Ping Mᴹ. *Kāipíng*.
14   Refer to Appendix I for detail on the connotations of this and other
      character names.
15   The 二豎 or 二豎子 "two sprites" are malevolent child spirits credited by
      Chinese mythology as being agents of illness. The expression is generally
      used in Chinese in a metaphorical sense.

馬氏知不可以理喻。乃露其哀懇之容。垂淚而言曰。姑病實
堪憂。姑雖妾姑。母是君母。不爲醫理。設有不測。將若之
何。(§1, 5/6/1909) 數日來君在外不預家中事。妾因姑病。求
神施治。羅掘俱窮。惟有市中醫生。未經延請。君知有妙術
者。何不請回診視。尚康瞑想半晌日。白沙墟有一著名醫
生。吳壽世。常自云能起死回生。日間到門診症者。戶限幾
穿。若得他診視。恐二豎子無處逃遁。但奈無孔方兄耳。馬
氏曰。無憂。妾尚有新棉衣一襲。留以禦寒者。丞往典之。
可爲醫藥之費也。康持往典肆。質銀六角。卽往請吳壽世到
家診脈。

---

16 孔方兄 "square-holed friends" is a humorous expression for money, the old
    style of Chinese coin having a square hole for its centre.

17 In the 1850s, pieces of eight—Mexican and Spanish silver dollars—were a
    highly popular currency in southern China. Because of their circular shape,
    these coins were referred to as 圓 Mᴹ. *yuán*, meaning "rounds", which is a
    coinage—no pun intended—that has stuck to the present day as the
    Chinese word for *dollar*. The name used in this chapter for a smaller
    corollary denomination to the piece of eight, the 角 *jiǎo* "corner/wedge-
    shape", was adopted as the word for dime in the decimal currency of the
    Chinese silver dollar that was introduced later in the *Qing* (Mᵒ. Ch'ing)
    dynasty. The word is still used today for *dime*, i.e. one tenth of a *yuán* or
    dollar. It would be wrong, though, to suppose on this basis alone that a 角
    jiǎo "corner/wedge-shape" meant a tenth of a silver dollar in 1850s China.
    Indeed, in many parts of the world, the piece of eight, which had a nominal
    value of eight reales, was divided into eight *bits*, the division sometimes
    being achieved physically by cutting the coin into wedge-shaped pieces.
    However, while the system of subsidiary specie for the piece of eight in
    China appears to be a somewhat neglected area of numismatics, all
    indications are that it was in fact a decimal one, i.e. one in which ten 角 *jiǎo*
    "corners/wedge-shapes" or dimes made a 圓 *yuán* "round" or dollar. Hence
    the translations given here.

When Mr Ng had finished the examination, he said, "The condition which afflicts your good mother arose from the contraction of a chill, which has spread inward on account of her old age and infirmity and the weakness of her internal heat, and because of haphazard prescribing. The dehydration of her tongue and lips is in fact no more than an outburst of deficient heat. If mistakenly treated with cooling preparations, her true inner heat would be immediately extinguished, which would be unthinkable. Fortunately, you engaged my humble self to come and make an examination early enough. If not, the situation might have been dire. The approach that is now required is treatment with a strongly warming and restorative preparation, to revive the vital vent's true heat, and so preserve the masculine pneuma; followed thereafter by treatment with sudorific medicines,[18] that will drive out the noxious airs and chills. With the two preparations one after the other, your good mother will be returned to her usual state of fitness and health." He then provided a prescription. Sheung Hong looked at it: aconite, ginger, cassia … warm and fiery medicines, at doses several times those usually prescribed. Yet Sheung Hong was convinced and paid the visiting fee of three dimes. With that, the doctor marched off. (§2, 12/6/1909)

Having returned with the purchased medicine, Sheung Hong again secreted himself in the opium den. His mother, when his wife had finished decocting the medicine, drank it. About an hour or so on, her temperature reached an extreme. Slaver ran from her mouth; her eyes bulged; her arms and legs flailed about; she yelled madly, grabbing at the mat[19] and tearing at the mattress, her state one of extreme suffering. Unbearably panic-stricken and

---

18   Sudorific medicines are medicines that cause sweating.
19   Sleeping mats woven from such materials as reed and bamboo are used in southern China in warm weather; they allow air to circulate beneath the skin and are wonderfully smooth and cooling to the touch.

吳先生診罷云。令壽堂之症。先由感冒風寒而起。緣因老人
體弱火衰。兼且方藥亂投。以致傳裏。其舌焦唇潤者。乃上
炎之虛火耳。若悞投涼劑。眞火立亡。不堪設想。幸得早些
請鄙人來診。不然。殆矣。惟今之計。須投以溫補大劑。生
囘命門眞火。以保陽元。然後再投以發散藥品。祛其風寒。
前後兩劑藥。令壽堂之體質。康健如常矣。說完授以方帖。
尙康視之。則附子薑桂之溫烈藥品也。其重度較於尋常方劑
數倍。尙康亦深信不疑。與步金三角。揚長而去。(§2,
12/6/1909) 康購藥歸。復藏烟竉。婦煎藥訖。母飲之。約一小
時許。達熱度之極點。口流涎。目裂眦。手足舞蹈。疾聲狂
叫。抓席擘褥。爲狀至苦。馬氏驚駭欲絕。

at a loss to know what to do, Ma called a few fit women neighbours, and they forcibly pressed her mother-in-law down on the
bed, face upwards. Presently, there was a noise in her throat, and
her eyes lost their light: she was, so lamentably, dead.

*The physicians of China have no diplomas of specialisation in
medicine, and those who play the role are all common and
illiterate good-for-nothings. Even were they to take the entire
country and poison to death everyone in it, the government
would show no interest. Alas, the tragedy! Sheung Hong's
mother's illness had been caused by exposure to the sultry heat
and was in fact a hot ailment. Treated though with the absolute
fieriest of warming medications, how could she escape death?*[20]

After Sheung Hong's mother's death, Ma wept in sadness and
grief, (§3, 19/6/1909) and remembering that in their penniless state
they had not the means to make the burial preparations, she could
not help but burst into tears and cry loudly, eventually fainting, and
taking a time to recover consciousness.

When Sheung Hong learned that his mother had died, he neither showed any sadness in his countenance nor wept nor cried. If
one wished to see him snivel, one would need to wait for the time
when his addict's cravings started up, for then he would make a full
display of himself in gushing condition.

Family, thinking on Ma's virtuousness and filial piety, did their
best to aid financially, so enabling rough burial preparations.

*Kwang Tung's traditional funeral rites involve misplaced belief
in superstitions. Buddhist monks and Taoist priests are engaged to
make observances to expiate the purgatory of the deceased's soul;*

---

20   In referring to "warming medications" and "hot ailments", the author is
      using the language of traditional Chinese medicine.

手足無措。卽呼鄰舍健婦數人。强按之仰臥榻上。俄頃。喉間作響。兩目無光。哀哉死矣。夫中國醫生。無專門醫學文憑。充當者俱是市井無賴。目不識丁。雖舉全國人而藥殺之。政府亦不過問。嗚呼。慘矣。蓋康母之病。原由感暑所致。實熱之症。乃投以極猛烈之温劑。焉得不死。母死之後。馬氏悲泣慘怛。(§3, 19/6/1909) 憶及家貧如洗。無以爲殮。不禁放聲5 大哭。以致暈倒。逾時復蘇。倘康聞其母死。無悲戚容。亦不哭泣。設欲見其涕淚。當伺其癮起之際。其滂沱6 之現狀乃畢露。斯時戚族乃念馬氏賢孝。力爲資助。方能草草殯殮。粵俗7 凡喪禮迷信邪說。延請僧道做齋超度。

5　原文倒作「聲放」，今正。

6　原文倒作「沱滂」，今正。

7　「粵俗」一語，可指全粵之俗，可指粵中某地之俗，其義如是。粵者，古域名也。約等於後代兩廣之轄地。故廣東昔有「粵東」之別稱。顧今有以粵為粵東之專名者。是非昔時之義，又非作者之意。然而譯曰「廣東」，蓋因英文無字與粵同義之故。

and their various performances—the breaking open of the Narakas,[21] the supplication of the ten kings,[22] the buying of face water,[23] the summoning of the lost soul—are side-splittingly farcical. After burial, a spirit chamber is also set up, for what is called the reception of the spirit. Paper is folded to form houses and vehicles, domestic servants and carriage horses, each and every item being laid out, with nothing absent from the arrangement. And on each occasion of worship, it is all burnt; and each time it is burnt, bonzes,[24] nuns and Taoists are engaged to chant from the scriptures and make vicarious repentance, the ear-grating noise of cymbals and gongs continuing throughout the night.

Then, after some days of mourning, a Taoist priest takes a flame and burns the soul's house and, with a sword, slashes the spirit board.[25] How queer! Is not the soul's house the residence of a father or mother's lost soul? Is not the spirit board that to which a father or mother's lost soul attaches? Yet bonzes are invited and Taoists engaged on promise of valuables to burn and slash them, which were one a judge, one might determine to be the crime of contracting another to commit arson and patricide: nothing could be more outrageously wrong. In our[26] Kwang Tung, over thousands of years, even the scholar gentry have held deluded belief in such things and have been unable to see the light. So they have no qualms about squandering great sums over these barbaric

---

21 The Narakas are the Buddhist hells. This ceremony is, however, also practised by Taoist priests.

22 The kings of the ten courts into which the Taoist hell is divided.

23 This is a reference to the practice of taking water from a river or well to wash the deceased's face and body, and throwing a little money into the water in thanks to its spirit.

24 A bonze is a Buddhist monk.

25 The author appears to be making reference to the funery custom of burning a paper house for the use of the deceased in the afterlife (燒靈屋). The

其破地獄。拜十王。買臉水。[8] 招亡魂。種種怪劇。最令人
絕倒。葬後又設一靈寢。名曰承靈。用紙紮成屋宇舟車。僕
人輿馬。凡諸舒具。莫不羅列滿前。故祭奠一回。必焚燒一
次。每次必延僧尼道士。誦經懺解。故鐃錢[9] 之聲。聒耳徹
宵。服闋日。道士用火燒其魂屋。用劍斬其靈牌。噫。異
哉。夫魂屋者。非用以居其父母之亡魂乎。靈牌者非其父母
亡魂所依託者乎。乃以金帛請延僧道而焚之斬之。吾爲裁判
官。決定以賄囑他人殺父放火之罪也。夫倒行逆施。莫此爲
甚。吾粵數千年來。雖士大夫亦迷惑而不知醒。不惜糜擲多
金。而爲此野蠻

8　指舊俗之所謂「買水洗面」。
9　按，此「鐃錢」之錢字，當指響盞，讀「盞」。俗字從金不從皿者，蓋以
　　響盞銅製故也。

---

deceased's temporary spirit tablet (a piece of cloth with his or her
name written on it), to which one of the deceased's three souls is held
to be attached, is placed in and then removed from the house prior to
its immolation. The spirit of the deceased is eventually transfered from
the temporary spirit tablet to a permanent wooden spirit board (神主牌)
—the reference to the tablet being slashed with a sword may reflect
part of an associated Taoist ceremony current at that time in the
author's region.

26　The character used here could be translated as either "our" or "my".

performances.[27] *The rich spend fortunes over them without the least hesitation; and even the poor require several tens of taels in order to orchestrate them successfully. And so, alas, throughout the land there is poverty and penury.*

After his mother's burial, Sheung Hong became yet more impoverished, to the extent that he could not put food on the table. Thinking of becoming a pedlar in order to get by, he applied repeatedly to relatives and neighbours for loans. However, it was a time that followed plundering by local malefactors in the name of King Hung,[28] after his revolt;[29] and then clashes between the Punti and Hakka[30] after his defeat;[31] and then destitution through the cumulative calamities of war; and then unexpected bad years[32] after the flames of war had passed by several times over. At this time rice cost seventy cash[33] a pint.[34] Hah! Where did people, in this period of disorder and desolation, who had not the ability to fend for themselves, have spare capital to loan to others? (§4, 26/6/1909)

---

27   In this strident and potentially offensive attack on traditional funery practices, the author appears to be displaying a degree of wilful misunderstanding of the religious significance of certain acts, such as the aforementioned immolation of a paper house.

28   洪秀全 Mᵒ. Hung Hsiu-ch'üan Mᴹ. *Hóng Xiùquán* was a self-proclaimed younger brother of Jesus and founder of his own Christian sect. He led the Taiping rebellion and became ruler of China's short-lived Taiping Heavenly Kingdom.

29   The expression translated here as "revolt" is an interesting one, and might indicate the author's support for King Hung or his beliefs—see related footnote in Chinese (footnote 13).

30   Kwang Tung's Hakka Punti War (廣東土客械鬥) was a series of very violent clashes between the Punti, which means "locals" or "natives" and refers mainly to Cantonese and See Yip people, and the Hakka, which means "guests" or "outsiders" and refers to people living in the same region who spoke the Hakka language (a distinct Chinese language) and who were descended from more recent immigrants. The war lasted from the mid-1850s to the mid 1860s and was reportedly bloodiest in the protagonist's district of s. Llin Nen, which it was late to reach.

之舉。故富者動費鉅萬。[雖]¹⁰　貧亦要數十金。方能葳事¹¹　。
嗚呼。國中。焉得不貧且瘠哉。尚康自葬母後。¹²　貧苦益
甚。甚且饘飦不給。意欲爲小販以度活。屢向戚里告貸。無
奈其時適當洪王反正¹³　之後。該處跳梁小醜。假洪王之名以
行劫掠。迫洪王失敗。而土客又復相鬨。是以兵連禍結。民
不聊生。不意幾次兵燹之後。復加以凶年。是時每升米售錢
七十。嘻。丁此荒亂之時期。¹⁴　各人自顧不暇。那有餘貲貸
人。(§4, 26/6/1909)

10　報中此字殘缺不全。按其殘跡及上下文義，似當作「雖」。因擬補，且加
　　框以標別之。
11　「葳」原作「臧」。蓋字之誤。今正。或說「臧事」與「葳事」「善事」
　　通，臧讀臧否之臧。按，世間文之以葳事作「臧事」，皆字之誤。臧事謂
　　襃其事，不謂葳事。葳事謂飭事，謂「善治事而已之」。葳，北方話讀
　　曰「產」，廣州話讀曰「淺」。
12　本續自此句以下，皆印異頁。該頁標句，用隙不用句號。今補句號，以求
　　劃一。
13　「反正」一語，有二義焉。一曰「投誠」。一曰「歸正」。參照下文之
　　意，可知此處「反正」乃指洪王反叛之事。然則作者容或兩字分用，言洪
　　王反叛於正統，容或存其歸正之意，以暗韙之。
14　此處本不分兩句。誤。今補句號。

31　The Taiping Rebellion was defeated in 1864.
32　Years of poor crops.
33　The Chinese copper coin, or "cash", had a nominal value of one lekin, or a
　　thousandth of a tael of silver (one tael weighed about thirty-eight grams).
　　However, around Canton in the years immediate to the defeat of the Taiping
　　Rebellion, the actual exchange rate was probably much higher (in Peking in
　　1865, for example, the rate was approximately 5,000 cash to the tael).
34　Rice was generally measured by volume rather than weight. The exact
　　volume of the Chinese pint, also referred to in nineteenth-century English
　　as the *shing* or *shêng*, varied according to place and time, but at the time and
　　place concerned, it would appear to have been approximately half a litre, or
　　around 0.88 of a British Imperial pint.

Sheung Hong rushed from one friend or relative's door to the next for days, but received nothing, other than tens of gratuitous white-eyed looks.[35] So he returned downcast and dispirited, and was forced to sell off, on the cheap, some clumsier ruder household items, so as to fund his opium habit. After a few days, even the hessian blanket that husband and wife wept to each other over,[36] was deposited at the pawn broker's.[37] Sheung Hong had by then been fully elevated to the rank of trouserless lord,[38] ensconced high within the Hibiscus City,[39] which he would not leave, despite its ruler's repeated attempts to oust him.[40]

Each day Ma picked wild herbs to sate her hunger. Her face jaundiced and cheeks swollen, her complexion pallid and wretched, she looked scarcely human. Examined close up, she was no more than a thin handful of bones covered in tattered cotton. Yet despite great hardship, Ma was not resentful.

One day, Sheung Hong returned surreptitiously to steal an old pot. He was making off with it when suddenly his wife spotted him. She stood to block the doorway, and then beseeched him, "Please come in and rest my husband. I have a few words of true counsel to give."

Sheung Hong responded bashfully, "Yes … Yes." Lost for alternatives, he was forced to follow his wife in.

---

35   Scornful looks.

36   牛衣對泣 "to weep to each other over a hessian blanket" is a classical Chinese idiom that describes husband and wife in a state of severe destitution; here the author uses it to literal effect.

37   There are many words for pawn brokerage (as for most things) in Chinese. Here, the author uses a term that has its origin in the 宋 Mᵒ. Sung Mᴹ. *Sòng* dynasty, when Buddhist monastaries ran their own pawn brokerages: 長生庫, the primary meaning of which is "perpetual-yield store" (in reference to the perpetual accrual of interest), but which has the auspicious double meaning of "long-life store", and, in the present context, could also be read as "life-extending store".

38   無袴公 "trouserless lord" appears to have been a comical expression at the time for a person in a state of absolute penury.

伺康於戚友之門。奔走 數日。一無所得。惟贈送白眼數十雙
而已。於是垂首喪氣而歸。不得已將粗笨傢具。賤售之以充
烟資。不數日。雖夫妻常對泣之牛衣。亦寄之長生庫中矣。
斯時伺康已晋封爲無袴公。高臥芙蓉城中。雖芙蓉城主屢逐
之亦不去。馬氏日採野菜以療飢。面黄腮腫。菜色淒其。不
辨人鬼。近驗之。瘦骨一把。蔽之以敝絮而已。馬氏雖艱苦
備嘗。然亦無怨懟。伺康一日潛歸。竊一破釜而逃。忽爲其
妻瞥見。故以身當戶而哀之曰。請君歸休。妾有一言忠告
也。 康怩忸[15] 以應之曰。唯。唯。無奈强尾其妻歸。

15   按，舊時之文有以「忸怩」作「怩忸」者。則此語或無誤也。

39   In Chinese mythology, 芙蓉城 "Hibiscus City" is another name for paradise.
     Here, though, the expression carries a double meaning. The other sense
     which is apparent is "the realm of hibiscus paste" (芙蓉膏之境). This sense
     comes about because 芙蓉膏 "hibiscus paste" is one of the Chinese
     monickers for opium, and because 城 "city" has the extended sense of
     "realm of" or "land of" in Chinese. The extended sense of 城 "city" can be
     seen clearly, for example, in the following line from a Cantonese folk ballad
     (尤二姐辭世): 恨我錯認愁城為樂土 "Woe that I mistook this city of angst
     for a land of joy", in which the "land of joy" and "city of angst" both refer to
     the household into which the singer, a spurned concubine, entered. The
     expression 愁城 "city of angst" or "city of saddness" appears later in this part
     and in §26. (Note that the 芙蓉 foo-yung "hibiscus" in 芙蓉膏 "hibiscus
     paste" is actually a contraction of 阿芙蓉 aa-foo-yung "opium".)
40   In other words, despite repeated attempts by the opium den's owner or
     supervisor to expel him.

They sat together on a little daybed. Ma tried to talk, but tears welled forth and her voice choked up and no sound came out. Falteringly, after a little while, she began to speak.

"Since I entered your door, five years have drawn to a close,[41] without a day well fed or a night of warmth. I have dwelt long in this city of sadness, not knowing the meaning of simple human joys. Of my fate being so mean, what more is there to say? My death will thus be nothing to pity, and now, haggard as I am, death's door is not far off. It is not out of any sense of attachment that I have saved my remaining breath to this day, but because I have not yet procreated. This worn frame I keep only out of the desire to bear the Wong family an heir. Otherwise, what difficulty would I have in shutting my eyes and ceasing to breathe, in parting forever from the world, ridding myself of all troubles, and ascending to the Realm of Bliss?[42] Why else should I stay as an addict's wife ever enduring this endless misery? As things now are, both our lives hang in the finest balance. What consideration can we give to progeny? How would it be anything other than surrendering to die not to devise a scheme through which to rescue things?

---

41   Traditional Chinese rhetoric identifies three main forms of expression: 賦
      "depiction", 比 "analogy", and 興 "evocation". 賦 "depiction" is direct language
      used for its literal or denotative meaning. 比 "analogy" is a broad category that
      includes smile, metaphor, synecdoche, etc.—language in which one thing is used
      for or compared to another. The third form, 興 "evocation", is language intended
      to elicit psychological associations. The author makes use of both "analogy" and
      "evocation" in the four-character four-syllable phrase 星軺五換, that is translated
      here as "five years have drawn to a close", but which literally means "the emissarial
      carriage has been changed five times over". To understand how the two meanings
      equate, a little further explanation is required: The only emmisary to which
      Sheung Hong's wife could be referring is 灶君 "the Kitchen God". In Chinese
      folk religion the Kitchen God is held to be Heaven's representative and observer
      in the house, and to return at the end of each year to report on the happenings
      therein. Prior to his departure, around a week before the year's end, sweet
      offerings are made to his paper idol (which is pasted up in the kitchen year
      round) and honey is sometimes smeared on his lips, all in the hope that he will
      say sweet things in his report. The paper idol is then burnt, and at the

並坐短榻中。馬氏欲言。而淚溢聲咽。不能成音。故稍間斷續而言曰。妾自入君門。星軺[16] 五換[17] 矣。日無一餐飽。夜無一宵温。長住愁城之中。不知人間世歡樂爲何物。妾薄命如斯。夫復何言。今憔悴若此。去冥路不遠矣。然妾一死何足惜。猶苟延殘喘。以至今日者。豈別有所留戀哉。亦緣未有誔育。故特留此殘軀。欲延黃氏一塊肉耳。設不然。又何難屏息瞑目。與世長辭。芟除一切苦惱。而登極樂之世界耶。又何必長作烟人婦。永受此無窮之悽慘也。今若此。吾兩人之生命 。 懸於俄頃。遑顧嗣續乎。若不設策營救。豈真束[18] 手待斃。

16　軺者，輕便之小車也，讀音同「搖」。星軺，使者之車也，又為使者之代稱。

17　「星軺五換」，疑言天之使者灶君，其已五升天堂，五降人間，而五易其車也，以喻室內五閱新年。蓋尚康婦為司灶者，故作者以此語而興彼女人口吻焉。實乃比興之佳語也。

18　此「束」字為「束」之俗體。餘同。

---

beginning of the new year, a new one is pasted up. Analysed from the Chinese rhetorical standpoint, the phrase "the emissarial carriage has been changed five times over" thus means, by 比 "analogy", that Heaven's emissary the Kitchen God has gone and returned five times, which, by another layer of 比 "analogy", means that five years have drawn to a close; and by 興 "evocation", by referring to the passage of years through reference to the coming and going of the Kitchen God, the identity of the speaker as woman and cook is highlighted. Phrases like this appear only occassionly in the present work, but high Chinese literature can consist almost entirely of this sort of language, and so, while extremely rich and elegant, it can appear utterly cryptic to readers unfamiliar with the full range of cultural and literary associations it plays on.

42　極樂世界 "The Realm/World of Bliss" is a Buddhist term, and the Chinese equivalent of Sanskrit's सुखावती *Sukhāvatī*, which, in 大乘佛教 Mahayana Buddhism, is the paradise of the 阿彌陀佛 Amitabha buddha.

When even ants and mole crickets know to forage[43] to preserve their lives,[44] why would a man in all his dignity willingly starve to death amongst the mulberry trees?"[45] On reaching this point, Ma's strength and voice failed her. Sheung Hong was silent, still gazing, with keen eyes, at the old pot.

After a pause, Ma spoke again. "The other day I heard a beggar woman say that my cousin has lately returned from the goldfields,[46] and is very wealthy. I implore you to go quickly to my mother's house, and relate my present circumstances to my cousin. He was always generous and chivalrous, and may still show pity."

Sheung Hong looked particularly uncomfortable on hearing this, but the proverb says *An ugly wife must in the end meet father-in-law*,[47] and he could do nothing about it. So he went in haste and spoke to her cousin as she had said to. Her cousin, on hearing the story, was sorely moved, and made him a gift of ten

---

43   The expression 覓食 "forage" has here the secondary meaning of *search out a living*.

44   This sentence is a reworking of a traditional idiom, which holds that even 螻蟻 "ants and mole crickets" do what they can to survive.

45   The phrase used, 甘爲桑中餓莩, means more literally "willingly become a corpse through death from starvation amongst the mulberry trees", there being a single word in Chinese for *the corpse of a person who has died from starvation*. There is a classical story about a man starving under a mulberry tree, which developed into something of a Literary Chinese trope, and is played on here. The expression 桑中 "amongst the mulberry trees" is also connected with romantic love.

46   The old word translated here as "goldfields" (金山) is one that is now commonly rendered as "Gold Mountain" (謂某一黃金所成之高岳), a fanciful pidgin-English calque that has taken on something of a life of its own. The oft misunderstood element within the expression is the second character, which has the primary sense of hill or hills, or mountain or mountains, but also an extended sense in Cantonese and the See Yip

夫螻蟻尚知覓食以全生。乃堂堂男子。甘爲桑中餓殍耶。馬
氏言至此。已氣竭聲漸矣。尚康默然不語。猶目灼灼注視破
釜。稍間。馬氏復言曰。妾曩聞丐婦云。吾堂兄近自金山
歸。饒有資財。懇郎君急往吾母家。將妾現今之狀況。訴之
吾堂兄。他素昔慷慨義俠。或猶見憐也。尚康聞言。頗有難
色。但諺語云。醜婦終須見家翁[19]。斯亦無可如何。乃遄往
如言以告。其堂兄聽罷。惻然動懷。即贈洋蚨田[20]

19　「醜婦終須見家翁」為粵間俗諺，意即卒不能不露醜。蓋其醜字兼含「短
　　處」之意，如「獻醜」之醜。家翁謂丈夫之父。家讀如其字。
20　原文「十」字本闕。今照下文「銀十元」等語擬補。

language, that of *land in general*, a metonymic jump that is quite natural given China and particularly Guangdong's hilliness. The expression thus means "goldhills" or "goldlands", i.e. goldfields. The second character is used in this extended sense in other Cantonese and See Yip expressions too, e.g. in the word for China, 唐山, which might be paraphrased as cº. "the Tong [Chinese] hills" or "Tong-land". The old Chinese names of specific Australian goldfields include (1) the 雪梨金山 "Sydney Goldfields", meaning the New South Wales goldfields, which encompassed, for example, (2) the 咯卩李巴 s. "*Lok-gee-lee-vaa* goldfields", or Rocky River goldfield, known colloquially in English as "The Rocky" and in Chinese as the 咯卩金山 "*Lok-gee* Goldfields"; (3) the 大金山 "Great Goldfields", meaning the Bendigo goldfields; and (4) the 新金山 "the New Goldfields", a term that was applied initially to the Victorian goldfields, then some decades later to the newly discovered Western Australian goldfields, and which eventually became a byname for Australia.

47　This is a Chinese proverb which means that one's shortcomings (or *ugliness* in Chinese) will eventually be revealed to others.

pieces of eight, to take back as temporary rescue from burning need. Sheung Hong was wildly pleased on seeing the coins, but in the act of receiving them, his limbs shook. The coins, cast ringing upon the floor, flew all about the house. Sheung Hong picked up each and every one and pocketed them close to his breast. He then sped back, making a detour to Pak Sha.[48] He went first to the opium den, where he lay upon a bed and puffed and sucked deeply, until he'd had a full feed of it, and was vital again. Afterwards, he shopped for some staples and vegetables and other items with which to return home.

When his wife saw him, she sprang to her feet. (§5, 10/7/1909)

Ma's gaze then fixed upon Sheung Hong's hands. "How have these things been come by!" she exclaimed in astonishment, "Could it be that my lord has been out burglarizing?"

On hearing this, Sheung Hong was enraged and scolded her gruffly, "Pah! On this globe there is no woman as stupid as you. How could it be that I, Wong Sheung Hong—whom, having been occasionally down through adversity in life, you recklessly brand a thief—will not eventually rise in the world?" Then, changing his tune, in order that he might brag to his wife,[49] he said, "Of course, the reason for these words of yours is no more than doubt as to this food's origins. Sit and I will tell you of it. I got up in the morning with the intention of going to meet with your cousin, but unforeseeably, I happened upon an old friend along the way. This man and I were once on the most intimate of terms, and when he was moneyless, I often came to his aid. Now, he has become an official, and has returned home on leave, and fortunately I ran into him. The two of us started talking of our present circumstances, whereupon he took out ten dollars and reimbursed me, adding that

---

48 This is the same market town previously mentioned in §2; see footnote 13.

49 This sentence contains an expression (驕其妻) from the same story in *Mencius* that was referred to in §1 (which concerned a cemetery-scavenging husband), and thus brings the same associations to the reader's mind.

翼。使持歸權救然眉之急。康見之狂喜。接授之間。手足震
動。擲地[21]鏘然。滿室飛繞。康一一俯拾之。揣之懷中。飛
馳而歸。迂道白沙。先往烟窟。橫臥榻上。大呼大吸。飽餐
一頓。躍躍如生。然後市些米糧菜蔬等項旋家。其妻見之。
亦霍然而起。(§5, 10/7/1909) 斯時馬氏之視綫。注射於倘康兩
手。作驚訝之詞曰。此物胡爲夫來哉。得毋郎君去作樑上君
子耶。康聞言怒甚。疾聲而罵之曰。咄。環球上蠢婦莫汝
若。我黃倘康近因命途乖舛。偶然落魄。就妄以穿踰目我。
余豈眞終身無發達之期哉。反又飾詞以驕其妻曰。汝爲此言
者。實疑此糧食之由來耳。坐。吾語汝。余晨起欲往晤汝堂
兄。不期於路途間。與一故友邂逅相遇。此人與我爲莫逆之
交。他前日貧乏時。我屢次周濟於他。現今出仕爲官。請暇
囘家。幸而相遇。大傢談起現時之境況。 他卽將銀十元。償
還於我。幷云。

21　原文「地」字半缺。今參別處地字擬補。

one day he would favour me by making me an official, to repay my benevolence. Stupid village woman, you could not have thought that I, Wong Sheung Hong, should stay an indigent gent forever? My only fear is that, with that face of yours, you do not look like a lady."

On hearing this, Ma gave a scornful snort, for she did not believe him, knowing that for him lying was the practised trick of a lifetime. However, she could not understand what the food's origin could have been, nor did she know whether or not he had seen her cousin. It was a little puzzle she could not work out, and so, forcing herself to revive her spirits, she went into the kitchen to rustle up a meal. When Sheung Hong had finished eating, pleased as Punch[50] he carried off the remaining money, and went again to his smoky den.

On the morrow, Cousin Ma[51] came to visit, and only then was it that Sheung Hong's foolhardiness and conceit became fully understood. Brother and sister cousin[52] had met each other in anguish. Ma, not having time for common pleasantries, had at once begun a tearful account of the whole story of their distress, over which her cousin also shed tears. Adding that, her husband's conduct being as such, he had lost all credibility in his social intercourse, and would definitely have difficulty making a living staying in the area, Ma pleaded for her cousin to take him to the goldfields.

Her cousin seemed to tacitly consent, but said, "The lazy are absolutely not up to the task of going overseas as hired labourers. Furthermore, with his addiction to opium, how would he weather the hardships and dangers? If he could summon the courage to quit

---

50 The author uses a Chinese expression here that is rhetorically and idiomatically close to the English expression given in translation.

51 "Cousin" is not the title used, but its addition seems necessary in translation, in order that this Ma might be distinguished from the other Ma—Sheung Hong's wife.

52 Male and female cousins can be referred to as "brother and sister cousins" in Chinese.

他日抬舉我做官。以報我之恩德。蠢村婆。我黃尙康豈終作
窮措大耶。但恐汝這副臉面。不像夫人耳。馬氏聽罷。嗤之
以鼻。知他說謊。乃其平生慣技。故不之信。然究莫明此糧
食之由來。又不知他曾見我堂兄否。一點疑團。總難打破。
不得已[22] 抖搜精神。往廚間弄飯。尙康食完。挾此餘賸。洋
洋得意。又往烟霞之窟矣。翌日。馬某到訪。始盡悉其謬
妄。斯時兄妹相見。不勝悲楚。馬氏不暇寒暄。卽將其家計
之困苦。哭訴一切。其兄亦爲之涕零。馬氏又云。其夫品行
如此。在社會交際上。已[23] 失其信用。居鄕定難謀生。力求
其兄挈之往金山。其兄似亦心許。但曰。出洋催工。慵懶者
斷難勝任。而況他又染有烟癮。何能冒此艱險。若能奮勇戒

22　此「已」字原作「巳」。誤。今正。
23　此「已」字原作「己」。誤。今正。後文凡「已」作「巳」作「己」之
　　誤，今皆改正，不復注明。

opium, if he could endure hardship with steadfastness and toil industriously in poverty, he might come to something; if not, it would be no more than vainly casting his body to its end in the world's nether regions. Bid someone fetch him back home. Before discussing it, I will question him."

Ma entreated a villager to go to The Clouded House[53] in the Pak Sha marketplace and call him back.

The day already near noon, Sheung Hong was still in the land of black comfort.[54] Once the villager had called and shaken him, he rose yawning and stretching, and began to make his hazy way back. On arriving home and seeing that Cousin Ma was present, he was shamefaced and uneasy, half delighted and half fearful: delighted that, in coming, Cousin Ma would certainly have some foreign biscuits[55] to give him; fearful that the lie he told his wife yesterday would today be exposed. So he did his best to say a few pleasantries, following which, Cousin Ma commenced to put one question after another to him, concerning his desire to aid him in going to the goldfields.

Sheung Hong agreed on each and every point, but had much difficulty in responding when questioned in the matter of quitting opium. After a while, he took his opportunity and said, "Giving up opium is something I have long wished to do. However, my

---

53   The translation of the opium den's name as "The Clouded House" is an attempt at preserving a pun in the Chinese name: an association with *crowds* (of customers) and with *clouds* (of opium smoke).

54   The land of dreams. 黑甜 "black comfort/black sweetness" is a Chinese expression for (sweet) sleep. (In Chinese 甜 "sweet/sweetness" has the sense of comfort when used to describe sleep.)

55   Foreign coins. The Chinese word 餅 "cake" has the extended meaning of "disc". The word has been used in this sense for many centuries, being applied early on to discoid pieces of silver and later to Chinese and foreign silver coins proper. The word is still commonly used in the sense of disc, e.g. in 鐵餅 "iron disk", which means *discus*, and 餅茶 "disc tea", which means *tea in pressed-disc form*. Naturally, the author plays on its double sense in this sentence.

烟。堅忍耐苦。積儉辛勤。或者有濟。不然。徒將此身斷送
於窮鄉絕域而已。命人尋他回家。余試問之。然後商量。馬
氏懇村人往白沙墟雲來居[24]　喚他。斯時日已向午。他猶在黑
甜鄉中。村人搖呼之。始欠伸而起。朦朧而歸。至家見馬某
在座。慙赧不安。喜懼參半。喜者喜馬某此來。必又有番餅
贈送。懼者懼昨日對其妻說謊。今日必然敗露。故勉强寒暄
幾句。於是馬某將欲資助他往金山之事。一一詰問之。他亦
件件答應。惟於戒烟一層。最難答覆。半晌[25]。乘機而言
曰。戒烟一事。余久有此志。緣余

24　「雲來居」之「雲來」字兼二義。一為「洋煙成雲而來」；一為「顧客如
　　雲而來」。蓋店號之詼諧者也。（洋煙即鴉片煙）
25　此字等，原作「响」，當作「晌」。二字形似，粵音無別，故易相混。今
　　皆改正，不復注明。

constitution being weak, it would be extremely difficult to quit without the aid of medication. Yet I am penniless: what can I do?"

"If my brother-in-law can indeed muster his strength and quit opium," said Cousin Ma, "I shall bear all the medicinal and other costs myself. Such trifling sums are of no concern."

Inwardly pleased, Sheung Hong answered, "If that is the case, please lend me another ten dollars for medicine: I have made my mind up to quit from tomorrow."

Cousin Ma gave him the dollars, and then another ten, instructing him: "These ten dollars are to purchase clothes, bedding and the like. Ten days from now, we head out together for Hong Kong to await a sailing. Over the next few months, I shall see to it on your behalf that there is food in your house. You need not trouble yourself over domestic concerns." Having finished speaking, he shook hands[56] with Sheung Hong, and departed. (§6, 17/7/1909)

The next day, Sheung Hong went again to The Clouded House, where he farewelled the men of the black milieu,[57] and had a good long smoke too, as a mark of feeling on their parting. Following this, he bought some opium-quitting pills—the preparation for his first attempt—and headed home.

Gentle readers, will Sheung Hong with this attempt indeed quit opium? Were it that with this he quit for good, henceforward

---

56 This expression—握手—could be read as "grasped hands", but it appears that the author is actually using it here in the modern sense of "shook hands", reflecting that cousin Ma had adopted this Western custom. The same phrase as is used here, 握手而別 "to shake hands and depart" appears in §16 and it is clear in that context that it does refer to the Western custom.

57 This expression—黑籍中人 "people of the black milieu"—means opium addicts.

體質薄弱。若無藥料補助。斷難戒除。但余一貧如洗。奈
何。馬某曰。妹丈果能奮力戒除。舉凡藥弭等費。眷弟一力
擔任。區區微資。何煩憂慮。尚康暗喜。卽應之曰。果如
此。請[26] 再借銀十元爲藥費。待余從明日起。決意戒除。馬
某果贈員。又再授十元。囑之曰。此十元購買衣服被蓋等
物。遲十天一齊出港。等候船期。近幾月汝家中糧食。弟代
爲料理。毋須內顧。說完。握手而別。(§6, 17/7/1909) 明日尚
康復往雲來居。與黑藉中人作別。兼且飽餐一頓。以誌分袂
之情。隨卽市些戒烟丸藥而歸。爲苐壹次戒烟之預備。閱書
諸君。尚康此次戒烟。果能[27] 戒除否。設若從此戒絕。嗣後

26　原文「請」字殘甚。今參別處請字擬補。
27　「果能」原誤倒作「能果」。今正。

never to touch it again, this book of mine could be ended here. In short, Sheung Hong's smoking of opium has a close relationship with this book, and so it is recorded in detail, without concern for its tediousness. In quitting opium, it is in the nature of us Chinese that when about to quit, we are like the chicken purloiner putting things off till next year,[58] *and after quitting, like Fêng Fu seeing a tiger and stripping back*[59] *his sleeves:*[60] *the resolve to persevere is highly lacking. Sheung Hong was a first-rate example of this.*

In the blink of an eye, the appointed tenth day arrived, and the clothing and bedding was bought in full. The day before setting out for Hong Kong, Ma's mother, having heard her son-in-law was to go overseas, put together some cakes, and a cock and pork and other things, and came to farewell him. Ma too dispatched a hen, and also bought sweet wine and joss candles and asked some village women to go to the Land God's altar, as well as the temples of the various deities, to pray for good fortune, in the hope that they might protect Sheung Hong, and see him profit and return in glory. Ma had prepared the day's evening meal beforehand, so that she might entertain her mother. When they had finished eating, her mother

---

58 The reference here is to a parable told by Mencius in response to a nobleman, who had agreed with him that taxes should be lowered to the ancient level of ten per cent, but asked if they might only be lessened for the present, and the full reduction put off till the following year. Mencius's response reads: 今有人日攘其鄰之雞者或告之曰是非君子之道曰請損之月攘一雞以待來年然後已如知其非義斯速已矣何待來年 "There is a man who each day purloins a chicken from his neighbours. Someone says to him 'This is not the way of noble men.' He replies, 'How would it be if I were to reduce to purloining one chicken a month, before stopping altogether next year?' Knowing what one does to be dishonourable, one should hasten to put an end to it. Why put it off till next year?"

59 The words for "purloin" and "strip back" are the same—攘—and the author uses this fact to his rhetorical advantage in this sentence.

60 The reference here is also to a story in *Mencius*: 晉人有馮婦者善搏虎卒為

永不沾染。則吾此書亦可由此絕筆矣。要之尚康吸烟。與此
書有密切之關係。故不厭繁瑣而詳記之也。夫吾中國人戒烟
之性質。當將戒之時如攘雞者之以待來年。及戒除已後。又
如馮婦之見虎攘臂。甚少堅持之毅力。尚康亦個中之一流人
也。轉瞬之間。十日之期已屆。衣服被蓋。亦經購辦完備。
出港之前一日。馬氏之母。聞婿往外洋。即弄些糕糍與雄雞
豬肉等物。到來與尚康餞別。馬氏亦割雌雞一隻。并買牲醴
寶燭。託村媼到社壇暨各神廟祈福。希冀保護尚康獲利榮旋
之意。是日馬氏早備晚膳。招待其母。食既。其母

善士則之野有眾逐虎虎負嵎莫之敢攖望見馮婦趨而迎之馮婦攘臂下車
眾皆悅之其為士者笑之 Mº. "There was a man of Chin, Fêng Fu, who was
skilled at catching tigers, and who eventually became a decent officer. When,
as an officer, he headed back into the wild, he came across a mob chasing a
tiger. The tiger was backed into a mountain recess, and none dared confront
it. The mob looked and saw Fêng Fu, and rushed over to welcome him. Fêng
Fu stripped back his sleeves and alighted from his chariot. The mob was
pleased. Those who were officers laughed at him." (From the officers'
perspective, Fêng Fu, on returning to his old less-civilised environment ("the
wild"), had reverted to behaviour that was on the level of the populace (the
"mob"), which, as an officer, should now have been beneath him.) The story
gave rise to a number of idioms—重作馮婦, 再作馮婦 & 又作馮婦—that
mean "to revert to one's old habits", but have the literal sense of "to go back
to being Fêng Fu".

turned to Sheung Hong and made various exhortations and expressions of regard and entrustment; nothing other than words intended to cause him to be industrious and frugal, to save his money, to return to China soon, and not to waste and so be forced to tarry in a foreign land. Then she said her farewells and returned home.

In the evening, Ma held Sheung Hong's hands and said to him sobbingly, "The pressures of poverty force my lord to make a sojourn far off in a barbaric wilderness. How can the love of husband and wife be severed so? Yet your leaving initially to return finally, that we might survive, is much better than our sitting opposite at the bed head[61] and awaiting death. My lord! At this time tomorrow you and I will be at other ends of the earth …"[62] Not finishing what she had to say, she cast her body into Sheung Hong's bosom, covered her face with her sleeve and cried alluringly.

Sheung Hong was also moved by feelings of sadness. Tears ran down his cheeks, and he wiped his wife's tears for her with his hand and consoled her, "Be not sad my dear, we are only parting temporarily, for no more than one or two years. Hopefully, god above will take pity and I shall meet with good fortune, and return with a hundred-million about my waist,[63] whereupon we shall reunite, to together enjoy our natural bond as husband and wife. Thus the happiness of those days to come, will be enough to compensate for these days of sorrow."

---

61 There is an old Chinese marriage custom known as 坐富貴 "sitting for wealth and honour" which requires newlyweds to sit opposite at the bed head, the husband to the east and wife to the west.

62 The Chinese idiom translated here as "at other ends of the earth" (地北天南) literally means "one at earth's north and one at heaven's south". There is another level of meaning that becomes apparent in this context though, which may have been intended by the author: The expression can be read yet more literally here as "earth at north and heaven in the south", and as women and wives are associated with the earth (which belongs to the

對尙康叮嚀致囑。不外使他克勤克儉。積蓄貲財。早日囘
唐。切毋浪費。以致勾留外地之詞。話完別歸。晚間馬氏執
尙康之手。嗚咽而言曰。因家貧所窘。致使郎君遠客蠻荒。
夫婦之情。何能割舍。但始離終聚。以圖生存。尤勝對坐床
頭以待斃也。郎君乎。明日此時。妾與君地北天南矣。語未
竟。卽投身於尙康之懷。以袖掩面而嬌啼。斯時尙康亦爲悲
情所感動。淚奔兩頰。卽以手代拭其妻之淚而慰之曰。卿毋
悲。不過暫別二兩載而已。望上帝見憐。遭逢美運。腰纏十
萬而歸。爾時夫妻團聚。共樂天倫。則後日之快愉。亦足償
今日之悲苦也。

---

feminine *yin* principle), and men and husbands with heaven (which belongs
to the male *yang* principle), the expression can also be read as connoting the
separation of a wife in the north from a husband in the south.

63 The Chinese idiom 腰纏十萬貫, or the abbreviated form used here 腰纏十
萬, literally means "with a hundred thousand strings of one thousand cash
about one's waist". English equivalents would include such saying as *as rich
as a lord* and *as rich as Croesus*.

Ma spoke again in her plaintive tone, "The ancients spoke of 'smitten women' and 'unfaithful men'. If when my lord becomes rich, he has lasses of Chin to the left and girls of Chao[64] to the right, I would be placed to the back of his mind, for why should he still remember that he had at home his wife from rougher days?"

Sheung Hong, beholding her fretful countenance, vowed in a loud voice so as to calm her: "I, Wong Sheung Hong, swear that even if I become as rich as Shih Ch'ung,[65] I will not take a concubine. Should I go back on my word, may it be that I come to a bad end—"

Ma, not waiting for him to finish, covered Sheung Hong's mouth with her hand and said, "Do not speak wildly. Tomorrow is the auspicious day of your sailing. What need is there to say such vile things? All I ask is that my lord thinks of me at home, without father- or mother-in-law, sons or daughters, lonely and impoverished and with only her shadow for company. And, I hope you will oft send letters and news to allay my concerns. Also, the sums of money that you make over the years, you will need to continually remit to cover the outlays at home. And, you should make your return at the nearest opportunity, and not suffer my longing eyes to wear out."

Sheung Hong assented on all points, and added, "To repay my dear one's former toil, no matter what happens, I will not make of my humble self an unfaithful man."

The two of them were still chattering away when the sky lightened. Ma at that moment felt a deep loathing for the rooster that heralded sunrise, urging on continually the dawning of the day, and leaving her unable to fully voice her emotions on separation.

---

64   Here, 秦娥 M°. "lasses of Chin" and 趙女 "girls of Chao" are, in their primary senses, simply different literary expressions for pretty women, *Chin* and *Chao* both being names of ancient realms. However, *Chin* and *Chao* are also surnames, so here the expressions take on an additional layer of possible meaning—women from this family and women from that.

馬氏又出哀慘之聲曰。古人云癡心女子負心漢。若待郎君發
達時則左秦娥。右趙女。即置妾於腦後矣。豈尚憶家有糟糠
之妻哉。尚康睹此愁悲之容。即大聲咒誓以安其心曰。我黃
尚康即使富若石崇。誓不娶妾。有背斯言。不得其死。馬氏
不待他說完。即以手掩尚康之口曰。毋亂言。君明日乃揚帆
吉日。何必作此惡語。總求郎君念妾在家。翁姑兒女。一無
所有。形影相弔。零丁孤苦。惟望頻寄書音。以慰妾之懸
念。逐年所入之歟。須要隨時滙囬。爲家中之用度。若稍有
機緣。即作歸計。毋使妾望眼將穿也。尚康一一應允之。復
曰。鄙人不論若何。決不作負心人。以報我卿往日之劬勞
也。時天已明亮。兩人猶絮絮而語。斯時馬氏深恨此報曉之
雄鷄。頻催天曙。令他不能盡吐其違離之心緒也。

---

65 石崇 M°. Shih Chʹung (Mᴹ. *Shí Chóng*) was a man of the third century of
the common era, who is renowned for his wealth, and as it happens, also for
his keeping concubines.

Alas! There be of joys, none so joyous as new friendship, and of sadnesses, [none so sad] as a far farewell.[66] *The most tragic of all things in the world is the parting in life of husband and wife. Yet the hills and waters*[67] *of Australia and America occupy the dreams of many a traveller to be, who in dawn frost, below the fading moon of morning, must abandon his wife's fragrant coverlets.*[68] *What man is without feelings and who can dispel them? This narrator too is a man who has been through it, and has long known the flavour of life apart. But men should make stout partings, and not have need to cry like children.* (§7, 24/7/1909)

Sheung Hong and his wife had been awake the whole of that night murmuring to one another, cherishing the precious time together. All of a sudden, Ma's eardrums were struck by a hubbub, formed from the sounds of cattle being called and of doors being opened and shut. She awoke with a start and stepped out onto the roofed walkway to look out. To her surprise the east was already light. The farmers were leading their oxen out to urinate, and the village women were carrying out water on shoulder poles to pour on the vegetable beds. Beyond their little lane, the figures of people making ready to go out into the fields to work could be seen flitting about. Ma knew it was past dawn and there was no time to prepare a meal. Yet fortunately there was no need for hurried commotion, as she had packed Sheung Hong's bedding and luggage in full the day before.

---

66 This line is a reworking of one in a well-known song, written around 2,300 years ago (楚辭·九歌·少司命). The rhyme is unfortunately lost in translation, but the antanaclasis is preserved as polyptoton (e.g. "of *sadnesses*, none so *sad*").

67 Here the expression "hills and waters" is used in their broader Chinese composite sense of *lands*.

68 In what here in translation constitutes a sentence, the author moves to a more literary style of expression, which in the space of fourteen syllables

嗟呼。樂莫樂兮新相知。悲[28] 莫悲兮遠別離。世間最可悲慘
者。莫若夫婦生離者也。而况美水澳山。常縈旅夢。曉霜殘
月。辜負香衾。人孰無情。誰能遣此。述者亦過來人。久嘗
此中况味。但丈夫當有壯別。無庸作兒女之悲啼也。(§7,
24/7/1909) 是夕尚康夫妻通宵不寐。喁喁細語。惜此可貴之光
陰。忽而叱犢聲。門扉開闔聲。喧騰耳鼓。馬氏驚覺。步出
迴廊一望。不料東方已白。農夫牽牛溲溺。村婦挑水灌菜。
矮巷之外。人影幢幢。將往田間操作矣。馬氏知爲時已旦。
炊黍不及。 猶幸昨日已將尚康之被蓋行李。檢点完備。斯時
不至忙亂。

28　此句原作「悲悲莫悲兮遠別離」。句首一「悲」字疑衍。今刪正。

(fewer in number than in "Yet the hills and waters of Australia and America") expresses its entire meaning succinctly, elegantly and subtly, through the combined use of a variety of rhetorical devices, e.g. the use of literary tropes like 殘月 "the fading moon of morning", which symbolises the fragmentation of the union between husband and wife (the moon is a symbol of union or togetherness in Chinese, partly on account of a semantic connection between roundness and unity—團圓), and allusions to poetry that concern the separation of husband and wife, through the use of expressions like 曉霜 "dawn frost" and 香衾 "(wife's) fragrant coverlets". Unfortunately, much of this rhetorical sophistication defies direct translation.

While washing, they heard the sound of knocking at the door. Ma knew it was her cousin and opened it to invite him in.

"Is the luggage together?" Cousin Ma asked in a panic. "If we are in the least bit sluggish, I fear we shall not make the ferry. The ferry to Hong Kong heads out from Tik Hoi[69] at one o'clock this afternoon. We are over fifty miles[70] from Tik Hoi and must walk to get there."

On hearing this, Ma passed the luggage to Sheung Hong, and uttering "Take care" was hurriedly parted from him.

Ma stood far out from the doorway, tears welling up around her eyes, wanting to let them fall but not daring to. Yet despite her every determined effort, the teardrops eventually streamed down like laced pearls, and spilled all over the bust of her dress. For when China's silly women see their husbands off on a journey, fearing that bitter tears might beget misfortune, they always try to hold them back, but are in the end unable. Deep at heart they suffer so. Yet utterly sincere are their true feelings of love for their husbands. Her unblinking willow eyes[71] fixed, Ma watched until Sheung Hong had passed out of the street gate and disappeared, before returning home bereft to sit aimlessly and pity her lone shadow. She thought to herself, *From this parting till I see my husband's face again, truly I know not how many months and years are yet to come and go. I shall from now onward dwell alone,*

---

69   The 荻海 c°. "Tik Hoi" (ᴹᴹ. *Díhǎi*) referred to here now forms part of the modern city of 開平 Hoi Ping (s. Hoy Hen, ᴹᴹ. *Kāipíng*), which straddles the confluence of the 潭江 ᴹᴹ. *Tánjiāng*, its largest tributary the 蒼江 *Cāngjiāng*, and a third river, the 茭江 *Jiāojiāng*, which flows from the city of 臺山 *Táishān*. See Appendix V.

70   At the time concerned, the length of the Chinese mile varied very widely across China. The official length was around 0.372 British Imperial miles or about 600 metres. But the local reckoning in this region may have been as little as about half this length.

盥洗間乍聞叩戶聲。馬氏已知其堂兄。故即開門迎入。馬某
遑遽而問曰。行李拾齊否。若稍遲緩。恐趕渡不及。香港渡
下午一點鐘在荻海埠開行。此距荻海五十餘里。須要步行。
方能趕到。馬氏聞言。卽親交行李與尚康。珍重一聲。匆匆
而別。馬氏遙立門外。淚盈兩眶。欲滴不敢滴。雖極力堅
忍。而似泉之淚點。已奔流如貫珠。浪浪滿衿矣。故中國無
智婦女。每送夫婿遠行。痛哭恐致不吉。往往欲忍其淚而卒
不能忍者。其中心亦云苦矣。其愛夫之眞情。抑何其懇摯
耶。斯時馬氏懸其不轉瞬之柳眼。直待尚康身出閘柵。望不
見影。始嗒然而歸。枯坐房中。顧影自憐。自思與丈夫此
別。實不知再更幾何年月。始得佀面。自此以後。獨棲獨
宿。實不知再更幾何年月。始得佀面。自此以後。獨棲
獨宿。

---

71   柳眼 "willow eyes" means shapely eyes. However, another association is
      apparent here, because the willow symbolises longing and reluctance to part.
      This symbolic sense is the reason for the ancient custom of giving a sprig of
      willow on a loved one's departure (折柳贈別), and is often played on in
      Chinese opera and poetry. It would appear to have its origin in the way in
      which willow leaves hold close to each other (the word used to describe
      this—依依—also meaning longing or reluctance to part), though some
      ascribe the association to the similarity in pronunciation between the word
      柳 "willow" and the word 留 "stay".

as a partnerless yeung-duck,[72] *as a flockless swan, sitting with only a lamp for company, sleeping in my shadow's embrace, through interminable nights, and days of three autumns' span.*[73] *The time when we wept to each other over a hessian blanket may turn out to have been more easily passed than that of these scenes and feelings to come.* Her thoughts reaching this point, she could not help but burst into tears and cry loudly.

On the road with Cousin Ma, Sheung Hong stayed silent, his mind muddled and thoughts confused, wondering when he might again behold the mountain flowers upon which his gaze alighted, and on what day he might next tread the ground he saw beneath his feet. Most people, it would seem, feel on the point of embarking on a far journey, that everything about the scenery of their homeland brings forth fondness and a longing to stay. Sheung Hong looked back towards his old home, but finding that, all of a sudden, it had been concealed by a confusion of hills, he heaved many a heavy sigh. Yet on seeing Cousin Ma ahead, he pondered that it would be cause for pride if one day he could, like him, return rich and victorious, and bring glory to his village. In consequence, a bold sense of hope burgeoned forth in him, sweeping beyond the highest heaven all sad thoughts of parting. Then, in the distance, they saw Tik Hoi and Cheung Sha, and a tapestry of sails and masts upon an expanse of limpid water. They raced over, and found the Hong Kong ferry just about to weigh anchor. So they flew down, and had not yet

---

72   Today, the bird name 鴛鴦, which one might translate as c°. "*yuen-yeung* duck", is generally considered to mean the mandarin duck. This is a misapprehension that has its origin in the M°. Sung dynasty, when the more highly coloured mandarin duck (properly called the 鸂鶒) began to be used in popular depictions of the *yuen-yeung* duck. The original identity of the *yuen-yeung* duck remains a mystery, because surviving descriptions and depictions do not match any extant species. The *yuen-yeung* duck is a symbol of a loving monogamous couple, a significance which is held to reflect the

如失侶之鴛。如離羣之雁。對燈而坐。抱影而眠。漫漫長
夜。一日三秋。此境此情。不若牛衣對泣時。猶爲易過也。
思至此。不禁放聲大哭。尙康與馬某在路上。悄然無語。心
亂神迷。觸目山花。何時方得再睹。俯首塗泥。何日方能重
履。大約人當遠別之際。祇覺家鄉境物。處處生留戀之心。
忽而廻望故居。已爲亂山所遮掩。於是不勝浩嘆。乍見馬某
在前。細思他日果能如馬某者。致富榮歸。光耀閭里。亦足
自豪。於是希望之雄心。忽而渤發。盡把別離之悲念。捲向
九宵雲外矣。遙見茨海與長沙。一水盈盈。帆檣如織。二人
疾奔而至。斯時香港渡適將拔錨。二人飛奔而下。行李猶未

bird's natural behaviour. The eleventh-century Sung-dynasty encyclopaedia the 埤雅 Mᵒ. P´i-ya ᴹᴹ. *Píyǎ* states that the male *yuen-yeung* duck is said to make the sound *yuen* and the female the sound *yeung*, which is the reason for the Chinese name, and the translations here given.

73　一日三秋 "days of three autumns' span" or literally "one-day: three-autumns" is an idiom that describes time passing sadly and slowly, autumn being the season most associated with sadness and loss, and three autumns representing three, or numerous, years.

deposited their luggage when, with the creak of wood and rope, the ship pulled away and merged with the midstream.

At that time, there were not yet any steamers on the river, so the ferries to Hong Kong and Macau were still all sailing ships, and it was not until five days and nights had passed that they arrived in Hong Kong. (§8, 7/8/1909)

After their arrival in Hong Kong, Cousin Ma and Sheung Hong stayed at the Kwong Wing Goldfield Agency in Sheung Wan,[74] a member of staff at that firm being a cousin of Cousin Ma's and the previous handler of his letters. Several days later, having given him detailed instructions in respect of rendering Sheung Hong aid in heading out for the New Goldfields,[75] and having entreated him to go to the shipping company to book his passage, Cousin Ma entrusted Sheung Hong to his cousin. His cousin having undertaken to see to everything, Cousin Ma explained all the arrangements clearly and gave Sheung Hong a few firm words of advice. He then returned home, for he had come to Hong Kong merely to send Sheung Hong off, as he had returned not long ago himself, and was thus unable to join him on the journey.

There was no boat to Australia for over ten days. When the time arrived, the Kwong Wing employee purchased Sheung Hong a sick pan,[76] foodstuffs and the like, and personally saw him aboard ship. Australia had not yet introduced prohibitions on Chinese people at that time, and so there were not the harsh regulations of today. The captain, having summarily checked names and tickets, attended to all matters, and then the ship set off.

---

74   Sheung Wan was one of the earliest areas of British settlement in Hong Kong. Today one of Hong Kong's better known commercial and residential precincts, it is still known by the same name.

75   See footnote 46.

76   Here we see what appears to be the colloquial expression used at the time for "sick bowl".

安頓。而欸乃一聲容與中流矣。是時河內猶未有汽船。故港
澳之渡船。猶是帆船也。歷五日夜然後到港。(§8, 7/8/1909)
馬某與尚康到港之後。全寓上環廣榮金山庄。緣該店司事是
馬某之族兄。曾代理馬某之書信者也。逾數天。馬某將尚康
託囑他族兄。並詳述他資助尚康往新金山事。又懇他代往船
行寫位。其族兄應允招待一切。馬某交代清楚。着實勸勉尚
康幾句。然後旋里。此次馬某[29] 到港。係專送尚康所致。緣
他返國未久。不能罫往也。越十餘日。方有開往澳洲之船。
居期。廣榮司事購備浪兜干糧等物。親送尚康落船。時澳洲
未禁華人。故無 今日之苛例。船主署爲點名驗票。諸事拚
擋。即便開行。

29 此字原誤印作陰紋「六」字。今據文義擬正。

In those days, steamers were not yet common; what Sheung Hong boarded was a sailing ship, known in Kwang Tung as a *mast-and-yard ship*. The passage of a sailing ship relies entirely on the winds. When the wind is wild it is rocked about; and when the wind is still it drifts about.

It happened to be winter at that time, and the sea wind was strong. Raging waves rose up like mountains, and the lone boat was lifted and dropped with the swells. Thrashed daylong by waves, it was as if the ship was a stone on which washing was being pounded. Apart from the sailors and seamen, those on board were all down with sea sickness, Sheung Hong very badly, for he was unaccustomed to heavy seas, and moreover, had ever been of a weak constitution. Beleaguered too by opium cravings, he was barely able to go on. During this time, all was quiet in the hold, except for the sound of vomiting. Sheung Hong, lying in his hammock, looked like he was long dead, pale in the face, spotted with spittle, in so wretched a state as not to bear beholding. And so he was for several days, not a morsel passing his lips.

Fortunately, when he boarded, Sheung Hong had made the acquaintance of two clansmen, a Pan Nam and a Ching Nam, who were both men of Wing On, Hoi Ping.[77] Pan Nam was a weakly scholar, who was also unused to rough seas. As to Ching Nam, he was a worthy man of magnanimous mentality, kindly and amiable disposition, and moreover, fit physique, and therefore better able to hold up. His bed happened to be close to Sheung Hong's, and he did his best to take care of him.

---

77   The 永安鄉 cº. "Wing On" referred to here, which has the literal sense of "forever peaceful", might be a veiled reference to Hoi Ping's northerly subdistrict of 長靜都 "Cheung Ching", which has the literal sense of "long calm". It might also be the name of a village. Recent historical discoveries suggest the latter.

當日汽船尚未大備。尚康所搭者。猶是帆船。粵人呼曰桅桁船。夫帆船放洋。全靠風信。風狂則任其簸盪。風靜則任其泛汛。其時適逢冬令。海風大作。怒濤如山立。一葉孤舟。隨波上下。船終日為浪所激。如搗布之石然。船內之人。除船員水手而外。莫不暈倒。而尚康尤甚。緣他未習風濤。而況體質素弱。又烟癮交迫。豈能支撐。此際艙內寂然無譁。惟聞吐嘔之聲。尚康則面色灰白。僵臥懸榻上。狀若陳死人。涎沫狼藉。其困頓之狀態。目不忍睹。如是者數日。餌不沾吻。幸得尚康落船之際。結識兩同宗系之人。一為賓南，一為程南。二人同是開平永安鄉人也。賓南乃質弱書生。亦不慣風波者。程南則志行磊落。稟性慈和。兼且體格完健。故稍可支持。其榻適與尚康相近。故力為看護。

Heedless of physical exhaustion, Ching Nam tottered back and forth between decks all day, fetching tea for him, and, taking no mind of the foulness, washing his sick pan. The ship went via Singapore and Port Darwin,[78] and only when at anchor did Sheung Hong manage to rise to his feet.

The voyage to Guichen Bay[79] took seventy-six days, and the scene of hardship over that time is impossible to explain in words. Whenever the sea was tranquil, Pan Nam would forget restraint and incant,[80] to give expression to his misery. He had one line that went—

From out the tips of hairs, the sweat it seeps;
while pillow-side, the waves are thundering.

—from which the situation can well be imagined.

Everyone was overjoyed on learning the ship was about to dock, and got together their baggage, and packed their bedding. The whole hold was in commotion, as if a swarm of bees was exiting a hive. After a short while the anchor was dropped, and the ship's ladder put ashore. Seventy-something Chinese labourers filed out, faces dirty, clothes ragged, with bamboo cases on their backs, their state no different from that of tramps.

Alas, swept thousands of miles by the pressure of poverty. *Quelle tragédie!*[81] (§9, 14/8/1909)

When Sheung Hong, Ching Nam and Pan Nam had come ashore, they saw everyone with no place to lodge, holding bags, shouldering cases and shilly-shallying by the roadside. Ching Nam asked, "Gentlemen, for what place are you headed?"

---

78   The Chinese names of Australian places often reflected early English names. Darwin, for example, continued to be known by the equivalent of the earlier "Port Darwin" long after the English name had been changed. See also the historical introduction, p. 22.

79   Robe, South Australia. See also the historical introduction, pp. 21–22.

80   In the author's day, as for thousands of years before, "incanting"—reading or reciting aloud in a manner akin to but nonetheless distinct from singing—was the normal way in which schoolchildren learnt poetry and passages from literature, and scholars read or recited poetry and the classics,

復不嫌穢褻。替他洗滌浪兜。[30] 取攜茶水。終日蹀躞於兩
間。不辭勞瘁。船經石叻澎打運各埠。每逢下錨。倘康始能
起立。船行七十六日。方到古慎尾。其中艱苦情形。難以言
喻。每遇風恬浪靜之時。賓南則肆意吟咏。以鳴其淒楚。故
有句云。汗從毛末出。浪向枕邊轟。其狀況亦可想見矣。諸
人聞船將泊岸。不勝愉快。檢点行篋。細疊被蓋。滿艙紛
擾。有如群蜂出房。無何。錨下。船梯駁岸。七十餘名之華
工。魚貫而上矣。垢面藍縷。背負竹笥。其狀態與流丐無
異。噫。因貧所迫。飄流萬里。抑何慘哉。(§9, 24.8.1909) 倘
康與程南等上岸之後。見各人攜囊負篋。徬徨于道左。無所
投止。程南問曰。諸君欲往何埠。

30　夫粵語謂暈動曰「暈浪」，暈車曰「暈車浪」，暈飛機曰「暈機浪」，暈
　　船曰「暈船浪」。此之「浪兜」，當謂暈浪時所用兜。兜者，兜之古字，
　　亦粵間舊俗常用之字也。兜之云盤。

or read their own work in the process of reviewing it. Like many Chinese
traditions, it has almost been lost. However, in recognition of its cultural
significance, and its merits as an aid to memory and to literary appreciation
and understanding, there are now efforts being made at reviving it.
Unfortunately, these are limited and sometimes misguided. Today, men and
women who have learnt to incant are mostly over eighty years of age.
Approaches to incanting differed between Chinese languages, dialects, and
regions. So if greater efforts are not made to record these various styles
before those still familiar with them pass away, they may be lost forever.

81　The author's concluding words translate roughly as "how tragic!", but as he
　　uses somewhat more archaic language in this expression, a French or Latin
　　phrase, in this case French, was considered a better rhetorical match than
　　plain English.

They replied, "In coming here, we had no definite destination in mind. We have merely heard that the gold deposits near Melbourne are good, and wish to make for them, except we do not know the route." There was one amongst them who spoke: "I once lived in this land, and am now coming back again after a return to China. The route, I could not well recognise, but the direction I can still remember. If you gentlemen wish to head there, might I act as a guide?" All nodded their agreement. So they formed a group and set forth on their journey.

Eating when hungry, drinking when thirsty, camping come nightfall, walking from dawn, they forded great waters, traversed wood and brush, scaled lofty mountain ridges, and passed across long land bridges,[82] but, after trekking for more than ten days, had still not sighted their objective. Moreover, in the vast wilderness there were no villages or shops. What dry provisions they had brought with them had been exhausted, and several men had already died along the way. Pan Nam and Sheung Hong, afflicted too by blistering of the feet, were unable to walk. So they lay rested up against a tree; but the cold wind cut to the bone, and they could not fall asleep. There was also a type of land leech in the ground, which extended forth its head to suck a person's blood. When one got up, the leeches would suck about the buttocks with their heads while hiding their bodies in the soil, as though they were the roots of the vegetation. The ant nests in the old trees were like hanging houses, and the ants the size of wasps. They would climb up trousers and enter sleeves, their bites causing the skin to swell. Yet fatigued in the extreme, the men could do nothing other than give themselves up for the poisonous insects to fill their bellies.

---

82 The word translated here as "long land bridges" (長堤) could also be translated as "long banks", and as the manmade structures "causeways" and "bunds".

簽曰。吾等此來。原無壹定之歸宿。惟聞美利彬附近金礦甚好。意欲壹往。但不識路徑。奈何。內有壹人曰。僕曾居留此地。前日歸國。今又再來。路徑不甚辨認。惟其方向。尙能記憶。諸君欲往。請爲先導如何。諸人首皆肯。於是結隊旅行而進。飢餐渴飮。夜宿曉行。涉大澤。穿林莽。踰峻嶺。度長堤。跋涉十餘日。猶未見到。茫茫荒野。又無村落商店。而所攜之乾糇已罄。死於半道者經有數人。賓南與尙康。亦足繭自疾。不能步履。于是枕樹而臥。無奈寒風砭骨。不能成寐。土內又有壹種旱蟣。伸首吮人膏血。若起立。旱蟣首吮股際。身藏泥裏。如植物之根蓫然。老樹上蟻窠如懸室。蟻大如蜂。緣袴入袖。咬膚欲腫。惟　時疲倦已極。壹任毒虫之裹腹而已。

The woods bleak, a cold moon on high, on guard against wolf's bite and tiger's chomp, fearful of savages' raid, they trembled with fear, scared out of their wits. All sat ringed about, sobbing, Sheung Hong and Pan Nam deeply regretting the misguidedness of the venture. Only Ching Nam seemed untroubled, incanting two poems, which he carved into a tree as a memorial:[83]

Across the boundless barb'rous wilderness, the road is long.[84]
　　Below which patch of white-white cloud[85]
　　does good-old home now lie?
For former land, the heart is rent, and vainly broken is the soul:
　　In frigid wind, one's bones are pierced, and body stiffened dies.
*We drink from mountain springs, and deem in thirst, they nectar
　　　yield:*
　　And feed on wild-fruit, that in hunger, as provisions tide.[86]
In this the land of treasures, we are now too deep to find;
　　Which year will realise hopes that in our hearts so deep reside?

83　This sentence is in some respects more specific in the Chinese. It indicates that before 刻 "carving (into wood)", Ching Nam first 削 "pared off the surface" in preparation.

84　These poems are written in a common traditional Chinese poetic form, which has strict requirements: A poem of this form must consist of four couplets, all couplets being of seven-character seven-syllable lines, the last character of each couplet and of the first line all having the same rhyme, with all lines arranged according to strict metrical rules, and the middle two couplets involving word-to-word antithesis. The word-to-word antithesis involves parallelism, meaning that if there is a verb, a noun, a conjunction etc. at one place in the first line of the couplet, then it must be matched by a word of the same type, and with a complementary sense, at the same place in the couplet's second line. A simple example of this in English would be "I am partial to pepper: she is fond of salt", in which "I" opposes "she", "am" matches "is", "partial to" complements "fond of" and "pepper" contrasts with "salt". Furthermore, the antithesis requires that the two lines must be more than independent opposites or structural matches, but rather that they complement each other in meaning, so as to form a whole that it greater than the sum of its parts, one which conveys a deeper, broader or different

惟時冷月當空。樹林蕭瑟。又恐野蠻劫奪。又防虎狼吞噬。
喪魄亡魂。股寒而慄。諸人團坐而啜泣。尙康與賓南深悔此
行之非計。獨程南坦然。復吟詩二章。削樹刻之。以爲紀
念。

莽莽蠻荒道路長。。白雲何處是家鄉。。傷心故國魂空斷。
。刺骨寒風體欲僵。。渴飲山泉勝玉酪。。飢餐野菓作餱糧
寶山已入難尋處。。夙願何年始克償。。

message through the combination of its pair of messages. As grammatical
English does not generally permit such concision and elegance of expression,
double the number of syllables have been used in the translation, which
consists of the same number of lines, each written in iambic heptameter
(and therefore perhaps better read aloud), with a rhyme or something close
to a rhyme at the end of each couplet, in an attempt to best mirror the
regular and harmonious sound of the original. An attempt has also been
made at reflecting, to a certain extent, the antitheses.

85 The expression 白雲 "white cloud" or, as rendered here to preserve the metre,
"white-white cloud", is commonly used in traditional Chinese literature and
song in connection with a longing for kin and home. It is reportedly an
allusion to the actions of one 狄仁傑 ᴹᵒ. Ti Jên-chieh (ᴹᴹ. *Dí Rénjíe* ᶜᴹ.
Dihk Yânh-giht) as recorded in the tenth-century history of the T'ang
dynasty, the 唐書 *Book of the T'ang*: The biography contained therein relates
that on one occasion Ti Jên-chieh ascended a mountain to look southwards
towards a lone white cloud, which he remarked was floating above the place
where his kin lived; and that he stayed staring in the direction of the cloud
until it shifted.

86 The verb "tide" is meant here in the sense of "tide over".

I pare these poems on a tree to leave a memory.
The hardship on this trip does go beyond all commentary.
We clutch at knives and group against attack from savage swift:
And chop up wood to fence from tiger's gulping bite more free.[87]
The first who ghosts become, along the way, the old and weak:
Their souls invoked by none, the lower world, a misery.
To drive away the cold, we have thanks be, a dry-twig fire;
Beneath the sombre moon, we facing sit, all speechlessly.

His carving complete, Ching Nam gave all a round of encouragement, and rallied them to push onward. (§10, 21/8/1909)

After walking on for several more days, Ching Nam, Sheung Hong and the others could see, on lifting their heads, only outstretched and open country, all green grass and dams[88] without roads to travel by. They looked at each other, the colour gone from their faces. Reluctant to advance, they thought of how they might make their way back. Yet the distance they had covered from Guichen Bay was already too great for them to return the same way. Furthermore, the contents of their travelling bags had been exhausted, and they had not the money for a journey by boat. So, on deliberation, they decided to discard all their bulky luggage, and to advance by fording through water. Fortunately the water was clear and shallow, passable with clothes peeled up. When deep, it reached the knees,

---

87   The fourth character of this line 柵 "fence" should, according to the metrical requirements of this type of poem, have a level tone (平聲), but the character used is pronounced, in the sense in which it is used, with an oblique tone (仄聲) in Mandarin, Cantonese and other Chinese languages, and according to the rhyme books employed in the composition of traditional poetry. However, in today's Hoisan (A.K.A. Toisan, Taishan) dialect of the See Yip language, it does have a colloquial pronunciation in the level tone. This is probably the sound the author intended.

88   "Dams" is meant here in the Australian sense of man-made water reservoirs of the type found on grazing properties.

削樹題詩紀念存。。旅行辛苦不堪論。。操刀結隊防蠻襲。
。斫木爲柵避虎吞。。半道老羸先作鬼。。重泉悽楚孰招
魂。。袪寒幸有枯枝火。。對坐無言月色昏。。[31]

刻完鼓勵他等壹番。復率之勉强而行。(§10, 21/8/1909) 程南與
尙康等。再進行數日。仰首一望。而彌漫曠野。盡是靑草陂
[32] 塘。無路可達。各人相顧失色。趑趄不前。欲圖歸計。無
奈此處離古愼尾不知已隔幾許路程。焉能復歸。矧旅囊已
罄。附舟亦無貲斧。於是羣相決議。盡棄其呆重之行囊。涉
水前進。幸其水淸淺。騫裳可渡。深者沒膝。

31   此律詩之頷聯，下句第四字「柵」，準式當叶平聲，乃其柵欄之意，依平
       水韻，與北方話、廣州話等方言之韻系，當讀仄聲。按，今臺山話，柵欄
       之柵別有平聲俗音讀曰「刪」者。詩中之音，疑即是也。
32   「陂」原作「坡」。蓋字之誤。今正。

when shallow it covered the ankles, and when it wet their clothing and bedding, they had not the time to pay heed. At nightfall, they chose a high bar on which to bivouac. And in the dead of night, extending their heads from tattered blankets to peer forth, they saw no more than lightless stars, and black clouds masking the moon, to the calls of hill falcons and the answering clamour of frogs croaking.

So for a week they walked on through swampland, and yet all was still lush and rampant grass and boggy terrain. They thought back on how, of the party of people who had come out with them, more than half had died along the route. Corpses discarded by the wayside had been pecked clean by crows in the twinkling of an eye. And amongst the party, there were those who walked carrying the sick and exhausted on their backs, crows circling above them, their beaks pointed down as if ready to swoop, for to the birds they must have looked like men long dead.

Seeing that ahead there was no place for them to encamp, and that behind lay nought but indistinct expanse, even Ching Nam's spirit was blunted and sapped. He thought to himself, *My country has not developed its manufacturing or exploited its minerals, and in consequence we poor are forced to risk death travelling to this remotest of isles, simply for the sake of our livelihoods. I recall how once, when living in my ancestral land, I bored wells and ploughed fields, going out to work when the sun rose and in to rest when it fell,*[89] *morning and night at home in the company of my two white-haired elders. What joy it was. Yet now things are as so. How pained and sorrowful would my parents be could they know my present hardship?* His thoughts reaching this point, this hero

---

89   The phrase "going out to work when the sun rose and in to rest when it fell" is conveyed here in Chinese through an idiom of a mere four syllables in length. The idiom was itself formed through the truncation of an existing expression (日出而作日入而息), which is a common trick of traditional Chinese rhetoric. This is one of many examples of rhetorical elegance within

淺者滅踝。雖衣被濡濕。亦不暇顧。夜擇高灘而露宿。夜闌
伸首破褥探視。但見黑雲障月。星斗無光。山鵑與蛙鼓之
聲。互[33]相答響而已。然行於瀦澤之中。已一星期。而蒙茸
碧草。猶是沮洳[34] 之區。廻顧同來隊人。沿途死亡。已逾其
半。道旁遺[35] 屍。轉瞬已爲烏鴉[36] 啄盡。隊中人有背負儓病
者而行。群鴉廻[37] 翔於上。垂喙欲下撲狀。蓋鳥意其陳死人
也。斯時程南見前無稅駕之地。而後顧又復茫茫。亦爲之意
阻氣奪。自念吾國工藝不興。礦產不闢。致使吾等窮民。不
顧生命。飄流絕島。亦爲生計所偪耳。遙憶前日住祖國時。
鑿井耕田。出作入息。與吾家中白頭二老。朝暮相依。其樂
何如也。今若此。 設使雙親得悉吾此時之苦狀。其哀痛又當
何如耶。思至此。

33 「互」原作「亙」。誤。今正。
34 「沮洳」原作「洳沮」。蓋倒文之誤也。今正。
35 「遺」原作「遣」。誤。今正。
36 原文「鴉」字半缺。今據其殘跡及文義擬正。
37 此字等，原作「逥」，當作「迴」。迴，遠也；逥，「回」之或體。今
   正，不復注明。

the work that challenge the translator anxious to preserve the writing's
meaning while also relating it in such a way as to produce an equivalent
effect upon the reader. The use of this idiom is also a good example of the
extreme concision and elegance of effect that the author achieves through
the use of Literary Chinese.

could not but shed a few tears, though he secretly wiped them away, fearing that his fellows might see and loose heart. Unexpectedly, Pan Nam happened to notice, and asked, "Since we set out from Guichen Bay, I have not seen a cheerless expression upon your face. Why now are you so sorrowful?"

Ching Nam replied, "We lost our country several hundred years ago and live under the authoritarian government of a foreign race,[90] which thinks only of its own licentious pleasure, and cares not for people's lives. And hence, in search of a living we meet today with this suffering. Is it not enough to hurt the heart and head?" He then wrote an All-the-River-Red tune poem[91] so as to give form to his sentiments:

Of the Yellow Emperor's line surely any average man is a scion.
How I rue that vast Cathay has to plunderers fallen,

---

90   The foreign race referred to are the Manchus. The Manchus are a Tungusic people, with a unique language and culture, whose leaders conquered China and established the ᴹᵒ. Ch'ing (ᴹᴹ. *Qīng*) dynasty in 1644. This, China's last imperial dynasty, was overthrown in 1911. Like some other periods of minority rule in China's history, the Ch'ing dynasty was characterised by initial brutality during and after conquest, in an attempt to subdue the Chinese population, followed by the relatively rapid sinification of its rulers, and marked throughout by underlying racial resentment on the part of a certain element of China's majority Han population. It was during this dynasty that Chinese men were forced, as a sign of submission to Manchu rule, to adopt the Manchu haircut—the queue and half-shaven crown—which English speakers so often consider quintessentially Chinese. However, it should also be noted that many Han Chinese were loyal supporters of Ch'ing rule, and that at the Ch'ing empire's powerful and prosperous zenith, Chinese art, culture and literature were supported and flourished.

91   The 詞 ᴹᴹ. *cí* ᶜᴹ. cih, which is translated here as *tune poem*, is a unique Chinese literary form that had its beginning as poetic song lyrics, and then developed into poems written according to song melodies but not intended for singing. (The name is generally given in English as "song lyrics", a problematic translation because it could be confused with other independent

不能不灑幾點英雄之淚。然猶暗自拂拭。恐爲同輩所見。以
灰其志。不意適爲賓南窺見。問曰。君由古愼尾首途以來。
未嘗有不豫之色。今何悲苦乃爾。程南曰。吾等亡國數百
年。處於異族專制政府之下。祇顧淫樂。不恤民生。今吾輩
因謀生而罹此痛苦。能不疾首痛心。故作滿江紅詞一首以見
志。

一介平民。。固猶是黃農遺冑。。恨莽莽神洲。。已淪盜
寇。。

---

forms such as 元曲, which are true song lyrics, and often share the same
titles as tune poems because many are written to the same tunes, or as "*ci*" or
"*ci*-poems", which are also ambiguous translations, because there is another
wholly unrelated literary form whose name is pronounced identically but
written with a different character: 辭.) Tune poems are also known as 長短
句 "long-and-short liners" because, unlike the 律詩 *regular poem* in Part §10,
they generally consist of lines of varying length. An explanation of their
other characteristics is not given here, save to say that they also make use of
rhyme and a measure of colloquial language, and may be divided into two
general classes, given by skilled translator Jiaosheng Wang as the *bold
romantic style* (豪放) and the *elegant restrained style* (婉約). 滿江紅
"All-the-River-Red" (M^M. *Mǎnjiānghóng*) is a traditional tune-poem title.
The most well-known example of an All-the-River-Red tune poem, both
today and in the author's day, is a work filled with wildly revanchist
sentiment (the O.E.D. defines revanchism as "a policy of seeking to retaliate,
especially to recover lost territory") that is credited to the M^o. Sung-dynasty
general 岳飛 Yüeh Fei (M^M. *Yuè Fēi* c^M. Ngohk Fēi), and which belongs
unequivocally to the bold romantic style. All-the-River-Red tune poems
consist of two stanzas, with the one rhyme repeated throughout both, and an
antithetical couplet of the same form as appeared within the poem in Part
§10 in each stanza. The translation given here is arranged to show the
stanzas, and into lines that in the original carry end-rhymes (unfortunately it
has not proven possible to reflect the rhymes in translation).

That neighbours strong have usurping roots long entrenched; and
    that men of our race do, to their own, pea-boiling injury.[92]
How it pains me that of the Great Ming's palace all but ruins
    remain, thick with millet.[93]

We are cruelly taxed, and to insult ever open; while they in games
    indulge, and fill the cup that funnels out.
Where's this godly grace, deep benevolence and rich provision?
Ferocious tigers in search of prey, they block the way: wailing geese
    enervated and thin, we cover the country.[94]
To the world's nether regions we are impelled to run, the bitterness
    of hardship to taste of fully.

When Pan Nam had finished reading, he asked surprisedly, "At a time of life and death, what leisure have we for the consideration of national affairs?"

"Since the Manchus came through the passes," replied Ching Nam, "our country has been host to a people of five million, who sit and feed but neither till nor weave. It is for no other reason but this that we, from out of impoverishment and bankruptcy, must today seek our living in foreign countries." He then heaved many a heavy sigh. (§11, 28/8/1909)[95]

---

92   The expression "pea-boiling injury" within this, the first stanza's antithetical couplet, is a common Chinese allusion based on an historical story that is still well known today: 曹丕 M°. Ts´ao P´i (M^M. *Cáo Pī* C^M. Chòuh Pēi), the first emperor of the state of Wei (220 to 266 C.E.) during China's Three Kingdoms period, ordered his younger brother, 曹植 Ts´ao Chih (M^M. *Cáo Zhí* C^M. Chòuh Jihk), on threat of death, to compose a poem in the course of seven steps. Ts´ao Chih composed a six-line poem, which moved his brother to shame. In the poem, Ts´ao Chih compares himself to beans boiling in a cauldron and his brother to bean stalks burning beneath, and ends by asking why, when they both sprang from the same origin, one should treat the other so fiercely.

強鄰僭竊久盤根。。同種相殘如煮豆。。痛大明宮殿剩頹
垣。。黍禾茂。。橫征斂。。任人詬。酖遊戲。。填巵漏。
。說甚麼天恩。。仁深澤厚。。猛虎當途思攫噬。。哀鴻遍
野盡癆瘦。。使吾民奔走到窮荒。。苦嘗透。

寶南讀罷。憮然曰。生死之際。何暇計及國事。程答曰。自
滿人入關以來。以五百萬之客民。不耕不織。而坐食於我
國。今日民窮財潰。使吾等謀食外國者。未嘗非此原因。說
完。不勝浩嘆。(§11, 28/8/1909)

---

93   On account of a song (黍離) in the ancient Chinese text 詩經 *The Odes*
     (A.K.A. *The Book of Songs*, the *Shi King*), wild and thick broomcorn millet
     on the site of a ruin symbolises vanquishment.

94   Some of the expressions within this, the second stanza's antithetical couplet,
     also warrant further explanation: (1) There is a link in Chinese between the
     ferocity of the tiger and the harshness of oppressive government, which is
     based in a story about Confucius coming upon a woman in mourning. She
     related that her father-in-law and husband had been killed by tigers, and
     now her son had been too. When asked why she chose to live where she did,
     she stated that the place was free from harsh government. Confucius then
     uttered the well-known line 苛政猛於虎 "Harsh government is more savage
     than the tiger". (2) 哀鴻遍野 "wailing geese cover the country" is a classical
     idiom in which the "wailing geese" represent people in a state of severe
     destitution.

95   In the *Chinese Times*'s serialisation of *The Poison of Polygamy*, it is 續
     "continuations", i.e. instalments additional to the first, that are numbered.
     The second instalment, or §2, is therefore Continuation One, and this
     twelfth instalment should be Continuation Eleven. However, it was
     incorrectly labelled as Twelve, and not given again correctly until §28, after
     which point, excepting the occasional aberration, it continued to be stated
     correctly through to the last instalment, which is §53 or Continuation 52.

"Hearing your words," said Pan Nam fretfully, "I am filled with resentment and hurt. Since stealing our country, those Strangers Strong[96] have not ceased to tax and levy through violence and extortion. Thus today, the money in the Great Within[97] is wealth sufficient to fight a Chü Lu;[98] and the palace of Rounded Brightness[99] rivals the Labyrinthine Mansion[100] in ingeniousness of design.[101] This draining of the Chinese people's fat and wealth to provide for the Tartars'[102] profligacy has ended in the destitution of the populace and financial ruin, and tumult throughout the land. The peasants of the fields have ceased their ploughing and risen up; and the champions of the sylvan hills have sworn blood oaths and formed alliances. A scene of devastation has followed, with nine in every ten houses empty,[103] and the fearful flames of war passing by several times a year. I aspired to till and weed with brush and tongue[104] yet found the inkstone field[105] gone to waste,

---

96   The Manchus.

97   The Forbidden City.

98   Mᵒ. Chü Lu (鉅鹿 or 巨鹿) is a place name and the site of a famous battle in Chinese antiquity, in which a small force vanquished a foe far superior in number. The historical account of this battle is the source of the Chinese idiom 以一當十 "one against ten", which is no doubt the association the author is playing on here.

99   The Summer Palace.

100 The 迷樓 "Labyrinthine Mansion" was a palace built by Mᵒ. Emperor Yang of the Sui dynasty (which lasted from 581 to 618 C.E.) that is renowned for its architectural excess and complexity.

101 This sentence forms a literary couplet. Its words are not intended to reflect the character's speech verbatim, but rather to reflect what he says and thinks through the clear and exact lens of refined language, as with a character who speaks in song or poetry in an English play.

102 The expression used here for Tartar (韃虜) is pejorative, and was much used by the early Chinese republicans.

103 This is a classical idiom that describes a state of disaster in which, through either the decimation or displacement of a population, houses are left empty.

賓南戚然曰。聆君言。使予懷悽感。溯自强胡[38]竊國[39]。無日
不橫征暴斂。大內金錢。富門鉅鹿。圓明宮室。巧競迷樓。
煎漢人之膏脂。供撻虜之揮霍。卒致民窮財盡。海內騷然。
隴畝農夫。輟耕而起。山林豪俠。歃血而盟。於是瘡痍滿
目。十室九空。兵燹驚心。一年幾度。欲圖筆耕舌耨。而硯
田已荒。

---

38   古稱北方之異族曰「胡」。至及清末民初，其俗義乃引伸，凡西方之洋
      人，與東方之倭人，皆得稱「胡」。故今之譯為「外人」，亦非失之。
39   原文「國」字模糊不清。既似「國」，亦似「關」。今參別「國」、
      「關」字，斟酌文義，擬為「國」。

---

104   This is another idiom, in which the earning of a living through writing and
      teaching is likened to the noble pursuit of agriculture.
105   Literary men are held to earn their living "ploughing their inkstones", hence
      the Chinese expression 硯田 "inkstone field".

and in consequence, my wife weeping, children crying and the
kitchen smoke no longer rising. Alack alack! Would that I knew,
in years gone by cooped up incanting,[106] the hardship of today's
long journey." Then, selecting a squarish piece of white rock, he
wrote out a T'ai-Ch'êng-Road tune poem,[107] so as to give form to
his heartfelt sorrow.

> *I turn my head: where lies my former land? A few sheets of white*
> *cloud curtain it.*
> *Crestfallen and adrift, as baldric girthed adventurer,*
> *I remember half a lifetime self trapped, like a silkworm bound,*
> *And think how many times, in ten years of grinding lead,[108]*
> *I offered up uncut jade.[109]*
> *How I rue, that in those years, China had iron*
> *yet cast only flaws.[110]*

> *For what do I seek shelter in this island waste, of salivating wolves*
> *and dholes,[111] and malevolent aborigines,*

---

106   For "incanting", see footnote 80.

107   The 臺城路詞 ᴍᵒ. "T'ai-Cheng-Road tune poem" takes its name and
character from a work by a renowned Sung-dynasty writer of tune poems
(周邦彥), of the elegant-and-restrained style, in which he gave voice to
thoughts and feelings of melancholy and longing, when far from friends
and home.

108   Ground lead was used in ancient China to erase written errors. The
expression 磨鉛 "to grind lead" thus grew to mean "to apply oneself
assiduously to written composition, either as an editor or author".

109   This is a reference to a well-known classical story: A man of the state of 楚
ᴍᵒ. Ch'u offers up a piece of uncut jade to his king. After it is determined to
be a rock and he a trickster, he has a foot cut off. When a new king ascends
the throne, the man again offers up his jade-in-the-rough, and the same
thing happens to him. Finally, his rock is recognised as jade by a third king.
The significance of the uncut jade as representing a person of talent or the
proposals of a person of talent should be clear in English too.

致使婦泣兒啼。灶烟不起。嗟嗟。昔年斗室吟哦。那知今日
長途之辛苦也。說完。擇一方白石。寫臺城路詞一闋。以誌
感慨焉。

迴頭何處故鄉是。。幾片白雲如羃[40]。。劍佩飄零。。征衫
落拓。。纔憶半生。。自困同蠶縛。。想十載研鉛。。幾回
獻璞。。悔恨當年。。九洲有鐵唯[41]鑄錯。。為何投奔荒
島。。豺狼涎滴。。土蠻性惡。。

40 「羃」音莫狄切，讀若「覓」，出韻。殆轉寫排印者之誤，本當印作「白雲
如幕」。幕音慕各切，叶韻。且幕之義，即「驟雨如幕」「幕天席地」
者，較羃為允。
41 此字原文作「雖」，應即「唯」或「惟」字之訛。今正。

---

110 鑄錯 "to cast or found (in the metalurgical sense) flaws" is a Chinese
expression for *committing errors*, the literal sense of which the author plays
on here through an initial reference to iron.
111 The 豺 dhole, A.K.A. the Asiatic wild dog, is a highly unique and now
endangered (i.e. very likely to become extinct) Asian canid, which plays a
significant though unpraiseworthy part in Chinese literature and the
Chinese language. Note that here the expression "wolves and dholes" is not a
mere misidentification of a couple of Australia's carniverous mammal
species: like the wolf of European fairy tales, both the wolf and dhole have
unpleasant figurative senses in Chinese.

Where hunger's fire grills the gut, and at one's shoulders,
        the cold wind jabs,
And where, carrying bags on shoulder poles and sacks on backs,
We walk through the evenings and camp come night.
'Tis all heartbreak at heaven's edge and tears dropped
        at world's end.
The road is long and indistinct, and I fear may end with
        my body in some ravine entombed.[112,113]

The poem written, his tears fell down like rain.

Then, Sheung Hong, who was lying splayed out by the way-side,[114] said in a feeble voice, "In risking our lives to get here, the only ideology we should keep is that money is all; and to reach our goal, we should be willing even to be enslaved. Why must you show such attachment over our old land's rise and demise? I may be uncouth and detestable, but the singular regard you gentlemen show for playing about with words at a time when our lives hang by a thread is truly exasperating. If you want to sip wine and engage in literary connoisseurship, wait till after we have returned wealthy and victorious and it will not be too late.

---

112 Mencius relates that, in antiquity, corpses were sometimes cast into ravines instead of being buried. He considered it an unceremonious and inglorious end, and a disrespectful act on the part of a deceased person's kin.

113 This poem does not rhyme in standard Mandarin, but it does in the See Yip language and Cantonese, which retain more of the sound systems of older forms of Chinese, according to which traditional poetry is written. The rhymes in standard Cantonese are as follows (in-rhymes shown in brackets): cᴹ. 幕 *mohk* "to curtain"; (落) *lohk* which forms a disyllabic word with the next rhyme; 拓 *tok* the second syllable of 落 *lohk* 拓 *tok* "crest-fallen"; 縛 *bok* or here the more literary pronunciation *fok* "bound"; 璞 *pok* "uncut jade"; 錯 *cok* "flaws" (this is also a literary pronunciation); 惡 *ok* "malevolent"; 髆 *bok* "shoulders"; 橐 *tok* "sacks"; 泊 *bohk* "to camp"; 角 *gok* "corner" (part of the expression for "world's end"); and 壑 *kok* "ravine" (note that the Hs in the romanisations do not indicate any change in the vowel, merely a lower-pitched pronunciation). In standard Mandarin, they become:

矧飢火煎腸。。寒風針髆。。又復擔囊負橐。宵行夜泊。
。儘淚墮天涯。。魂銷海角。。渺渺長途。。恐葬身溝
壑。。

書罷。淚下如雨。斯時尙康挺臥道傍。作微弱之聲曰。吾等
冒險至此。但存唯一金錢主義耳。苟能達其目的。雖爲奴
隸。亦所甘願。何必沾⁴²沾於故國興亡乎。吾雖鄙俚可厭。
君等於生死一髮之時。祇顧舞文弄墨。真是令人懊惱。若欲
杯酒論文。待富足榮歸後。猶未晚也。

42   此字原作「沽」。誤。今正。

ᴍᴹ. 幕 *mù*; (落) *luò*; 拓 *tuò*; 縛 *fù*; 璞 *pú*; 錯 *cuò*; 惡 *è*; 髆 *bó*; 橐 *tuó*; 泊 *bó*; 角
jiǎo; and 壑 *huò* or *hè*. The reason for the significance of the discrepancy is
that the rhyme employed in this poem is of the clipped tone, that northern
Mandarin, upon which standard Mandarin is based, has lost. The clipped
tone is a tone that ends abruptly, in this case (in Cantonese) in an unaspi-
rated K, like at the end of the first syllable of the English word *mocking*.
Here and elsewhere, the author chooses to use traditional rhymes that also
rhyme in the See Yip language.

114 There is a Confucian dictum that one should not sleep splayed out like a
corpse (寢不屍). The author's description of the way Sheung Hong sleeps,
here and elsewhere, appears to reference it.

It is now over a day since we ate. Our famished bellies are rumbling and we are soon to become hungry ghosts.[115] Can you gentlemen indeed stave off starvation with poetry?" Finished, he went into a sulk. Knowing him to be contemptible, Ching Nam and the others did not argue. (§12, 4/9/1909)

Having received an earful from Sheung Hong, Ching Nam, while detesting what was said, felt an unbearable hunger in his belly on hearing him talk of their having run out of food. So he conferred with the guide, saying, "We who, out of the pursuit of gain, have hazarded our lives by casting ourselves into this barbaric wilderness, have today reached this place. Yet while we have relied on your effort to lead us here, our food was exhausted a full ten days ago, and all that we have relied on to keep us from death has been the presence, in the land we have passed through, of hill farms run by white graziers, from whom we have been begging scraps of bread, so we might preserve what breath remains us. Now we find ourselves in the middle of this vast swamp devoid of human habitation, with no one to beg food from. I would ask you to tell me clearly how long a journey it is from here to Melbourne."

The guide replied, "I declared when we first set out that I could only roughly tell the direction, and that I had no firm grasp as to the route. Surely you must have heard."

Ching Nam responded sorrowfully, "The time of our arrival is still unforeseeably distant, and we are tired and fatigued in the extreme, and finding it difficult to walk. What can be done?"

---

115 In Chinese, the word 鬼 "ghost(s)" is an antonym of the word 人 "human being(s)/person(people)/man(men)", and for this reason it is often used in terms of abuse to infer that the object is the opposite of human. Consequently it is sometimes translated as "devil" or "devils", e.g. in the expression *foreign devils*. "Hungry ghosts" also means souls that have no one to propitiate them.

今吾等不食。已日餘矣。飢腹雷鳴。行將作餓鬼矣。君等果
能以詩詞療飢耶。話完。悻悻然。程南等知其卑鄙。亦不之
較 (§12, 4/9/1909) 程南因尚康絮聒一番。雖甚可厭。及聞糧盡
之語。始覺腹餒難堪。卽與嚮導相商曰。吾 等 [43] 擲生命以投
蠻荒者。欲圖獲利計。今日得到此地。雖賴君引導之力。然
絕糧已經旬日。所賴以不死者。實緣前日所經之地。尚有白
人畜牧山壩[44]。屢丐其麵飽餘瀝。以救殘喘耳。際此茫茫一
潴澤之中。渺無人烟。無從乞食。此地距離美利伴爲程尚幾
許。願明以告我。嚮導曰。吾於首途之時。已經宣言。祇能
畧辨其方向。至路線一層。實無把握。君豈不聞耶。程南悄
然曰。到埠尚遙遙無期。而吾等困疲已極。艱於步履。奈
何。

43   原文「等」字半缺。今據其殘跡及文義擬正。
44   「壩主」、「羊壩」、「蔗壩」等語，在奧洲舊華文報上，屢見不鮮。按，
      凡此諸「壩」，蓋皆英文farm之音譯，意即「農牧之場」是也。

The guide climbed up a highish hillock, and craning his neck, looked all about. Then he pointed out a hill in the distance and said, "The dusky green patch at that hill's foot would perhaps be forest. There might be fellers or firewood collectors camped within and we might get something if we went there. Even if there are no woodcutters, we might still hope for fruit with which to fill our famished mouths." So the group then resolved to head for the forest.

En route, Pan Nam lifted his head to gaze afar and said, "The clouds up there are black as ink and this cold wind is howling. We might walk quickly as rain will be coming." Where they were was around forty or fifty miles from the forest, and after a mile or so's hurried walking, heavy rain did indeed bucket down. Only a few of the group were carrying [bamboo] hats; the rest were fortunate to have baggage with which to cover their heads so that their breathing was not obstructed by the rain, but they were soon dripping wet from head to toe, like the proverbial dunked hens.[116]

On reaching the forest the weather cleared and the rain stopped, and they sat down ringed about under the trees. Ching Nam and the guide investigated the surrounding area, but to their great disappointment, found no evidence of any people. Fortunately, their explorations took them to a place where they saw bunches of grapes hanging from a tree.[117] The group were amazed, as pleased as if they had come by a rare treasure, and after eating several each, they recovered some vitality. Suddenly, just as they were chewing, a strange sound came out of the wood. They were all startled. A moment later, a beast shot out, bear-headed and

---

116 The proverb or expression 沐湯之雞 "dunked hens", which refers to the appearance of birds that have been dispatched and dunked in boiling water prior to plucking, means "people drenched to the core".

117 A highly unlikely sight in the Australian bush.

嚮導登高阜翹首四顧。遙指一山而言曰。此山麓下青青葱葱
者。非森林耶。此處或有採薪伐木者棲息其間。吾等到此。
或有所獲。縱無樵者。尤[45]冀有果實。暫充飢吻也。是以羣
相決議。向森林而進。途間賓南仰首眺望曰。空際黑雲如
墨。寒風怒號。雨將至矣。可速行。該處與森林相距。可四
五十里。而遄行里許。果然大雨傾盆。携笅笠[46]者祇居少
數。餘人幸以行囊幪首。呼吸不爲雨水所窒。然上下淋漓。
已如沐湯之雞。甫抵森林。雨亦晴歇。諸人圍坐樹下。程南
與嚮導週圍窺探。不料杳無人迹。大失所望。幸而探至一
處。見有菩提子纍纍然懸於樹上。羣相驚喜。如獲異寶。各
啖數枚。始有生機。方咀嚼之際。忽有異聲。出自林間。諸
人咸駭怪。俄而一猛獸瞥然而至。熊首而

---

45 按，俗有以「尤」代「猶」者。古則多以「由」字代之。蓋古今假借
    異，而其理一。
46 此「笅笠」之「笅」字，與二十一續者，疑皆誤，應作「篛」、「箬」、
    「筠」之類。

tiger-bodied,[118] and with eyes that cast a fiery radiance all around. Having no time to run, Ching Nam shinned up to a tree top. In fright, the group darted for cover in all directions. Several people fell and lay prone on the ground. Those lying at the rear were immediately savaged by the beast. Spotting this from his tree, Ching Nam's eyes bulged with rage and the desire came on him to summon all his strength and go down to save them, but he knew he was no match for the beast. Exigency inducing sudden ingenuity, Ching Nam pulled out a sharp blade from about his waist, and focusing on the beast threw it down with force, striking the animal right on the back. Blood spurted forth, and it gave a loud howl, before retreating into the undergrowth.

Ching Nam jumped down and inspected those who had been savaged.[119] But, their skulls crushed, they had already expired. He then picked up the blade he had thrown and went to look at the two people lying ahead. It was Pan Nam and Sheung Hong. They were pressed, eyes closed, to the ground, mumbling, as if in a state of prayer. Listening carefully, Ching Nam heard one saying "O Savior of Those in Hardship Most Miraculous Avalokitasvara Bodhisattva,"[120] and the other "No-Noble of Han Shou"[121], stuttering as they spoke through trembling lips, their faces ashen. Beholding this state of affairs, Ching Nam was filled with both pity and anger. He rebuked them: "What kind of a time is this to keep up such medieval behaviour!"

---

118   The beast described is a close match for the now extinct thylacine (A.K.A. Tasmanian tiger, 袋狼), a marsupial carnivore that had a striped body similar to a tiger's and a head that was also likened to a bear's in early European descriptions. Thylacines were very shy animals and reports of attacks on humans were rare and often of doubtful veracity. Nevertheless, some accounts do suggest that thylacines were capable of attacking people when either they or the people concerned were in a debilitated state. However, the thylacine is believed to have been extinct on mainland Australia by the time of European settlement, a fact which makes the story given here all the more improbable.

虎身。目如懸鈴。光芒四射。程南奔避不及。猱升樹杪。諸
人四散驚竄。有數人踣於地上。後踣者已爲猛獸所嚙。時程
南在樹上瞥見。怒目裂眦。欲奮身下救。知難與敵。忽而人
急智生。在腰際拔一利刃。注射此獸。力擲而下。適中獸
背。血液如注。大嗥一聲。即向叢莽而逸。程南一躍而下。
審視此人。已顱碎氣絶。即拾回擲獸之利刃。復顧前踣之二
人。知是賓南與尙康。伏地閉目喃喃。似祈禱狀。細聆之。
一云救苦救難靈感觀世音菩薩。一云漢漢壽亭侯。語時脣顫
音澀。面如土色。此際程南睹此狀況。又憐又惱。即斥之
曰。此何時乎。尤作此酸腐之態耶。

---

119 Actually, it is unclear in the original whether one or more people are
     savaged, as Chinese grammar does not require the author to indicate the
     number.

120 This is the title of the Buddhist Goddess of Mercy 觀音 Mᵒ. Kuan Yin (Mᴹ.
     Guānyīn), whom Taosim also reveres.

121 This is the title of the Taoist god Mᵒ. Kuan Kung (A.K.A. Mᴹ. *Guān Gōng*,
     關聖帝君), often referred to in English as the Chinese Mars or God of War.

They then opened their eyes a little and, quailing, said, "T-t-the b-b-beast?" Ching [Nam] cut them off, "Enough talk. Up quickly and on. Otherwise we will be in peril." While speaking, he hurriedly grasped their arms, and propping themselves on his, they each got up.

One to his left and one to his right, Ching Nam then pulled them desperately onward, and they caught sight of ten or so shocked people by the wayside half a mile away. Knowing them to be of their group, they pushed themselves to catch up. "We thought you had no hope of coming out alive," said the others. Then the group's members started asking after each other's condition.

"This is no place to chat," said Ching Nam. "We should walk hurriedly for another distance, until we are free of danger, and then choose a good place for a brief rest."

On hearing this, they continued on. Then, finding a flat area of grass, they rested, and Ching Nam recounted the perilous circumstances under which he had thrown his blade. They all bit hold of their tongues, speechless. Pan Nam and Sheung Hong's shocked souls had [by then] settled slightly, but on hearing Ching Nam's words, their faces turned pale once more. All said praisingly, "If it had not been for you, the two of them might [not have] escaped the beast's jaws." Then all lamented and grieved for those who had been killed. Ching Nam went on [to describe] the farcical scene of Pan Nam and Sheung Hong chanting. He said to Pan Nam, "You are not an ignorant man, [why would you] engage in this antiquated [behaviour]?"

"Our Chinese deities are the most miraculous of all," responded Pan Nam. "When one meets with misfortune, [through summoning the strength to] chant [devoutly] from the scriptures, one can be freed from jeopardy. Had we not been chanting, who can say, we might now already be beast's dung."

Ching [Nam] gave a scornful snort, and thought to himself, *China is a country of polytheism, and this superstitious faith in*

斯時二人微張其眸。瑟縮而言曰。獸丨獸丨。程南卽[47]攔絕
其語曰。毋多言。速起前進。不然。殆矣。言時急以手掖
之。二人扶手而起。程南即左右[48]扯拽。效命前進。遙望半
里之外。有十數人愴惶道左。知是本羣之人。極力趕及。僉
曰。吾輩意汝等無生還望矣。於是[49]羣相詢狀。程南曰。此
非細談之所。再遄行一程。待脫離險惡。擇一善地。稍爲休
憩。言之未晚。衆復前進。果覓得一平陽草地。羣息於此。
程南詳述當時擲刃之險狀。諸人莫不咋舌。賓尙二人此□[50]
驚魂稍定。聞程南言。面復死白。衆讚曰。微君一擲。他二
人□[51]逃獸吻矣。衆復傷悼遇害者。程南又□容□[52]二人誦經
之怪劇。對賓南曰。君乃通人。□[53]作此迂腐之□[54]何爲。賓
南曰。吾中國神聖。最彰靈異。若逢災難。果□□[55]心誦經。
可脫險厄。設非誦經。此際吾兩人已成獸糞。亦未可知。程
南[56]嗤之以鼻。復自念中國爲多神教之國。即此迷信

47 原文「南卽」二字殘損。今據其墨跡及文義擬正。
48 此字原倒作「右左」。疑誤。今正。
49 「於是」原誤倒作「是於」。今正。
50 此字全缺。按其文義，當作「際」或「時」字。
51 此字幾乎全缺。審其殘跡、文義，或為「難」字。
52 「容」字前後二字全缺。推其文義，原文蓋當作「形容其」。
53 此字殘缺之甚。審其殘跡、文義，或當作「竟」。
54 此字全缺。按其文義，或當作「語」。
55 此二字亦全缺。按其文義，原文或當作「果能誠心誦經」。
56 此字全缺。今據文義擬補。

supernatural power alone is more than enough to cause its demise. If even Pan Nam, an educated and learned man, is so superstitious, what of silly women and children. Then he heaved many an audible sigh. (§13, 11/9/1909)

A short while later, the trees of the forest, now distant to the eye, all turned to fire, and looked under the marbled splendour of rosy clouds spread wide, just like the ruby liquidambars[122] of July. In the other direction, the setting sun in the far heaven formed the semblance of a fiery ball, fresh from some furnace, that had been cast amongst the misty expanse of grassland, its residual rays producing the illusion of this lovely evening scene. Yet in a few moments, the red orb halved and then gradually sank and disappeared, and in a twinkling the vastness of the open country filled with thick fog, and the world began to slip into darkness.

Facing the group, Ching Nam declared, "Tonight's camp will be different from those of previous nights. This place is a no man's land and undoubtedly the abode of wolves and tigers.[123] We will be doing naught but providing for the nourishment of these beasts unless we institute some method of defence." Ching Nam then called on the group to head over to a stand of small trees, which was about a hundred yards away. He then directed them to take their knives out from their belts and to fell saplings and chop up branches, and to plant posts in the ground, and form an enclosure in which they could rest, defended against the savage beasts. Then he exhorted them to make the strictest preparations for their security, and to take shifts in which to doze but not dare slumber.

In the deep of the night, Ching Nam leaned against the fence and gazed about. The low moon was clasped between mountains

---

122 For readers who are unaware, liquidambars are deciduous trees with maple-like leaves that are known for their beautiful autumn foliage.

123 Whether or not the author knew that wolves and tigers are not Australian animals is unclear. It is possible he was simply using the phrase in the general sense of ferocious beasts.

神權一端。已足亡國而有餘。賓南爲讀書明理之人。尙且迷信若此。何況無智婦孺乎。欷歔者久之。(§13, 11/9/1909) 無何遠望之森林。盡成火樹。流霞散綺。恰似七月之丹楓。廻顧天外斜陽。有如離冶之火球。抛擲於蔓草荒烟之中。其返照餘光。幻成此可愛之暮景焉。俄而紅輪半缺。漸漸而歿。轉瞬間茫茫曠野。濃霧四塞。將變爲黑暗之世界矣。程南對衆宣言曰。今夜之棲宿。與前夜不同。此処爲人跡罕到之地。決爲虎狼之窟穴。若不設法捍衛。徒膏獸吻耳。約離百碼之外。有小樹一叢。程南卽呼羣人同趨於此。指揮他等出佩刀伐樹砍枝。埋椿於地。圍成柵檻。羣息其中。以禦猛獸。先戒羣人。嚴爲守備。輪流假寐。不敢熟睡。夜闌程南憑檻而眺。斜月啣山。

and the southerly wind pierced to the bone. (Australia's northerly winds are warm and southerly winds cold, the coldness resulting from their coming off the Antarctic Ocean.)[124] All was silent, but for the miserable *caw caw* of calling crows, seemingly voicing the dolour[125] of these displaced travellers. The sound provoked Ching Nam's feelings of separation and, disconsolate, he began to weep. Then, turning the words over in his mouth, he made up a new ballad[126] of a few stanzas, and turned his filial thoughts to song:

> *Miserable be the sound of the crow's cries.*
> *I think of my old father watching from village gate with expectant*
> *eyes.*
> *Since his journeying son left home his whole heart must agonize.*
> *That which cannot be repaid are his kindnesses as infinite as*
> *limitless skies.*[127]
> *How am I to dance for him in multicoloured disguise?*[128]

---

124   The text within the parentheses is an author's note. N.B. The north wind (朔風) is associated in China, as in other countries in the northern hemisphere, with cold air.

125   Great sorrow or distress (from the Latin for pain or grief).

126   What is given here as "ballad" (樂府詩, or simply 樂府 in Chinese) is generally translated directly as *music-bureau poem*. This Chinese literary form is a style of rustic narrative poetry of popular origin. The Chinese name comes from the fact that during the Han dynasty (circa 203 B.C.E. to 220 C.E.) these folk songs (they were originally songs) were collected by the Imperial Bureau of Music. The traditional poems, which are of unknown authorship, concern a wide variety of human themes, such as love, betrayal, and feats on the battlefield. They therefore share some characteristics with the European ballad, and like the European ballad, they were later written by literati, as were what are called "literary ballads" in English and "new ballads" or "new music-bureaus/music-bureau poems" in Chinese. These Chinese "ballads" admit of greater flexibility as to line, stanzaic and overall length than other poetic forms, and while rhyme is central to their structure,

南風刺骨。（澳洲朔風温而南風寒風由南冰洋而來故寒也）
萬籟無聲。祇有羣鴉啞啞而鳴。其音凄楚。似與無家可歸之
旅客。訴其哀苦焉。程南聞之。觸動離緒。愴然泣下。口占
新樂府數章。爲思親之歌焉。

烏鴉啼。。聲悽楚。。思我倚閭懸望之老父。。遊子去故
鄉。。中心徒悲苦。。昊天罔極恩難補。。焉得綵衣爲親
舞。。

there is also a great deal of flexibility as to the types of rhyme that may be
employed and no limit on the number of changes in rhyme that may occur
in a single poem. The rhymes used in this "new ballad" are reflected in the
translation that follows, though it has proved necessary to reuse some of the
rhyming words, which was not done in the original.

127 The phrase 昊天罔極 "as infinite as limitless sky(ies)" is a classical idiom,
which is used to describe the greatness of parental benevolence.

128 This sentence makes use of a literary reference (彩衣娛親). It is said that at
the age of sixty-nine (or seventy by the traditional Chinese reckoning, which
starts, like the Western calendar, not from zero but one), м°. Lao Lai Tzŭ
(老莱子)—a contemporary of Confucius and Lao Tzŭ and one of twenty-
four traditional exemplars of filial piety—started dressing in the colourful
attire of a child, and dancing about in a childlike way, so that he might spare
his aged parents the distress of seeing him grow old.

Far beyond myriad layers of clouded trees[129] where his face is not to be seen, I vainly ascend holts from which to gaze with longing eyes.[130]

Miserable be the sound of the crow's cries.
I think of my old mother watching from home door with expectant eyes.
The raiment of her journeying son is of the thread that betwixt her fingers lies.
So innumerable were her labours in her rearing nurturing enterprise.
How am I to offer up dried venison that it might her vitalize?[131]
That windblown tree is now already fading, and I fear that by my return it may have met its demise.[132]
I think on mother and son each at different corners of the earth and deep in breast do agonize.

---

129 The expression 雲樹 "clouded trees" can be translated as meaning *trees on mountain tops that reach into the clouds*, which thus represent the mountains they crown, which in turn symbolise the obstacle of geographic distance between people. The classical idiom 雲樹之思 "clouded-tree thoughts" means thoughts of friends or family far away, and there are many other classical phrases based on the expression that share similar senses.

130 *Holt* is an archaic English word for a tree-topped hill, and is used here to translate an archaic Chinese word that means the same (岵). This phrase is a reference to a song (陟岵) in the ancient Chinese text 詩經 *The Odes*, which tells of a person far from home ascending various hills, from which he looks out, thinking at different times of his father, mother and brother. (Actually, classical exegeses differ as to whether 岵 meant a wooded hill or a bare hill, and its definition is still the subject of debate among scholars today.) *The Odes* was a fundamental text of traditional Chinese education.

131 This sentence clearly makes use of another literary reference on the subject of filial piety. The story alluded to may be that of 李維則 M°. Li Wei-tsê (Mᴹ. *Lǐ Wéizé*), who, after his sick mother requested dried venison, which he was unable to procure, is said to have offered up flesh cut from his own thigh instead, and to have thereby effected a cure.

遠隔雲樹幾萬重。。不見親顏空陟岵。。

烏鴉啼。。聲悽楚。。思我倚門懸望之老姥。。遊子身上
衣。。慈母手中縷。。千萬劬勞育與撫。。焉得爲親進鹿
脯。。此時風木已堪危。。又恐歸來風木古[57]。。兒兮母兮
各一方。。思之令人痛肺腑。。

57   風木古，言風木作古也。作古者，死亡也。

132   風木 or 風樹 "windblown tree" is a literary trope whose origin lies in a
        conversation between Confucius and a man named 皋魚 M᷂. Kao Yü (M᷂. *Gāo
        Yú*) that is recorded in a Han-dynasty collection of anecdotes and literary
        miscellanea (韓詩外傳). During the conversation, Kao Yü, who is explaining the
        reasons for his sorrow, utters the following line: 樹欲静而風不止，子欲养而親
        不待也 "I am a son who wished to support his parents but whose parents waited
        not, as a tree that wished for still but for which the wind abated not." Here,
        the author uses "windblown tree" in reference not to himself but to one of
        his parents: While traditional scholars familiar with the original sense might
        not have approved of such imprecise usage, the common reader familiar only
        with the idioms in which the expression occurs would most likely have seen
        no issue with it. Such idioms include 風樹之悲 and 風木之悲 "the sadness
        of the windblown tree", which mean the grief of a person who has lost his
        parents and the privilege of supporting them in their old age.

O Crow! O Crow!

Thou who canst regorge in return.[133] *Why dost thou crow?*

I have a high hall which is my parents' reserve.

Who will tureened broth there serve?

My hunger, that can be;

My parents' hunger is the death of me.

O Crow! O Crow!

Thou who canst regorge in return. Thy admirable filial heart so.

If even birds such virtue exemplify,

What of the sons of man like I?

Would that I had wings to fly,

To be to my parents' chamber anigh.

O Crow! O Crow!

Thou hast parents thou oft sees. I have parents beyond the sky.

The song's heart-rending sound provoked misery in its listeners, and all amongst the group were moved to tears; all save Sheung Hong, who, like a silly hog, laid splayed out within the fence snoring thunderously. Pan Nam consoled Ching Nam, "You have an honest unaffected nature and have acted outstandingly filially.[134] Heaven will surely bless you and enable you to provide for your parents in their old age. Why must you still be so sorrowful?"

---

133 The phrase "regorge in return" is used here to translate the classical Chinese expression 返哺 "(of a juvenile bird) to regurgitate food back to a parent bird", a filially virtuous behaviour that Chinese lore ascribes to the crow.

134 Filial piety has been, for much of Chinese history, not only a governing principle in everyday life, but a principle of governance and ethical doctrine for the Confucian state. In its refined form, it is a far deeper concept than standard English definitions and common Chinese conceptions, which tend to focus on obedience and deference to one's elders, might lead one to believe. Indeed, Confucius is recorded to have railed against the suggestion

烏鴉。。烏鴉。。汝能返哺。。何用啞啞。。我有高堂。。
誰奉壺漿。。我飢猶可。。親飢殺我。。

烏鴉。。烏鴉。。汝能返哺。。孝心可嘉。。禽鳥尚如此。
。何況爲人子。。焉得兩翼飛。。歸伴雙親闈。。

烏鴉。。烏鴉。。汝有親兮常見面。。我有親兮隔天涯。。

歌聲慘惻。悽動肝脾。羣人聞之。亦皆感泣。獨尙康蠢然一
豕。挺臥柵內。鼾聲雷動。賓南慰之曰。君天性爛漫。孝行
卓著。皇天決然福汝使終養雙親。何自悲苦乃爾。

that filial piety should entail blind obedience. Some traditional definitions focus on the shared pronunciation of 孝 the Chinese character for filial piety and the character 效 "to imitate". In this imitative sense, filial piety extends from care and concern for one's parents and forebears, in like fashion to their instinctual care and concern for oneself, to the emulation of their qualities, which is connected with the idea that a descendent is a representative of a long line and as such has a natural duty to that line.

Ching Nam replied, "Who is not someone's son? Who is without parents? Left without any alternative but to take leave of those one holds dear and cast oneself into the world's nether regions, if misfortune should strike, the loss of one's own person would be no cause for pity, but what would it mean for one's parents? Thinking on this, how can one be indifferent?" Finished, he could not help but cry bitterly. This startled the roosting crows, which proceeded to fly about their tree calling plaintively, the ceaseless *caw caw* adding to the sense of untold bleakness.

The sky was only barely light when they limped off again on their way. "The grapes in the forest yesterday," said Pan Nam, "were indeed as Ch'ên Chung Tzŭ's well-side grub-ridden plums,[135] set in place by Heaven to save us. But how are we to get by today?"

All the group could do in response was sigh. Then, looking far off, they saw smoke spiraling up from sparse woodland, and with a look of delight upon their faces they remarked amongst themselves, "There are people there!" and "What harm can there be in heading over to search for them?" So they made straight for the sparse woodland to investigate where the smoke was coming from.

By the twisted roots of an old tree, they found, still burning, the remains of a fire of crisscrossed dry logs. All wondered if there might be hunters camped about, but just as they were conjecturing, they suddenly saw two black savages[136] arrive with deft speed, hair tangled, bodies naked and eyes ugly, one armed with poisoned arrows,[137] the other grasping a throwing stick. The savages grinned hideously at them, as if they were about to grab and eat them.

135 The story of Mº. Ch'ên Chung Tzŭ coming back from the brink of starvation after eating grub-ridden plums he found by a well is recorded in *Mencius*, and other old texts.

136 The translations "savages" and "aborigines" that appear in this and other instalments are quite close in sense to the Chinese terms used.

137 Evidently the author was unaware that Aboriginal Australians did not use bows and arrows.

程南曰。誰非人子。誰無父母。不得已而割慈忍愛。投身於
窮荒絕域。設有不測。一身不足惜。其如雙親何。思念及
此。豈能恝然耶。言罷不禁痛哭。驚動樹上烏鴉。又復繞樹
哀鳴。啞啞不止。益增無限之悲涼。斯時天已微明。各復跋
行就道。賓南曰。昨日森林之菩提。正是陳仲子井上之螬
李。[58] 天特設以救我等者。今日又將若何。諸人嗟嘆不已。
遠望疎林之中。火烟裊裊。羣人喜色相告曰。此處有人烟。
可無妨碍。趣往尋之。於是直抵疏林。探火烟所從出。果見
古樹蟠根之側。枯株縱橫。餘燄[59]尙烘。衆疑有獵者棲此。
正猜擬間。忽見有二黑蠻。飄然而至。蓬首裸體。雙睛鶻
突。其一挾持毒矢[60]。其一手執飛標。向人獰笑。欲攫噬
狀。

58　事見西晉《高士傳・卷中・陳仲子》與《孟子・滕文公下》。
59　「燄」，焰之或體。
60　「挾持毒矢」之挾，當言搭矢張弓而持之也。蓋「挾」字之古、今義有
　　別。其今義與文意不甚當，而古義中則有正相合者。如《儀禮》〈大
　　射〉曰：「挾乘矢於弓外」。漢鄭玄注曰「方持弦矢曰挾」。清段若
　　膺《說文解字注》曰「方持弦矢曰挾，謂矢與弦成十字形也」。又如
　　〈鄉射禮〉曰「凡挾矢於二指之間橫之」。鄭玄注曰「此以食指將指
　　挾之」。又如《詩經》〈小雅・吉日〉第四章曰「既張我弓，既挾我
　　矢」。宋嚴粲《詩緝》引《儀禮》注曰「方持弦矢曰挾」。又如〈大
　　雅・行葦〉第六章曰「敦弓既句，既挾四鍭」。皆謂已搭矢持之也。
　　至於「挾持」一語，既可連讀作「挾而持之」之意，又可分讀作「挾
　　一毒矢」而「分持所餘」之意。

On seeing them, the group was frightened witless and collapsed into panicked disorder. In the blink of an eye, the savages had already caught two of them, and pressed them down against the ground as if preparing to cut them up and eat them. Ching Nam and the guide took them by surprise, giving them each a forceful stab from the side with their knives, whereupon they released their captives and raced after the two of them, and the two of them bolted off.

The savages were in a hideous rage, and were leaping about like gibbons, but fortunately their wounds were serious and they could not reach them right away.[138] They then puckered their lips and each made a loud whistle; following which, another two savages, with stone axes in their hands, came out from the bush and joined in pursuit. Ah! How could these starved, exhausted people with little breath remaining them contend against these powerfully built savages? Two poisoned arrows were then shot off one after another and, with a *whoosh whoosh*, grazed passed their ears. Right at this perilous juncture, they suddenly saw a white man coming towards them, with a double-barreled gun over his shoulder, and a hunting dog following behind. Witnessing this state of affairs, he took careful aim at the savages with his gun, and with a *clap*, they were struck by shot and fell. (§14, 18/9/1909)

As soon as the pursuing aborigines further back heard the sound of the gun, they darted back into the wood, and in a flash concealed themselves without trace.

Ching Nam and the guide stood dazed by the wayside, like stunned birds,[139] their backs drenched in the sweat of terror.[140] With a wave of his hand, the white man beckoned them over and

---

138 This instalment is patently loaded with racist and dehumanising content. However, while it might sound strange to the English reader to say so, the comparison of Aboriginal people to gibbons might not be an example, because it was not unusual in Chinese to compare a person of great agility to a monkey or gibbon.

羣人見之。破胆亡魂。咸相驚擾。轉瞬已擒二人。按之於
地。將欲擘食。程南與嚮導。出其不意。從旁猛刺一刀。他
卽棄擒者而奔二人。二人狂奔而逃。土蠻怒態獰惡。跳躑如
猿。幸而傷勢頗重。不能驟及。他復撮口作響。一聲呼嘯。
又有二蠻從林莽而出。手執石斧。同爲奔逐。噫。以彼飢疲
殘喘之人。焉能當此雄健之蠻鬼。又連放二毒矢[61]。嗚嗚從
耳邊擦過。正在危急之際。忽見前來一白人。肩荷孖鎗。後
隨獵犬。睹此狀態。卽以鎗準擬土蠻。轟然一聲。應彈而
倒。[62] (§14, 18/9/1909) 後追之蠻人。[63] 一聞槍聲。復竄入林
裏。閃藏無蹤。程南與嚮導。呆立道旁。如木雞然。汗流浹
背。白人以手招之而

---

61 此中述土人用弓矢之語，失實之甚，蓋是器，及毒鏢、毒針之類，乃奧洲
    之土俗所未曾有者。

62 昔者，夫奧洲之土人分數百族，散居其大洲各地而生息。察其風俗，雖則
    古樸，亦不無倫理、法律、禮儀之文物焉。察其社會，雖與中國上古不
    同，亦必有如堯舜之聖人焉。不知幾千萬世之後，英國之人侵略其地，據
    為己有。進而殺戮其人，奴役其人，姦污其人，剝削其人，而不以圓顱方
    足儼然人類相視之。土人遂墜塗炭，甚則罹滅族禍，而永絕跡於天地之間
    矣。今作者將土人形容為禽獸者，似有違于「己所不欲，勿施於人」之理
    者也。此譯者之所不可不言，以為奧洲之土人雪冤也。

63 此續之文皆散文，然每句後原有二句號。今皆省，以求劃一。

---

139 This (木雞) is a standard expression, which literally means "wooden hen(s)",
     and is an equivalent to English's *stunned mullet(s)*.

140 This is a set idiom in which the word "terror" is not used but implied.

asked, "How come you are here in this wilderness? This place is the haunt of savages and fierce beasts, and save for the occasional hunter, people seldom venture into it. You gentlemen are fortunate to have come across me, otherwise you would have fallen into the ruthless hands of the savages."

Ching Nam, who was newly arrived in Australia and did not yet know any English, could not comprehend and looked baffled. Fortunately, the guide had previously resided in Australia for several years and understood the overall gist. He approached and performed the rites of greeting, thanking him for his kindness in rescuing them. Then he related the causes and story of their adventures, gesticulating all the while with his hands, as an aid to his organs of speech.

On hearing the tale, the white man exclaimed in astonishment, "You gentlemen truly have no less an adventurous nature than us whites, but I think you must have been mistaken, for to go from Guichen Bay to Melbourne there was no need to take that route. While this place falls within the province of Victoria, it is still several hundred English miles from Melbourne. Bendigo is relatively close by, and the gold deposits there are very rich. If you gentlemen wish to take up mining, it might be better to walk to Bendigo first." The two of them nodded in agreement, and then entreated him to go with them into the wood to search for the two men who had been taken captive. The white man generously consented, and reloaded his firearm.

Ching Nam and the others walked behind him, and nearing the wood's edge, they caught sight of a man staggering towards them. When he reached them, they saw it was one of the men who had been captured, his clothes torn and his hands and feet injured. They asked after the other man.

"When the two aborigines went after you," he replied, "we attempted to escape, but another aborigine suddenly came and we were again seized. I fought with all my strength and fortunately broke free. The other man was taken off."

問曰。汝等緣何到此荒野。此地為土蠻猛獸出沒之區。除少
數獵人偶然涉此之外。人跡罕到。君等幸而遇我。不然。必
遭野蠻之毒手矣。程南初到澳洲。未諳英語。惘然不解。幸
而嚮道前居澳洲數年。畧曉其大意。即趨前為禮。謝其援救
之恩。並陳述歷險之緣由。語時復以手作勢。為口舌之幫
助。白人聞之駭曰。君等冒險之性質。誠不亞於吾白人。但
由古慎尾而之美利彬。不需經此程途。君其誤耶。此地雖屬
域草利省。而距美利彬埠。尚隔數百英里。此去品地高埠較
近。而況金礦甚富。君等如有意礦物。不若先到品地高一
行。二人頷之。復懇其同入林內。覓尋被虜之二人。該白人
概然允諾。復整理其鎗枝。裝納子彈。程南等尾之而行。將
到林際。遠望一人踉蹡而來。及前。即前被虜者。衣服破
裂。手足損傷。問其一。答曰。當二蠻人逐君之時。吾等正
欲逃避。忽又來一蠻人。復被拿獲。吾死力抵抗。幸脫於
難。其一已捉去矣。

Ching Nam again entreated the white man to assist them in a search. But, knowing it would be to no avail, the white man firmly declined his requests. So they had no choice but to follow him back out of the wood. "While the others have escaped," said Ching Nam, "we still do not know whether or not they will survive. What can be done?"

"I expect they will not come to harm," replied the guide. "I only fear that they might have fled in all directions, and that there is little chance we shall be reunited."

However, contrary to expectation, when they made their escape, they had raced off in each other's company. Turning their heads to glance back, the sight of the white man shooting the savages dead, and of everything that had happened on entering the wood with him, had all met their eyes. So they had squatted down at a far off spot to await news. When they saw their companions approaching, they shouted out loudly. Ching Nam heard them, and knowing they had come to no harm, was all the more relieved. And as soon as Pan Nam and Sheung Hong saw Ching Nam, they were as overjoyed as young children on seeing once more their adorable caring mother. On taking a tally of those present, it was apparent that they had only lost the one person who had been caught. Again, they breathed long sighs. Yet there was nothing they could do.

"Ten or so English miles from here," said the white man, "is a Chinese market garden. I have long known its owner to be an honest and reliable man, and a most chivalrous one. Were I to take you gentlemen to him, as you are men of his own race, he would undoubtedly receive you." On hearing this, all in the group were elated. Their deflated spirits buoyed, they hobbled off on their way. Filled with heroic vigour, the white man seemed just like a courageous general, leading off this broken band of soldiers after an ill-fated battle, and beating a retreat into the wilderness. (§15, 25/9/1909)

程南復懇該白人協力搜尋。白人知無濟於事。力卻其請。於
是數人不得已跟隨白人出林而去。程南曰。彼等雖已逃脫。
而生死存亡。依[64]然未卜。奈何。嚮導曰。料彼等不及於
禍。但恐四處逃竄。勢難復聚耳。誰料彼等脫逃之時。聯袂
而奔。回頭瞻顧。當時白人鎗斃土蠻。暨同入林裏諸事。盡
入諸人眼簾。故蹲坐遠處。以待消息。及見他等前來。故大
聲疾呼。程南聞聲。知羣人無恙。益加寬慰。而賓南與尙
康。一見程南。如幼孩復見其可愛之慈母。欣忭無既。查點
人數。祇失去被捉之一人。復羣相太息。然亦無可如何。白
人曰。去此十餘英里。有華人菜園一所。吾素知該人誠實可
靠。且甚義俠。吾送君等到彼處。他念同種之人。決然招
待。羣人聞之。甚為歡躍。各復鼓其頹敗之精神。蹣跚就
道。該白人英氣勃勃。一如勇敢之將官。偶然戰挫。率此敗
殘之兵士。落荒而走。 (§15, 25/9/1909)

64   原文「依」字半缺不清。今擬正。

The white man knew the route well and was, moreover, sure and nimble footed. Ever fearful of falling behind, the debilitated group strove to keep pace; though whenever he reached a fork in the way, the white man would stop to wait. After a little while they came upon a farm. The white man waved to signal them to wait for the moment, and then went in ahead.

From outside, Ching Nam and the others gazed about. It all had a highly bucolic air: within were several smallish plank buildings; grazing on the pasture beside them was a flock of sheep, which seemed unafraid of the visitors; outside the door, two huge mastiffs, thickly furred and long tailed, with heads like those of young lions, barked gruffly at them; a flock of hens clucked about inside a scrub fence. Along the fence line apple trees and grape vines spread shade about the farm's sides, and their fruits hung in abundance, the group salivating in hunger at the sight. The garden was a view of pure verdancy, with plots of melons and patches of greens, amongst which several Chinese people were working. On seeing the visitors though, they discontinued their labour and stood to look, with expressions of utter astonishment on their faces.

Presently, the white man emerged with a Chinese man following behind him. The Chinese man bade them enter. Then the white man exchanged some kindly words with him, shook his hand and took his leave. The guide, Ching Nam and the others also saw him off nodding their thanks. Ching Nam and the others then considered the Chinese man: he was near forty, and appeared natural and unaffected, kindly and genial. After they had passed through the door he let them settle their luggage. Then, pointing to chairs and beds, he said "You gentlemen are fatigued and starved. Please rest a little before we speak."

They seated themselves and then Ching Nam ventured to speak, "Thank you for so honourably receiving us here like this.

該白人所歷之程途。俱是熟悉。而況步履矯捷。羣人力疾追逐。時虞落後。該白人每於歧路[65]之處。必貯足[66]以待。無何。至一壩。白人揮手示意。使羣人暫待。他卽先入。程南等在外瞻眺。內築板屋數間。不甚軒厰。屋側羣羊齧草於地。似不畏客者。戶外有二巨獒。茸毛修尾。頭如乳獅。向客狺狺而吠。籬落間羣鷄喔喔。大有鷄犬桑蔴之風。壩傍菩提與苹果樹。巡欄[67]布蔭。子實纍纍。羣人見之。幾致涎滴。園內瓜畦菜町。一望葱綠。有數華人工作於其間。見客輟業[68]竚望。狀甚驚訝。俄頃。白人出。一華人尾其後。華人肅客入。白[69]人與該華人殷勤數語。握手而別。嚮導與程南等。亦點首相送。程南等相此華人。年近四十。狀甚純樸。慈靄可親。入戶之後。與羣人安頓行李。復指椅榻而言曰。諸君勞頓飢疲。請稍憩。而后傾談。羣人就坐。程南進言曰。感君高義。如此招待。

65　此歧路之「路」字，原文似誤印作「潞」。今正。
66　「貯足」二字，疑卽「佇足」之誤。佇足者，止步也。蓋臨印版之時，或無正字可用，故擇與音同形似者為通假字。
67　「巡」當作「循」。循者，沿也。不作循而作同音字巡，蓋亦手民之苟且也。
68　原文「業」字模糊不清。今據其殘跡與文義擬正。
69　「白」原作「臼」。誤。今正。

My humble self and my companions are indescribably appreciative. Might we enquire as to your good surname and style?[141]"

The Chinese man replied, "My surname is Chan and my name[142] Leung, and I am a native of Ning Yup's lower three.[143] I have sojourned in Australia these last seven summers and winters[144] and have farmed a garden here for over three years. I know some English and so have much intercourse with my Western neighbours. Just now I heard George relate that, hunting in the wild, he had come upon you as you were falling into the hands of the aborigines, and that had it not been for him coming to your aid with his firearm, you might not have escaped calamity. Later, after I enquired further, I learned more, including about you coming from China to Australia, landing at Guichen Bay, and becoming lost. And on hearing all this I felt much pity and sadness for you. George also said that if these Chinese people he had come across did not find a good place in which to settle, they would end up homeless wanderers, the consequences of which would be unthinkable. So he said he had taken it upon himself to bring you to me. Then he asked whether I was able to accommodate you. I exclaimed 'Hah! What are you

---

141 In traditional Chinese culture, taboos exist around the given names of adults: see Ching Nam's entry in Appendix I for details.

142 His given name.

143 At that time the district of s. Llin Nen (A.K.A. o. Sinning, 寧邑 c°. Ning Yup s. Nen Yip) was divided into six 都 M^M. *dū* c^M. dōu "subdistricts": the more northerly 平康, 德行 and 文章 were referred to collectively as 上三都 "the upper three" or 上新宁 s. "Upper Llin Nen", and the more southerly 潮居, 矬洞 and 海宴 as 下三都 "the lower three" or 下新宁 "Lower Llin Nen". (Actually, "subdistrict" is an over-simplification of the meaning of the word 都 c^M. *dōu*. It really means something closer to *conurbation*, and was one of a number of types of zones into which districts at the time were subdivided. During the M°. Ch'ing dynasty, the administrative structure at the subdistrict level was not standardised and differed widely. Llin Nen had a comparatively simple structure, in that it was subdivided into half-a-dozen of the same type of administrative zone.)

令鄙人等感激莫名。敢請君之姓字。華人曰。弟姓陳名亮。
寧邑之下三都人。僑寓澳洲。寒暑七易。在此種園。亦經三
載。因弟稍諳英語。鄰近之西人。時相過從。頃間聞佐治君
言。因野獵。遇君等陷於蠻人之手。他以火器相助。始脫君
等於厄。後詢悉始知君等由華來澳。在古愼尾登岸。誤入迷
途等語。弟聞之甚爲悲憫。他又云。此等華人。若無善地安
頓。決至流離失所。不堪設想。故擅自帶來君處。復問弟能
否容納。弟曰。嘻。君何

---

144 Here "summers and winters" is merely a more elegant alternative to the word
    "years". In Chinese, polite formulae are often formed from concise poetic
    language. The literal meaning of the expression used in this passage (寒暑七
    易) is actually "the winter cold and summer heat have cycled seven times
    over", though it is so concise that it contains fewer syllables than the words
    "summers and winters".

saying? Am I not the patent round-skulled square-footed[145] teeth-concealed hair-bound[146] picture of a human being? How could I do other than come to the rescue of those in danger? And moreover, they being my countrymen, even were they a group of hundreds or thousands, let alone a mere ten-or-so people, I should still do all in my power to see them provided for!'" As he spoke these words, a chivalrousness of spirit showed through in his brow.

"You are a good man and a gentleman," said Ching Nam, "and you inspire respect. Who says Chinese people have no sense of altruism?"

"One need pay no heed to such notions," replied Chan. "But I have not yet learned your names, surnames, clans and native places. I beg you relate them in full."

Ching Nam responded, "My surname is Wong and my name Pang. Ching Nam is my style. I am a native of Wing On, Hoi Ping." Then he pointed to Pan Nam and said, "This man, who is known as Pan Nam, is my clansman."[147] He then pointed to Sheung Hong and said, "This is a man of my greater clan[148] named Sheung Hong, and a man of your district."[149] The others in the group then introduced themselves in turn. After this Ching Nam gave a detailed account of their adventures,

---

145 圓顱方趾 "round-skulled (and) square-footed" is a classical Chinese idiom used to describe human beings, because: Chinese lore holds that the universe contains 三才 "three potentials", namely *heaven* above, the *earth* below, and between them, *man*; and that 天圓地方 "heaven is round and the earth square". And thus, man's round skull and square feet, at the upper and lower ends of his body respectively, symbolise his unique identity as the "potential" that falls between heaven and earth. (N.B. the words round and square have other senses in Chinese unrelated to shape and some traditional commentators state that the expression 天圓地方 "heaven is round and the earth square" is purely a reference to the nature of these entities. Nevertheless this symbolic association of circles and squares is frequently drawn on in traditional Chinese art.)

言。余亦圓顱方趾。嚙齒束髮。居然人類。豈有見難不救之
理。而況盡屬鄉親。縱使千百爲羣。余亦要盡平生之力以處
置之。何況區區十餘人乎。言時義俠之氣。溢於眉表。程南
曰。君乃善人君子。令人起敬。誰謂華人無愛羣心耶。陳君
曰。此何足介意。君等之族貫姓名。猶未賜教。仰道其詳。
程南曰。弟黃姓名鵬。程南其字。開平之永安鄉人。指賓南
曰。此爲余族叔號賓南者。又指尙康曰。他是弟之同宗。名
尙康。君之同邑人也。其餘諸人。挨次自道。程南復縷述歷
險之狀況。

---

146   嚙齒束髮 "teeth-concealed hair-bound" is a slightly altered form of a
      Chinese idiom used to describe human beings, and to connote manliness.
147   The word translated here as "clansman" specifically refers to a clansman of
      one's father's generation, who is younger than one's father.
148   There is a distinction in Chinese between 同族 "clansmen of one's own clan"
      and 同宗 "clansmen of one's greater clan or tribe". All have the same
      surname, but the former share a more immediate ancestor, and the latter
      generally live in different places. From Ching Nam's perspective, Pan Nam is
      an 同族 "immediate-clan clansman" and Sheung Hong a 同宗 "greater-clan
      clansman".
149   The district of s. Llin Nen (新寧縣).

moving between sudden sadnesses and joys, and from beginning to end he did not tire in the telling. Afterwards, Chan continued to exclaim in surprise, shock and sorrow for some time.

While Ching Nam had been speaking, the group had seen a Chinese person placing cutlery upon a table, dispatching hens and preparing a meal of the most extreme sumptuousness. Chan said, "I knew you gentlemen to be exhausted and famished as soon as you arrived. So I instructed my worker to hastily prepare a meal. In this wilderness markets are far; I expect you gentlemen will forgive me for the lack of delicacies."

Ching Nam replied, "There is no need for such modesty sir. We survivors of hunger and fatigue hope for no more than to fill our bellies. Indeed, favoured now with this great feast, we feel nothing but guilt." They then sat and ate. The group had not eaten cooked food for over twenty days all added, merely sating their hunger and thirst at streams and springs and with wild fruits along the route. Now, beholding these fine victuals, they began to chomp and feast away with the same rapaciousness as the proverbial hungry tiger on seizing a sheep, and they did not stop till their bellies could fit no more.

When they had finished, Ching Nam said, "Since setting off from Guichen Bay we have walked for forty-six days and have been beset repeatedly by misfortune, finally escaping danger today. From over seventy people, only we thirteen remain, and we are fortunate to have survived. Yet recalling all those men who met their doom, one cannot but lament most deeply."

"Do not be downhearted sir," said Chan. "You gentlemen have thankfully survived and have reached your goal. You should now hasten to convey news home to comfort your families. I pray that you will stay with me for a little, until you are each fully recovered physically. There will be time enough to plan for your livelihoods thereafter." They all assented and felt at heart most grateful. (§16, 2/10/1909)

After several days' convalescence, they all recovered their full strength, and Ching Nam spoke on behalf of the group to express their thanks: "We

忽而悲。忽而喜。自始迄終。娓娓而談。陳君亦爲驚歎悲悼
者久之。言次。見一華人按餐具置桌上。殺鷄爲黍。俻極豐
腴。陳君曰。自君等屈臨時。弟已知君等勞悴飢憊。故吩咐
夥計。亟爲炊爨。野荒市遠。無甚下箸物。料君等決能恕
余。程南曰。余等疲餓餘生。但求裹腹[70]。於願已足。况復
叨此盛筵。能不疚心。君何謙抑乃爾。說完。就坐而食。默
計羣人。不火食已二十餘天。在路上溪泉野菓。充飢渴耳。
今睹此精良之食品。正如餓虎搏羊。大餐大嚼。盡其食量而
後止。食旣。程南曰。吾等自古愼尾首途以來。步行四十六
天。迭罹劫難。今日方得脫險。七十餘人之中。祇餘吾等十
三[71]人。亦云幸矣。但追憶罹難諸君。言之實堪哀悼。陳
曰。君勿悲。君等幸已出險。目的亦達。亟宜賫音囘家。慰
安家人。懇君等在弟處暫住。待各人體格完健。然后隨圖生
計。未爲晚也。羣人唯唯。心甚感佩。(§16, 2/10/1909) 逾數
天。各經休養。體質復原。程南代表群人申謝曰。僕等

70 俗間有將果腹之果書作「裹」者，非是。裹者，纏也。果，實之也。顧文
 思義，其理明矣。
71 原文「三」字原缺下橫。今據其殘跡與文義擬正。

have foisted ourselves upon you so unreasonably, and with many mouths and numerous meals, have consumed a great deal, yet you sir have steadfastly refused our repeated offers to work for you. We feel terribly uncomfortable over this, and though you might most honourably refrain from reckoning such things, we cannot continue to trespass on your hospitality."[150]

Chan said, "This is not the case sir, for indeed I have calculated it all! But, I am no miser, and a little food and drink is too paltry a thing to mention. Were you gentlemen willing, despite the crude conditions, to condescend to stay for a year, I should be all the more pleased. However, you have been through much trouble and many dangers, and have survived impossible odds, in order to come here. You must harbour infinite hopes, and I should not dare, with such coarse fare, to prevail upon you to stay longer, and waste your precious time. I imagine there is much of which you gentlemen, being new to this land, are unaware. So I would beg to lay out a plan for you, and, if you were willing to accept, I might further seek out for each of you a place of employment. I don't know what your thoughts on this might be though."

"We accept," said Ching Nam, "for having been delivered by you from death's door, we should not dare do other than you instruct."

Thus, of the ten people besides Ching Nam, Sheung Hong and Pan Nam, some were sent into mining, and some into horticulture, a suitable occupation found for each.

A fair number of that group who worked industriously and saved thriftily later returned home, pockets brimming, to lead a life of peaceful enjoyment. Yet tastes are many and varied, and a half of that number stayed on in this land.

---

150 Some of the polite language here and in the following paragraphs sounds quite flowery and obsequious in translation, whereas in Chinese it is much more formulaic in flavour. This is the effect of direct translation, in which formulaic expressions, such as English's "I beg your pardon", take on a far

無端叨擾。口眾食繁。銷耗甚夥。屢欲替君操作。而君又堅
不之許。吾等撫心自問。殊形不安。雖君雲天高義。了不之
較。但吾等豈可長坐而食。陳曰。靡君言。弟亦籌之熟矣。
然弟豈慳吝者。區區飲食。何足詡齒頰。如君等不嫌齷齪。
肯屈留經年。余心更爲愉懌也。雖然。君等蹈風波。歷艱
險。萬死一生而來者。其希望正無窮。弟豈敢以粗糲慰留。
誤諸君可貴之時月。料君等初到此地。諸多未稔。故敢借箸
代籌。如肯俯就。弟亦可代謀一棲身處。未識尊意若何耳。
程南曰。如君言。正是生死人而肉白骨也。敢不如命。於是
除程南尙康賓南而外。其餘十人。或從事礦業。或從事種
植。莫不部署妥當。其後群人中勤奮儉積。囊橐充牣。囘國
安享者。大不乏人。而嗜好多端。勾留此地者。亦居半數。

more literal meaning when translated into non-formulaic equivalents.
Chinese has a much richer range of polite formulae than English, and
semantically compatible equivalents are thus not always available to the
translator.

Today, in the few plank houses on the little hill at Bendigo,[151] there are three or four old men, weary and decrepit, blind and hunchbacked, who, with canes in their hands go in file, pulling hold of each other's clothes, to the old people's home to collect their relief rice. They are those stout adventurers of yesteryear. What tragedy!

Gentle readers, think not that this humble author's narration is unrelated to its title, for if one is to tell the story of Sheung Hong's taking of a concubine, one cannot but find its origins in his going abroad. Nor can one not detail the hardships he faced. Do not be impatient gentle readers, the characters[152] in the title will appear in time. (§17, 9/10/1909)

Seeing that Chan Leung had sent off all in the group but them, and not knowing what to make of this, Sheung Hong spoke with Ching Nam. "Since coming here," he said, "Chan has treated us all equally liberally. Yet now, through his recommendations, all the others have found some means of support, while the three of us are left cast aside. Could it be that Chan thinks us frail and unfit for hard labour, or is it that he has less of a fondness for us?"

Ching Nam responded, "Why should we look to others to lay plans for us? Real men should be self-reliant. But Chan has displayed in his treatment of us a much greater cordiality of affection and views us with higher regard. I should think that he has some other motive."

---

151 The same transliteration for Bendigo as appears in this novel can be seen in a Chinese dedication that accompanies a photograph of the Bendigo district's long-standing Mining Registrar Mr H.S.V. Busst, which was presented to him by the Bendigo Chinese Association after he made a donation of £50, and is on display in Bendigo's Golden Dragon Museum. It also appears in Australia's early Chinese newspapers.

至今品地高埠小山頂上。板屋數椽。有三四老人龍鍾衰憊。
盲目駝背。牽衣執杖。魚貫而往領養老院之賑米者。原是昔
日歷險之壯夫也。噫慘矣。閱書諸君。毋謂鄙人敍述此事。
與題無干。然欲敍尙康之納妾。不能不溯源於出洋。又不能
不詳述其苦況。諸君稍安毋躁。題中人將次出現矣。(§17,
9/10/1909) 尙康見陳亮派遣羣人。不及於彼等。心甚疑惑。語
程南曰。吾等到此。蒙陳君一例優待。今羣人俱蒙陳君薦
引。得所依託。獨於吾等三人。淡焉置之。豈以吾等文弱。
難任苦役耶。抑別有所愛憎耶。程南曰。大丈夫當謀自立何
必依人作計。況陳君對於我等。別具靑眼。其待我等之情
素。較於羣人。倍形欵洽。察其用心。當別有所在。

---

152 The word polygamy in the serial's Chinese title translates literally as "many
wives". The "characters in the title" referred to here are therefore Sheung
Hong's wife and concubine, to whom the story will turn in time.

The following morning, Chan Leung said to Ching Nam, "You may believe me when I say sir, that I know you gentlemen to be other than mediocre sorts. I would especially concede that you sir, are a man of open and decisive mind. I have some earnest words for you, which I shall be so bold as to speak, though I know not whether they will meet with your acceptance."

"Do not wait to speak them. I shall do whatever it is you ask that is in my ability to do," replied Ching Nam.

"It is no more than that I wish to forge an association with you in a shared business," said Leung.

"Since you see fit to honour me with such high approval," said Ching Nam, "I should do all in my miserable power to comply. Having drifted all this way though, I and the others have not a penny to our names, let alone capital with which to co-perate with you in business."

"Do not worry," said Leung. "The business I speak of is a primary industry and can be embarked upon without any principal to begin with. It is not long since this continent was opened up and metal deposits are to be found all over. Furthermore, the land is wide and people are few and a discoverer can take and work what he finds. I have a Western friend[153] who has found a gold deposit where the veins are very rich, but he lacks capital and has no man power either, so he has come to me for both. I regret though, that I am hampered by this garden. Often I have wished to abandon agriculture and turn to mining, but this garden returns rich profits and I have not been able to sever my attachment to it. I should like to manage this garden in addition, but should find it difficult to spare the time, and would likely risk losing sight of one business for the other. I fear all the more that if the mining venture were not

---

153 Actually it is unclear in the original whether Leung is referring to one or
more Western friends.

翌朝。陳亮對程南曰。君得毋疑弟耶。弟知公等非碌碌者。
君胸懷慷爽[72]。尤爲弟所輸服。弟有衷曲之言。不嫌冒昧。
未識君肯容納否耳。程南曰。趣言之。如弟力所能逮。無不
遵命。亮曰。願與君締交。共圖商業耳。程南曰。蒙君不
棄。敢不竭棉薄。但弟等颺流到此。不名一文。焉有資本與
君協圖商業。亮曰。毋憂。弟所云之商業。乃是實業。雖無
母金。亦可興辦。本洲開闢未久。五金礦產。隨處皆有。而
況地博人稀。探得者即可據爲己業。余有西友探出一金礦。
金苗甚旺。他乏資本。又無人力。謀之於弟。余恨爲此園囿
所羈絆。屢欲拋棄農業。而轉事礦業。顧此園獲利殊豐。眷
戀不捨。意欲兼治此園。又難以分身。勢將顧此失彼。更恐
礦務無

---

72   「爽」字原係字底朝天倒印。凡顯屬此例者，今皆正，或不一一注明。

kept well in hand, it might reach a profitless end and I might instead lose this garden, which would be a great pity. So I am presently vacillating. If you would deign to consent though, my mind will be decided."

"Some sum would still need to be raised to cover procurement costs," said Ching Nam. "One cannot cook without rice."

"You need not be overly concerned sir," said Leung. "The mining can be done without machines, man power alone is enough; and I should naturally assume responsibility for purchasing the picks, shovels, water chutes[154] [and other] equipment needed. Furthermore, I would make an agreement with the Westerner that absolutely all profits made from the day of commencement are to be divided equally."

"I have never learnt anything of the business of mining though," said Ching Nam.

"That is no impediment," Leung replied. "I worked at mining back when I first arrived in this continent, though due to adverse fortune I reaped but negligible profit, and so had to abandon it and take up gardening. Mining is actually the business in which I excel. But there is one other thing I have to say, something my lips seemingly ought not to utter. Today though, since you are accepting me as a confidant and I am laying a plan for you, and a plan for myself, I cannot [do other than] share it with you directly."

"What is it?" asked Ching Nam.

"Your kinsmen Pan Nam and Sheung Hong," said Leung. "In my humble opinion Pan Nam is a perfect gentleman, reliable and sincere; whereas Sheung Hong has a cunning and deceitful nature, and is in fact nothing other than a wicked and indolent fellow. In the forming of friendships it is wise to exercise the most prudent consideration. The repercussions of indiscrimination can be most dire. I should like to find some other enterprise in which to install Sheung Hong. What do you say?"

甚把握。他日倘無所獲。反失此園圃。殊爲可惜。是以正在
躊躇。如君肯俯就。吾意決矣。程南曰。採辦之費。亦要籌
集多寡。斷難爲無米之炊。亮曰。君毋過慮。不用機器開
採。祇需人力足矣。所需用之水槽與鋤鏟□[73]器具。弟自然担
任購辦。吾更與西人立約。後日不論若何。利益決然均沾
也。程南曰。治礦一事。弟未曾問津。奈何。亮曰。毋傷。
弟前日初到本洲。曾從事於礦務。惟命舛時乖。所獲殊屬稀
微。故棄之而種園耳。此事實弟所優爲也。但弟尙有一言。
此言似不應出於弟之口。今日君許弟爲心腹交。然爲君計。
亦爲弟計。又不能[74]直捷剖露。程南曰。如何。亮曰。君之
昆季。賓南尙康二人。以鄙意察之。賓南一彬彬之君子。誠
懇可靠。尙康生性狡詐。實一邪廨[75]之夫耳。大凡交友。最
宜審愼。倘涉泛濫。拖累正復不淺。弟意欲別覓一業。以安
置尙康何如。

73　此字全缺。按其文義，似應作「等」。
74　「又不能」三字後，似脫一「不」字。
75　「廨」疑為「懈」之訛。

154　水槽 "water chutes" could also be translated as "water troughs".

"Your consideration is most appreciated," replied Ching Nam, "but Sheung Hong and I have met difficulties and dangers together and have become comrades through adversity. I could not bear to send him off elsewhere. My only hope is that he will not disappoint us in the future."

"These are the words of a benevolent man," said Leung. "If you are of such a mind, I shall show him no ill will. However, keep a careful guard against him, lest you should give yourself cause for regret."

So it was that the few of them came to work a mine together near Bendigo. Chan also gave each of them one pound sterling to remit back to China to settle and maintain their families. (§18, 16/10/1909)

At that time in the south of China, where the villages were arrayed like honeycomb,[155] there lay, at the foot of a confusion of hills, a certain village, and at its centre was an old house. A cold moon shone under its low eaves, a chill breeze blew through its little windows, and the pea-like flame of a single lamp lit its forlorn midnight hours. Within, leant against a bed panel[156] was a woman clothed in coarse cloth, with a pin of bramble in her tangled hair.[157] Her pretty face was gaunt, and in her shapely eyebrows regret was locked. She was silent, as if lost in contemplation. What woman was this? Sheung Hong's wife, Ma.

---

155 Thickly dotted.

156 Most likely the panel of a traditional Chinese canopy bed.

157 The 布裙 "coarse skirt" or "coarse cloth" and the 荊釵 "bramble hairpin" are mere literary tropes used in Chinese to describe the appearance of poor women. Furthermore, the expression 裙釵 literally "skirt and hairpin" is actually a metonym for "women", and this sense is played on in the idiom here employed which combines the aforementioned tropes, 布裙 荊釵 literally, and only literally, "coarse skirt and bramble hairpin".

程南曰。君意足感。但弟與尙康。同歷艱險。已成爲患難之
交。奚忍令彼他適。但願此後尙康無負於我等足矣。亮曰。
此仁者之言也。君若此。弟復何懟於彼。雖然。愼防之。勿
貽後悔。於是數人在品地高附近同治一礦。陳復各予以英金
一磅。令彼等郵寄回國。以賉家人。(§18, 16/10/1909) 此時支
那之南部。村落綜錯。有如蜂窠。亂山之麓。有一村焉。村
之中央。有陳舊之屋。時則矮簷月冷。小牖風寒。子夜凄
淸。一燈如荳。中有一婦。布裙荊釵。首如飛蓬。斜靠床
欄。桃臉銷瘦。柳眉鎖恨。默然無語。若有所思。此婦何
人。乃尙康之妻馬氏也。

Ma thought to herself, *From the time Sheung Hong left for over-seas seven months have passed, yet I have not had the slightest news or indication concerning him, and cannot surmise whether he has survived or died. If misfortune were to strike my husband, to whom in a shadowy future might my person come to belong? I have no parents-in-law above and no children below*[158] *and would be all alone in the world. Worry could fill my bosom, but none would offer consolation. All there would be to do would be to wash my face each day with tears. Inside this house's walls the scene is stark, and without, there is not a miserable inch of land.*[159] *While, to provide for my sustenance, I collect firewood by day and spin and weave by night, were I to fall ill, who would take pity on me? My cousin might come to my aid for a little while, but prolonged poverty taxes a benefactor,*[160] *and how could I spend a lifetime bowing and scraping for help from others? Thinking on that, there have been times when I wished to hang myself, but I have remembered that I am still childless, and my husband brotherless and alone; were I to die and desert him, who would offer up incense in the hall to keep his ghost from hunger, and how should I face his ancestors in the afterworld?*[161] *I only hope that God above might pity me and see my dear husband reach his destination safe and well, and one day return rich to China, to be as my cousin of today. How great would my joy then be!* Thinking on this, she started a silent and ceaseless recitation of *Gods and Saints offer Your protection.*[162]

Her tender insides turning with wild thoughts, and tiredness slipping over her, Ma wrapped the coverlet about her seated legs and fell asleep. Passing through a haze, she suddenly saw Sheung Hong, clothed in brilliant colours, sitting opposite her at the bedside.

---

158 The words "above" and "below" indicate social precedence in this context.

159 Cultivatable land on which to subsist.

160 長貧難顧 "prolonged poverty taxes a benefactor" is a Chinese idiom that means it is difficult to care for or support people whose poverty is prolonged or indefinite.

馬氏默計尙康出洋後。已七閱月矣。尙杳無音兆。生死存
亡。難以臆度。倘黃郎或有不測。然後顧茫茫。此身又將誰
屬。而況上無翁姑。下無兒女。孑然一身。縱滿胸愁緒。無
人慰藉。祇日以眼淚洗面而已。加以四壁蕭條。貧無立錐。
雖日則採樵。夜則紡織。以自贍其口腹。設罹疾病。誰可憐
儂。76 縱吾堂兄暫爲週恤。然長貧難77顧。又焉能畢世低首求
人。思念及此。幾回意欲自經。廻念膝下猶虛。而丈夫又是
鶺原隻影78。如妾死却不顧。一堂香火。誰爲供奉。而黃氏
之鬼。不其餒而。妾又焉能對黃氏先人於九京也。望天公可
憐妾。使兒夫平安抵埠。他日致富旋唐。一如妾堂兄之今
日。那時妾之歡樂。又復何如。於是默誦神聖庇祐不休。此
際馬氏正是柔腸九轉。胡思亂想之時。不覺神思困倦。擁衾
而眠。朦朧間忽見尙康對坐床沿。衣裳鮮艷。

76　此處等，原文留隙而漏句號。今皆補。不復注明。
77　原文「難」字全缺。而所屬之詞語分明。今據補。
78　此乃「鶺鴒在原、形隻影單」之省文也。

161　In Chinese folk religion, incense in the form of joss sticks is burnt to supply
the means of delivery of not only a worshiper's words and wishes, but also of
food and drink offerings that provide for the sustenance of an ancestor or
loved one in the netherworld.

162　The "Gods and Saints" referred to are Taoist deities.

The room was piled full of bags and cases and other luggage, and successive calls of "Goldfielder! Goldfielder!"[163] came resounding up the laneways. Overcome with joy, Ma was speechless. Then, anon, she saw a raggedly clothed haggardly faced Sheung Hong stretched recumbent across a wide bed, smoking opium through a short bamboo pipe, just as he had been in former days. In the midst of these fancies, Ma suddenly heard from beyond the door the sound of people calling swine and woke. Only then, her senses restored to clarity, did she realize that it had all been a dream of Han Tan.[164] She rubbed her eyes and looked out through the doorway. The beams of an ever brightening dawn sun had already struck the top of the chicken coop.[165] (§19, 23/10/1909)

Ma woke from apple-blossom sleep[166] in a charming springtide languor,[167] to a still and empty chamber, within which, companionless and alone, she felt keenly the regret of *one that once did tell her husband dear to seek a title grand*.[168] She turned her thoughts to last night's dream, and found its scenes so distinct in her memory that they might have been before her very eyes.

---

163 金山客 "goldfielder" was a vernacular name for people born in China who were resident in or had returned from the Australasian or North American goldfields and which generally connoted wealth.

164 邯鄲一夢 M°. "a Dream of Han Tan" means a believed experience of life events that are in fact illusory. The idiom is based on a story set in the district of Han Tan, which tells of a hapless 盧生 scholar surnamed Lu who, in the space of a dream, lives out the long and full remaining span of his life, and on death wakes to discover his old self and surroundings and that almost no time had elapsed. There are various versions of the story recorded in old texts: one that dates from the Yüan dynasty (a 雜劇 play about the story, written by 馬致遠 and entitled 邯鄲道醒悟黃粱夢) introduces Lu's dream with the exact same phrase as the author uses here to introduce Ma's—不覺神思困倦 "… and tiredness slipping over her/him …"

165 The motif of the rooster heralding the coming of day is common to Chinese too.

而行囊箱篋⁷⁹。纍積滿室。又聞金山客金山客之聲浪。轟傳
里巷。馬氏喜極。不能出聲。俄而又見尚康衣服襤褸。容顏
憔悴。橫床短竹。臥吹鴉片。一似昔日在家時之狀態。此時
馬氏正在猜思。忽聞門外呼豕之聲。豁然而醒。方知邯鄲一
夢。揉目望戶。已是杲日曈曈。影射鷄塒上矣。(§19,
23/10/1909) 馬氏此際海棠睡醒。春態嬌慵。而寂寞空幃。塊
然無偶。大有悔教夫婿覓封侯之恨。迴憶昨宵夢境。歷歷如
在目前。

79　此字等，原作山麓之「麓」，當作箱篋之「篋」。蓋從林者，山足也；從
　　竹者，竹高篋也。今皆正，不復贅注。

166　海棠睡 "apple-blossom sleep" means the sleep of a beautiful woman whose
　　appearance while asleep is disheveled yet charming. The expression
　　reportedly has its origin in the 唐 Mᵒ. Tʹang-dynasty emperor 玄宗 Hsüan
　　Tsung's description of his beloved concubine 楊貴妃 Imperial Consort
　　Yang, when on one occasion she was brought to him in a drunken slumber.
　　(The type of apple blossom referred to is specifically that of the Chinese
　　flowering apple *Malus spectabilis*.)

167　The author is describing Ma as a woman in her springtime. The word 春
　　"spring" in Chinese connotes youth, romance, and sexual relations.

168　The author is quoting the last line of a Tang-dynasty poem entitled 閨怨
　　"Lament of the Bower-bound Lady": 悔教夫婿覓封侯 "regret I so that
　　once I told my husband dear to seek a title grand". The poem concerns the
　　regret and resentment felt by a lady long separated from a husband who has
　　gone into the army. The "title grand" means a feudal title, and wealth and
　　power attendant thereto, which military success could bring.

Though whether this was for good or ill she did not know. Having forced herself up, she attended for a little while to her sundry women's tasks, before opening the door and going off to wash with cold water. Then she walked back to her dressing table. Seeing it strewn with cobwebs and her toilet case covered in dust, she felt no inclination to wipe or brush. She took up a broken mirror,[169] but regarding in it a countenance pale with worry she could only look at her image in misery, and before she knew it her bodice and sleeves were covered in tears. Anon, she lifted a split comb to tangled hair and gave it a few haphazard brushes, while thinking to herself *Even if I had pomade for it, there is no one for me to charm; and as things are, I have not pomade either!* She then walked over to the steps, got the chicken and dog food in order, and did a round of feeding. Then she searched out her daily companion, a steel sickle, and rushed over to the side of the lane, where, with a *scrape scrape,* she set about sharpening it on a gutter-side whetstone. Having finally attended to everything, Ma lifted up a pair of baskets on a shoulder pole, closed the double doors, and left. Where then was Ma going? She was off to collect fuel with which to cook.

Having walked in her delicate and graceful totter into the countryside, she lifted her gaze and looked about. The scenery was bright and beautiful and the chatter of birds and the fragrance of flowers was in the air, but all of it only added to the heartache she felt as the fretful wife of a man far away. So she set off, wending her way towards the feet of that confusion of hills. But the hill road was rugged and as she trod Ma was ever at risk of falling. Having had to

---

169 The phrase "broken mirror" has a strongly allusive meaning in Chinese, because of the well-known classical story of the 破鏡重圓 "broken-mirror reunion", which tells of a husband and wife forced to separate in war but who find each other again by means of the broken halves of a mirror, which they employ as tokens of their identity. Note: broken mirrors do not connote bad luck in Chinese as they do in English.

不知是吉是凶。強起料理其婦女瑣碎之事。半晌。開戶。以冷水盥漱。迴步至粧臺前。見鏡匣塵封。蛛絲斜罣。亦無心拂拭。試取破鏡一鑑。而愁容慘淡。對影悽然。不覺淚盈襟袖。尋將半折之梳。舉向如蓬之髮。糊亂掠了幾掠。自思雖有膏沐。亦無容悅之人。況並膏沐而亦無之乎。復步至堦畔。檢點雞犬之食料。喂飼一畨。後然覓其日常爲伴之鋼鐮。馳至巷側。向渠邊之礪石。霍霍而磨。諸事拼擋已畢。肩挑兩筐。闔其雙扉而去。噫。馬氏何往。往採彼炊食之燃料也。於是孃孃婷婷。行至野外。舉目一覽。而山明水秀。鳥語花香。適足增思婦離人之悽惻也。故望亂山之麓逶迤而進。而山路又復崎嶇。步履時危傾跌。不得已

walk on her knees to a cliff edge, she summoned all her strength and started cutting straw. Before she realised it, it was near noon, but looking back at her baskets, Ma saw that she still did not have a sheaf's worth.[170] So she kept on, paying no heed to the fire of hunger burning in her. Her feet became unbearably painful though, and bending her head to inspect them, she found that her bowed shoes[171] had been pierced by the cliff-side rocks and that blood was pouring from her toes. She cast her sickle aside, sat back in a daze on the stones, and began to quietly sob.

For Ma was a woman whose feet had been bound. In our Kwang Tung, through its vile traditions, women whose feet are not bound are regarded as servant women and as unmarriageable. In wealthy and noble families girls' feet are bound from a young age; but in impoverished families engaged in domestic service or agricultural labour, a girl's feet are not bound until she is nearly come of age, by which time her muscles and bones are already rigid, so binding must necessarily be done with great force. Yet even if ligaments are snapped and toes broken, the parents of these girls show no pity. Nevertheless, ignorant women boast amongst each other of their stylish minuteness and consider them to be toys to pleasure men, for which they are happy to endure the most extreme pains. Alas that pairs of plain and natural feet should be thus transmuted into these putrid ulcerated appendages! Of what are our Chinese women guilty that they should suffer this

---

170 Straw, usually rice straw, was then the standard cooking fuel. Rice straw was a fast-burning hot fuel well suited to Chinese cooking but which produced thick smoke.

171 Curved shoes, this being the Chinese name for the short shoes used by Chinese women with bound feet, which are generally referred to in English as *lotus shoes*.

膝行而至崖邊。極力芟刈。不覺日已向午。迴顧兩筐。猶不
盈一束。斯時飢火中燒。亦不暇顧。無奈足痛難堪。俯首檢
視雙趺。而一對弓鞋。已爲崖石擦穿。足指鮮血淋漓。乃抛
棄鐮刀。呆坐石上。嚶嚶啜泣。蓋馬氏者。纏足之婦[80]也。
吾粵陋俗相沿。如婦女不纏足。謂爲僕婦。無人肯娶。故富
貴家之女子。自小與他裹纏。而貧苦家或從事井臼。或從事
耕耘。迫至將及笄時然後纏足。斯時筋骨已堅。勢不得不極
力裹束。雖使筋折指斷。其父母亦不哀憐。乃無智之婦女。
復羣以纖小誇尚。以爲取悅男子之玩具。雖痛楚萬狀。亦樂
爲忍受。噫嘻。一雙天然白足。變而爲臭腐潰爛之肢骸。[81]
吾中國婦女何辜。而受此

80　「婦」，原誤印作「歸」。今正。
81　此句之後，原有二句號。其一疑衍，今刪去。

punative amputation?[172] *Perhaps the wicked practice's instigator Li the Last*[173] *eats thereby his fill of flesh.*[174]

"What blackguard created this scourge which causes me such trauma!" cursed Ma tearfully. Then, a chest full of worries now stirred, she started to cry uncontrollably. After some time she thought to herself that crying would do no good. So she stemmed her tears and tore a length of fabric from her undergarment with which to bandage herself. Then she picked up her sickle, shouldered the straw and made her battered way back towards home. Her feet unbearably sore though, she could not help but stumble with each step, so it took several hours along a road of only half a mile before she reached the village gate. (§20, 30/10/1909)

Having returned home, relieved herself of her burdens and rested for a little, [Ma] rose and prepared her breakfast.[175] A short while later,[176] a hobbling old woman approached, wearing a [bamboo] hat, and carrying in her left hand a basket of the same, whilst supporting herself on a dove cane[177] with her right. Ma looked out at her: it was her mother. Ma rushed to relieve her mother of the things she was carrying and then invited her in to sit.

---

172 The word used by the author—刖—means foot amputation, and was one of various corporal punishments inflicted on criminals in Chinese antiquity.

173 李後主 M°. "Li the Last" was the third and last emperor of the 南唐 Southern T'ang, one of many small and short-lived states that sprang up in the interlude between the collapse of the T'ang dynasty and the establishment of the Sung in the tenth century, in what is known as the 五代十國 Five Dynasties and Ten Kingdoms period. The author's attribution of the invention of foot binding to Li the Last was a popular version of its origin. (See Dorothy Ko's book *Every Step a Lotus: Shoes for Bound Feet* for more on foot binding and its origins, and for images of the type of lotus shoes worn by women in Kwang Tung's See Yip region.)

174 The author is satirically suggesting that the notional amputated parts, produced by what he describes as the amputative practice of foot binding,

刖刑[82]也。作俑之李後主。其肉焉足食耶。斯時馬氏含淚而
罵曰。誰家天殺。造此禍胎。使儂受此慘痛。復觸動滿腔愁
緒。放聲大哭。良久。自思悲啼亦是無益。始收涕裂其內衣
一幅以裹之。俯拾其鐮刀。肩荷芻草。狼狽而歸。無奈兩足
痛苦不堪。一步一蹶[83]。半里之路。歷數小時方至里
門。(§20, 30/10/1909) 歸家。釋負稍憩。起治晨餐。食頃。有
一老婦頭戴笭笠。左携竹藍。右扶鳩杖。龍鍾而至。視之乃
其母也。馬氏急接所携之物。乃延之坐。

82　「刑」，原誤印作「形」。今正。
83　原文「蹶」字模糊不清。今參同報別處蹶字擬正。

might serve as offerings that provide for the sustenance of the practice's
instigator in the afterworld. Note: (1) As with German *fleisch*, the Chinese
words for meat and flesh are the same. (2) In Chinese, the consumption of
meat has traditionally connoted wealth and power, the ancient expression
肉食者 "meat eaters", for example, means members of the ruling class.

175　Ma is actually not named in this first sentence, which consequently sounds a
little odd in Chinese. The reason was perhaps a printing error.

176　The idiomatic expression the author uses for "a short while later" (食頃) has
the literal sense of "in a meal's time", i.e. in the time it takes to eat a meal.
Its use is therefore wittily apposite given the context.

177　Chinese lore holds that the 鳩 "dove" is 不噎之鳥 "a bird that does not
choke", and for this reason it has featured for millennia as a propitious motif
on walking sticks for the elderly.

"Have you had any news of late from that fine husband of yours?" asked her mother.

"None as yet," replied Ma.

Her mother knitted her brow. "There has been no news of Sheung Hong since he left," she said. "If he is not interred in the guts of the river fish, then he has died on an island of savages, and will never return. His family too has come to an end. Why is it my child that you must persist in living like this? Why cause yourself to suffer such vexation, going on worrying that you will not have a mouthful of food to eat, while you are still in the prime of life?"

"Huh! What are you saying mother?" exclaimed Ma. "It has not yet been a year since my husband went overseas, and while there has been no news of him, there has neither been any reliable report of his death. How could I leave so heedlessly? Moreover, I am mean-fated and suspect I shall never enjoy good fortune. Even if some mischance does befall my husband, I should hope for no more than to die and bring an end to it all. Go back home and rest mother. Do not go on about things."

On hearing this, a palpable anger pervaded her mother's face and she scolded her in a quaking voice, "You ungrateful incorrigible wretch! Your mother gives you kindly advice, but you counter her in such a way. If this is how you are going to be, you need not hope that your cousin will come to your aid hereafter." Finished, she made her way to the door and left, fuming; and she was still muttering and cursing away when she reached the neighbourhood gate. After her mother had gone, Ma shut the doors and drank of tears.

Several days later, Ma's cousin came bearing a letter, and five Mexican dollars,[178] which he said had been sent by Sheung Hong.

---

178   See footnote 17 for more on Mexican dollars.

母曰。近間若個好兒郎。曾有音問否。馬氏曰。未。其母蹙
額曰。尚康一去。消息渺然。非葬於江魚之腹中。定死於蠻
鬼之島。那有還家之日。況黃家人跡已絕。吾兒尚守此胡
爲。以吾兒如此好年華。愁無啖飯處。何苦自尋煩惱。馬氏
曰。嘻。母何言。兒夫出洋。未够一載。雖無音兆。而生死
未有確耗。豈可輕去。況兒命薄。自顧不能享厚福。縱吾夫
有長短。兒惟一死以了之而已。母歸休。毋喋喋爲。其母聞
之。怒容可掬。顫聲而罵曰。賤骨頭了不長進。母以好言告
汝。反如此衝突耶。汝誠如此。嗣後毋望汝兄周恤矣。罵
完。憤憤出門而去。及至里閈。猶喃喃咒罵不休。馬氏自其
母去後。掩戶飲泣[84]。逾數天。其堂兄持書一封。并墨銀五
員。云是尚康寄回。

84   此二字原誤倒作「泣飲」。今正。

On hearing this Ma was wildly joyous. "Since your husband went to sea," said Cousin Ma, "no blue-bird message or brown-hound news has reached us,[179] and there are wild rumours floating about in town of bad news. So I have been exceedingly concerned. Today though, I unexpectedly received a piece of mail from Hong Kong. Hurriedly opening it up to read, I discovered that it was a letter posted by my brother-in-law, and that inside it was a letter for home, and one pound sterling, which had been changed for five Mexican dollars at Hong Kong. This gave me some consolation and so, knowing you have been intensely worried for him, I hastened to bring it to you.

"What does he say in the letter?" Ma asked. "Is he safe and well?"

"Yes," her cousin replied. "The letter to you I had no right to open and read, but according to the letter sent to me—"

At this point Ma interrupted: "I have no time to listen to your letter, please open up the letter to me and read it out for me to hear."

Cousin Ma unfolded the letter and began to read aloud. The letter read:

Since our teary parting at village gate, a year has now fleeted by, and with every thought of home, my insides are cut to shreds.

After setting to sea last year, it took over seventy days to reach Guichen Bay. From there we headed straight out, journeying for over forty days before we reached Bendigo. Only thirteen of the more than seventy people with whom I headed out did not die on route. In the end we had the good fortune to come upon a man of our district named Chan, who rescued us from danger; but the scene of hardship on that journey is more than brush and ink can describe.

---

179 青鳥 or as here 青鶯 "blue bird" and 黃犬 "brown hound" are literary names for *messengers*. The blue bird's status as a messenger comes from Chinese folk religion, which credits 西王母 the Queen Mother of the West as possessing three. The brown hound is based on an historical dog named 黃耳 "Brown Ears" that belonged to third-and-fourth-century literary giant 陸機 M°. Lu Chi (M^M. *Lù Jī*), and was employed to run messages over vast distances.

馬氏聞之。歡忭若狂。馬某曰。自妹夫放洋而後。靑鸞信
杳。黃犬音乖。而市上浮言。妄傳凶耗。余殊爲憂慮。今日
忽接港信。急爲拆閱。知係妹夫郵函。內有家信一封。並英
金一磅。在港換墨銀五員。余心稍慰。知吾妹懸念殊切。故
忽忽持來耳。馬氏曰。函內詞意云何。他平安否。馬某曰。
平安。寄汝之信。我無拆讀之權。惟寄我之函所云————[85]言
至此。馬氏即攙言曰。吾不暇聆兄函。懇速將寄我之函[86]拆
閱。念給我聆。馬某即將該函披讀。函曰。

里門泣別。倏忽經年。每思故園。肝腸寸斷。憶自舊歲放
洋。歷七十餘日。始抵古愼尾。即由該處首途。旅行四十
餘天。方抵品地高地方[87]。同行七十餘人。沿途死亡。只
剩十三人。後幸遇同邑陳君救援。方能出險。途中艱苦情
形。非筆墨所能罄也。

85　報中破折號原作二「｜」。
86　原文「函」字半缺。今據其殘跡與文義擬正。
87　「地方」原誤倒作「方地」。今正。

*At present I have found a position for myself mining a gold
deposit near Bendigo. Alas, though, that I am forced by the pressure
of penury to leave that which I love and go afar, to cast myself to a
remote island in the world's nether regions, where one is fortunate
to hold on to life against impossible odds of its loss at the claws
and mouths of savages and beasts. Thus, in the silent and empty
hills, or when coverlet is cold and pillow chill,[180] I think always of
forsaken lute and zithern, that sound not their happy harmony.[181]
How can it do other than pain one to the core? Alas that if you and
I wish to meet, we must leave it to our dreaming souls. I expect
that you dear [share] the same feelings.*

*I am living now fairly well: you need not trouble yourself
thinking of me. I send herewith one pound sterling to cover, for
a time, the housekeeping costs. I hope that you will keep it to use
when you have need. There is more I wish to say, but allow me to
relate it in detail another time.*

When her cousin had finished reading, Ma bid him explain the
letter through line by line.[182] Tears of anguish ran down her face
when she heard the explanation of the lines about the hardship on
the journey. However, when Cousin Ma reached the letter's end,
seeing that it was talk of love, he considered that he and she being
cousins it would not be proper for him to explain fully. Seeing her
cousin gloss over the lines, Ma grew puzzled, and so pressed him
once more to explain it over in detail. [Cousin][183] Ma was left with
no alternative. His cheeks flushed red, and he summed it up with
the words "thinking of home". But seeing her cousin respond in
this fashion Ma was most dissatisfied. On account of this, Cousin
Ma rose, excused himself and headed back.

---

180 The phrases 空山寂寞 "the silent and empty hills" and 衾寒枕冷 "coverlet is
cold and pillow chill" are both literary quotations.

現在品地高附近。採掘金礦。以謀株棲。嗟乎。爲貧困所
迫。以致割愛遠離。投身於窮荒絕島。乃在蠻人猛獸之爪
吻。拾回萬死一生之殘命。亦云幸矣。然每於空山寂寞之
境。衾寒枕冷之時。廻念靜好瑟琴。置而不御。能不令人
痛煞耶。噫。欲圖相會。両憑夢魂。料卿亦□[88]同情也。
居處粗安。毋勞注念。茲付來英金壹磅。暫爲中饋之貲。
仰收需用。不盡欲言。容再細達。

馬某讀罷。馬氏使他逐句解釋。解至途中艱苦之句。馬氏聆
之。悽然淚下。及讀至信末。馬某見是情話。自思屬在兄
妹。不便詳解。而馬氏見其兄含糊讀過。心滋疑惑。復迫其
詳細再解。馬某[89]無可如何。祇得紅漲両頰。以思家二字了
之。而馬氏見其兄如此。心殊快快。於是馬某興辭而歸。

88   此字殘缺尤甚。細審之，疑當為「表」字。
89   「馬某」二字原作「馬氏」，與文義不合。疑植字之誤，今正。

181 The much-celebrated euphony that exists between the Chinese 琴 "lute" and
     瑟 "zithern" symbolizes loving harmony between husband and wife, both in
     Chinese literature and in various spoken idioms based thereon. The present
     line references a phrase (「琴瑟在御，莫不靜好」) within a particular folk
     song in the ancient Chinese text 詩經 *The Odes* that concerns this associa-
     tion. The words "happy harmony" are taken from William Jennings's 1891
     translation of the song, the title of which he translated rather freely as "The
     Good Housewife".
182 The letter is written in Literary Chinese, the grammar and diction of which
     differs from all forms of spoken Chinese. Therefore, while it could be read
     out according to the pronunciation of any vernacular, it would not necessar-
     ily be understandable, especially if the hearer was unfamiliar with literary
     language. A rough analogy to this situation would be an expression in
     mathematical notation, which can be read out in many languages, but would
     not necessarily be understandable to the hearer if he or she was unfamiliar
     with the terms used.
183 馬某 "Cousin Ma" appears to have been misprinted as 馬氏 "Ma" in the
     original. It has been corrected in the transcription with a note.

Alas that as China has not developed female education, Chinese women are illiterate, and thus even husbands and wives cannot communicate their feelings between each other. What is most bitterly regrettable though, is that when one party is at world's end, and they are thousands of miles apart, every confidence and every expression of love within their correspondence is disclosed in full to others.

Her cousin having headed off home, Ma was still unsettled at heart. So she took the letter to a local scholar. Then finally, after it had been deciphered for her over and over, Ma was consoled. (§21, 6/11/1909)

Sheung Hong is a man of devotion not some faithless fellow, thought Ma to herself after receiving the letter. So with patience and calm she awaited her husband's return; and as Sheung Hong sent back a small sum each year, she worried not that she would want for rice or salt.[184] Ma became all the more frugal too, and used the resultant savings to support her mother. Sharing in this profit, the old woman not only stopped urging her daughter to remarry, but never ceased in praising Sheung Hong for his virtue.

There was of course nothing unusual in this, for such is the disposition of our country's uneducated women.

---

184 The expression 米鹽 "rice or/and salt" also has the idiomatic sense in Chinese of *minor necessaries.*

憶。中國女學不興。婦女不識文字。雖夫妻之間。猶不能通情素。而天涯萬里。尺牘往還。一切秘密之言。道情之語。盡宣洩於外人。最堪痛恨。馬氏待其兄歸後。心猶未釋。復將此函持往該鄉之學究處。反覆推解。方始慰帖。(§21, 6/11/1909) 馬氏自接函之後。自念尚康爲情篤之人。決非薄倖者可比。故甯心耐意。以待其夫之歸來。而尚康每年亦有微資寄囘。米鹽無虞缺乏。馬氏益加儉積。每以餘資贍養其母。而老婆子沾有餘潤。不但不勸其女之別醮。反稱道尚康之賢良不置。此吾國無教育婦女之常態。不足爲怪。

Time slipped by as Sheung Hong, Ching Nam and the others worked the deposit near Bendigo, and all of a sudden three years had passed, but with no great improvement in the mine's output. One day in summer, one on which the weather had fined somewhat after a downpour that had lasted a third of a month, Sheung Hong, Pan Nam and Chan Leung were lunching together in a tent, while Ching Nam was apart, supervising several white men as they laboured in the mine. Suddenly there was a strange rumbling sound. Leung and the others raced out to look and found that the whole mine had collapsed. Knowing Ching Nam and the others were buried alive inside, they panicked, and all rushed to attack the ground with picks and spades. After three hours, to their great distress, they dug out the white men, who were beyond saving, their corpses already stiff to the touch. Still they had not found where Ching Nam was. So they dug in search of him for over two hours, but throughout came upon no sign or clue as to his whereabouts. Then Sheung Hong said, "Even if we recover him, he'll be no different to the white men. We are doing no more than taxing our strength in vain."

"No no," replied Chan sternly. "Ching Nam and I are closer than kin. No matter what I must find him."

"There is a little crib-room that has been newly cut, off to the side of the mine," said Pan Nam. "Might he not be there?" Leung was struck with realisation, and on close inspection determined its location.

On that spot they dug concertedly till around ten or so feet down.[185] Then they heard a sound coming from underground, a muffled *buzz buzz*, which on close scrutiny they could tell to be a human voice.

---

185 The author could be referring to a British or Chinese foot. The latter, also known as the Chinese covid, was slightly longer.

尚康與程南等在品地高[90]附近治礦。荏苒光陰。倏忽三年。
該礦無甚起色。一日時當夏令。霪雨經旬。是日稍霽。尚康
與賓南陳亮等同在帳內用午膳。獨程南督率數白人在礦內操
作。驟聞怪聲隆隆。亮與尚康等趨視。始知全礦崩陷。知程
南等生葬礦中。大驚。諸人急以鋤鑱攻土。歷三小時始起出
數白人之尸。撫之已僵。施救無及。大慟。尤失程南所在。
搜掘移時。皆無跡兆。尚康曰。雖獲之。亦與西人一例耳。
徒勞心力爲。陳正色曰。否否。吾與程南情逾骨肉。不論如
何。須要尋獲。賓南曰。礦傍有新開小窟窨。得毋在是乎。
亮大悟。於是細加審視。認定其處。向此地點合力掘挖約至
十餘尺。聞有聲自地下出。嚶嚶如蜂鳴。細辨之。人聲。

90　此處「在品」字下本無「地」字，今據下期〈刊誤更正〉補之。

"Ching Nam's alive!" exclaimed a joyous Leung. Changing hurriedly to wooden tools, so as to prevent injury by pick or spade, they dug about a foot deeper.

Then they again heard a person speak.

"I'm still alive. Please be careful gentlemen, lest you should injure me."

They all responded, and each discarding his wooden tool began to scrape at the earth with his hands. Soon they saw a board. This they forcibly loosened and then lifted. Ching Nam could be seen curled up within the cavity. Beside him were two upright supports of strong timber, which had prevented the earth from crushing him. Leung then rushed to lift Ching Nam up by the arms and bring him out. Seeing him unharmed they were all relieved and elated.

"Having been struck by this calamity, I thought my number was surely up; but owing to your rescue I am able once again to see the light of day. Till my dying day, I shall never forget this kindness," said Ching Nam thankfully.

"We did no more than our duty. What talk is this of kindness?" replied Leung. "Though we had not the time just now even for guilt, it was work in our collective enterprise that brought this hardship on you."

The group then discussed the matter of the Westerners' bodies, following which they promptly made a report to the police station for investigation. It was determined that the earth around the mine had been gradually broken down by the prolonged rainfall, and that the mine owners' failure to take preventative steps in advance had caused the disaster. Accordingly, they were ordered to pay an indemnity so as to bring the matter to an end: everything they had saved over several years was lost in a day.

Thereafter, they agreed to abandon the mine and relocate to the diggings near Ballarat, to again work at mining. The veins in those diggings were particularly rich and their earnings were considerable.

亮大喜曰。程南尙生。急易以木具掘土。免爲鋤鏈所傷。再
深尺許。始復聞人語曰。余未死。諸君稍慎。幸勿傷我。諸
人應之。各棄木具。以手抓土。俄而見一板。力撼而起之。
見程南蜷伏在內。傍有二堅木豎支[91]。故程南得免爲泥土所
迫壓。亮急以手掖之起。見程南無恙。咸相歡慰。程南謝
曰。弟罹此危難。自分已死[92]。賴諸君相救。復得重見天
日。此恩沒齒不敢忘。亮曰。此吾等應盡之義務耳。況諸人
共事。致君獨罹此苦。吾等方疚心不暇。何恩爲。於是羣相
商議西人尸首之事。卽報警署檢驗。官判礦土爲積雨所浸
攻。礦主不先事預防。故罹此劫禍。判補囘恤欵。以了此
案。諸人數年積蓄。一旦又蕩然無存。故僉謀[93]棄此礦遷往
孖辣附近各坑。再治礦業。此坑金苗殊暢旺。入欵豐裕。

91　「豎支」原作「支豎」。蓋倒文也。今正。

92　「自分已死」一語，本出《漢書・蘇武傳》：「武曰『自分已死久矣』」。
　　顏師古注曰「分音扶問反」。按，分猶言料想也。蓋安分之分之引申義，
　　死字活用也。

93　「僉」原作「簽」。誤。今正。

Later, Ching Nam bought a deposit independently of them with a Westerner, and also opened a shop in Melbourne, named San Tung Yuen, which supplied Chinese foods to the various towns.[186] Then, after several years of such enterprise, and the attainment of a certain prosperity, they began to plan their return home. (§22, 13/11/1909)

"Now that we have been overseas for six years and have accrued some wealth," said Ching Nam, "I should like to make a trip back to our ancestral land."[187]

"I am delicate and cannot stand hardship," said Pan Nam. "My being here feels quite pointless, and the thought of returning does not leave me for a moment. However I often feel uneasy at heart over my inability to achieve my aspirations in one matter."

"What matter is that?" asked Ching Nam.

"Our compatriots residing in this continent presently number over a hundred thousand,"[188] replied Pan Nam, "and even in Victoria, in excess of several tens of thousands. (Forty years ago there were indeed these numbers, but, through restrictions of the most extreme severity, they have grown ever smaller.)[189] Nevertheless, while great in number, they are disorganised. Internally, they lack the concept of solidarity; and externally, they lack a plan of approach. So the white people demean and humiliate them, which is truly a matter for concern. However, if a plan of approach is to be established, the concept of solidarity must first be established; and to produce this concept of solidarity, we must first establish a place of congregation. Of those from our country sojourning here, See

---

186 The Chinese word for "digging(s)" (坑) became the word for "town(s)" amongst Australian and North American speakers of the See Yip language. It can therefore be translated as either depending on the context of its use.

187 祖國 "ancestral land" is the Chinese equivalent to *fatherland* or *motherland*, and can carry the same chauvinistic connotations that the word fatherland has acquired in English.

後程南與西人獨購一礦。又往美利伴開一商店。名新同源。
專辦各坑華人食料。經營數載。囊橐稍裕。於是羣謀歸
計。(§22, 13/11/1909) 程南曰。吾等航洋六載。今積有微貲。
願回祖國一行。賓南曰。吾文弱。不能力任艱苦。在此殊屬
無謂。回國一念。刻不能忘。但尚有一事。未能竟志。中心
時覺不安耳。程南曰。何事。賓南曰。目下吾國同胞。僑寓
本洲者。十餘萬人。以域多利而論。亦逾數萬。(四十年前確
有此數自禁例蔡嚴日形減少耳)人數雖衆。而散漫無紀。對於
內無聯結之觀念。對於外無對待之方略。故白人矬辱。是誠
可憂。然欲求其對待之方略。須先求聯結之觀念。欲生其聯
結之觀念。不可不預求壹合集之地點。吾國之旅寓此地。
以四

---

188 The figure given, 十餘萬, means over ten 10,000s but fewer than twenty, i.e.
     over 100,000 but below 200,000.
189 The restrictions imposed on Chinese people under the White Australia
     Policy. Note that the sentence within the parentheses is an author's note and
     does not form part of the story's text. The note makes it clear that the
     author is writing forty years after the events he is describing, and from his
     reference to "forebears" later in this part it is clear that he considers the
     characters to belong to an earlier generation than his own.

Yip people are the greatest in number.[190] I wish to advocate for the building of a See Yip clubhouse.[191] A point of unity and structure. What do you gentlemen think of this?"

"I am in full favour of such an endeavour," said Ching Nam, "but it is not within the strength of one or two people to see it through."

Accordingly, they sent out invitations to all those See Yip people who had some sense, and, after several rounds of discussion, each assumed responsibility for a portion of the funds for the building.

A few months on, they succeeded in collecting several thousand pounds. They then selected a strip of land in Melbourne's *Bee-loo Park*,[192] and in the space of several months constructed a grand, tall and spacious See Yip Association building, the text of the panel, couplet and stele inscriptions for which was all composed by their hands.[193]

It can be seen from this that our forebears were not without communal thinking. Ah! This endeavour of Pan Nam and others can be said to have been one of extraordinary vision. Unfortunately, the building venerated idols, and so annual

---

190 People from Kwang Tung's See Yip region: see Appendix V.

191 The expression used by the author, 公所 cᴹ. *gūngsó* Mᴹ. *gōngsuǒ*, generally translates better as "community organisation", "association" or "society", but as it can also refer to the physical building used by such an organisation (in fact, this is its primary sense), and as this sentence relates to its physical construction, the word "clubhouse" was considered a preferable translation; in a slightly different semantic context later in this part, it is given as "See Yip Association building".

192 The placename 彼露帕 s. "*bee loo park*" is a transliteration from English, in which the character 帕, which is pronounced *park* (but means something wholly unrelated), is clearly used to represent the English word park. Albert Park was, and still is, the approximate location of Melbourne's See Yip temple, so it would appear that the characters 彼露 "*bee loo*" are intended to

邑人爲最多數。吾欲倡建壹四邑公所。整齊而統壹之點。君
意以爲何如。程南曰。斯舉余甚贊成。但非壹二人之力所能
逮也。於是柬邀四邑士人之稍有識者。磋商數次。各人担任
建款。不數月果集金數千磅。即在美利伴彼露帕地方。擇地
壹段。建築壹四邑公所。軒崇宏廠。數月落成。檻聯碑文。
皆其手撰。此可見前人非無團體思想也。嘻。賓南等此舉。
可謂有特[94]識者矣。惜乎崇祀偶像。每年

94　原文「特」字半缺。今參別處特字擬補。

reflect the pronunciation of the word Albert. A printing error may explain
why they do not: "Albert" is generally transliterated in the *Chinese Times* as
亞露弼 "*aa-loo-bit*"; the transliteration which appears in this instalment may
be a mutilation of something like 亞露彼 "*aa-loo-bei*", with the first syllable
lost and with the second two reversed. Transliterations appear to have been
particularly susceptible to such mutilations in early Chinese newspapers,
probably because the typesetters were unfamiliar with the English words
they represented. Alternatively, the name may have been changed by the
author intentionally, consistent with his statement in the preface that he
would make slight changes to names.

193 Lines that form an antithetical couplet and are inscribed on paired vertical
plaques are a common feature of Chinese temples.

expenditure was colossal.[194] *Yet, constrained by the old mindset*
of several decades ago, they could hardly be blamed for this.[195]
(§23, 27/II/1909)

Once everything had been seen to, Sheung Hong, Ching Nam
and Pan Nam boarded a ship back to China. This ocean voyage was
very different from the last. The sailing ship they boarded at Melbourne took them back to Hong Kong directly. The winds being
fortunately calm, the ocean's surface was as flat as a mirror,[196] so
there was little danger or difficulty. After sailing for fifty or so days,
they arrived safely in Hong Kong. It happened that a paternal
cousin of Pan Nam's there was an employee at Kwan Cheung
Hing,[197] and had directed people to welcome them off the boat and
see to their luggage. The employees in the shop were likewise exces-
sively welcoming.

The snobbishness of that place[198] *is enough to provoke the most*
intense indignation. They subject everyone going overseas to
white-eyed looks,[199] *and yet go out of their way to fawn on those*
returning. What is the reason for this earlier haughtiness and
then later deference of theirs? It is their focus on Chi Tzŭ and
all his gold.[200] *Our country's merchants are, alas, vile and*
contemptible, and exceedingly short of vision. Unable to

---

194 The author is presumably referring to the expenditure involved in traditional
Chinese religious practices, such as the burning of incense and the making
of offerings.

195 This phrase has a double meaning: "they could hardly be blamed for this/be
found blameworthy for this" and "this was hardly surprising".

196 "As flat as a mirror" is a Chinese cliché equivalent to English's "as flat as a
millpond".

197 One might also read this phrase as "at *a* Kwan Cheung Hing", though the
translation given, which suggests that the business name should be familiar
to readers, seems the most natural.

198 Hong Kong.

耗費不資。此亦囿於數十年前之舊腦筋。無足爲怪也。(§23,
27/11/1909) 諸事已畢。賓南與尙康程南三人。同附海舶回
國。此次航洋與前次大異。在美利伴附帆船直囘香港。幸而
風恬。浪靜。波平如鏡。無甚艱險。舟行五十餘天。已安抵
香港。適值賓南之從兄。在港均祥興司事。先命人到舟迎
迓。料理行李。店中夥計。亦極意歡迎。港地人情冷煖。最
令人憤悶。凡出洋之人。莫不加以白眼。而回國者則曲意逢
迎。彼何以作此前倨後恭狀態。實則注意季子之多金。噫。
吾國商人。卑鄙齷促。眼光如豆。不能

---

199 Scornful looks.

200 The Chinese idiom 前倨後恭 "earlier haughtiness, later deference" has its
origin in the story of the same Mᵒ. Chi Tzŭ who is referred to here. He was a
political strategist of China's Warring States period, once poor and
unsuccessful, who, on later returning home wealthy and influential, is said to
have asked his sister-in-law the reason for her earlier haughtiness and later
deference, and to have received the frank response that the reason was "all
his gold". The Chinese words for silver and gold can both be used in the
sense of money. It may be that the author used the word gold here advisedly,
with respect to his "goldfielder".

*improve our own goods and compete against Western merchants,
they pride themselves purely on the oppression of Chinese
labourers and the exploitation of their blood and sweat.[201]
Instead they ridicule them and label them at every turn
chumps[202] (meaning they are foolish), which is most bitterly
regrettable. This is due to their undeveloped business acumen.
How can their ever continuing commercial downfall do other
than invite the affronts of Westerners?*

Sheung Hong and his two companions spent the night in
Hong Kong, and the following day caught boats[203] back to their
villages. Ching Nam, who had not yet taken a wife, returned to his
parent's home to find his father had passed away. After crying and
weeping in pain and sorrow, he forced himself to smile for his
mother, who was doing her best to comfort him.

Pan Nam became all the more determined in his endeavours
after returning home. He had successes in that year's district and
prefectural examinations, and before long entered a regional university.[204] Thereafter he applied himself to education, and dared not
think again of heading out over the seas.

Night had already fallen by the time Sheung Hong reached the
village gate. Returning home, he found his wife with a bamboo
pole in her hands, driving the chickens back to their perches.

---

201 汗血 "blood and sweat" is the Chinese equivalent to English's "blood, sweat
and tears".

202 This colloquial term's (羊牯) sense of "chump" is an extension of its narrower
sense of "a green gambler ripe to be taken advantage of", which is itself an
extension of the earlier sense of "a lamb for slaughter".

203 The Chinese text is in fact ambiguous as to whether the characters took
separate boats or travelled via the one boat.

204 Under China's civil examination system, successes in District and Prefectural
Examinations qualified one to sit the 院試 "Chancellor's Examination",

改良土貨。與西商相角逐。徒朘削華工之血汗以自豪。反從
而嘲笑之。動加以羊牯之徽號。(謂其愚蠢)最堪痛恨。此緣
商智不開。商務之墮落。每況愈下。焉得不招西人之侮辱
耶。尚康三人。在港經宿一宵。明天即搭船旋里。程南尚未
有家室。歸家父亡母在。哀痛號泣。母力撫慰。始強顏爲
笑。賓南歸家益加奮勉。是年縣府試皆利。旋入邑庠。此後
從事教育。不敢作出洋之想矣。尚康及抵里門。維時已暮。
入戶見其婦。手持竹竿。驅鷄歸榤。

which was superintended by a high official known as the 學政 Literary Chancellor. Success in this examination earned one the first literary degree, holders of which were referred to in English as *civil licentiates* (or as Mᵒ. Hsiu-tsʿai, which reflects their colloquial title—秀才). Qualification as a civil licentiate gained one admission to a government-run 學宮 "university", specifically either a 郡庠 "prefectural university" or, as is referred to here, a 邑庠 "regional university". A highly talented licentiate might go on to sit for the second, third and fourth degrees at the provincial, national and palace examinations respectively.

She raised her head and saw him, but taking him for a burglar, took several steps back and began to raise the pole in her hands, ready to drive him off. Witnessing this state of affairs, Sheung Hong realised that on his returning back so unexpectedly, after a parting of six years, his wife had not immediately recognised him. So he called out loudly, "It's me!" Stopping the pole mid air and inspecting him, his wife then realised it was Sheung Hong. Startled, she dropped the pole and remained, for a while, speechless. Meeting so suddenly after such a long parting, she became embarrassed and awkward. Her cheeks flushing red, she withdrew to her room.

Anon, a scene of piled cases presented itself, to the sound of successive calls of "Goldfielder!", just as in her dream. Ma thought to herself *Could I be doing other than dreaming?* But beyond the bedroom curtain, the house was filled with commotion. The sounds of Sheung Hong conversing with the village folk, and of women and children racing to each other with news, all reverberated in her ears. Discerned clearly, it was plainly not a dream.

Suddenly two or three old women raised the curtain and poked their heads in. One said, "Why not come out and help your man settle his luggage?" Another woman cut in, "You've worn your eyes through gazing out for his return.[205] So we've come especially to give our congratulations, as well as to extract some biscuits and cakes for our grandsons." Blushing all the more with embarrassment, Ma could do no more than nod and smile. The women backed out and began recounting to Sheung Hong the village events that had occurred after his leaving. Then Sheung Hong told them of the hardships he had encountered during his adventures. The women then enquired as to

---

205 The Chinese word for "gaze" or "look" (望) also means "hope for" and a number of Chinese sayings, such as the one used here, play on this double sense.

舉首見尙康。意以爲暴客。卻立數武。欲揚手中竿逐之。尙康睹此情狀。知相別六載。猝然歸來。驟難識認。故大聲疾言曰。是我。其妻停竿審睇。方知是尙康。斯時心怔竿墮。半晌無言。曉違日久。忽然見面。反形羞澀。紅漲兩頰。移步入房。俄而金山客之聲浪。與箱篋之堆積。一如前日之夢境。馬氏自思。得毋夢耶。然房幃以外。滿室喧攘。婦孺之奔走相告聲。尙康與鄉人寒暄聲。震動耳鼓。審視明白。又明明非夢。忽有二三老嫗。搴幃探首而言曰。嫂嫂何不出來幫哥哥安頓行李。又一嫗攙言曰。嫂嫂望穿眼睛。望得哥哥歸來。吾等特來道喜。並索餅果與吾孫兒。馬氏越加羞赧。惟點頭微笑而已。數婦退出。與尙康緬述別後之鄉事。尙康告以歷險艱苦。數婦又詢

the customs of the Westerners and the scenery of the foreign lands. And so, over several hours, they prattled on incessantly, showing no signs of fatigue. Hah! Were these old women so unworldly? Or were they playing at pranks?[206] (§24, 4/12/1909)

Ma paced back and forth in her room, her state of desperateness just like that of a ravenously hungry man whose mouth waters in passing a butcher's stand, and who is pained by the impossibility of getting a taste. Suffering through this hunger, for several hours she waited, though time passed not merely as if there were three autumns in one day, but rather half a lifetime in every hundredth.[207] Over and again she scratched her head as she searched for a plan to see them all off, and then stamped her feet when none came to her. But all she could do was grind her teeth in anger and resentment, and curse her husband's greed for talk and the village women's thoughtlessness.

It was not until the second watch was nearing its end that the villagers gradually dispersed.[208] When they all had, Sheung Hong walked slowly into the room.

A smiling Ma then berated him in a petulant tone, "Faithless husband of mine, six years apart must still feel not so long to you, that you should intentionally dilly-dally on your return. Did you think it would have been for my benefit alone if you had come to bed a little earlier?"

"Deranged woman, you are too unreasonable by far," responded Sheung Hong. "When neighbours pay a visit to someone returned home from afar, how can one simply show them the door?"

---

206 In other words, were they intentionally keeping Sheung Hong from his wife, who was waiting so expectantly for him in another room.

207 The word 刻 translated here as "hundredth", which actually literally means "notch (as on a gauge)", was a unit of time, equivalent to one hundredth of a day, or 14.4 minutes. This decimal unit was later adopted, with the introduction of non-decimal Western timekeeping, as the word for a unit of very similar duration, namely a quarter of an hour or fifteen minutes, in which new sense it is still in common use.

外國之風景。西人之習俗。剌剌不休。歷數小時。毫無倦
容。嘻。老婆子不知事耶。抑故惡作劇耶。(§24, 4/12/1909) 馬
氏徘徊房中。其急遽之狀。正如餓夫過屠肆。饞吻流涎。苦
難到口。其佇待數小時。豈徒一日三秋。實則一刻半世耳。
幾番搔首頓足[95]。又無計遣去羣人。徒切齒怨恨。罵其夫之
貪言。與村嫗之不曉事而已。二更向盡。其村人始陸續散
去。尚康徐步入房。馬氏含笑帶嗔而罵曰。薄倖郎相別六
年。尤未覺久。歸至家猶故意俄延。若早些歸寢。偏益儂
耶。尚康曰。癡婦大不近情。遠人歸家。鄉鄰到訪。豈便下
逐客令耶。

95 搔首者，極力想方設法之兒也。頓足，終恨束手無策之兒也。搔首頓足，
    設方法恨無策之總兒，是也。又作「捫耳頓足」。捫，抓也，粵音蔴（即
    輆學之輆音）。

208 The night-time was divided into five equal divisions, called 更 "watches", the
    arrival of each of which was announced by means of the beating of
    percussive instruments, such as bells or large drums in cities, and hand-held
    鑼 gongs or 柝 wooden clappers in villages. The end of the second watch and
    the beginning of the third therefore fell three-fifths of the way through the
    night. The system of dividing and marking the night in this fashion existed
    in China for thousands of years and continued into the 1930s.

"You men," said Ma, "know not whether one is alive or dead ..." Touching at that point on her daily hardships, Ma's eyes reddened and her voice choked up. Burying her head in Sheung Hong's shoulder, she began, faintly but deeply, to sob. But after Sheung Hong had offered a little consolation, she stemmed her tears and cheered up.

As they sat facing each other, chatting happily, Sheung Hong looked over his wife, studying her, and felt that while she still retained her charm, she was already a Hsü Niang past her prime.[209] Then that wicked thought sprang forth in him, and startlingly diminished, several times over, the feeling of true love that he had all along had for her. He calculated to himself, *I have several hundred in silver and could make myself comfortable thereby, would that my wife were not already old and her face detestable to me. Living day-to-day with an old woman, what interest will the rest of my life have? But I am no poor scholar: what is to stop me from buying some pretty young thing for a concubine, so I might enjoy my remaining years?* His thoughts reaching that point, Sheung Hong experienced a sudden rush of happiness and could barely help himself from jumping for joy. Then he contemplated to himself, *I have only a few hundred in savings, just enough to cover the price of a concubine. If I exhaust this and am in need of funds in future, where am I to come by them?* His thoughts reaching that point, so great was his disappointment his whole body broke out in a cold sweat. And so with those thoughts, his mind like a windlass[210] revolved ceaselessly throughout the night.

---

209 徐娘 м°. Hsü Niang was a wife of the Southern Liang dynasty's 元帝 Yüan Emperor (who reigned circa 552 to 555 C.E.) who was known for her promiscuity in later life, for which reason she features in a Chinese saying: 徐娘半老丰韻猶存 "a Hsü Niang past her prime: she still retains her charm". Here though, the author uses the saying to somewhat different effect by inverting its phrases.

210 The 轆轤 "windlass", for obvious reasons, is an object that often features in Chinese analogies to the turning of a person's mind or gut. The analogy was therefore a clichéd one.

馬氏曰。汝等男子。不知人生死。言至此。忽觸動其平日之苦況。眼紅音咽。以首伏在尙康肩上。嗚嗚啜泣。尙康稍爲勸慰。始收淚作喜。夫妻對坐笑談。尙康端詳審視。覺馬氏丰韻猶存。已是徐娘半老。其惡念忽生。竟將平素摯愛之心。減去數倍。私心默計。吾有白金數百。可爲小康。無奈內人已老。面目殊覺可憎。日與老嫗同居處。下半世有何趣味。此時我非窮措大。何妨買⁹⁶一少艾爲妾。以樂餘年乎。思至此。喜從天降。不禁手舞足蹈。細自忖量。吾囊中祇有區區數百金。僅够一妾之價值。若將來用罄。需費何著。思至此。又遍身冷汗。大爲失望。徹夜心似轆轤。輪轉不休。

96　「買」原作「賣」。「賣」字悖於文義，應爲「買」之訛字。今正。

Unaware of the collection of concerns on Sheung Hong's mind, Ma kept chattering on about all manner of things, sometimes laughing joyously, sometimes crying charmingly. Sheung Hong though, was not of a mood to listen attentively. With the exception of a few words of greeting when they had first met, the only sounds he issued were replies of "Yes, yes." Reunited that one day having been separated six years, on what was for others a night of grateful love beyond pen and ink's description, Sheung Hong had, alas, other things in mind. While he let his wife tell tearily of her deepest sorrows and pains, and relate fully her feelings through their separation, he stayed indifferent, showing not the slightest feeling for her over their marriage bed.

Observing [his] demeanour closely, Ma perceived that something was amiss. She thought to herself, *My husband is not long returned and there has been no opportunity for me to have given offence. Might it be then that aspersions have been cast against me when he was overseas so as to force us apart? Or could it be that when we first met I spoke too brusquely?* ***[211] considering things for a moment, she fell into a five-mile fog,[212] through which she could conceive no explanation. So with renewed tenderness, she cuddled up against him and enquired carefully, but Sheung Hong uttered not a word of response. Weeping, Ma said, "With you abroad for six years I have been all alone in the world. I have cut fuel by day and woven cloth by night, and have been through who knows how much hardship. Yet when rumours of bad news circulated and my mother pressed me to plight a new troth, I resisted with all my strength and swore

---

211 The three asterisks represent a mutilated character in the original text, the exact sense of which cannot be determined.

212 五里霧 "five-mile fog" is a Chinese expression which can mean, as here, a place of extreme cloudiness and uncertainty.

尚庚揣此一腔心事。而馬氏不知。祇顧細語喁喁。說長說短。時而歡笑。時而嬌啼。尚康無心諦聆。除初見時寒暄數語。餘外應聲唯唯而已。噫。六載暌離。一朝聚首。在他人此一夜之恩情。實非筆墨所能形容者。乃尚康別有心裁。一任其妻之泣訴苦衷。緬述離緒。彼則淡焉置之。毫無感情於床第之間也。馬氏細察其[97]狀。知覺有異。自思夫歸未久。無從開罪之處。得毋在外洋時。被人讒間耶。抑初相見時語太唐突。□[98]思量半刻。如墮五里霧中。無從懸忖。故愈加溫柔。偎抱細詢。尚康默無一言。馬氏泣曰。君往外洋六載。妾伶仃一身。晝樵夜織。不知歷盡幾許苦辛。復謠傳凶耗。母偪易節。妾力拒。誓

97　原文「其」字殘甚。今參別處其字擬補。
98　此字殘缺難辨。

to keep faith till death. I had not expected that today I would see your face again, and with the warmth of my affection, I was almost driven mad. You on the other hand have looked on me as a thorn in your side. Had I known you would show no fondness for my haggard face, I should rather have died and had done with life." Finished, she rested her head against Sheung Hong's arm and cried in sweet and charming tones, her tears welling forth in streams which were soaked up by the mattress. But, savage-natured, this intemperate and mean fellow had not a stone for a heart but a heart that could turn.[213] He gave no words of reassurance, but instead lifted his arm away and hurriedly pushed his wife's head onto the mat, before scolding her, "I see you have grown wicked of heart, and would say that our shared destiny has now come to an end. Who *** you to make another scene?"

Ma cried loudly till her voice went, by which time Sheung Hong was already snoring thunderously. (§25, 18/12/1909)

Her eyes not closing, all through the night Ma cried, while thinking to herself, *Through so much hardship I longed with the utmost eagerness for my husband's return, expecting that with it the walls of this city of sadness would come tumbling down.*

---

213   This phrase is a play on a line from a well-known song within 詩經 *The Odes* (邶風·柏舟): 我心匪石不可轉也 "My heart be not a stone, One cannot turn it". A declaration of constancy of will, the line relies on the dual senses of the word 轉 "turn", namely "to revolve", and "to change". The stone to which it refers is possibly a quernstone (磑石), which would mean that it forms an ancient analogy similar to the aforementioned one involving the 轆轤 "windlass". Here the author flips the line on its head, by asserting that while Sheung Hong's heart is not a stone, it can nevertheless turn. In the author's line, the word "stone" is not a quernstone but rather a symbol of steadfastness. This symbolic sense comes about because stones are an obvious manifestation of hardness, and because the Chinese word for "hard" (堅) also means steadfast. (The symbolic sense is old and may in fact have been used to produce a twist in the original song, because the listener would expect a steadfast heart to be likened to a stone.)

以守死。不圖今日復見君面。妾歡愛熱度。幾致發狂。乃君
視同眼釘。早知憔悴容顏。不爲君憐。不如死休。說完。以
首枕尙康之臂。宛轉嬌啼。淚泉沾褥。乃猥薄子豺狼成性。
匪石可轉。並無慰解之詞。反將臂掀去。丞推其妻之首於蓆
上而罵曰。吾見汝心頭滋惡。料此後緣分已盡。誰復□[99]汝
撒潑耶。馬氏大哭失聲。而尙康鼾聲雷動矣。(§25, 18/12/1909)
馬氏啼哭一夜。不曾合眸。自念艱苦備嘗。翹盼綦切。企望
夫歸。而愁城自破。

99　此亦為字之殘缺模糊者。細審其迹，似「又」底者。

Who would have thought that by forgetting the love he once held for his wife of poorer days,[214] *he would become indifferent to me, thus betraying my confidence, dashing my hopes and leaving me to rueful regret.* Before she realised, it was almost daybreak. Ma got out of bed, washed, and began attending to the housework as usual.

It was not until the sun had risen high in the sky that Sheung Hong yawned and rose. Ma, all the more respectful and attentive, waited on him as he washed and rinsed, holding his towel for him and wiping him therewith. Yelling at her at his pleasure, Sheung Hong acted as though he were ordering some lowly maidservant about.

Alas, our country's women are possessed of an especially subservient nature. Holding to the dictum Thou shalt not disobey thy husband, they are wont to steadfastly endure, without the slightest feeling of resentment, whatever insults and beatings their husbands care to mete out. Their claim to a feminine virtue of feebleness unique throughout the globe stems in fact from the inability of education to spread, as a result of which their intellects have not been fired. One of the causes of this is the sorry state of women's rights. Alas the path of wifehood is hard! Where might there be found a women's revolutionary army to beat the bell of freedom, strike the

---

214 The expression 糟糠之妻 and the abbreviated form used here 糟糠 "wife of poorer days" literally mean "chaff wife" and "chaff" respectively, and have their origin in the words of one 宋弘 м°. Sung Hung (мᴹ. *Sòng Hóng*), a high official in the Han-dynasty imperial court, who lived around the turn of the Christian era. Chinese records relate that a certain Han-dynasty emperor, who was considering offering his younger sister to Sung Hung in marriage, quoted him an adage to the effect that when a person achieves status he changes his acquaintances and when he becomes prosperous he

誰料負心人恝情糟糠[100]。令儂失望。自怨自艾。不覺天已遲
明。馬氏下牀盥洗。依然料理家政。日上三竿。尙康始欠伸
而起。馬氏伺候盥漱。執巾侍幘[101]。愈加敬謹。尙康任意呼
喝。如役下婢然。噫。吾國婦女。具一種特別服從性質。守
無違夫子之戒。縱任其夫如何詬罵。如何鞭撻。堅心忍受。
無少嫌怨。擅地球獨一無二之柔糯[102]婦德。實緣教育不能普
及。故婦智不開。女權不振。有以致之也。嗟乎。夫婦之道
苦矣。焉得女界革命軍。敲自由之鐘。擊

100 因心已忘之而無動於衷曰恝。因忘情而無動於衷，是曰恝情。「恝情糟
糠」者，恝情於糟糠之妻也。按，《聊齋誌異》之〈二商〉篇，有「恝情
骨肉」句，謂恝情於兄弟。兩語如出一轍。恝，音戛。

101 此句蓋仿成語「侍執巾幘」而作。幘者，以巾拭物，音節。幘者，梳篦
也。音與幘同。

102 「糯」當作「懦」。

changes his wife. Sung Hung is reported to have responded: 臣聞貧賤之知
不可忘糟糠之妻不下堂 "Your subject has heard that acquaintances from
when one was poor and mean cannot be forgotten, and that from one's high
hall, a wife with whom one once subsisted on chaff must not fall." In the
author's day, literate people were highly familiar with such classical
anecdotes. While the author's frequent allusions to them add greatly to the
quality of the original, only a small number can be highlighted and
expounded upon in the present translation.

drum of awakening, and erase the hierarchy that makes husbands superior and wives inferior, thus rendering them equal?[215]

As soon as he had finished breakfast, Sheung Hong headed off for the Pak Sha market, to search out his old smoking friends and suck and puff away unrestrainedly. Then he headed off to all the old shops he had once frequented to chitchat. Those within who had once subjected him to white-eyed looks[216] now flattered him in the highest terms; and those who would not extend him a cash[217] on credit now humbly sought his custom. With peddlers and shop-keepers pestering him from left and right, Sheung Hong was overwhelmed. It was not until evening that he meandered back home, the flames of his hubris blazing all the more brightly.[218]

After several months, he had squandered more than half of his several hundred taels in savings. Reckoning that he could not reach his objective of taking a concubine immediately, he wanted to plan a return to Australia. His wife considered his motives and said to him, "I have been wed to you ten years and feel ashamed that I have not been able to bear you a child. What is to be done about the continuation of your line? Why not seize this chance and, with the money that yet remains, buy an unwanted child for me to raise, that we may not meet with Po Tao's sorrow?"[219] Sheung Hong agreed.

---

215 There is a theme that lends this sentence a rhetorical flair and that is lost in translation: The word used for "erase" also has the sense of "render level"; the word for "hierarchy" also has the sense of "steps" or "different planes/tiers/levels (physical or social)"; and the word for "equal" also means "at the same level".

216 Scornful looks.

217 A cash was a copper coin of very low value. See footnote 33 for further detail. Cash in this sense, as a countable noun, has a different etymology to cash in an uncountable sense, i.e. money.

覺迷之鼓。劃夫尊婦卑之堦級。而使之平等哉。朝餐已畢。
尚康卽往白沙市塲。尋其舊時烟霞之友。大肆吞吐。復往舊
識各店談話。昔以白眼相加者。今則極口恭維矣。昔日一文
不賒者。今則卑詞求售矣。行商坐賈。左右纏繞。令尚康應
接不暇。日晡始施施而歸。其氣燄愈驕。過數月。囊中數百
金。揮霍已過半矣。娶妾之目的。料難遽達。欲作返澳計。
其妻廉得其情。謂之曰。妾於歸已經十載。自愧不能作繭。
君之嗣續。將若之何。趁尚有餘資。買一螟蛉。使妾撫養。
不致同傷伯道也。尚康可之。

218　This description of Sheung Hong's haughty return home contains an
　　　allusion to the parable in *Mencius* about a cemetery-scavenging husband:
　　　see footnote 11.

219　ᴍᵒ. Po Tao was the courtesy name of a man of the fourth century named
　　　鄧攸 Têng Yu (ᴍᴹ. *Dèng Yōu*), who, through various twists of fate, died
　　　childless, on account of which he features in a number of Chinese idioms
　　　concerning childlessness (如伯道無子伯道之憂等).

Several days later, an old woman with a child for sale presented herself at the door. He had already come of age, but Sheung Hong took a liking to his handsome features. However, the asking price was high and no agreement could be reached. (§26, 25/12/1909)

Just as Sheung Hong was haggling with the old woman, a villager reported that a stranger had come to visit, and had been waiting for some time by the earth-god shrine. Sheung Hong followed the villager out to meet him, and discovered it was Ching Nam. He promptly conducted him into the house, and after the two of them had exchanged a few pleasantries, Ching Nam said, "Since we returned to China, several months have suddenly passed by, and we have not yet managed to *trim the candle by western window*[220] and talk heart-to-heart. There can be no excuse for my remissness, but of late I have built a lodge[221] and taken a wife, and have been occupied with my own lowly affairs. So while I have wished to engage in an elegant escapade from north of the hills, a lack of time has kept me from visiting *Tai*,[222] and at heart I have felt ill at ease. I expect that you will forgive me. Today, being somewhat freer, I have come especially to pay my respects."

---

220 This is a literal translation of a Chinese idiom that has its origin in a Tang-dynasty poem. It means to meet with an intimate friend and converse at length.

221 The word Ching Nam uses here, 廬 c^M. lòuh M^M. *lú*, which is translated as "lodge", was often used in the names of large houses, particularly those situated in country settings. In the twentieth century it was frequently applied to the See Yip region's Western-influenced multi-storeyed mansions, such as can be seen in its UNESCO World Heritage Listed sites. In the timeframe in question, however, the word would refer to a more traditional style of building, and not a tower.

222 This sentence contains allusions to an anecdote in the perennially popular fifth-century work 世說 "*Hearsay*" (a book better known to latter ages under the revised title of 世說新語 "*Hearsay Retold*" or "*New Hearsay*", which is given in Richard Mather's English translation as *Shih-shuo Hsin-yü: A New Account of Tales of the World*). The anecdote appears under the heading of 任誕 "Whimsical and Unrestrained Behaviour" and relates the following:

逾數天有老嫗携一童。踵門求鬻。年已弱冠。尙康愛其貌
美。但索價昂。未有成議。(§26, 25/12/1909) 尙康方與老嫗爭
價。適有村人報告。謂有外客到訪。在社旁久候。尙康卽隨
村人往見。方知是程南。旋卽導入屋內。二人寒暄數語。程
南曰。吾等囘國已來。倏忽數月矣。未得剪燭西窗。暢談心
曲。弟疎懶之罪。無可辭咎。惟是近間築廬納婦。賤務冗
忙。屢欲作山陰之雅舉。奈無訪戴之時間。撫心自覺不安。
我哥料能原諒。今日稍暇。特來[103]參謁耳。

---

103 「來」原作「未」。按,「未」應為「來」之訛。蓋「未」不合文義, 而
　　來字相合,「未」「來」二字又形似易混。今據改。

When residing in 山陰縣 the district of ᴹ°. Shan Yin (modern-day 紹興
ᴹᴹ. *Shàoxīng*), 王子猷 Wang Tzŭ Yu woke on a night of heavy snow. He
rose from his bed, imbibed, looked all about at the whitewashed scene, paced
fretfully, incanted 左思 Tso Ssŭ's poem 招隱 *"In Quest of Reclusion"*,
remembered his friend 戴安道 Tai An Tao, who was to the south in 剡縣
the district of Shan, and then went off by boat to visit him. Having travelled
through the night he reached Tai's door, but then turned back. When asked
why, he responded that he had gone on a whim, and it having passed, there
had been no need for him to see Tai. This anecdote is the source of the
Chinese expression used here, 訪戴 "to visit *Tai*", which means to visit a
friend. The name of the district in which Wang Tzŭ Yu was residing, Shan
Yin, also appears here, but is translated literally, as "north of the hills",
because the author may also have been using it with reference to the real
hills that separated Ching Nam's locality (開平 ᶜ°. Hoi Ping) from Sheung
Hong's (新寧 s. Llin Nen).

"It has been the same for both of us," replied Sheung Hong, "there is no need for such politeness." Then, in an effort at hospitality, he bade his wife brew tea and cook a meal.

With the earnestness of true friendship, the two of them talked freely of how they had been lately; but when talk reached the subject of progeny, Sheung Hong looked woebegone.

"You have been home some time now," said Ching Nam. "I should reckon that your good wife must have made a happy announcement?"

Sheung Hong shook his head and said, "To this day she is still a barren field from which no harvest can be anticipated. I am just about to select an unwanted child to adopt."

"Your good wife is yet young," said Ching Nam, "what need is there for such haste?"

Sheung Hong replied, "If she is keen, how am I to refuse?"

"Might it be then that you have already settled on one?" asked Ching Nam.

"Just now an old woman arrived with a child she said she wished to sell. He has a very pleasant face, only he is somewhat advanced in years," replied Sheung Hong. "It would seem that my wife finds him very appealing, and if in a moment all is agreeable on discussion, I shall accept the offer."

"This is a matter of your family affairs and I should not meddle," said Ching Nam. "However, the two of us have lived together through adversity and are closer than kin, so I shall shy not from the risk of giving offence and offer some faithful counsel. In our country's several-thousand-year-old society, nothing has been of more consequence than bloodline or of more importance than succession. When someone is heirless, a branch from their clan tree is grafted on to succeed them, so that the line of lineage is preserved. Nowadays, those of us See Yip people who adopt unwanted children forget their roots and turn their backs on their ancestors, purchasing boys from different clans and thus sullying their genealogies. How is it that they all refer absurdly to the sons of any of the whole world's people as their own?

尙康[104]曰。彼此如是。何用客氣。卽命其妻煮茗炊黍。稍盡
殷勤。兩人推心置腹。縱談近況。及談至子嗣一層。尙康愀
然不樂。程南曰。君抵家許久。量尊嫂決有喜信。康搖首
曰。終是石田。難期收穫。吾正欲擇一螟蛉也。程南曰。尊
嫂尙屬靑年。何必躁[105]切若是。康曰。彼自好之。我又奚
辭。程南曰。信如君言。曾擇定否。尙康曰。適間一嫗率一
童至。云求鬻者。貌甚好人。但年齡稍長耳。窺吾內人意。
似甚愛悅者。待稍頃相商。若適意。無復挑剔也。程南曰。
斯事乃君家政。僕不應越俎。但吾二人患難相處。情逾骨
肉。故不嫌唐突。而有所忠告。夫吾中國數千年之社會。最
重莫血統。最要莫嗣續。如有絕嗣者。則裁宗枝以繼續之。
猶不失爲一脈相傳也。今吾四邑人之育螟蛉者。忘本背祖。
購取異族兒童。以亂其宗祧。何不盡指全世界人之子。妄稱
己子乎。

104　原文倒作「康尙」。今正。
105　原文「躁」字結構左右相反。今正。

What is more, silly women especially choose boys who are fully grown for sons, so as to fulfill their desire to take in a daughter-in-law early, and so, incredibly, make of themselves and their husbands parents-in-law who are neither deaf nor barmy.[223] Hah! Having gone through life without the pain and suffering of child-birth, they yet boast to their fellow villagers of unicorn trail and katydid young.[224] One could say they truly achieve what is described by the Kwang Tung proverb *She who bears a son in the morning is a mother-in-law by evening*;[225] but the harm done is beyond what one can bear to state. Orphaned young, the great majority of these adopted children end up seeking a living amongst bands of beggars. With the absence of home education and the lure of bad habits, such an outcome is assured. Where in the world is there an upright warm-blooded male who would willingly call a different man Father and a different woman Mother? At the dire end, they reduce families to bankruptcy and ruin, and bring disgrace to their houses; at the minor end, they thieve and pilfer, abscond and run away from home. The results are no other than these. Occasionally there are those who bring greatness and glory to their villages, but they are the rarest of the rare. If you wish to adopt and raise an unwanted child, you might choose one of tender years from within your own clan, expose him to education in the home, and stimulate his natural filial instincts. Only then will there be hope. If you do not heed my words, regret will come too late."

---

223 This is a re-working of the Chinese saying 不癡不聾不成姑翁 "those neither deaf nor barmy, make not [also do not for] parents-in-law", a rhyming phrase which has the idiomatic sense that at times parents-in-law must feign deafness and dementia so as to give a younger couple the space they need.

224 麟之趾 (or 麟之止) "The Unicorn's Feet/Hooves/Footsteps/Trail" and 螽斯 "The Katydid" (a large green grasshopper with long legs and horns) are both names of songs within *The Odes* that are associated with virtuous and numerous offspring. In the case of the katydid, Chinese lore asserts that each individual gives rise to ninety-nine young in its lifetime, and

尤有無智婦女。尚擇成年之童子。以爲之子。以償其早娶媳
婦之願望。居然成爲不癡不聾之翁姑。嘻。半生無坼副[106]之
苦痛。反以螽斯麟趾。誇耀於鄉鄰。粵諺云。朝生子。晚作
姑。計誠得矣。其禍害豈勝忍言哉。夫螟蛉子者。少失怙
恃。在乞兒隊裏求生活者。居大多數。無家庭之教育。有惡
習之引誘。可斷然矣。世豈有血性男子。而肯謂他人父。謂
他人母耶。故大則傾家蕩產。牆茨貽臭。小則鼠竊狗偷。奔
匿逃亡。其結果不過如是也。間亦有光大門閭者。然而碩果
僅存矣。君如欲養螟蛉。可在本族中。擇一年齡幼稚者育
之。施以家庭之教育。感發其父子之天性。方有期望。若不
聽吾言。則悔無及矣。

---

106 按，「坼」字誤，當作「坼」或「㘽」等。坼，裂也。國音撤，粵音
策。「副」字正，古作「疈」。謂剖。讀若偏僻之僻。坼副，指孕婦難
產，裂身割身而後能產是也。如《史記·夏本紀》〈正義〉引《蜀王本
紀》曰「禹母吞珠孕禹，坼副而生」，言言禹母之坼疈而生大禹也。
如《詩·大雅·生民》曰「誕彌厥月，先生如達。不坼不疈，無菑無
害」，言薑嫄生后稷之易。

---

the song which concerns it ascribes virtuous qualities to that progeny,
such as harmoniousness. In the case of the unicorn, Chinese mythology
holds that it is a benevolent creature (it does not crush other creatures
beneath its hooves when it walks, and has a flesh-tipped horn that
causes it pain if used), and one traditional interpretation of the symbolic
meaning of its 趾 "feet/hooves/footprints/trail" in the aforementioned
song is *the offspring of a benevolent person.*

225 The words morning and evening in the proverb refer to the morning
and evening of a woman's life.

Ching Nam's argument left Sheung Hong fearful to the point that his hairs were standing on end, and he immediately sent the old woman away. Ching Nam then added, "In coming here I had an important matter to discuss with you."

"What matter is that?" enquired Sheung Hong.

"I am to open a cloth and grocery shop in the Pak Hap[226] market with a man named Tam,"[227] said Ching Nam. "There are ten shares in all. I hold four. What would you say to you and Tam each holding a half of the remaining six?"

"How much would be required in funds?" asked Sheung Hong.

"Around a thousand taels," replied Ching Nam.

"What can be done though if my pockets are empty?" asked Sheung Hong.

"That is no impediment," replied Ching Nam, "I shall borrow at first to establish it."

"Very well then," agreed Sheung Hong. The two of them then discussed the finer details, and when all was resolved, Ching Nam rose and excused himself. Sheung Hong walked with him out of the village. Then they shook hands and parted. (§27, 15/1/1910)

Several months later, the shop in Pak Hap opened under the name Yee Loong, with Tam charged to act as its manager. Ching Nam had met Tam in Australia and knew him to be honest and

---

226 "Pak Hap" is a riverside market town in the district of cº. Hoi Ping, which faces Centipede Hill (yet to appear in the story) from the other side of the 潭 江 Mᴹ. *Tánjiāng* river. In Australia's early Chinese-language newspapers and in the novel, its name was written interchangeably as either 北合 or the now-standard 百合, both renderings sharing the same pronunciation in the See Yip language. "Pak Hap" was also, coincidentally, the surname of that distinctively moustachioed white Australian and active member of the Chinese-Australian community Senator Bakhap, a Commonwealth parliamentarian from Tasmania who was raised by a Chinese stepfather, spoke the See Yip language, and who was—at least by 1918—known to our author (according to reports in Australia's Chinese-language newspapers). See http://biography.senate.gov.au/thomas-jerome-kingston-bakhap

程南一番議論。說得尚康毛骨悚然。即遣老嫗他去。程南復
曰。弟此來有一要事。與君相商。尚康曰。何事。程南曰。
吾與譚某在北合市場。開設一商店。專售雜貨布疋。共十
股。弟認四股。餘六股。君與譚某各認其半。若何。康曰。
需基本金幾何。程曰。約千金。康曰吾囊已罄奈何。程南
曰。無傷。吾先假資開辦。康曰。可。於是二人妥議。程南
興辭。康送至村外。握手而別 (§27, 15/1/1910) 遲數月。北合之
商店。經已開張。店名怡隆。專託譚某司理店務。程南與譚
某在澳時相結識。知其誠實

---

227 Tam (pronounced *tarm*) is the man's surname. The expression used by the
     author actually equates to "Tam X" or "Tam something", by which it is to be
     understood that Ching Nam has informed Sheung Hong of both the man's
     surname and personal name, but that the personal name has not been made
     known to the reader. This is possible in Literary Chinese because the reader
     implicitly understands that dialogue is not necessarily verbatim and as such
     the author can decide to give the reader the same level or more or less detail
     than is actually contained in a quotation of natural speech. The author uses
     this approach to naming elsewhere too, e.g. in respect of Ma's cousin.

reliable, which is why he had entrusted him with the heavy responsibility. Ching Nam being decent, amiable, and highly regarded by his fellow villagers, and Tam scrupulously proper, the business did exceptionally well.

One day, Ching Nam received a card from Sheung Hong, which he could see was an invitation to a dinner. On closer reading, inside were the words *has the honour to host a ginger banquet on the occasion of his son's first-month birthday.*[228,229] With a look of delight on his face, he realised that Sheung Hong was celebrating the arrival of a son as his first child. So he assembled various items and hurried off to deliver them with his congratulations.

When he reached the village, Ching Nam learned that Sheung Hong had bought a one-year-old boy from nearby to be his son and heir, and that he was nevertheless following the tradition of holding a soup-noodle party after a full month had passed. So neighbours and relatives had all gathered, *the young and the old, the rustic and the ravishing-to-behold,*[230] crowding the house, and leaving behind them a jumbled mess of shoes.[231]

---

228 Chinese boasts a highly sophisticated written etiquette, though nowadays few speakers have much knowledge of it. There is an entire lexicon of elegant literary expressions, and a complex set of prescriptions as to layout and phraseology, that are specific to such things as formal invitation cards. This phrase is written in the parlance appropriate to an invitation of its type.

229 It is a Chinese tradition to celebrate a child's first-month birthday with a banquet. Amongst speakers of Cantonese and the See Yip language this is refered to colloquially as 擺薑酌 "putting on a ginger banquet" and a dish of ginger and pork knuckles stewed in sweet vinegar is an essential feature.

230 This (老的少的村的俏的) is a quotation from the celebrated Chinese play 西廂記 *The Story of the Western Wing* (also known as the *Romance of the Western Chamber*). Literally translated, the words form the seemingly plain and unmemorable phrase "the old and the young, the rustic and the pretty". But in this phrase, as is often the case with language, it is not the exact sentiment that is important so much as the way in which it is expressed, i.e.

可靠。故委以重任。程南忠厚和藹。爲鄉鄰所信重。而譚某
又復謹愿。故商業異常發達。一日程南接一柬。知是尙康邀
飲者。細閱之。內有小兒彌月。寅具薑酌字樣。方知尙康有
一索得男之慶。爲之喜色。備物走賀。及抵里。始悉他在近
处買一週歲之兒。以爲子嗣。尙康亦依俗例於彌月之後。開
湯餅之會。故戚里咸集。履舄交錯。老的少的村的俏的。擠
擁滿室。

---

the rhetoric: The rhetorical punch in Chinese comes from the fact that the
words 村 "rustic" and 俏 "pretty" alliterate, and the words 少 "young" and
俏 "pretty" rhyme. An attempt has been made at preserving these rhetorical
features in translation, through the change of "the pretty" to "the ravishing-
to-behold" and "the old and the young" to "the young and the old": "rustic"
and "ravishing" alliterate, "old" and "behold" rhyme. The result is the
euphonius "the young and the old, the rustic and the ravishing-to-behold",
as opposed to the pedestrian "the old and the young, the rustic and the
pretty", which fails to reflect the original's rhetoric.

231 The "jumbled mess of shoes" is a Chinese idiom that connotes a scene of
revelry and the loss of decorum.

Shortly, with the clattering of cups and bowls, an assortment of viands was laid out. High in the precedence, hosts and guests attempted to give away their seats, pulling at sleeves and grabbing at garment fronts in like manner to officers making arrests; while low in the precedence, village children vying for seats almost came to blows.[232] Shortly, the sounds of soup being sipped and bones being chewed; of people playing *chai mui*[233] and draining their cups; of people forcing others to imbibe and of wine[234] flowing like water formed into a tremendous racket, and the scene turned to one of exceptional liveliness. Ching Nam did his best to join in with the group; after a time, though, his back drenched in sweat from the strain, he had to escape the drinking and go for some tea. A little while later, the dinner came to an end.

Local custom required the new mother to hold her infant before the guests, and for them to give *lai see*[235] for the benefit of his good fortune and long life, and to deliver their good wishes. Ching Nam filed forward with the group, and, inspecting the little child, found that he was already *gaga*-ing and on the verge of speech.

"What has he been named?" he asked Sheung Hong.

"Kam Ngau," replied Sheung Hong.[236]

"This boy's features do have a rough bovine look about them, a perfect match for his name," said Ching Nam by way of hidden mockery; following which he forced out a few perfunctory remarks, nothing other than such things as how the boy might one day succeed in shouldering the affairs of the family, and how he might one day surpass his father.

---

232 In other words, those banqueters seated higher in the precedence were attempting to convey respect by forcibly exchanging places with those seated lower down, the latter resisting pugnaciously out of similarly self-deprecatory motives.

233 *Chai mui* is a Chinese finger-guessing game in which drinking serves as a forfeit. The game of rock-paper-scissors is an equivalent with which many Western readers would be familiar, though *chai mui*, in its traditional forms, is far more complex, and bears a strong resemblance to the Western game of morra.

俄而餚饌紛陳。杯盤撞擊。上席主客。推讓座位。而牽袖捉
襟。有如差役拿人。而下席村童互相爭座。幾致用武。俄而
嗑湯聲。嚼骨聲。豁拳聲。乾杯聲。強迫飲酒聲。卮盞淋漓
聲。喧譁震天。異常[107]熱鬧。程南隨衆人竭力應酬一番。已
是汗流浹背。不得已逃席飲茶。逾時席終。鄉例初生娘抱嬰
兒於賓客前。衆賓客以利市增福壽。并致祝詞。程南亦隨衆
挨次而進。審視小孩。已牙牙學語矣。問尙康曰。是何命
名。康曰。名金牛。程南暗哂之曰。此兒骨相粗呆。恰與命
名相肖。故勉強敷衍幾句。總不外他日如何克家。如何跨灶
等語。

107　「異常」原誤倒作「常異」。今正。

234　Chinese wine, not fermented grape juice.

235　Gifts of money in paper envelopes, which are generally auspiciously coloured
　　　and decorated.

236　金牛 "Kam Ngau" translates directly as "Metal/Gold(en) Ox". The author might be
　　　implying with this name that the boy was born in the Chinese year of the metal/
　　　golden ox (the second of the sexagenary cycle), which in the period in question would
　　　have been the one that started in early 1865 and ended in early 1866.

All the guests then dispersed in a twinkling.

"My plan is to sort out my home affairs and return to Australia within a month," said Ching Nam. "What do you think?"

"If you are returning to Australia," said Sheung Hong, "I should like to follow along. Though I am not sure whether or not you would be willing to take me?"

"Of course I would be willing," replied Ching Nam, "but you would need to put your family affairs in order beforehand, so as not to cause any delay come time of departure."

Sheung Hong agreed, and then asked, "What of the business of the Yee Loong shop?"

"I have a thorough plan for the Yee Loong shop," replied Ching Nam. "My suggestion is that we charge Tam to run it. Furthermore, I suggest that it would be a great comfort to us while we are overseas if Tam could take care of all our women and little ones on our behalf, as otherwise they would be without anyone to look after them and we most uneasy at heart. We would bear all responsibility for additional injections of capital into the shop and for its support of our families.[237] What do you think?"

"So be it," responded Sheung Hong.

That settled, the two of them further agreed to set off in the first decade[238] of the next month. Ching Nam then headed back home.

When the appointed time arrived, they had their travelling bags fully prepared, and the familiar path making the journey light, the last trip was no parallel.

---

237 Monetary and/or material support.

238 Traditionally, the Chinese month was broken into thirds called 旬 cᴹ. chèuhn "decades". This unit once played a similar role in China to the *week* in Europe. The first decade ended on the tenth of the month, the second on the twentieth and the third on the twenty-ninth or thirtieth, depending on whether the month was long or short.

轉瞬諸客星散。程南曰。予拚擋家事後。擬於月內返澳。君意云何。康曰。如君返澳。弟願附驥。未審肯提挈否。程曰。有何不願。但吾兄家政預爲整頓。勿致臨期延悞爲要。康應之。復曰怡隆店務。何如。程南曰。怡隆[108]一店。余已籌之熟矣。鄙意欲專託譚君掌理。況吾等出洋。婦女小弱。無人照料。心甚不安。如得譚代爲照拂一切。至爲慰藉。若本店接濟附充[109,110]一層。統歸余等担任。君意以爲如何。康曰。唯。於是兩人復約定動程之日期。在下月初旬。程南方歸。屆期兩人預將行囊檢点完備。此同駕輕就熟。非前次之可比。

108 「怡隆」原誤倒作「隆怡」。今正。

109 「附充」原誤倒作「充附」。今正。

110 按，凡商業經營中，有股東附投新銀數，以充填本銀之不足，舊謂之「附充」。欲審其用法，可搜奧洲國立圖書館之Trove網站，參考《廣益華報》西曆千八百九十五年一月五號刊第七頁〈銀行附充〉一則，及該報與他報別錄。

Cradling Kam Ngau, Ma had said to Sheung Hong, "You, Daddy (a customary expression in Kwang Tung by which a wife with a son may address her husband), have today a very different family from before. Even if you will not think of me, you must think of this little baby." Reaching that point, weeping, she had covered her face with her hands, unable to look up.

Ma's emotions on separating had been especially painful, [beyond] what the pen can describe. Alas! How is a person to feel when faced in life with the prospect of prolonged separation and indefinite return, for the second or third time over?

Ching Nam and Sheung Hong had made a wistful departure, taken a boat to Hong Kong, and then boarded a new Taikoo-company steamer.[239] Once at sea, the toots of the horn and the clacking of the engine the only sounds to be heard, they traversed a thousand miles of boundless sunlit ocean in the blink of an eye. And in fewer than twenty-or-so days they arrived safely in Melbourne. (§28, 22/1/1910)

After their arrival in Melbourne, Sheung Hong put up at China Street's San Sui Shing, a store that formed part of Ching Nam's assets;[240] while Ching Nam went about on his own, checking on his businesses, and before long, headed off to Ballarat to inspect his gold mine. Then, seeing that all his businesses had shown improvement and that the employees who had been acting for him had been exceptionally industrious, Ching Nam rewarded all for their efforts. Seeing as he had returned, the store staff promptly passed the stores back into Ching Nam's charge; and after they had been handed back, Ching Nam worked hard to expand them. He also purchased a mining site on Ballarat

---

239 太古 Taikoo is the Chinese equivalent to "Swire" common to the Chinese names of firms in the Swire group, ever since the establishment of Butterfield & Swire in 1866.

240 The word translated here as *assets* is generally translated today as *capital*, and this was a sense it already possessed at the time the novel was written.

斯時馬氏抱金牛。謂尚康曰。汝阿爸（粵俗有子之婦呼夫之
語）今日之室家。與前日大異。君縱不念妾。要念此呱呱
者。語至此。已掩泣不能仰。此際馬氏之離情別緒。非常慘
痛。筆難[111]描述。噫。人生離別。至再至三。而歸期又遙遙
無定。當斯境者。其何以爲情也。程尚二人。悵然出門。附
舟抵港。卽搭太古公司之新輪船。放洋後。但聞汽笛嗚嗚。
機聲軋軋。萬頃晴[112]波。瞬息千里。不銷二十餘天。已安抵
美利畔矣。(§28, 22/1/1910) 程南與尚康旣抵美利伴後。尚康暫
住釵拿街之新瑞勝。此店亦屬程南貲本。程南獨自調查所屬
之商業。旋往孖罅辣檢驗金礦。見各商業。俱有起色。署理
夥計。異常勤奮。程南獎勞一番。各店伴見程南復囘。卽將
各商業退囘程南掌理。故交代之後。程南極力擴張。又在孖
罅辣購得礦地一所。

---

111 原文「難」字本殘缺不清。今據其殘跡與文義擬正。
112 原文作「晴」，爲「晴」字之誤也。今正。

that had very rich gold veins; and furthermore, with a Chan and a Wong, he opened a shop on Little Bourke Street, which dealt in comestible Chinese medicines and was called San Yuen Shing.

Aware that he had reaped quite handsome profits and that Sheung Hong was still without any occupation, Ching Nam looked over his stores for him, but there was no fitting position. So he established a carpentry workshop especially, which he named Tak Yuen, and [appointed Sheung Hong] to manage. This was a shop close to Little Bourke Street that made Western furniture, tables and chairs, sold widely, and reaped very handsome profits.

Ere long, time's stallion speeded on, and in the blink of an eye another six years passed by. Ching Nam wanted to grow old carefree, amongst the woods and springs of his old country.[241] So he checked over each of his businesses, installed people to manage them, and then boarded a steamer back to China.

The Tak Yuen shop had been fully entrusted to Sheung Hong's control, and a year later, Sheung Hong was unequivocally living the life of a lord.

Meanwhile, in a village in China, several unruly children had gathered by an earth-god shrine, and were getting up to all sorts of mischief. A woman, her dress of coarse cloth, her hairpin of bramble, a bamboo pole in her hands, was trying to drive her son off to school; her boy being the one who, unwilling to make for the schoolhouse, was yelling insults and charmingly crying. Huh! Who was this woman? She was Sheung Hong's wife. And who was this boy? He was Sheung Hong's son, Kam Ngau.

Six months after parting from her husband, Ma had given birth to a daughter. The apple of her eye, Ma's elation and relief had been exceptional, and she had immediately sent off a letter

---

241 This phrase is a reworking of a set literary expression for retirement.

金苗暢旺。復與陳某黃某等在小博街開設一商店。曰新源勝。專辦中國食用藥品。程南自覺獲利稍豐。而尚康尚賦閒在此。迴顧各店。又無相當之位置。於是特開辦一木廠。名曰德元。使[113]尚康[114]司理。該店在小博街附近。專造西人傢私椅桌。銷售甚廣。獲利極豐。無何駒光迅逝。轉瞬[115]又是六年。程南欲養老林泉。優游故國。於是点查商業。命人紀理。故卽附輪囘國。而德元一店。專委尚康掌握。逾年。尚康儼然稱素封矣。惟時支那之村落。有三五頑童。團聚社前。作諸種之惡戲。有一婦布裙荊釵。手持竹竿。驅兒返學。該童嬌啼詬罵。不肯就塾者。嘻婦何人。尚康之妻也。此兒何人。尚康之子金牛也。馬氏自別夫而後。越六月而產一女。歡慰異常。視若拱璧。卽馳函

113　原文「使」字甚為模糊。今因單人旁可辨，而形頗似「使」，擬正。
114　「尚康」原誤倒作「康尚」。今正。
115　「轉瞬」原誤倒作「瞬轉」。今正。

informing Sheung Hong of the news. However, unforeseeably, after several months the child died. Unbearably grief-stricken, Ma had depended from dawn to dusk, to pass the time and to dispel her melancholy, on Kam Ngau alone. In such a fashion, the days had turned to months and the months had passed by. This year he was already seven,[242] and studying under the village primary teacher. But he was exceptionally dull and frequently skipped school. Today he was again playing at truant, and at pranks, with the other boys. His mother had seen him and had wanted to drive him off to school, but seeing him charmingly crying, she could not bear to be too forceful.

Alas, our country's women are ignorant and silly, no different to the savages of the various islands. How, on deduction, might a country produce good people when there is no education in the home, only the selfish love of a parent for its young? Her husband at a far corner of the earth and her chamber still, all Ma knew to do was to depend on this unruly son to survive.

Sojourning in Australia, Sheung Hong's circumstances grew ever more affluent, and his carnal desires ever more intense. Indeed, coverlets cold in still of night, no stranger in this land could be free from an ill sensation of forlornness. Furthermore, within the public gardens and the playhouses were all the Western men and women in gay attire, their arms interlinked and heads together, like pairs of love birds, their deep and sincere affection meeting a person's vision, and their soft chatter prickling his ear drums. Men are not made of wood: how can they forget love? In such a setting even a man of iron or stone would be moved.

---

242 Six years old by the Western reckoning.

報告尚康。不期數月而殤。馬氏哀痛欲絕。所藉以度晨昏。
解積悶者。惟金牛而矣。而日居月諸。今年已七齡。就學於
本村之蒙師。然異常頑鈍。屢次逃學。今日又是私逃。與羣
兒惡作劇。其母見之。欲驅而就學。見他嬌啼。又不忍過爲
強迫。噫。吾國婦女。不學無智。與各島之土蠻無異。無家
庭之教育。祇有舐犢之私愛。推其結果。焉有良善之國民
乎。馬氏與其夫地角天涯。房幃寂靜。祇知與此頑兒相依爲
命而已。尚康寄旅澳洲。囊橐日益充裕。肉慾日益增加。而
況作客他鄉。夜靜衾寒。不無凄清之惡感。加以公園之內。
劇塲之中。西人之紅男綠女。莫不交臂並頭。如比翼之鳥。
故深情欵欵。觸我眼簾。細語喁喁。刺吾耳鼓。人非草木。
豈能忘情。此間縱是鐵石人。亦生感觸。

How could Sheung Hong, being, moreover, of Têng T'u Tzǔ's ilk, be indifferent?[243] So his fervor for taking a concubine grew ever more inflated.

He thought to himself *Amongst the powdered and rouged there is no shortage of swollen-breasted, slender-waisted[244] Western Venuses.[245] Yet people of different races are wont to mistrust one another, which would indeed make for difficulty. And even if this would not bother some, with the Western system of monogamy, it would be highly unlikely that one would esteem me and accede. Easiest of all would be to take a woman of the shameful profession, but they live on beer and are also unbearably dirty.* His thoughts wild with infatuation, Sheung Hong slept uneasily. (§29, 29/1/1910)

Happenstance had it that a certain Kung Lok was chatting one day with Wong of Yuen Shing.[246] The former was, like Sheung Hong, a man of Llin Nen,[247] one who had gone overseas in his youth, and had been sojourning in Australia for over twenty years. Now over forty years of age, he had some savings, but had not yet married.[248]

243　登徒 M°. Têng-t'u is a disyllabic surname and 子 Tzǔ an archaic title. The person referred to as 登徒子 Têng-t'u Tzǔ was a man of the third century B.C.E. whose name has, perhaps unfairly, become synonymous with the word *lecher*.

244　The Chinese expression translated here as *slender-waisted* (蜂腰) literally means "wasp-waisted". It is not translated as such because the English expression wasp-waisted was and is generally used only to describe clothing, or waists that are extremely thin as a result of tightly laced clothing, whereas in Chinese, the expression simply means slender-waisted. The Victorian women so described would no doubt have been corseted and wasp-wasted.

245　The word "Venus" here is a translation of the name of a Chinese beauty of antiquity whose name is synonymous with beauty, as is the name of the goddess Venus in English.

246　Yuen Shing is presumably a contraction of the business name San Yuen Shing referred to in the previous instalment, and Wong the surname of the business partner mentioned in connection therewith. (Note that the protagonist Wong Sheung Hong shares the same surname.)

何況尙康乃登徒子之流。豈能恝然。於是娶妾之熱度。日益
膨脹。自念粉白脂紅。不少鼓乳蜂腰之西子。[116] 而非類相
猜。實生阻力。縱有等不以此爲介介。而西人一夫☐[117]妻之
制。斷難隆心而從我。最易者莫如醜業婦。但日以啤酒爲
命。其齷齪又是不堪。尙康妄念痴心。睡[118]不貼席。(§29,
29/1/1910) 適有龔洛者。亦甯人。年少出洋。旅澳卅餘載。時
已年逾不惑矣。稍有蓄積。而未有室家。壹日與源勝之黃某
談。

116　「西子」一語，兼含兩義：一則西施之流；一則西洋女子。有鑒於是，故
　　　譯如左，以並達之。
117　原文「一」字全闕。今因所屬之詞語分明擬補。
118　原文睡字顚倒。今正。

247　A native of the district of s. Llin Nen, like protagonist Wong Sheung Hong.
248　The Chinese does not express the sense of *over forty years of age* through the
　　　use of a number, but rather through the phrase 年逾不惑 "past the age of
　　　delusion". This is a reference to a passage in 論語 "*The Confucian Analects*",
　　　in which Confucius states that by forty he was no longer deluded. Similarly,
　　　the sense of *fifty* in the next line is expressed through the use of a term with
　　　this significance that appears in the ancient 易經 *Book of Changes*. This
　　　instalment is liberally peppered with such literary references, many of which
　　　would require lengthy explanation and cannot therefore all be footnoted.
　　　The translation is consequently a somewhat paler version of the original.

"You are approaching fifty, sir, yet still want for a wife,[249] to say nothing of offspring," said Wong.

"I have long wanted to find a woman and thus fulfill my heart's desire," replied Kung. "But living overseas it is very hard to find one who is suitable."

"Tell me sir, what type of woman is it that would suit your liking?" asked Wong.

"Who knows how many of our countrymen residing overseas have married Western women," replied Kung. "In my humble opinion, though, it is at heart a source of displeasure for them. Why? Upper-class Western women are constrained by racial boundaries, and would almost never lower themselves to accede to intermarriage. Harlots from the lower class, one would not wish to marry. And while those of the middle class do occasionally marry, they are as rare as morning stars.[250] If men should come by them, though, they show in the end too exalted a sense of feminism, and no sense of frugality, so scarcely any such couples keep by each other into their white-haired years. As to the daughters of Chinese fathers and Western mothers, in the extravagance to which they are accustomed to aspire, and their unbridled feminism, they do not fall short of Westerners, but tend rather to exceed them. However, they lack the comprehensive education[251] of the Westerners, and the subservient nature of the Chinese. And their barbarous liberty is not dissimilar to that of the so-called women of liberty[252] in China today.[253]

---

249 The sense of "still wants for a wife" is expressed here through the use of a classical idiom, which carries certain overtones. The idiom (中饋猶虛), which is based on a passage in the *Book of Changes*, implies that a wife's role should be limited to the provision of food for the sustenance of those in the home and ancestral and other spirits.

250 寥如晨星 "as rare as morning stars" is a Chinese saying.

251 完全之教育 "Comprehensive Education" was an educational approach promoted by prominent Mᵒ. late-Ch'ing intellectual and educational theorist 王國維 Wang Kuo-wei (Mᴹ. *Wáng Guówéi*). Strongly influenced by Western educational theory and philosophy, the system consisted of an integrated tripartite approach to education, through 智育 "intellectual

黃曰。子年將大衍。而中饋尚虛。其如後嗣何。龔曰。余久
欲物色壹婦。以了宿願。但處外洋地方。甚難中選耳。黃
曰。君以爲何等人。方適君意。試言之。龔曰。吾國人僑居
外洋。與西婦結婚者。亦不知凡幾。據僕鄙意。心滋不悅。
何則。西人上流婦女。限於種界。決難降格相從。而下流娼[119]
妓。我又不願就。而中流者間或亦有。但如晨星之寥寥。苟
得之。究亦女權過尊。不知儉約。白頭相守者無幾人。而華
父西母之女子。其習尚之奢華。與女權之驕泰。較之西人。
有過之無不及。但無西人完全之教育。又無華人服從之性
質。其野蠻之自由。 與中國現今所謂自由女者。大致相類。

119　原文「娼」字全缺。今因「下流娼妓」幾屬成語，非此語則難通，擬補。

education", 德育 "moral education" and 美育 "aesthetic education",
combined with 身體之訓練 "physical training", and was focussed on the
ultimate aim of forming of the student a 完全之人物 "Complete Person"
(the same Chinese word being used for both *comprehensive* and *complete*, its
sense being inclusive).

252　This was the term applied to a new class of women in M°. late-Ch'ing
China, who, under the influence of education and Western ideas, were
challenging widely accepted Confucian ideals of womanhood, by doing such
things as acting assertively in their interactions with men, and insisting on
assessing potential husbands as they saw fit before deciding for themselves
on marriage.

253　The phrase at the beginning of this sentence (其野蠻之自由) might also
have been translated as "their barbarous freedom", which would clearly
sound awkward in English given the words that follow. The reason for this is
that the Chinese word generally taken to be synonymous with the English
word *freedom* (自由) actually differs slightly from it in meaning, because the
Chinese word emphasises the exercise of individual will, whereas the
English word emphasises the absence of restrictions on its exercise. The
word liberty, which carries more of this sense, is thus often a closer match.

I should not have anything to do with them. As to women born here of Chinese parents, they are harshly selective, and conduct themselves with too much superiority. The bare belly of one who asserts to be a wealthy man would be very difficult for someone of my age and means to come to possess.[254] So there are dropped plums that have missed their time,[255] but whose parents, seemingly delusional, still think them rare commodities worth stockpiling.[256] I have wanted to return to China to take a wife, but it takes time to cross the seas. Furthermore, men who live overseas are likely to be unable to stay for long; and if so, must sing a song of parting before the curtained chamber is yet warm. Thus leaving a young woman to live idly in married widowhood. At heart, it would be too much to bear. However, if a Chinese woman was willing to come overseas to marry, even if she were as lowly as a bondmaid,[257] I would willingly wed with her, and should not begrudge a grand sum to do so."

---

254 This sentence relies on an allusion to a well-known anecdote concerning the fourth-century great 王羲之 M°. Wang Hsi-chih (Mᴹ. *Wáng Xīzhī*), a man who might be described as being even more to the art of Chinese calligraphy than Mozart is to Western classical music. The story relates that Wang Hsi-chih's future father-in-law, a man surnamed 郗 Ch'ih, sent a messenger to his father requesting one of his sons for his daughter. Wang's father informed the messenger that all his sons were to be found in the hall's eastern side room, and that he was welcome to view and select any one of them. Having viewed the sons, the messenger reported back to Ch'ih that, on hearing why he had come, all of them had put on airs and graces, with the exception of one who had lain on a daybed eating, with his belly exposed, as if oblivious. Ch'ih exclaimed with confidence that he was the son-in-law he wanted, and after establishing who he was—Wang Hsi-chih—the marriage was brought about. The anecdote is the source of a number of idioms and expressions relating to sons-in-law. Here, the author does not quote any such idiom in full, the reference to the coming into possession of a bare belly being enough to signify entry into the state of being a son-in-law, or a prospective son-in-law. Regrettably, the line is far less elegant, or easy to comprehend, in translation.

僕甚不取也。而華人土生女子。又遴選過苛。自處過高。以
僕之年齡與家資而論。甚難當自稱富翁者之坦腹。故有摽梅
[120]愆期。其父母尤以爲奇貨可居者。不其惑歟。僕屢欲返國
完娶。而跋涉重洋。煞費時[121]日。況且出洋之人。勢難久
居。乃房幃未煖。卽唱驪歌。致使青年婦女。空守有夫之
寡。撫心自問。情何以堪。如有中國女子。肯到外洋就婚
者。雖婢女之賤。僕願與之締婚。雖千金不靳也。

120 「摽梅」之「摽」，原文作「標」。蓋手民之誤也。今正。
121 原文「時」字殘損。審之，字之殘跡似「時」，而文句似當作「煞費時
    日」。今據正。

---

255 The expression 摽梅 "dropped plums" has its origin in *The Odes* and means
    women of a marriageable age. The expression that follows, 愆期, translated
    here as "that have missed their time", is used in both *The Odes* and the *Book
    of Changes* in respect of women missing the time for marriage.

256 奇貨可居 "a rare commodity worth stockpiling" is a common classical idiom.

257 婢 "bondmaids" are described in the following passage from sinologist
    Herbert Giles's 1900 *Glossary of Reference on Subjects Connected with the Far
    East:* "Slavery in China is now chiefly confined to the purchase of girls for
    use as servants in large establishments. These girls are on the whole well
    treated; and when they reach a marriageable age, their owners are bound by
    custom to see that they are suitably married and started in life on their own
    account." They were known colloquially in Cantonese and the See Yip
    language as 妹仔, which is generally transliterated according to its
    Cantonese pronunciation as *Mui Tsai*, and is a term that would still be
    familiar to most Cantonese and See Yip speakers.

On hearing this, Wong slapped the table and rose to his feet. "If so, this matter can be concluded happily!" he exclaimed.

"What do you mean?" asked Kung.

"I have a bondmaid, a most clever and pretty one, who has come of age and is now awaiting a match. If you wish sir, I could write to my cousin and instruct him to bring her over with him, so that she can be married to you.[258] What do you say?"

"Fairness of face is not important to me," said Kung. "I would only ask you as to what her character is like."

"She has a most refined and virtuous nature," replied Wong.

"I love our country's women for no other reason than that I value their subservience," said Kung. "If her disposition is indeed refined and virtuous, what more could I require of her?"

So they fixed a price for her and parted. (§30, 26/2/1910)

Ere long, time's stallion speeding on, the great formic mill turned about its axis,[259] and in a twinkling, several months passed by. And within this period[260] Wong did indeed write to his family, directing them to ask the bondmaid whether or not she was willing.

The bondmaid's name was Tsiu Hei, and while in fact of middling looks, she was endowed with the nature of a seductress, and given to behave with abandon.

She had, below the end of her left eyebrow, a little wrinkle, and when she smiled a dimple would appear on each of her cheeks.

---

258 The translation "be married to you" is a simplification of the actual phrase used (諧花燭), in which, by metonymy, the name for the ornately decorated candles that light the traditional Chinese wedding chamber form a substitute for the word marriage. This, like the expression "to walk down the aisle" in English, serves the rhetorical purpose of representing the whole act of marriage through reference to a single vivid aspect of it.

259 One theory of old Chinese astronomy held that the heavens move westward and the sun and moon eastward, but that because the heavens move faster, the sun and moon appear also to move westward. This was analogised to an ant walking on a hand mill: the hand mill is turned in one direction and the ant

黃某聞之。拍案而起曰。果如此。事可諧矣。龔曰。何謂。
黃欣然曰。吾有壹婢。甚秀慧。年及笄。正待擇人。君如有
意。弟即函囑吾族弟。挈之同來。與君諧花燭。如何。龔
曰。吾不重妍媸。但問其德性如何耳。黃曰。性甚嫻淑。龔
曰。吾之所以愛吾國婦女者。重其馴服耳。果若品性嫻淑。
我又何擇焉。於是訂明身價若干而別。(§30, 26/2/1910) 無何駒
光迅速。蟻磨[122]如輪。轉瞬已閱數月矣。黃某果函囑其家
人。問該婢願意否。婢名俏喜。貌本中姿。然賦性妖冶。舉
止輕狂。左目眉梢下有壹小痕。笑時兩頰露二酒窩。

122　原文「磨」字模糊不清。今據其墨跡與文義擬正。

walks in the other, but because the mill turns faster, the ant moves with it. In Literary Chinese, the words *sun* and *moon* being the same as the words for *day(s)* and *month(s)*, their ant-on-a-mill movement—which might be described in English as one that involves swimming against the tide—symbolises the passing of time. Here the author uses one of a number of literary expressions that are based on this analogy. Note: *formic* is a rarely used adjective for *ant*.

260　This phrase does not appear in the Chinese text, but is necessary in translation if the sense of implicit temporality is not to be lost.

Slender, shapely, willow-waisted, pretty of face and graceful of form, she would often strike coquettish poses and regard her figure admiringly. Now of eighteen summers,[261] Tsiu Hei counted petals[262] and supplicated the moon,[263] thoughts of romance ever on her mind. Yet when holding up her mirror or refreshing her perfume, she would often feel sullen regret for her lack of liberty, and inability to realise her heart's desires.

Chan was her family name. Wong had purchased her when she was little to act as his mother's personal maid. But Tsiu Hei's parents had by now passed away. So in the matter of choosing her a spouse, her master was entirely free to act.

Having received his letter, Wong's wife called Tsiu Hei to her and [said],[264] "Come forward. I have some exceedingly good news for you."

"Your maid is lowly, what good news could there be for her?" [asked] Tsiu Hei. "May I trouble madam to relate it? Or might it rather be that madam is teasing her maid?"

"No," responded Wong's wife. "Your master sent back a letter the other day, saying that he wishes to wed you to a rich man and for you to go to Australia soon to be married. Are you willing?"

"Madam is most fond of jesting," said Tsiu Hei. "She often plays games with her maid ..."

---

261 Seventeen years of age by the Western reckoning.

262 The counting of flower petals was a form of romantic augury, which might be likened to the European game of *he loves me, he loves me not*; plucking, however, was not necessarily involved.

263 Like the practice of praying on the seventh day of the seventh month for deftness of hand in needlework, moon worship was engaged in by young women who hoped to secure a fine match in life.

264 There would appear to be a misprint in the original text: the character for "asked" appears here, when it would seem rather to belong with Tsiu Hei's question immediately below. The translation has been adjusted accordingly, with the changes highlighted in square brackets.

柳腰苗條。花容孃娜。時常搔首弄姿。顧影自憐[123]此時俏喜韶
華已逾二九。故卜花拜月。盡屬懷春。把鏡添香。時常惜恨。
無奈身不自由。不能償其宿願而矣。其母家陳姓。黃某自小購
來。爲其母侍婢。俏喜之父母。時已亡過。所以擇配之事。其
主人儘能自由舉動。黃某之妻。自領函之後。即呼俏喜問[124]
曰。汝來前。吾有一極好消息報汝。俏喜曰。婢子賤人。有何
好消息。煩夫人報。[125] 夫人得毋捉弄婢子耶。黃妻曰。否。汝
主人昨付囘一函。云欲將汝配壹富人。不日到澳洲結婚。汝願
意否。 俏喜曰。夫人大好諧語。常以婢子爲戲。

123　此語原作「願影自憐」。「願」蓋即「顧」之訛。今正。
124　「問」字與文意悖。疑爲刊誤，本應植下文「曰」字之前。
125　原文疑脫一句號。今擬補。

"No," replied Wong's wife sternly. "This is no game. It is the matter of your lifelong commitment. You had best tell me directly whether or not you are willing."

On hearing this, Tsiu Hei answered unabashedly, "So, my master has given consideration to this matter: I had thought your maid would wait lifelong on madam. But being mean-fated and unlikely to wed a rich man, it would have been enough for your maid were her master willing to take pity and select for her some melon seller or vegetable peddler. As to marriage in Australia, if her master so orders, though it is the end of the earth, your maid would not dare refuse."

Seeing that she had given her nod of acceptance, Wong's wife wrote in reply to her husband, and a month later a local named Song Tak was charged with the task of taking Tsiu Hei across with him. At that time, though, under English law, only married couples were permitted to land. So when they went to the shipping firm to purchase tickets, the two of them concerted to attest that they were husband and wife. Thus, when they boarded the steamer, its kitchen staff, passengers and crew all took them to be a real married couple in the full sense. Furthermore, Song Tak, not leaving her side, affected an interest in associating with her. He a Têng-t'u,[265] she a trollop, the two exchanged affectionate [glances], and in the space of the first few days, performed the conjugal act. Joined as harmoniously as are fish to water, twenty-or-so days of fine time under a calm sea breeze came and went, alas, as quickly as a spark off a flint. Ere long, a blast from the ship's horn signalled its arrival in Melbourne, and a pair of new acquaintances felt only regret for the speed of the voyage.

When he received a letter of reply from his wife stating on which boat Tsiu Hei would be coming, Wong immediately advised Kung Lok. Overjoyed, Kung Lok at once rented out a golden house

---

265 A lecher: see footnote 243.

黃妻正色曰。否。此非戲言。乃你終身事。願意與否。不妨
值告。俏喜聞言。并不羞澀答曰。主人亦計及此事耶。吾以
婢子終身侍老夫人矣。婢子命薄。難配富人。主人果肯憐
儂。爲婢子擇一販瓜挑菜者。於願已足。若從婚澳洲一層。
主人有命。雖天涯海角。婢子亦不敢辭。黃妻見他首肯[126]。
即函覆其夫。逾月。卽托其同鄉人爽德者。挈之同行。斯時
英例非夫婦不准登岸。是以往船行購票。二人約定口供。認
爲夫婦。故登輪以後。船中廚役與搭客等。俱認他爲眞夫
妻。無猜無忌。爽德又假意周旋。不離左右。此是登徒。彼
屬蕩婦。眉目[127]傳情。不一二日間已實行其夫婦之事矣。噫
嘻。魚水和諧。海風平靖。二十餘天之好時光。迅如石火。
無何一聲汽笛。已到美利伴矣。一對新相知。反恨舟行之迅
速。黃某得其妻覆函。云俏喜搭某船前來。卽刻知會龔洛。
龔洛喜不自勝。卽租一金屋。

126　原文「肯」字之上端殘損。今據其下部與文義擬正。
127　此字殘甚。今據其殘跡與文義擬補。

in which to keep his A-chiao,[266] before making every arrangement for the wedding proceedings, as well as procuring a ring, adornments, utensils, furniture and all the other appropriate items. The newspapers he bought and read regularly, surveying them for the time at which the steamer was to dock, so that he could prepare his bride's welcome. In the few days leading up to the steamer's arrival, Kung Lok neither slept nor ate. The days passed for him like years, and it was with no little difficulty that he lasted till the one in question.

Kung Lok had hired a Chinese servant woman to act as his bride's chaperone (what in Kwang Tung is referred to colloquially as a *bride-woman*). This Chinese woman was named Lin Neung, and while a Hsü Niang past her prime,[267] she was nonetheless silver-tongued, worldly and highly personable.

He had also hired two carriages: one for himself and Wong to take, the other reserved to seat his bride, accompanied and attended to by Lin Neung.

Being the groom, Kung Lok had naturally polished himself up, taking his snake-bean-length[268] pig tail[269] and coiling it atop his crown, placing a new felt hat upon his head, and changing into a suit of new Western clothes.

So it was that he went proudly off to the dock to receive his bride. And when there, looking out at the steamer approaching the shore, he danced about in a state of mad delight.

---

266 These are literary references to a story about the 漢 Mᴼ. Han dynasty's 武帝 Emperor Wu, who is said to have been asked as a child on his aunt's lap whom he would like to marry, and to have responded that he would like to marry her daughter, whose pet name was *A-chiao*, and to build a golden house to keep her in. The story is the source of the idiom 金屋貯嬌 "to keep Chiao in a golden house", the golden house meaning a resplendent house and Chiao meaning a beauty—that being the name "Chiao's" actual meaning—and the whole phrase taking on the sense of taking a wife or a concubine, or building or decking out a house for one.

爲貯阿嬌之所。所有一切結婚之儀式。與及傢私器皿釵釧約指
等項。置備妥當。時常購閱報章。查探某輪泊岸之期。以爲歡
迎新娘之準備。將泊輪之前數日。襲洛寢食都廢。度日如年。
好容易方捱至是日。隨即催一華人僕婦。爲攙扶[128]新娘之用。
（粵俗名衿姨）該華婦名練娘。雖徐娘半老。而口角慧利。態
度風流。最可人意。又催馬車二輪。自與黃某乘一輛。留一輛
坐新娘。使練娘陪侍。襲洛身爲新郎。自然修飾[129]壹番。即將
長如荳角之豚尾。蛇盤頂上。頭戴一新氈帽。換過一套西式新
衣裳。昂然到碼頭迎迓。遙望該輪將次到岸。則喜極若狂。手
舞足蹈。斯時澳洲未禁華人。

128　原文作「抉」，爲「扶」字之訛也。今正。
129　「修飾」原誤倒作「飾修」。今正。

267　See footnote 209.
268　The word used here, 荳角 or 豆角, is the Cantonese and See Yip word for
　　snake bean: in Mandarin the same word simply means *bean*. The proper
　　Chinese name for the snake bean is 長豇豆.
269　*Pig tail* is the derogatory term for the Manchu *queue*, in both Chinese and
　　English.

Australia had at that time not yet restricted the Chinese. So once a ship had dropped its anchor, people could embark and disembark freely. Wong and the others boarded the steamer together and firstly searched out Song Tak. Song Tak led Lin Neung to Tsiu Hei's room; he and Wong then settled the luggage ashore.

Kung Lok was anxious for [a] sight of his bride, [and so] stood leaning at the side of a table, staring intently. Tsiu Hei was also anxious for a sight of her groom, and stole frequent peeks from within her room. Perceiving her intent, Lin Neung pointed out Kung Lok and said, "That is my mistress's husband-to-be." On hearing this, Tsiu Hei fixed her gaze and looked. Presently, her pretty face went red, her shapely brows bristled, and her tears fell down in beads. She rested her head on Lin Neung's shoulder. Then, after a little while, she stamped her foot and angrily exclaimed, "Pah! So that toad dreams of eating swan![270] I swear I would rather die than marry the foreign devil!" Finished, she started to quietly sob. (§31, 5/3/1910)

Lin Neung was uncommonly quick-witted. "Worry not, mistress," she said comfortingly. "In this land there is freedom of marriage. If he does not suit your liking, I would ask you to go to your people: this old handmaid is capable enough of panicking and flustering over it between the parties on her own."[271] This said, she escorted her off to board the carriage.

Kung Lok, having been outside the room, had no idea of the circumstances behind this turn of events. While he had heard

---

270 This is a Chinese idiom used of people who fantasise about possessing someone far above them. It has its origin in the famous Ch'ing-dynasty novel 紅樓夢 the *Dream of the Red Chamber* (A.K.A. 石頭記 *The Story of the Stone*), though the word used for "eating" in that novel is the Peking vernacular 吃, whereas here the more literary 食 is used, this also being the common word in Cantonese and the See Yip language.

271 This is verbal irony. Lin Neung's actual meaning is that she is capable of the opposite of panicking and flustering, i.e. that she is quite capable of managing everything.

船若下錨。即可自由上落。黃某等一齊登輪。先尋着爽德。
爽德即引練娘到俏喜住房。隨即與黃某料理行李上岸。斯時
龔洛急欲□[130]見新娘。姑[131]斜立餐檯之側。目不轉睛。此時
俏喜亦急欲一見新郎。在房內頻頻窺視。練娘會其意。即指
龔洛言曰。此是姑爺。俏喜聞言。定睛一看。登即桃臉發
赤。柳眉聳翠。淚落如荳。伏練娘肩上。半晌始頓足罵曰。
咄。癩蝦蟆想食天鵝肉耶。儂甯死誓不嫁此洋鬼子。罵完。
復嚶嚶啜泣。(§31, 5/3/1910) 練娘甚乖覺。勸之曰。姑娘毋憂
慮。此乃婚姻自由之地。如不適意。請至家。老身自能周張
[132]於其間也。於是攙之登車。龔洛在外。尤不知其中底蘊。
雖聞

---

130 原文「一」字全缺。今據文義及下文「俏喜亦急欲一見新郎」之語擬補。
131 「姑」字似當作「故」。此或為魯魚之誤，或為四邑話不分陰平、陰去二
　　聲，兩字同音而故意通假也。
132 「周張」或作「周章」，謂驚慌而失措之貌也。如言「事先計劃周詳，庶免
　　臨時周張」是也。今則引伸其義，直謂驚慌失措。句意即謂「老身自能慌
　　忙無措一番於其間」，有自謙之語氣。

chattering from within, he was vague as to what had been said, and seeing Tsiu Hei cover her downcast face with her sleeve as Lin Neung assisted her ashore, he took her to be bashful, and held no concern that there might be anything else on her mind. He moved over to the bulwark, and leaning against it, staring out with gleaming eyes, regretted that he could not return with her in the carriage. It was not until Song Tak and Wong had finished set-tling the baggage, and returned to the boat to call him, that he sauntered over to the carriage and took it back.

They arrived together at Kung's house, its curtained rooms silent, which Kung thought odd.

"Have they arrived?" he asked the newly hired Western maid.

"I haven't seen them," she replied.

Wong, thinking that the carriage driver had got lost, raced back to his shop.

Finding women's cosmetic boxes and such piled up within, the realisation struck that they had gone there instead. Wong cursed Lin Neung under his breath for the improperness of her arrange-ments, and then went upstairs. There he found Tsiu Hei sitting silently in a corner. Her head hung low, she did not speak, nor even greet him.

"Why did you not go directly to Kung Lok's house?" Wong asked Lin Neung.

"My mistress instructed me to come here," replied Lin Neung. "She said she wished to have a word with her master."

Wong was about to enquire as to what she wished to have a word about, but just then he heard the sound of leather shoes,[272] and turning his head saw Song Tak leading Kung Lok in. Wong made way for him to sit. But as soon as Tsiu Hei sighted Kung Lok,

272 This is a reference to Kung Lok's Western dress, as Chinese shoes were typically made of cloth.

房中絮絮而語。但不甚了了。見練娘扶俏喜登岸。垂首掩
袖。意彼羞澀。不虞其有他也。乃移凭船欄。目灼灼注視。
恨不得同車而歸。及爽德與黃某料理行囊妥當。回船呼之。
始施施然坐車而囘。數人同到龔屋。簾幙寂然。心竊怪。問
新僱西人僕婦曰。他等到否。答曰。未見。黃某意車夫失
路。復奔囘店中。見有婦女飾匣等物。堆積店內。方知彼等
到此。陰罵練娘措置失當。即登樓。見俏喜默坐一隅。低頭
不語。亦不請安。黃某問練娘曰。何不直到龔屋。練娘曰。
姑娘吩咐來此。云欲與主人一言。黃欲詢何事。乍聞革履之
聲。囘首見爽德引龔洛而來。黃即讓坐。俏喜一見龔洛。

a palpable anger pervaded her face, and she neared a point of manic frenzy.

Fearing the situation would become awkward, Lin Neung seized the brief window of opportunity and said "This place is a clutter with so many people, and miss says there is a family affair on which she is yet to report. How about coming to my cottage for a little?" Then, with a furtive movement of the tip of her eyebrow, she signalled her meaning.

[Wong] comprehended, and hired a carriage to deliver Tsiu Hei to Lin Neung's residence.

Lin Neung then egged her on further, saying, "To me, your husband-to-be has the appearance of a man who is not a man and a devil who is not a devil.[273] His cheeks are whiskered; his face is ugly; and moreover, he is already nearing life's eventide. It is no wonder my mistress is angry and resentful. Were it this old hand-maid, even she would not be willing to marry him."

On hearing this, in her desire to break off the marriage, Tsiu Hei became all the more decided.

Lin Neung then said to her in a low voice, "Worry not miss, here men and women must be willing before a wedding can take place. How about, if my mistress can find it in her to persevere, this old handmaid selects again on your behalf for a fine match?"

Tsiu Hei nodded in agreement and, clearing the anger from her complexion, thanked her, saying, "In this matter I rely completely on you Auntie."[274]

---

273 In other words, he looks neither Chinese nor Western. Here, a 鬼 "devil" means a "foreign devil", i.e. a foreigner, and a 人 "man" means a Chinese man specifically. Note that the word "devil" is used in derogatory and racist Chinese expressions to mean the opposite of a human being, though this overtone has weakened in some set expressions: refer to footnote 115.

274 Chinese makes extensive use of kinship terms as addresses for non-relatives. It is to be noted, though, that only certain kinship terms are capable of such extended application.

怒容可掬。幾發狂易。練娘恐難以爲情。即乘間曰。此處人
多龐雜。娘云尙有家政稟達。不如到敝廬一坐如何。說完。
復暗以眉梢遞意。黃[133]某心會。即催一車送他到練娘住宅。
練娘復愚之曰。儂觀姑爺模樣。人不人。鬼不鬼。兩腮鬍
鬢。面目醜惡。而况年已將暮。無怪姑娘憤懣。雖老身亦不
願從之也。俏喜聞言。悔婚之意益決。練娘復低聲語之曰。
姑娘毋憂。此處要男女願意。方准行婚禮。姑娘果能堅持。
老身代汝再擇佳耦如何。俏喜領之。又霽顏謝曰。此事全仗
姨姆。

133　此字殘甚，不可復識。今因文義分明擬補。

Presently, Wong knocked at the door. Lin Neung conducted him into the parlour[275] and said to him, "Why is it that you have been so rash sir? My mistress is most dissatisfied with her husband-to-be, and has utterly refused to marry him. I have done my best to dissuade her, but she is still determined not to consent. What can be done?"

Wong was greatly shocked on hearing this, and told Lin Neung to bring Tsiu Hei into the parlour.

"I hear that you are not willing to marry Kung: is this so?" he asked.

"It is," she replied.

"You have come thousands of miles to marry him, why would you have second thoughts now?" asked Wong.

Tsiu Hei replied righteously, "When would your maid dare intentionally disobey her master's orders? But Kung is past fifty, over forty years your maid's senior, and even if he should enjoy great longevity, he would last no longer than ten years. When the time came, your maid would have nothing on which to rely. Would my master be able then to again extend the favour he showed in rearing me? Where moreover would I be left if misfortune should strike while residing on this remote isle without kin or neighbours?"

"But I have already received your bride price from Kung," said Wong. "I can hardly change things now."

"My master's only concern is money; he shows none for whether his maid lives or dies," said Tsiu Hei. "If things go unchanged, all that will be left for your maid to do will be to die and have done with this life."

---

275 The Chinese name for a Western parlour (a pleasantly decorated front room generally reserved for entertaining visitors), which has today been largely forgotten, was 花廳 "fancy room". Here only its second character is provided, a character that can be variously translated as "living room", "drawing room", "morning room", "sitting room" or "parlour", the last being the most fitting in this context.

俄頃。黃某扣門。練娘引到廳上語之曰。老爺何太鹵莽。姑娘甚不滿意姑爺。抵死不嫁。經妾力勸。依然執意不肯。奈何。黃某聞言。大驚。即呼練娘引俏喜出廳問曰。聞汝不願與龔某結婚。然耶。曰。然。黃曰。汝萬里從婚。何故中悔。俏喜侃侃言曰。主人之命。婢子敢故意違逆。但龔某年逾大衍。長婢子四十餘年。縱有上壽。亦十年之間耳。到此時婢子無依。主人能再任養育之恩否耶。況寄居絕島。無親無鄰。設有不測。將焉置妾。黃曰。吾已受龔某之聘。決難更改。俏喜曰。主人祇顧金錢。不顧婢子生死。若無更改。婢子惟有一死以了此生耳。

Lost for words, Wong signalled to Lin Neung to work on her, and then made a reluctant exit from the house. (§32, 26/3/1910)

Kung Lok sat bedazed within the shop after Tsiu Hei left, his head turned down and eyes closed in contemplation. All of a sudden he was met by the sight of Wong returning alone, with a dismayed look on his face. He had been feeling like he was in a five-mile fog over Wong and Lin Neung's actions, and had been wanting to question them, but had been at pains over what words to use. Now though he could hold back no longer.

"My humble dwelling is all fitted out," he said. "Why not instruct Lin Neung to take her there?"

Wong was then still hoping that circumstances might take a turn, and so he replied vaguely, "Yes, yes," and after lingering for a little while, went off again to Lin Neung's to check for news, thinking that she would doubtless have been working on Tsiu Hei for him.

Little did Wong know that after he left the house, rather than attempting to dissuade Tsiu Hei, Lin Neung had been instructing the monkey on tree climbing,[276] and devising with her a stratagem of withdrawal from the engagement.

Lin Neung heard Wong return and went to speak with him first. "My mistress is unlikely to change her mind about the marriage," she said. "My best efforts to dissuade her have been utterly ineffective. It might be simplest and best overall, and avoid discord, if you were to respond to Kung quickly and directly, and prompt him to take another."

Wong shook his head and breathed a sigh. Then he raced to Tsiu Hei's side, where, in the hope of piquing her interest, he told her in tender tones of how rich and populous, how frugal and

---

276 教猴升木 "to instruct a monkey on tree climbing" is a classical Chinese idiom that has its origin in *The Odes* and means to encourage an already wicked person towards further wickedness.

黃語塞。陰使練娘婉勸[134]。逡巡而出。(§32, 26/3/1910) 鞏洛自
俏喜去後。呆坐肆中。垂首瞑想。忽見黃某獨囘。顏色喪
沮。覺他等舉動。如在五里霧中。幾欲詰問。難苦措詞[135]。
此際勢難忍耐。乃言曰。敝舍已佈置妥當。何不命練娘挈彼
到此。斯時黃某猶望有轉環。故含糊應之曰。唯唯。躊躕半
晌。復至練娘處討探消息。意練娘決爲婉勸。豈知自黃某出
後。練娘不徒不勸。反教猱升木。與他籌畫退婚之策。聞黃
復到。先語之曰。姑娘婚事。勢難囘意。儂已力勸。毫無效
用。不若直捷答覆龔家。使他另娶。免致兩歧。較爲簡當。
黃某搖首嘆氣。奔至俏喜身旁。復柔聲甘言。冀圖聳聽。謂
龔某如何富庶。如何儉積。如何

---

134 「勸」原作「勤」。兩字形近之誤。今正。
135 原文「詞」字半缺。今據其殘跡與文義擬正。

honest, and how young in years Kung was;[277] and how, if she missed this chance, she would one day most certainly be regretful. And in such a fashion he pained and strained himself in trying, in every way possible, to get her to see sense. But it was to no avail, for Tsiu Hei sat facing the wall and uttered not a word, not until he had finished speaking, when she said with a sneer, "If you want your maid to accede, you will have to go to court and have a magistrate rule it."

Realising that she was utterly decided, Wong made a disgruntled exit, and then a hesitant return to the shop.

"Have they gone yet?" asked Kung Lok as soon as he saw him.

Wong was at a loss for words, and so he reluctantly answered, "I know not why, but my maid has vowed she would rather die than accede to the marriage. What can one do?"

Kung, on hearing these unexpected words, looked the very image of a little child that had been frolicking merrily but was now on the verge of bawling, its senses having abandoned it at the sudden sound of a clap of thunder.

"I expect you must have written to your maid to inform her of our agreement," he said after a fair time had passed. "How could it be then that she would have second thoughts now, with the date upon us? And how am I to show my face to friends and relatives, my black yurt[278] already prepared and my bride nowhere to be seen? I hope, sir, that you will do your utmost to take matters in hand." (§33, 2/4/1910)

"Contrary to what I expected, this matter has gone awry," said Wong, his forehead knitted with exasperation. "I am now at my wit's end and the limits of my strength. All I can do is hire a Chinese woman who is a good talker, to try again at persuading her to

---

277   The word 富庶 cᴹ. fu-syu means "rich and populous" or "having much wealth and many members". A region can be *fu-syu*, a family or a clan can be *fu-syu*, but an individual cannot. The word's usage here therefore consitutes a malapropism, which the author appears to deliberately put into the mouth

誠樸。如何年少。如汝錯此機緣。他日決然怨悔。苦口苦
心。開導萬端。無奈俏喜面壁而坐。默不一語。待彼說畢。
始冷笑曰。欲婢子見從。除非到衙裏。待長官裁判耳。黃某
知其決絕。始恨恨而出。徬徨返肆。龔洛一見。即問曰彼等
去未。黃某無詞可答。始勉强而言曰賤婢不知何因。誓死不
從。奈何。龔某驟聞此語。酷似小孩酣嬉之際。忽然霹靂一
聲。神魂喪失。幾乎大哭出聲。良久纔曰。先生前日與弟約
言。料必函告令婢。何以臨期中悔。況弟青廬已備。而新婦
渺然。有何顏面見戚友。望先生力爲主持。(§33, 2/4/1910) 黃
某蹙額曰。此事變生意外。非我意料所及。我已智窮力竭。
惟有催一善言之華婦。再爲勸

of his character Wong, so as to produce the rhetorical effect of highlighting
that some of the compliments he is paying Kung Lok in his attempt to
persuade Tsiu Hei of his desirablity are hollow.

278 From the late M°. Han dynasty to the T´ang, the foreign custom of holding
the marriage ceremony in a yurt or similar canopy of or dressed in cloth of
indigo-black was adopted in some parts of China. The term "black yurt"
thus came to mean *wedding canopy* or *wedding room*, and by extension,
wedding.

see sense. If the matter cannot be settled, I shall simply restore the bride price to you." Kung, hanging his head, did not speak.

Wong acted according to his plan, and after a good while, the Chinese woman he had hired for her ability to talk reported back on her assignment, "The little wench is iron-willed and the matter cannot be settled." A discontented Wong then surrendered up the bride price to Kung.

Kung Lok had no choice but to pocket the money and return home, despairingly despondent. Afterwards, ruffled by the event, he would oft *my-oh-my* while tracing air.[279] A year hence, he returned to his village to take another. Unsuccessful though, he finally consigned himself, in a fit of madness, to a drowning death in a pond.[280]

Wong had sat morosely in his shop after Kung left. Meanwhile, the news that Tsiu Hei had broken off the marriage had filled the Chinese street. When Sheung Hong learned of it, he danced about like a madman, before taking his opening and going off to see Wong.

"I hear your bondmaid has come here to marry Kung. What a splendid thing!" he said, in a pretense aimed at provoking him. "I imagine that that pair of *yuen-yeung* ducks[281] is now joined as harmoniously as fish to water. Why then, sir, are you here all silent in your shop, worry locked betwixt your brows?" Wong merely shook his head.

---

279 This classical idiom is an allusion to a story recorded in 世說 *"Hearsay"*, the book previously mentioned in footnote 222. The story (which is set in the 350s C.E.) relates that after the great general 殷浩 Mᵒ. Yin Hao was dismissed from office and residing in the district of 新安 Hsin An, in the province of 楊州 Yang Chou, he spent all his time tracing characters in the air. Officials and common people from the province spied on him, and by following the movements of his hand discerned that he was writing four characters over and over: 咄咄怪事, which translate to "MY OH MY, IT IS THE STRANGEST THING."

導。如事不諧。祇將聘金歸趙而已。龔某垂首不語。黃某果
依此策而行。良久。所僱之能言華婦復命曰。小妮子心如鐵
石。事不諧矣。黃某始怏怏將聘金繳回龔某。龔洛不得已囊
金而歸。懊喪欲絕。後爲此事所刺激。時常書空咄咄。逾
年。旋里另娶。無奈瘋顛大作。卒蹈塘而死。黃某自龔洛出
後。悶坐肆中。斯時俏喜悔婚之事。已洋溢華街。尙康聞
之。舞蹈若狂。乃乘間往見黃某。故託詞以挑之曰。聞令婢
到此與龔某結婚。最大佳事。料此際一對好鴛鴦。已諧魚水
矣。君何以默在肆中。愁鎖眉尖耶。黃祇是搖首不語。

---

280 Large fish ponds are a ubiquitous feature of the See Yip region.
281 鴛鴦 *"yuen-yeung* ducks" symbolise a loving monogomous couple: see
     footnote 72.

Sheung Hong spoke again, "One discerns from your face sir that something is perhaps not as you would wish. Why not open up your breast to your unworthy clansman?"

Wong proceeded to explain from beginning to end how Tsiu Hei had been stubborn, and how she had broken off the marriage.

Sheung Hong affected sympathetic sighs, and then asked, "What will you do with her now?"

"I can do nothing about her now," replied Wong. "I've already returned the bride price to Kung."

"Then where, fine sir, is your bondmaid presently residing?" asked Sheung Hong.

"She is staying at Lin Neung's house," answered Wong.

On hearing this, Sheung Hong was inwardly pleased. And having made a hasty departure, he went off to pay Lin Neung a visit.

"The northwest wind is strong tonight, it's blown a *maa-jin*[282] here!"[283] said a smiling Lin Neung on meeting.

"I've come expressly to cadge a place at the wedding banquet," replied Sheung Hong.

"Deranged fellow!" cursed Lin Neung. "People haven't even a bit of mutton to swallow down and you come here speaking nonsense."

"It's you who's speaking nonsense, not I," said Sheung Hong, affecting ignorance. "Why this vague retort, which leaves one utterly in the dark?"

"Come, I shall tell you," said Lin Neung. And moving her cherry-like mouth close to Sheung Hong's ear, she said in a low voice as she pointed to the room:

---

282 孖氈 o. "*maa-jin*" (Cantonese pronunciation) were traders of substance who dealt with foreigners, and who were accorded considerable status in the popular sphere. This name is held to have originated as a transliteration of the English word "merchant", a conclusion that the etymological evidence would appear to support. Lin Neung's mention here to the northwest wind

尚康又曰。辨君顏色。似有不如意事。弟與兄忝屬同宗。何
妨剖懷相示。黃某果將俏喜如何倔強。如何悔婚。表白一
次。尚康貌爲嘆惜。復問曰。現下當作何處置。黃曰。我亦
無如他何。我已將聘金還囘龔某矣。尚康曰。令婢現寄居何
處。黃曰。暫住練娘家。康聞言暗喜。亟辭去。往訪練娘。
甫見面。練娘笑曰。今晚西北風大。吹得孖毡來也。尚康
曰。我特來討喜酒飲。練娘咒罵之曰。風狂郎。[136] 人家一塊
羊肉咽不下。還來打誑語。尚康復貌爲不知曰。我非打誑
語。汝是打誑語。何以言詞閃鑠。令人悶胡廬耶。練娘曰。
來。吾語汝。果以櫻口接近尚康耳鼓。復低聲指房內曰。

136　此處本無讀號。疑當有之。今擬補。

---

is presumably a reference to Hong Kong or Canton, which were places
associated with "*maa-jin*" that lay to the northwest of Melbourne.

283　The motif of unexpected guests being blown (by accident) to one's door is
something of a conversational trope in Chinese, equivalent to an English
expression like "To what do I owe the pleasure?"

"That lovely bright pearl inside there is now in the palm of my hand, and we shall see for which lucky gentleman I might give her up." Then she began to retell[284] [the whole of] Tsiu Hei's story.

But in the midst of Lin Neung's telling, a long and charming call of "Auntie!" came from within the room, and with it Sheung Hong's spirit flew beyond the highest heaven. He stopped Lin Neung and said, "There is no need to state any more. If you can effect this match for me, I shall forever hold and knot for you."[285]

Lin Neung complicated matters for the moment, "Refrain from wild fancies sir: she thinks highly of herself, and may not be the type who is willing to be made a small star."[286]

On hearing this, Sheung Hong, almost going down on his knees, implored her further: "Pity me. I shall not blame you if the matter cannot be brought about. But if it is settled, I shall wish you long life with a gift of ten sovereigns."[287]

"Why such eager impatience, sir?" said Lin Neung with a smile. "I would not baulk at any trouble if compensated with a substantial premium. You might, on settlement of the matter, reward me with twenty sovereigns."

---

284 "Retell" is the closest translation to the word the author uses, but in the context, the equivalents to "recount" or "tell" would be more appropriate. It is given as such, however, because the translation does not attempt to disguise the flaws present in the original.

285 In other words, I shall be eternally grateful. The expression "to hold and knot", or more precisely "to hold in the mouth, and to knot", which the author gives as
啣結 but which is more properly written 銜結, is a combination of two unrelated classical stories—with which the author and much of his audience would have been familiar—that concern the repayment of kindnesses. The first is the story of a ten-year-old boy named 楊寶 ᴍ°. Yang Pao, who, for rescuing an injured Eurasian siskin (a yellow-and-black feathered species of finch) and nurturing it back to health, is rewarded with the gift of four magic rings of white jade, which the siskin delivers held in its beak. The second story concerns a general of antiquity named 魏顆 Wei K'o: Shortly

此中一顆好明珠。已在妾掌握之中矣。看誰家郎君有福氣。
便可捨得。復將俏喜始末。覆述殆[137]遍。言次。房內長呼姨
姆。其聲嬌婉。此時尙康魂靈兒已飛去九天矣。乃止練娘
曰。無庸多述。果能成全於我。生死啣結。練娘姑難之曰。
彼高自位置。未必甘作小星者。君毋妄想。康聞言。幾乎雙
膝跪下。復懇之曰。卿憐我。事之成否。我不怨卿。若果
諧。當以十金磅爲壽。練娘笑曰。君何性急乃爾。果以厚値
償儂。妾又何敢憚煩。事果諧。當酬妾以二十金磅。

137　原文「殆」字全闕。今據文義擬補。

---

before his death, Wei K´o's father had instructed that a particular concubine
should be buried with him. When his father died, Wei K´o ignored that
instruction in favour of one given earlier, when his father was still lucid, to
the effect that he let the concubine live and find a new husband for her.
Later in life, in 594 B.C.E., Wei K´o and his brother lead an army which
defeated that of an enemy state in battle and captured its famed commander,
a Hercules named 杜回 Tu Hui. When on the battlefield, Wei K´o had seen
an old man knotting grass. This knotted grass had tripped Tu Hui and
enabled his capture. Afterwards, the old man visited Wei K´o in a dream and
stated that he was the concubine's father, and had knotted the grass to repay
him for saving his daughter.

286　In Chinese, a 小星 "little star" is a nameless star, and a literary term for *concubine*.

287　The sovereign was a gold coin with a nominal value of one pound sterling,
and an actual value dependent on the gold price. The Chinese name for this
coin translates as "gold-pound."

"I shall dare do as you command! I shall dare do as you command!" declared Sheung Hong, repeatedly bowing his head. (§34, 9/4/1910)

A moment later, repeated calls of "Auntie! Auntie!" issued from the room. Lin Neung turned, pushed through the doorway, and entered.

"What is the cause of this incessant howling? In the grip of a convulsion are you?" she exclaimed. "A certain person is working hard for you. Why the need to interrupt with these antics while she is engrossed in conversation?"

She then continued in a lower voice, "Sour shrew, I have found a fine man for you: hasten to reward your matchmaker."

"Might it be the one just now with the white clothes, scholar's shoes, pointy nose and bearded cheeks?" snapped Tsiu Hei. "On comparison, how far is he from Kung! Worse still, he frequently shuts his eyes when speaking, which makes him look frightening, like a corpse that has been long in the grave. Given that he is not far from death's door, I would ask that you marry him."

"How is it that you know him?" replied Lin Neung, as though struck by realisation.[288]

"Peeping out, I got a thorough view of him," said Tsiu Hei. "Your[289] furtiveness of speech could not escape my gaze. I guessed eight-or-nine-tenths of it when you first met."

Lin Neung berated her, "Imp of a maid, do not look on him so scornfully. He is a Chinatown *maa-jin*:[290] Tak Yuen's proprietor.[291]

---

288 The expression 爽然 "as though struck by realisation" can be interpreted in two ways given the context: (1) as indicating that Lin Neung genuinely realised all of a sudden what an apt description of Sheung Hong the one given by Tsiu Hei was; or, (2) as indicating that Lin Neung was simulating innocent realisation for the sake of humour. Regardless, her response appears to cleverly combine an acknowledgement of the issue of Sheung Hong's looks with an overall attempt at redirecting Tsiu Hei's focus elsewhere, by making light of them.

尙康頻頻點首曰。敢如尊命。敢如尊命。(§34, 9/4/1910) 俄而
房內疊呼曰。姨姆。姨姆。練娘反身排闥入內曰。子癎發
耶。何故狂號不休。人家與汝操勞。何苦惡作劇。以斷人談
興。旣而低聲曰。酸丫頭儂與汝擇一鴛侶矣。速酬媒。俏喜
亟曰。豈適間之白衣儒履。齙腮尖鼻者耶。彼較龔某。相去
幾何矣。況彼言談間屢瞑其目。如癸窀內之陳尸。令人可
畏。彼去冥路不遠矣。請子從之。練娘爽然曰。子何以識
之。俏喜曰。儂已窺之熟矣。汝二人言談鬼祟。豈能逃我之
眼光。汝等初晤時。儂已猜度八九矣。練娘罵曰。刁婢毋賤
視人。彼爲華街之孖毡。德元之店東也。

---

289 This is a plural "your", inclusive of both Lin Neung and Sheung Hong.

290 For "*maa-jin*", see footnote 282.

291 See Appendix III for speculation on the identity of this and the other real businesses that appear to feature in the novel under slightly changed names.

What disgrace would he bring on you? So far as [appearance] is concerned, there is a world of difference between him and Kung. Furthermore, his fondness for you my lady being as the longing of a thirsty horse for a spring, if you were to marry him, he would take you for a Kuan Yin and worship you.[292] Furthermore, when we choose commitment,[293] money should be our guiding principle. Living in prosperity in a land where women's rights are especially strong, you would have the freedom to act as you pleased."

Tsiu Hei's heart skipped a beat. "Has he taken a wife yet?" she asked. "I would not stoop to concubinage."

Lin Neung laughed heavenward. "How can you be so very naïve!" she exclaimed. "Men detest the familiar and love the new, for their affections change according to their encounters. I have a wide experience of people. Of those men who have drifted beyond the seas, none cares to spare a thought for his wife of poorer days. Even if there was one that did, it would simply be to regard her as he would a dry skull. Furthermore, she would be bound to her quarters, while thousands of miles away at the world's end, you would lie upon his bedroom mat. What obstruction would you face? And if, after some time had passed, you were to acquire a little master,[294] how disparate would your position be from that of a wife by marriage? I fear that by that time, that village woman back home would already have transformed into a Husband-gazing Rock."[295] And with that, she clapped her hands and laughed.

---

292 ᴹᵒ. Kuan Yin (A.K.A. ᴹᴹ.*Guānyīn*, 觀音) is the Buddhist Goddess of Mercy. See footnote 120.

293 Use of the idiom translated here as "choose commitment" (擇人而事) is generally associated with prostitutes and courtesans.

294 A baby boy.

295 An influential collection of fantastic tales entitled 幽明錄 *"A Record of the Concealed and Manifest"*, which was compiled in the earlier half of the 400s C.E. by the same man who compiled the aforementioned 世說 *"Hearsay"*,

何辱歿汝爲。若論形[138]貌。與龔某有霄壤之別。況彼之愛慕
娘子。如渴馬思泉。子若從之。行將汝作觀音供奉矣。況吾
等擇人而事。當以金錢爲第一主義。苟囊橐充切。処此女權
特重之地。何愁舉動不自由。俏喜此際已怦然心動。乃問
曰。渠有家室未。若抱衾裯者。妾不屑爲。練娘[139]仰天大笑
曰。子何不達之甚。男子厭常喜新。隨所遇而轉移。妾閲多
人矣。飄泊外洋者。誰肯一念糟糠之婦。雖有之。直作髑髏
觀耳。況彼守房闈。子當寢席。天涯萬里。有何窒礙。倘再
過幾時。得一小哥子。又與結髮何殊。吾恐爾時故鄉之村
嫗。已化作望夫石矣。說完。復鼓掌大笑。

138 原文「形」字殘缺之甚。今據其墨跡與文義擬補。
139 「練娘」原誤倒作「娘練」。今正。

and a similar work written two-hundred years earlier by 曹丕 M°. Ts'ao P'i
(Mᴹ. *Cáo Pi*) the aforementioned first emperor of the state of Wei, record the
story of a woman, who, with child in hand, bid farewell to her far-journeying
husband on a mountain, and standing and staring out at him turned to stone.
The name of the real and still-extant anthropomorphic stone at the story's
centre, the "Husband-gazing Rock", consequently became a literary
appellation for a steadfastly constant wife who longs for her husband's return.
Here, Lin Neung's tone in her use of the expression is decidedly spiteful.

"Do not prattle on," said Tsiu Hei. "I have my own considerations. For the moment, I shall go along with you, for I want to take advantage of his doltishness."

"Sour shrew, you are not truly a woman of the world,"[296] said Lin Neung. "I see clearly what inhabits the recesses of your heart and mind. Do not take this old handmaid for your puppet."

So they joked and jibed between themselves, and Sheung Hong, who had stepped outside, lingered about beyond the door, awaiting good news.

Lin Neung then came out and said with a smile, "Impatient one, I see you are still around. I have already pulled that piece of flesh from out another's throat to cast towards your ravenous jaws. With what will you reward me?"

"If that is so," replied Sheung Hong, "then I am, from my head to my heels, a beneficiary of your great kindness, and I swear, through all my lifetimes, to never dare forget."

Lin Neung responded with a faint smile, "I've heard sweet words like those many times before, but as the Kwang Tung proverb says, *A matchmaker after marriage is a fan after Autumn.*[297] Come that time when lute and zithern play in joyful harmony,[298] were this old handmaid to approach your door she would be taken to be bothersome, harsh words would follow, and there would be no great kindness to speak of. Watch only that you do not renege on the agreed twenty sovereigns."

---

296 The expression given here as "woman of the world" (曠達者) means "one who is 曠達 cᴹ. *kwong-daat*". The word *kwong-daat* is very rich in meaning and appears to have no English equivalent. It denotes the possession of a particular understanding, outlook and mentality, characterised by a strong sense of the ways of the world and the insignificance of one's life in the greater scheme of things, and by a light-heartedness that stems from the depth and breadth of that outlook. Its equally rich connotations include the following: a pessimistic view of the world; Taoist as opposed to Confucian

俏喜曰。子毋信口開河。妾自有裁度。姑順子。儂正欲利用
其憨態。練娘曰。酸丫頭非眞曠達者。汝之心曲。我自能燭
照。毋以老身爲傀儡也。二人互相笑謔。尙康趨出而後。猶
徊徘戶外。以待好消息。適練娘出戶笑曰。急性兒猶在此間
耶。妾已抽人喉間肉。投汝饞吻矣。何以報妾。尙康曰。果
爾。自頂至踵。皆卿深恩。生生世世。誓不敢忘。練娘微哂
曰。此等甜言。儂已司空見慣。粤諺云。婚後媒人秋後扇。
爾時一對瑟琴。和樂並奏。老身再登門。以爲騷擾。呵斥及
之矣。何深恩之足云。但二十金磅。切勿爽約。

thinking; a certain lack of propriety and a degree of deviation from the path
of moral rectitude; a preference for enjoying life and a disinclination to the
pursuit of fame and power. Its sense can be positive or negative depending
on the view of the speaker. Here, Lin Neung's positive use of the word says
much about her own mentality.

297 This proverb is typically used in its non-literal sense of "none give any
thought to one who has finished serving his/her purpose."

298 See footnote 181.

Laughing and chatting, the two of them then went off to see Wong. (§35, 16/4/1910)

"Were I to speak right off," said Sheung Hong, "it would be too abrupt. So I would ask that you go in first. To avoid any slips that might give the game away, I shall arrive later. You have a wonderful way with words too and speak compellingly."

Lin Neung nodded in assent, and then went in ahead.

"In what state is that ungrateful wretch?" asked Wong.

"My mistress is most unwilling to wed," replied Lin Neung, her whole forehead knitted with worry. "She wants to rid herself of her three-thousand strands of trouble[299] and go off as a disciple of the Great Being.[300] And she has been asking me questions, which I have declined to answer, about Western nuns. Just before, the *Saa-low-vay-san Aa-mee*[301] (which means "Salvation Army" in translation)[302] passed by, and she asked me about it. I gave her an outline, and, looking on it approvingly, she vowed she would join to redeem her liberty. It is fortunate she does not yet know English, otherwise, it would have been dangerous."

Wong was shocked. He thought, and was about to speak when Sheung Hong suddenly entered.

---

299   This (三千煩惱根) is a Buddhist expression for *hair*, in which "strands" has the double sense of "roots" or "causes", and what is translated here as "trouble" refers specifically to the Buddhist afflictions of the mind or *kleshāh*, such as desire and pride.

300   大士 "Great Being" is the Chinese equivalent of the Sanskrit *mahāsattva*, which is the Buddhist term for a highly enlightened bodhisattva. Here the term is used specifically in reference to the Avalokitasvara Bodhisattva (觀世音菩薩) or Buddhist Goddess of Mercy ᴍᵒ. Kuan Yin.

301   This reverse transliteration reflects an educated guess as to the pronunciation of the original transliteration in the dialect of the See Yip language of the author's day, according to which it would have been fashioned.

302   The author gives in this note what was, and still is, the Chinese name for the Salvation Army, in which the word 救世 "salvation" has the specific sense of *salvation of the world*.

二人談笑往見黃某。(§35, 16/4/1910) 尙康曰。吾遽言。語太唐突。請卿先。我後至。免露破綻。況卿言詞婉妙。易動人聽也。練娘頷之。果先往。黃某曰。賤骨頭如何者。練娘[140]攣蹙曰。姑娘甚不願適人。欲掃除三千煩惱根。從大士作弟子去。屢以西人女尼之事詢妾。妾已婉却之。適間沙露威慎阿彌經過。（譯言救世軍）彼詢妾。妾語其梗槪。彼羨之。云誓欲入斯會。以贖其自由之身。幸其未諳英語。不然。殆矣。黃某大驚。思欲語。尙康忽入。

140 「練娘」二字原作倒文。今正。

Feigning unfamiliarity, Lin Neung greeted and freed her seat for him.

"You two are speaking of something, I should not stay," said Sheung Hong.

"It is only an idle matter," replied Wong, "you are not intruding."

Sheung Hong seated himself, and then asked, in full knowledge of the answer, "Has the matter of your bondmaid been settled yet?"

"Others' worries are not yet over," replied Lin Neung. Then she smiled, "You had a mind to pick this topic, though. If you are so concerned, why not take her for a little star?"

"Who am I to engage in such wild fancies?" replied Sheung Hong.

Wong reckoned to himself that were Tsiu Hei to succumb to prompting from elsewhere, he could very easily lose his tidy little bride price for good, and he might as well take this opportunity to bring about a match, thus preventing any mishap. Suddenly, it dawned on him that Sheung Hong did not yet have any children, and had repeatedly tried to take a concubine. So he urged him by saying, "As you are still without [progeny] sir, what Lin Neung suggests is most sound."

Not waiting for Sheung Hong to reply, Lin Neung said, "If you were so inclined sir, I should do for you my utmost as a matchmaker."

Sheung Hong gave a faint smile.

"I shall go off to act as your Cupid,"[303] said Lin Neung, rising to her feet, "and I shall not be found wanting in the fulfillment of my mission." Then she hurried out.

---

303 Naturally it is not the Cupid of Greek mythology that is mentioned here, but the equivalent in Chinese mythology, the 月下老人 "old man of the moon", who ties together those who are predestined to marry by means of invisible red threads.

練娘佯爲不知。讓坐請安。尙康曰。汝等語事。余不便留。
黃曰。無傷。閒事耳。尙康就坐。故問曰。令婢之事。已妥
辦否。練娘笑曰。他人愁煩未了。汝故意拈題兒。汝如此關
切。何不納作小星。尙康曰。吾豈敢生此妄想。黃某暗忖設
若俏喜受他聳動。不難將偌大聘金。付之流水。不如乘機撮
合。免生意外。忽悟尙康未有兒女。屢次納妾。因慫恿之
曰。君嗣 續 [141] 尙虛。練娘 [142] 斯言大是。練娘不待尙康答言乃
曰。如君有意。妾竭力作伐。尙康微哂。練娘起立曰。妾往
代君作月老。決有以報命。愴遽 [143] 而出。

141　原文「續」字模糊不清。今據其墨跡與語義擬正。
142　「練娘」二字原作倒文。今正。
143　「愴遽」之「愴」，必爲「囪」字之同音假借也。按，四邑話之寧邑話、新
　　　邑話等，其愴、囪字似皆屬異音字，唯有開邑話讀作同音耳。以此觀之，
　　　則著書人所操，當爲開邑話也。

Shortly, Lin Neung returned and said, "It's the strangest thing, my mistress would not consent to any number of invitations to wifehood, but did on hearing one to concubinage. It must be that our *maa-jin* has earned this through self-cultivation in his last life, or that his and her names are registered in the *yuen-yeung* catalogue."[304]

Sheung Hong feigned incredulity. "She has been overly severe in her selection of a candidate, how could it be that she would deign to consent? Don't play with people Lin Neung."

Wong, singularly ignorant of their prearrangement and mutual artifice, then enquired of Lin Neung, "Is she or is she not in fact willing?"

"I've never been capable of telling lies," replied a straight-faced Lin Neung.

"How are you disposed?" asked Wong of Sheung Hong. "Yea or nay, decide."

Sheung Hong, after deliberately hemming and hawing for a good while, replied, "Since you have set the ball rolling like this, who am I to decline?"

Lin Neung looked askance and said with a smile, "Making himself look fully sated while three feet of drool hangs from his ravenous[305] mouth, just as most of the men of this world." There was an uproarious outburst from all present.

Lin Neung then reconciled the parties to agree that what bride price there was to be paid should be in accordance with the previous agreement with Kung. (§36, 23/4/1910)

---

304 鴛鴦譜 Cº. "the *yuen-yeung* catalogue" is, in Chinese folklore, the comprehensive register of couples' names which is kept by the "old man of the moon." For *"yuen-yeung"*, see footnote 72.

305 The word translated here as "ravenous" (饞), which could also be translated as "gluttonous" or "voracious", has the secondary meaning of "lustful".

俄而練娘復入曰。此大怪事。姑娘多少正配悉不就。聞爲側
室則就之。定是孖毡前生修得到。不然。鴛鴦譜上。註有二
人姓名也。尙康佯作不信曰。彼遴選過苛。焉肯俯就。練
娘[144]毋作弄人。黃某尤不知彼等先有成約。互相巧弄。乃詢
練娘曰。彼實願意與否。練娘正色曰。妾從來不會說謊。黃
某對尙康曰。汝意向如何。諾否決定。尙康故作沉吟。良久
始曰。汝等如此作興。我又奚敢推辭。練娘斜盼笑曰。饞涎
三尺。尤作飽態以示人。世間男子。大抵如是耳。滿座哄
然。於是練娘從中調劑。所有聘金。悉依龔某前約。(§36,
23/4/1910)

144 「練娘」二字原作倒文。今正。

Thinking to himself that the betrothal money would now not end up being redirected to the land of nowhere,[306] Wong was secretly delighted. Lin Neung and Sheung Hong, too, parted pleased.

Thereafter, it was Lin Neung who saw to each and every arrangement.

First, she went to a lane which came off of the Chinese street and rented a large house, one that had a No. 4 address plate.[307] The next day, she collected Tsiu Hei in a resplendent lady's carriage, and took her there to live. Lin Neung then temporarily filled the role of house servant. But she and Tsiu Hei were compatibly foul of character, and relied on each other more in the manner of mother and daughter.

On the evening on which they were to plight their love for one another, Sheung Hong, wanting by every means to ingratiate himself with his precious concubine, said, "We were both born in China, where we lived but a stone's throw apart, and yet were never destined to meet. Who would have known that eventually, living thousands of miles away, we would become husband and wife. There must be some fine destiny in all of this."

Tsiu Hei calculated to herself, *Should I want to secure his lasting favour, I shall have to strike pre-emptively.*[308]

---

306 This expression for an imaginary or nonexistent place has its origin in the first chapter of the work of the ancient Chinese philosopher 莊子 Mº. Chuang Tzŭ. This well-known chapter (逍遙游) also contains the story of the Chinese roc: see the explanation of Ching Nam's name that is given in Appendix I.

307 Like the number thirteen in English, the number four carries ominous connotations in Chinese. The association, specifically, is with death.

308 In modern Chinese there are many short idioms taken from classical Chinese that function as or in a similar way to individual words, and do indeed have individual word equivalents in English. The expression used here for "pre-emptively" is an example. It has its origin in the words 先發制人後發制

此時黃某私心竊喜。以爲此項聘金。不致歸於無何有之鄉。
練娘與尙康。亦欣然而別。由是一切部[145]署。悉由練娘主
裁。即往華街橫巷租一大四號門牌之屋。翌日以油碧車。迎
俏喜居之。練娘暫充僕婦。然俏喜與練娘。猶臭相投。兩相
依倚。如母女焉。定情之夕。尙康欲在寵妾之前。多方獻媚
曰。我兩人同生於中國。相居咫尺。反無一面緣。不料居留
萬里。卒成夫婦。此中迨[146]有良緣。俏喜默計欲圖固寵。不
可不先發制人。

---

145 原文「部」字模糊殘損。今參別處部字擬正。
146 此「迨」與「殆庶」之「殆」音義皆同。

於人 "The early subdueth: the late are subdued." This line, in the ancient
history of the Mᵒ. Former Han dynasty entitled 漢書 "*The Han*" (more literally
translatable as "*Writings on The Han*" but generally translated as the "*Book of
Han*"), is attributed to a certain 項梁 Hsiang Liang. Hsiang Liang's words
loose some of their rhetorical clout on translation into English, but are similar
in style and force to those attributed in *The History of the Peloponnesian War* to
Athenagoras of Syracuse (as translated by Jowett *c.* 1881): "If a man does not
strike first, he will be the first struck." (Hsiang Liang was a nobleman of the
ancient vassal state of 楚 Ch'u, who was descended from a line of generals and
was uncle and tutor on military strategy to the famous and infamous 項羽
Hsiang Yü. Hsiang Yü, A.K.A. 項籍 Hsiang Chi, who is immortalized as the
self-styled hegemon of the Chinese folk story *Farewell My Concubine,* fought
劉邦 Liu Pang for the imperial crown after the collapse of the short-lived and
tyrannical 秦 Ch'in dynasty in 207 B.C.E. in a famed but ill-fated campaign
that is recounted in *The Han.*)

For regret will come too late if I do not now bring all the devices of charm and coercion to bear, and make him commit utterly to the bounds I set. So she said, with tears running, "My fate is as mean as a peach flower's,[309] and my frame is as a drifting twig. What more is there to say than that it is for fear of a fate inhuman that I find shame in concubinage. There is a senior woman[310] in your home. When to your former garden you return, how will this mean-fated servant girl[311] be able to escape the claws and jaws of that raging lion?[312] Should I seek death it will be denied me, and should I want to live I shall be unable. I know not when this retribution for the sins of three lifetimes might come to an end.[313] What fine destiny is there to speak of?" This said, she cast herself into Sheung Hong's embrace and began, faintly but deeply, to sob, in a state most piteous.

Even a heart of stone would at that moment have been turned to putty in her hands.[314] And Sheung Hong's was, moreover, that of a devil of the carnal realm.[315] So he endeavoured as best he could to comfort her, and said, as he licked away her tears with his tongue, "Worry not, my dear, for I have cast off that old village woman back home as one casts off a worn slipper."[316]

---

309 Comparison of a person's meanness of fate to a peach flower is a common Chinese literary trope that relies not only on floral transience but also on the double meaning of the Chinese word for "mean/ness" (薄), a word which also means "thin/ness," in which sense it describes the thinness of the flower petals. For this reason meanness of fate is also likened to paper, and, to the thinnest of thin (double meaning: meanest of mean) things: peach flowers drawn on paper.

310 大婦 "senior woman" is one of many expressions in Chinese for lawful wife, as opposed to concubine.

311 The expression 小青 "servant girl" translates literally as "little blue", reflecting the fact that Chinese maidservants once dressed in blue.

312 This analogy between a termagant wife and an enraged lion was not a novel one: it featured in popular literature and drama.

313 Chinese folklore holds that destiny selects one's partner in marriage in this lifetime on the basis of one's behaviour and/or contacts in one's previous

若不逞[147]此時施以種種柔媚要挾手段。使他死心塌地。就我
範圍。後悔無及。於是泫然泣曰。妾命薄如桃。身飄似梗。
衾裯慙抱。徒恐命不猶人。夫復何言。君家有大婦。他日故
園歸去。爾時命薄小靑。豈能逃怒獅爪吻。此際欲生不得。
求死不能。三生孽冤。不知何時得了。何良緣之足道。語
畢。投身尙康之懷。嗚嗚啜泣。狀甚可憐。此時雖鐵石心
腸。已化作繞指柔矣。況尙康爲色界之魔耶。於是撫慰備
至。以舌舐其淚曰。卿勿憂。吾家老村嫗。我已棄如
敝屣矣。

147 「逞」蓋字之誤也。當作「乘」。

three lifetimes. The reference to a marriage as retribution is likewise clichéd,
the term used here being one of several that characterise, often humorously,
a relationship, spouse or lover as the agent of retribution for the sins of
previous lifetimes.

314 The Chinese phrase rendered here as "turned to putty in her hands" is a
quotation from a line in a 晉 Mᵒ. Chin-dynasty poem written in 318 C.E.,
which describes how a will as hard as 百鍊鋼 "swordsmithed steel" has faded
to one of 繞指柔 "finger-wrapping softness".

315 The words used here for "devil" and "carnal realm" both carry Buddhist
overtones.

316 The worn-slipper analogy is given in the form of a common classical idiom,
and is thus clichéd language.

Tsiu Hei replied with simulated outrage: "Your faithlessness is truly beyond Li Lang's![317] If you would cast aside even a wife by marriage, then what of a concubine? And if today you take me and discard your rightful spouse, how can I know that tomorrow you will not take another and discard me? Faithless are men!" And as she spoke she turned her head to face the wall and wept.

Sheung Hong looked blankly for a little while, wanting desperately to justify himself, but in pains over which words to employ. "Do not worry unnecessarily my dear," he said. "My heart is all yours, and will ever be, though the seas may dry and the rocks decay.[318] If you do not trust me, I shall swear it before the gods: from here on, I shall treat you in the manner that befits a wife; all the affairs of home will be at your discretion to direct; and, as I am still able to protect you with my life, hereafter, no person whatsoever will dare offend you in the slightest."

Fearing Tsiu Hei might still have doubts, Sheung Hong then brought out all his worldly possessions, producing the gold coins he had saved up over time. And after he had collected up and exhibited each one, he took the keys to their cases and handed them over to Tsiu Hei.

---

317 The Ming-dynasty collection of vernacular stories entitled 警世通言, which is translated as *Stories to Caution the World* in the full modern translation produced by Shuhui Yang and Yunqin Yang, contains a story about a courtesan known as 杜十娘 M°. Tu Shih-niang and her lover 李甲 Li Chia, A.K.A. 李郎 Li Lang (郎 *lang* being a title of address used by a woman for a husband or male lover). The story tells of how Tu Shih-niang wins her freedom in order to be with Li Chia, and how he then betrays her love for him, an act which results in her consigning one priceless treasure after another, and then her own person, to the murky waters of the Yangtze. The story is often recounted or alluded to in traditional literature and folk ballads. "Du Shiniang Sinks Her Jewel Box in Anger" is the title given to it in the aforementioned translation; the Chinese title is 杜十娘怒沉百寶箱.

318 This (海枯石爛) is a Chinese idiom commonly used in declarations of undying love.

俏喜佯作怒態曰。君之薄倖。真李郎不逮也。結髮者尚且拋
棄。何況媵妾。今日君娶妾而棄嫡偶。焉知後日君不娶他人
而棄妾。薄倖哉男子。語次即移其首面[148]壁而泣。尚康呆視
半晌。欲極力剖白。苦難措詞。乃曰。卿毋過慮。我之心
肝。已經全副給卿。雖海枯石爛。永永不移。卿如不信。予
當誓之神明。此後當以嫡禮待卿。一切家政。任卿主裁。吾
猶能以性命保卿。不論何人。嗣後無敢以片言干犯卿者。尚
康猶恐俏喜不堅信。復將平日所積蓄之金幣。傾囊倒篋而
出。逐一撿示畢。即將該箱篋之匙。交與悄喜。

148　原文「面」字稍殘。今擬補。

Tsiu Hei pretended not to take any notice. She knew, though, that Sheung Hong had fallen into her net. So she turned her head to reveal a delicately limpid gaze, and said disdainfully, "No things on earth are more untrustworthy than men. To win women's favour, they show no hesitation in making solemn pledges of eternal love and spouting all manner of nonsense, and in putting it all to the back of their minds before they even turn on their heels."

Then, biting her lip, she struck Sheung Hong's cheek with her fingers and said, "Tonight you take your vows for the first time.[319] You must bear it firmly in mind, sir, that should you go back on your word, I have sworn not to stay by you."

"Yes, yes," consented Sheung Hong. And through multifarious false acts of gentleness and beguilement, he then made to forge a sense of strong attachment between them.[320] Henceforth, he was an infatuated insect, which passed its days in a drunken dream, amidst fallen flowers and spent catkins.[321] (§37, 30/4/1910)

---

319 The expression translated here as "take your vows" (受戒) refers to a Buddhist initiation ceremony in which the initiate accepts to afterward abide by certain religious dictates. Tsiu Hei uses this expression in reference to the promises Sheung Hong makes in respect of his future conduct.

320 The word translated here as "false" can also be read as "vain".

321 (1) 癡蟲 "infatuated insect" is a set expression, which means *infatuated creature*. The literal sense of "insect" has been preserved in translation to highlight both the alliteration present in the Chinese expression, and the semantic connection between the word insect and flowers and catkins. (2) The phrase 亂花殘絮中 "amidst fallen flowers and spent catkins" can be interpreted in other ways, e.g. with only one "fallen flower", Tsiu Hei, and the "spent catkins" taking on the sense of her spent bedding. (In English, the connection between catkins and bedding is hardly obvious, but the Chinese word specifically means catkins of the fluffy variety, as are produced by the pussy willow, and also other forms of botanical fluff, such as kapok floss and cotton. It is in the sense of *cotton/kapok wadding* that the word is associated with bedding.) (3) The idiom 醉生夢死 "to pass one's days in a drunken

俏喜故作不理。然知尚康已入彀中。乃迴首流波送盼而唾之
曰。世間最無信行者。莫若男子漢。欲買婦人之歡心。不惜
誓山盟水。肆口亂道。誰料不旋踵而已置之腦後矣。復咬唇
以指批尚康之頰曰。今夜爲初次受戒。君要牢牢緊記。如有
食言。儂誓不依汝。尚康唯唯應命。由是千柔百媚。虛作綢
繆。從此一隻癡虫。已醉死於亂花殘絮中矣。(§37, 30/4/1910)

---

dream" or "to live between life and death in a drunken dream state" is here
reduced to its first and last characters, 醉 "drunken" and 死 "death." Such
elliptical constructions are common in Literary Chinese, and the educated
reader immediately identifies the meaning of the full expression in them.
Here, the choice of characters serves to emphasise the senses of death over
life and drunkenness over dreaming.

Alas, alas! *A wilting melon late in fall, whose young fruit split in yesteryear; a faded flower deep in spring, whose ruby petal early dropped.*[322] Only a bleary-eyed dolt could have taken her for a maiden chaste![323]

The following morning, friends and relatives gave gifts to mark the occasion. One of the guests, Chau Sui Hing, had composed a long couplet satirizing how they were not matched as a couple.[324] Sheung Hong, though, was oblivious.

To himself he thought this charmed life of fleshly pleasure had come out of self-cultivation in his last lifetime,[325] and that now he had this A-chiao,[326] he would not swap places with a king on high. Accordingly, he provided for his guests a banquet of the most extreme sumptuousness.

There was the clatter and bustle of horse and carriage, the toasting and exchanges between guests and host. Then, once the shoes were a jumble,[327] when ears were hot with wine and drunken merriment prevailed, Chau turned to face Sheung Hong and said,

---

322 This poetic but uncomplimentary description of Tsiu Hei contains a number of innuendoes that are not evident in translation: (1) The expression 落紅 "to drop red" can be used in reference to the breaking of the hymen, as well as to the dropping of red petals. (2) The expression 破瓜 "split melon" is used in reference to a woman's coming of age, or loss of virginity. It has its origin in the first half of the first millennium of the common era, the character for 瓜 melon, written in one form of the 隸書 so-called *clerical script* then in use, looking like two 八 eights superimposed, and the splitting of this character indicating its division into those two eights, which together indicated the sum of sixteen, sixteen years being then considered the time at which a girl came of age. The expression was thus originally a visual conundrum, along the same lines as are still popular amongst Chinese riddlers today. The English word "yob", which originated as "boy" spelled backwards, has a similar etymology. Here, however, the author, having already used the character for melon in the preceding phrase, replaces it in this one with the character 瓞, which means a small melon specifically. He thereby avoids

噫。嘻。秋老瓜殘。早曾破瓞。春深花謝。久已落紅。何物
懵丁。猶作處女觀也。翌晨戚友贈物誌慶。有周遂卿者撰一
長聯。諷刺其非偶。而尚康恬不之怪。自以爲此生艷福。前
世修來。得此阿嬌。雖南面王無以易也。於是作筵餉客。備
極豐腴。斯時車馬喧闐。主賓酬酢。當履舄交錯之際。酒酣
耳熱之餘。周某對尚康[149]曰。

---

149 「尚康」二字原作倒文。今正。

---

repetition and succeeds in emphasising, poetically, the tender age at which
Tsiu Hei ceased to be "a maiden chaste."

323 懵丁 "bleary-eyed dolt" is a vernacular expression (in Cantonese and the See
Yip language) and is not used in Literary Chinese or Mandarin. The author
uses this language switching to good effect here and elsewhere. In this case,
it serves to create a sharp and slightly comical contrast with the preceding
line of ornate Literary Chinese.

324 Calligraphically rendered literary couplets that express good wishes are often
presented as gifts on such occasions.

325 前世修來 "had come out of self-cultivation in his last lifetime" is rather a
mouthful in English, but in Chinese it is no more than a clichéd way of
saying, through reference to the Buddhist concept of karma, that something
had been *earned*.

326 An м°. "A-chiao" is a beautiful wife or concubine: see footnote 266.

327 As observed in footnote 231, the Chinese idiom 履舄交錯 "jumbled mess of
shoes" connotes a scene of revelry and a loss of decorum.

"Happy you may be sir, but do you not fear the roar of a Ho Tung lion upon your return home?"[328]

Sheung Hong replied loudly, "Why such cowardice sir? We were born in an authoritarian state whose government is as harsh as the tiger is ferocious, and whose officials are as ruthless as wolves are savage; hands shackled, feet fettered, there is not one matter in which we are free, save for this system of polygamy. Each man, from the most venerated above to the multitude below, can thus fulfill his desires. It is indeed our supreme good fortune as men. Would it not be a relinquishment of our rights to be daunted by it like you? A real man displays his might, and does not fear the continued opposition of any Ho Tung lion."

"I disagree," replied Sui Hing. "Polygamy is to human decency and universal principle most harmful. Our compatriots have been habituated to fallacies that value men over women; so they have always taken women to be toys. Matters have developed to such a point today, that womanhood's dismal state is one of abject wretchedness.[329] And yet the lords and ministers of this world fan the flames, and encourage others, in order to advance their private ambitions. At every move they invoke a few outmoded lines of preceptive scripture,[330] which say how women ought to be heedfully respectful and acquiescent,

---

328 Mᵒ. "Ho Tung lion" is a Chinese equivalent to "shrew" in English, i.e. in the sense it has in Shakespeare's *The Taming of the Shrew*. See §37, footnote 312. Here, it is a reference to Sheung Hong's wife back home in China. Note also that the phrase translated as "return home" could be translated more literally as "return to China" or "return to your/our home country."

329 This phrase contains a rhetorical flourish that is lost in translation: The author uses a Literary Chinese idiom (慘無天日) for "abject wretchedness" that literally means "(of a social state) wretched beyond the light of day," the expression "light of day" or "heaven's sun" also meaning "the law of the land." The rhetorical play made is between this idiom's connection with the absence of daylight and the preceding phrase 女界之黑暗 "womanhood's dismal state," which could be more literally translated as "the blackness/

君樂則樂矣。後日返國。不畏河東獅吼耶。倘康大言曰。子
何恇慷[150]乃爾。吾等生於專制之國。猛虎苛政。凶狼酷吏。
梏手桎足。無一事可以自由。惟此一夫多妻之制。上自至
尊。下達庶人。可以如願相償。實爲吾等男子無上之幸福。
氣餒如君。豈不自放棄其權利。大丈夫肆其雄威。雖有河東
獅子。橫生阻力。亦何足畏。遂卿曰。不然。一夫多妻。於
人道公理。最有妨害。吾國人狃於輕女重男之謬說。往往以
女子爲玩具。馴至今日。女界之黑暗。慘無天日。而當世之
王公大卿。又復吹波揚厲。以便其私圖。動引幾句迂腐經
文。謂女子當如何敬戒。如何從順。

150 「恇慷」者，恇怯也。「慷」與「怯」，音義同。

---

darkness of womanhood." It may be of historical interest to note that the
first recorded usage of the aforementioned idiom for "abject wretchedness" is
in an essay written by the prominent м°. late-Ch'ing Chinese intellectual 梁
啟超 Liang Ch'i-ch'ao (мᴹ. *Liáng Qǐchāo*) entitled 中國專制政治進化史論
"*The Historical Development of Authoritarian Government in China*," which
was first published in 1902. While the possibility exists that the author of
this novel coined the expression independently—it is simply a slightly
modified version of a similar earlier idiom (暗無天日)—it seems quite likely
that Liang's essay was his source.

330 The word "scripture" is used in translation in reference to the classical
writings that Confucianism most venerates.

or that in a woman an absence of talent is a virtue. So they repress their intelligence, and deprive them of their rights. They themselves, contrarily, fill their intramural entourages with painted beauties,[331] who, in the end, vie amongst each other for favour, in a contest of charm that throws a sea of jealousy into violent upheaval.[332] Beyond enumeration is the catalogue of those who have lost their families or countries on this account. How lamentable that is. Only through a sense of true love can a married man and woman enjoy family happiness. With one husband and many wives, there can be no sense of true love, as in a marriage between one wife and many husbands, which a man would find difficult to suffer silently; the case is the same for both men and women. In polygamy, envy secretly grows, love necessarily dissipates, and, alongside, ill feeling arises. When ill feeling has accumulated in a family, what happiness is there to speak of?"

"No, no," replied Sheung Hong. "Yao gave Shun two daughters in marriage, and his household was harmonious.[333] King Wên[334] had numerous consorts, and they were as happily matched as lute and zithern. How is it that Shun and Wên did not lose their family happiness because of their many wives? Might it not rather be that it hinges on who holds the reins?

---

331 後陳 "intramural entourage" means, in this context, a group of women kept deep within the walls of a residence, i.e. a harem.

332 醋海翻波 "a sea of jealousy in violent upheaval" is a common Chinese idiom that hinges rhetorically on a play on the word 醋 "vinegar," which has the secondary sense of jealousy.

333 Mᵒ. Yao and Shun are legendary Chinese sage-kings of remote antiquity, a 聖人 sage being a human being of the highest moral category.

334 Mᵒ. King Wên is a posthumous title accorded by its holder's son, King Wu, who was the first emperor of the ancient 周 Chou (Mᴹ. *Zhōu*) dynasty. King Wên is also credited as having been a sage.

又謂女子無才便是德。姑[151]抑壓其智慧。剝奪其權利。自己
反粉白黛綠。充實後陳。卒至爭嬌奪寵。醋海翻波。因此而
喪家亡國者。曷可勝道。可慨也已。夫男女婚配。有摯愛之
感情。方能享家庭之幸福。若一夫多妻。決無摯愛感情。亦
猶一妻多夫。而男子勢難啞忍。男女之間。易地皆然。故妒
心潛生。愛心必弛。惡感亦緣之而起。家庭之內。惡感坌
集。何幸福之足云。尚康曰。否否。堯以二女妻舜。而家室
雍和。文王姬妾衆多。而瑟琴靜好。若舜若文。何以不因多
妻而喪失其家庭幸福者。大約在乎駕馭之人耶。

---

151 「姑」應為「故」之通假字。蓋其二字之四邑話讀音同。

"Furthermore, the phrase 'his concubines were not clothed in silk' appears in *The House Accounts of Confucius*.[335] Therefore, sages, too, took concubines.[336] What harm is there then in having many wives?"

Seeing his verbal subterfuge and irrelevant analogy for what it was, Sui Hing dismissed the matter with a laugh, and took leave of his fellow guests. (§38, 7/5/1910)

Sheung Hong lived henceforth in a haven of comfort.[337]

With willow stem's gentle charm, and peach-tree leaf's perfume strong,[338] enwrapped in sheet and quilt,[339] in bedroom sanctum sheltered head to foot, and sequestered in a splendid smoke, with leisure lamp and little pipe, he held his lovely concubine, and exhaled fine clouds.[340] A rosy face,[341] the black

---

335 The book named here (孔子家語 M°. K'ung Tzŭ Chia Yü Mᴹ. *Kǒngzǐ Jiāyǔ*) is one whose title has been translated into English in a wide variety of ways, owing to the ambiguity that surrounds the exact significance of one of its characters in particular, a character that has the everyday senses of home(s), house(s), household(s) or family(ies), but also a set of somewhat less common and rather different significations, such as "a set of people who espouse the ideas articulated by a thinker or teacher whom they follow", or what is likely the later sense of "a set of scholars who espouse ideas that are similar, but who are not necessarily followers of the same thinker or teacher", which senses are often translated as "school" or "school of thought". The translation of the title that is given here is an original one. *Sayings of the Confucian Family*, *The School Saying of Confucius*, and *Sayings of the House of Confucius* are other examples, given by sinologists James Legge, R.P. Kramers, and Michael Hunter, in the nineteenth century, the mid-twentieth century, and 2017 respectively. The translation of ancient book titles is often a difficult task, which necessitates thorough semantic, etymological and historical investigation and consideration, and considerable time was accordingly spent in the formulation of the title given here.

336 Sheung Hong is quoting a phrase from an ancient Confucian text out of context and thereby seemingly suggesting that Confucius, who is esteemed the greatest of sages, kept concubines. But the phrase he quotes actually relates to someone else. (Note: in its original context, the phrase 妾不衣帛 would be read "thou hast not clothed thy concubines in silk," but taken out

而況孔子家語。妾不衣帛。然則聖人亦曾娶妾者。雖多妻何
害。遂卿見他強詞奪理。擬不於倫。故一笑置之。與眾賓告
別。(§38, 7/5/1910) 從此尚康居於安樂窩中。柳枝柔媚。桃葉
香濃。一幅衾裯。全身覆幬。加以短笛閒燈。烟霞寄隱。抱
嬌妾。吐輕雲。紅顏黑

---

of this context, it could be interpreted as "his concubines were not clothed in silk", as is given here.)

337 安樂窩 "haven of comfort" or "comfort haven" was the name given by Mᵒ. Sung-dynasty polymath 邵雍 Shao Yung (1011–1077 C.E.) to his residences. It later developed into a general expression for a particularly comfortable place or situation, a sense similar to that of the phrase *bed of roses* in English.

338 桃葉 "Peach-tree Leaf" or "Peach Leaf" and 柳枝 "Willow Stem" are names of famous historical concubines that are commonly used allusively, as is the case here. Like many allusive names in Chinese, they are not distinguished orthographically as proper nouns (unlike *a Venus* for a beauty and *a Scrooge* for a miser in English) and are well suited, by virtue of their natural—in this case botanical—senses, to use in traditional Chinese poetry, in which the human often hides behind a naturalistic veil.

339 The archaic expression 衾裯 "sheet and quilt" is also allusively connected with concubinage.

340 The "fine clouds" and "splendid smoke" are references to opium smoke. Likewise, "leisure lamp" and "little pipe" are references to instruments used in opium smoking.

341 紅顏 "a rosy face" or "a reddish complexion" is a Chinese expression for "a pretty face", i.e. a beautiful woman.

milieu,[342] and a great sense that someone was *so joy-struck as to have forgotten Tsuák.*[343]

Word was, ere long, conveyed afar.

On hearing the news, his old wife Ma, whom time had rendered haggard of face, thought resentfully, *That unfaithful fellow has left me nothing but four low walls and a smokeless stove gone cold. It is solely thanks to my cousin, who took pity and came to my salvation, that I am here today. I had only hoped that soon, having made some savings, he would hoist his sail for home, that thereafter we should enjoy the evening of our lives together, as a white-headed pair of* yuen-yeung *ducks.*[344] *Who could have foreseen that, having attained a certain prosperity, he would turn his thoughts to becoming a man of* Ch´i *with his one wife and one concubine?*[345] *Now in the soft warm land of sensual delight, holding his A-chiao*[346] *in his arms, how would he even know that he still had at home a wife by marriage who had suffered the pain and bitterness of a thousand trials and tribulations? And should*

---

342 "The black milieu" is the world of opium smoking. Though technically the expression so translated (黑籍) refers not to a black milieu, environment or world so much as to membership or inhabitation of such a world. See footnotes 54 and 57.

343 This is an idiom. 劉禪 Mᵒ. Liu Shan (207/208–271/272 C.E.) was the last ruler of the state of 蜀 o. "Tsuák" (Mᵒ. Shu Mᴹ. *Shǔ*) during China's tumultuous three-kingdoms period. The state of Tsuák was eventually conquered by the rival state of 魏 Mᵒ. Wei. Liu Shan surrendered and soon relocated to Wei's capital, where he was created a duke and was able to live a life of material comfort. Old Chinese histories record that the king of Wei gave a banquet for Liu Shan to the accompaniment of Tsuák performances, which left his compatriots desolate with thoughts of their vanquished homeland, but had no effect on him, a display of apathy that did not escape the scrutiny of the king. At a later meeting, the king asked Liu Shan 頗思蜀否 "Dost thou think greatly of Tsuák?", to which he is recorded to have replied 此間樂不思蜀 "Here I am joy-struck, and so think not of Tsuák." This utterance was contracted into the pithy idiom that appears here and is still in common use today, which has the derogatory sense of "too happy to think of home". It seems highly likely that the reason the phrase 此間樂不思蜀 "Here I am

籍。大有樂不思蜀之意。無何風信迢遞。故園老荊。已憔悴
容顏矣。馬氏聞信。恨曰。負心郎四條壁立。寒灶無烟。幸
吾兄憐而拯恤之。始有今日。祇望他稍有積蓄。早理歸帆。
從此一對白首鴛鴦。共樂桑榆晚景。豈料室家晷爲贍裕。便
思作一妻一妾之齊人。此時在温柔鄉中。擁抱阿嬌。那知故
鄉尚有千磨百[152]折。茹苦含辛之髮妻乎。就令

152 「百」字原缺上畫。今參別處百字擬正。

joy-struck, and so think not of Tsuák" was so catchy was that it rhymed. This
rhyme would appear to have been lost in most of today's Chinese languages
(e.g. Mandarin and Cantonese) but to be very well preserved in the most
archaic of them, 潮州話 Teochew, a language which is, in the opinion of the
translator, ever a source of insights into ancient literature and linguistic
developments. "Tsuák", a transliteration of the Teochew pronunciation of the
name of Liu Shan's former state, was accordingly chosen for the purposes of
this translation. "Tsuák" rhymes in Teochew with the idiom's 樂 o. "lák", which
means "happy" or "joyous". Here, the expression "joy-struck" has been used
instead, so as to preserve a sense of the rhyme.

344 Paired 鴛鴦 c°. "*yuen-yeung* ducks" are a symbol of a loving monogamous
couple. See footnote 72.

345 The M°. "man of *Ch'i*" referred to here is the same cemetery-scavenging
husband who appears in the parable in *Mencius* alluded to in §1: see footnote
11.

346 An M°. "A-chiao" is a beautiful wife or concubine: see footnote 266.

he tire one day and the instinct to return stir,[347] *when in his home village he rested his luggage down, she would be in her dazzling prime, an apple blossom*[348] *in springtime, whereas I would be old and doddering, a willow after autumn.*[349] *That fickle man, with his hatred for the old and fondness for the new, would see me for a bristle in his back, and a thorn in his eye.*[350] *What, oh what, can I do?*

Her thoughts reaching this point, she could not help but burst into tears and, on the verge of hanging herself, cry till her voice was spent.

Withdrawn to her bed, a coverlet wrapped about her seated form, like smoke from her stove she rose not for several days, her tears coursing down as she cried and choked in resentment and regret.

Those several days later, their adopted son Kam Ngau, who was now nine years of age[351] and crouching before the bed, began hopping about and crying in hunger.[352]

On learning all of a sudden that her husband had taken a concubine, Ma had been moved to reflect on her predicament and to

---

347 The classical idiom here used that denotes the stirring of an instinct to return (鳥倦知還) has the literal sense of "as a bird that when tired knows to return". The idiom has its origin in a very well-known piece of classical literature (歸去來辭), written in 405/406 C.E., in the line 雲無心以出岫鳥倦飛而知還 "Where the clouds lack cores they let mountains protrude, and when the birds tire of flight they know to return." (Taken on its own, this line's first phrase, "Where the clouds lack cores they let mountains protrude", appears to paint a simple picture of mountains reaching through a layer of cloud. However, through its juxtaposition with the second phrase, "and when the birds tire of flight they know to return", which concerns the concept of instinct or intuition, it becomes apparent that, due to a wordplay, it can be read quite differently, so as to form a phrase that concerns the related concept of *unintentional action*. This secondary meaning is "The clouds unintentionally let mountains protrude" or "Where the cloud is unwitting it lets mountains protrude". The secondary sense comes about because the word 心 "core(s)" also has the sense of "mind(s)" or "heart(s)" and therefore the expression 無心 "lack cores" carries the secondary meaning of "without heart/mind" or "unheartedly/unmindedly", which is a Chinese word for "unintentionally" or

他日鳥倦知還。息裝故里。彼則年華方艷。恰如春候之海
棠。儂則老態婆娑。一似經秋之楊柳。二三其德之男子。憎
舊憐新。直視妾如背上芒。眼中釘矣。奈何。奈何。思至此
不禁失聲大哭。幾欲自經。連數日擁衾而臥。炊烟不起。咽
恨啼怨。淚漣枕席。時養子金牛。年已九齡。伏在床前。跳
躍啼飢。馬氏本賦性賢淑。驟聞夫婿納妾。乃自悲身世。感
懷苦況。

"unwittingly". Through this wordplay, the line forms a description not only
of a visible scene of nature, but of one that is redolent with the invisible
intuition and unintentional action at play within nature.)

348 Specifically the blossom of the Chinese flowering apple *Malus spectabilis.*

349 The Chinese word 婆娑 "doddering" can also be used to describe the flailing
motion of windblown willow stems. Furthermore, there is a connection
between old age and bare willow stems, words used to describe the withering
of plants also being used in Chinese to describe human aging. There is thus
a strong semantic connection in Chinese between the phrases "old and
doddering" and "a willow after autumn" that is not apparent in English.

350 These are set expressions similar to English's "a thorn in one's side" or "a
dagger in one's breast".

351 Eight years old by the Western reckoning.

352 The single character 時 at the beginning of this sentence indicates a scene
change to a period of time inferred in the preceding text, i.e. several days
later. In Chinese this change is effected quite smoothly without mention of
where the boy has been in the preceding days, e.g. away at school, or with
friends, relatives, etc.

lament her lot in life, which was only natural; but she had ever been endowed with feminine virtue, and seeing her child now crying in hunger in a state most pitiable, she reassured herself, *I am wrong. I am wrong. What is done is done. Of what avail can death or despair be? Though I should wail till I were a cuckoo coughing crimson,*[353] *which in my spittoon turned to turquoise,*[354] *that faithless fellow beyond the seas would not consider for a moment, as he and his sweetheart hugged and spoke heart-to-heart, that he had yet a spilornis-poison-preferring Hsüan-ling wife.*[355] (§39, 14/5/1910)

Furthermore, a husband being his wife's guide-line[356] *and a woman's duty being to obey him, even if he forsook me, I ought not to utter a word in dissent. I am now approaching forty, yet remain childless. And while I enjoy the gratification of having an adopted son, and while he is nominally a son, when all is said and done I am really* Po Tao *without*

---

353 This is an allusion to a Chinese fable, which holds that the cuckoo is the reincarnation of an ancient king who coughs out blood as he cries in sorrow. The Chinese name for the rhododendron and azalea, the 杜鵑花 "cuckoo flower", comes from the story that the red or red-flecked flowers of certain varieties are stained with the blood of this king-cum-cuckoo.

354 Chinese legend tells of a righteous minister of antiquity (萇弘) who was wronged, and whose loyal blood, which was preserved after his suicide, turned into turquoise. The expression used here, 化碧 "to turn to turquoise", is one of a number of Chinese expressions that have their origin in this legend and concern the undying loyalty of a wronged party. It should also be noted that traditionally the relationship of a wife to a husband was often paralleled with that of a minister to his sovereign. Ma is invoking this parallel.

355 This line references a well-known story: One day the first emperor of the 唐 ᴍº. T'ang dynasty decided to bestow a gift of several beautiful women on his distinguished minister 房玄齡 Fang Hsüan-ling. Fang Hsüan-ling, who is said to have lived in abject fear of his termagant wife, declined the gift on account of her objection to him taking any concubines. The emperor later summoned Fang Hsüan-ling's wife and presented her with the option of either drinking wine infused with the deadly poison of the serpent

此亦常情。忽見孺子啼飢。情殊可憫。乃自相慰解曰。妾悮矣。妾悮矣。事已成矣。悲亦何益。死亦何益。雖哭到杜鵑啼紅。唾壺化碧。爾時海外薄倖郎。方與意中人。兩相偎抱。談心曲事。又遑計及尙有甯甘鴆毒之玄齡婦耶。(§39, 14/5/1910) 況夫爲妻綱。婦人有從夫之義。縱使將妾棄置。亦復何道。妾年將四旬。而膝下猶虛。雖有養子承歡。名詞上雖稱有子。事實上究是伯道無

eagle (a bird of the genus *Spilornis*) and dying jealous, or of permitting her husband to accept his gift. Fang Hsüan-ling's wife proceeded to drain the cup of poisoned wine, which was in fact only vinegar. This act caused the emperor to dismiss his idea and earned Fang Hsüan-ling's wife a place in history as an archetypal jealous wife and indomitable woman.

356 Confucian moral philosophy holds that 君為臣綱夫爲妻綱父為子綱 "a sovereign is [or *formeth*] a subject's guide-line; a husband is a wife's guide-line; and a father is a son's guide-line", and that these 三綱 "three guide-lines" are of key importance to ideal social structure. ("Guide-line(s)" is an original translation that is intended to reflect the word's base meaning of *a net's guide rope*, i.e. a line that comes off of a net which is held and used to guide it when casting, or tied to anchor it in place when it is left out-stretched. It is one of a large set of ancient terms in Chinese relating to governance, tradition, and social organisation that have a metaphorical connection to threads, nets, strings and cables. Existing translations, which include "headship(s)", "bond(s)", and "norm(s)", do not adequately reflect this association, which is key to the traditional analogies in which it features.)

a boy.[357] *Should that beauty come here one day and bring forth offspring in my stead, ensuring the continuance of the Wongs' oblations,*[358] *it would be some consolation to me. The proverb says it is a senior woman's*[359] *good fortune when a junior wife bears a son.*[360] *Why must I adopt this small-mindedness and deficiency of spirit, and give the denizens of this place cause to sneer? Furthermore, the laws and statutes on the taking of concubines are writ large and clear. The men of my country who have trains of consorts and concubines must number many millions. How, then, am I alone? And why, then, must I imitate the mean and peculiarly jealous women of this world, who compete for preeminence in beauty and fight for love and favour?* Her thoughts reaching this point, Ma's troubled breast calmed.

This sour wife's full breast of bayberry wine having now cleared completely of its lees,[361,362] she stroked her son Kam Ngau's back and said, "Cry not my son, mummy is getting up." She then inspected Kam Ngau and said, "You know don't you, son, that you now have a concubine-mother? If mummy should die," and at this point her voice turned to a teary whisper, "misfortune will surely meet you." When she had finished crying, she wiped her tears and straightened her bodice, before forcing herself up to begin on the housework.

357　晉書 Mº. "*The Chin*" (a history of the Chin dynasty published in the T'ang dynasty, whose head compiler, incidentally, was the 房玄齡 Fang Hsüan-ling named in the previous part) contains the biography of a man named 鄧伯道 Têng Po Tao, whom it describes as a selfless and principled official, who, through various twists of fate and choices based on principle, died without a son and heir. It adds that people at the time, who lamented this fact, coined the saying 天道無知使鄧伯道無兒 "Heaven by a fool's ploy left Têng Po Tao without a boy." Later, this saying was contracted into the expression used here, 伯道無兒 "(to be) Po Tao without a boy", which means to be without a son.

358　Offerings for the sustenance of deceased ancestors in the netherworld.

359　大婦 "senior woman" is one of many expressions in Chinese for lawful wife, as opposed to concubine.

兒。倘他日彼姝歸來。代妾作繭。而黃氏血食。不致將斬。
心亦稍慰。諺云。小妻[153]生子大婦福。儂又何必作此淺狹之
量。貽鄉黨笑乎。況娶妾之律。載在明條。吾國男子。姬妾
成列者。何啻萬萬。何獨於儂。又何必效世間之齷齪奇妒婦
女。爭妍媢。奪寵愛乎。思至此。胸次又爲之坦然。此際酸
娘子滿胸楊梅。已渣滓盡淨矣。乃撫其子金牛之背曰。兒勿
啼。阿娘起矣。復諦視金牛曰。兒亦知兒多一庶母乎。阿娘
死。兒必無幸。言至此。聲復爲之幽咽。於是拭淚整襟。强
起而理家政。

---

153 原文「妻」字模糊不清，既似「妻」又似「妾」。今參別處妻、妾字擬
正。

---

360 The words "senior" and "junior" refer here to seniority of precedence only. 小
妻 "junior wife" was another expression for concubine.

361 (1) The word 酸 "sour" has here its secondary Chinese sense of "jealous." (2)
The word "wine" does not appear in the original sentence, the name of the
liquid referred to being omitted by an act of ellipsis not permissible in
grammatical English.

362 楊梅 the *Chinese bayberry* or *red bayberry* is a red fruit, about the size of a
macadamia nut, that can be used to make a fruit wine. This wine is red, but
when its somewhat sour bayberry sediment sinks, it clears. It is probably this
rather graphic change that the author is alluding to in this analogy, the sour
sediment representing jealousy, on account of the aforementioned dual
senses of the word sour.

Meanwhile, Sheung Hong was egregiously enamoured of Tsiu Hei. At times, having viewed himself in the mirror and seen in reflection the hair which hung down from his temples flecked with frost, he could not help but feel ashamed that he was ill-matched as a partner, and appreciate the atmosphere of the bedchamber. When by pillow screen or dressing table, the object of his affections would oft cast cold looks to fright him. So he had no choice but to be accommodating and forgiving, and not to pick holes when he found them, in order that he might win her favour.

But sly Tsiu Hei advanced with each window of opportunity, at times displaying a bewitching charm to secure his indulgence, at times unleashing a coquettish innocence to intensify his affection, by way of which she was free to amuse herself as she pleased in the tea rooms and public bars, and the theatres and picture galleries. Consequently, neighbours cast criticism, and she became well known for her immorality. But while Sheung Hong knew of people's tuts of disapproval, there was nothing he could do, for he dared not voice his displeasure.

Huh! He who spoke previously of a real man's masculine might had been subdued by feminine might! And he who spoke previously of not fearing any Ho Tung lion now feared a rouge tiger!

When our country's uneducated women reside in a land where there is liberty of action, it is lawless liberty to which they adapt most readily. Furthermore, those who are their heavens[363] have neither a fine formula for reining them in, nor the ability to reform their wild natures, or to check and prevent insidious developments. Instead, they ingratiate themselves in every possible way, in order to please them.

---

363 Their husbands. (Traditionally wives were associated with the earth, representing the feminine, or *yin*, principle in nature, and husbands with heaven, representing the equal male, or *yang*, principle in nature.)

乃尙康對於俏喜。孾[154]愛殊甚。有時對鏡自照。兩鬢星霜。
未免自慙非偶。領畧閨中況味。枕屛粧畔。而所歡時作冷觀
以驚人。不得已姑爲涵量[155]。不摘小疵。以買其歡心。而狡
猾之俏喜。蹈隙而進。有時肆其狐媚。以固其恩寵。有時
撒[156]其嬌癡。以增人愛憐。於是茶亭酒肆。畫院劇塲。任意
遊嬉。因此而街鄰指摘。穢德彰聞。尙康雖知人言嘖嘖。無
奈敢怒而不敢言。嘻。疇昔所謂大丈夫之雄威者。已爲雌威
所箝制矣。疇昔所謂不畏河東獅者。而今反畏一胭脂虎矣。
夫以吾國無敎育之婦女。居留於舉動自由之地。其不法律之
自由。最易沾染。況爲其所天者。旣無駕御之良方。又不能
防微杜漸。潛消其野心。反復百般獻媚。以博其歡愉。

154 原文「孾」字模糊不淸。今審文義、報別孾字擬正。
155 「量」蓋「諒」字之誤。二字音同易相溷也。
156 「撒」原作「撤」，字之訛也。今正。

Whenever, over their marriage beds, they act slightly contrary to their wives' wishes, or utter a few words that occasion offence, they willingly bend their knees and take their vows,[364] *or unhesitatingly bear their torsos and sue for peace.*[365] *It is Chou's wife who frames the laws of conduct,*[366] *and her husband, insensible of shame, who bears a cane on his back.*[367] *So these uneducated women are continually indulged, and consequently their sense of immoderation continually grows, and their sense of shame continually diminishes. They go off on pleasure outings without hesitation, starting with sweetmeat shops, then gradually moving to liquor shops*

---

364 The expression translated here as "take your vows" (受戒), which appeared also in §37, refers to a Buddhist initiation ceremony in which the initiate accepts to afterward abide by certain religious dictates. Here, as in §37, it takes on a broader sense of making promises in respect of one's future conduct. See footnote 319.

365 This is an allusion to a well-known story recorded in the universal history of China compiled by 司馬遷 Mᵒ. Ssŭ-ma Ch'ien circa 100 B.C.E. entitled 史記 *The History*. (This is how the present translator would render the short title by which this book is and has been known for more than 1,500 years. Reading its characters as individual words instead of as one, it might also be translated as "*The Record Keeper's Chronicles*". The simple two-character title was likely formed from a contraction of the longer earlier title 太史公記 *T'ai-shih-kung Chi*, which this translator would give as "*The Chronicles of His Lordship the Grand Record Keeper*". The shorter title has been translated into English in numerous ways, many of which appear to be attempts at reflecting the full significance of the book's earlier longer title, rather than the simpler significance of the later, presumably contracted, title. Recently, the translation "*Records of the Historian*" has been proposed, which seems, to this translator, to be a somewhat unreflective amalgam of both possible readings.) The story relates how 廉頗 Lien P'o, a general of the state of 趙 Chao, stripped to the waist, had his hands bound behind him, and, with a whipping cane held against his back, presented himself at the door of the

每於床第之間。稍拂其意。自行屈膝受戒。片言獲罪。不惜
肉袒求成。周婆制禮。丈夫負荊。不知愧赧。故無教育之女
子。日受驕縱[157]。則侈心日生。恥心日泯。冶游無忌。始而
飴糖店。寖[158]假而酒水店。

157 「驕縱」與「嬌縱」通。蓋嬌者，驕之通假字也。
158 此「寖」字於「浸」，音、義同。

---

prime minister, 藺相如 Lin Hiang-ju, in a display of sincere contrition for
his earlier resentment of the same, which he had recognised was unjustified.
This story, which concludes with forgiveness and the establishment of a firm
friendship, gave rise to a number of classical idioms that relate to sincere
contrition. The words 肉袒 "bare their torsos" are a contraction of one of
these idioms: 肉袒負荊, which has the literal sense of "to bare one's torso
and carry, on one's back, a cane".

366 儀禮 *The Book of Etiquette and Ceremonial* is a central text of Confucianism
that is known by a variety of names, including 禮 *The Rites*, a name which
could also be translated as "*The Laws of Conduct*". Traditional wisdom holds
(contrary to historical evidence) that 周公製禮 M°. "*The Rites* were framed
by (the) Duke (of) Chou," the sagacious son of the King Wên and younger
brother of the King Wu mentioned in footnote 334. *The Rites* are also held
to enshrine China's first marriage code, for which reason 周公之禮 "The
Duke of Chou's Rite" is an epithet for marriage. Here, the author uses the
(pre-established) phrase 周婆製禮 "Chou's wife frames the laws of conduct",
which suggests, derisively, a wife's usurpation of her husband's role as the
ultimate arbiter in matters of social conduct, and in marriage particularly.

367 This is another allusion to the story referred to above in footnote 365.

(the tavern and the sweetmeat shop—or in Western speech lo-lee shop[368]*—being refuges of the vile and unsavoury), which they come and go from of their own accord, and in the end they engage, brazenly, in all kinds of unruly behaviour. Yet if one traces the causes of this wickedness,*[369] *they lie in fact not with women but with men.*

My chronicle having reached this point, I cannot bear to commit more of it to paper, for I love my fellows, and it would shame them. Yet neither can I bear not to commit more of it to paper, for I love my fellows, and it would warn them. Thus pressed, I shall attempt a general outline, that it might act as a Zen shout and bat-thwack[370] *about the heads of my fellows residing in foreign lands.* (§40, 21/5/1910)

Brought near to his last breath under the entrancement of smoke and flesh, Sheung Hong was like a man long dead. And before each act and utterance it was to Tsiu Hei's face that he looked for his lead.

---

368 This is clearly a transliteration of the English words *lolly shop*. The expression's last character was, by the author's time, a well-recognised and standard transliteration of the English word *shop*, for which reason it is not hyphenated in translation. Actually, by the author's time, this transliteration of shop had taken on its own somewhat extended sense in the See Yip language, being used, for example, in respect of canneries in Canada. It also appears, in respect of cookshops, in Ballarat's *English and Chinese Advertisers*, which date from the 1850s.

369 Though its primary sense is not so specific, the word 罪惡 "wickedness" was used at this time, as it still is today, as a translation of the Christian word *sin*. The Buddhist word for sin, in contrast, originated not with the adoption of an existing Chinese term, but with a new coinage, 罪孽 "wickedness that is met with karmic retribution".

370 The expression translated here as "a Zen shout and bat-thwack" (棒喝) is a Zen Buddhist term for the controlled use of shouting, and striking with a form of bat, the purposes of which include such things as the dispelling of delusion and the triggering of spontaneous realisation.

(飴糖店西語拉利澀與酒店同爲藏污納垢之地) 私自往來。卒至明目張胆。作種種不規則之行爲矣。溯其罪惡之原因。實不在婦女而在男子。吾紀至此。吾[159]愛吾同胞。實不忍形諸筆墨。以爲吾同[160]胞羞。吾愛吾同胞。又不忍不形諸筆墨。以爲吾同　胞儆。無已。試舉其大畧[161]。以爲我居留外地之同胞。作當頭之棒喝也歟。(§40, 21/5/1910) 尙康爲烟色所迷。奄奄一息。如陳死人。而一言一動。無不仰承俏喜之顏色。

159　原文「吾」字模糊不清。今參他處字擬正。

160　原文「同」字模糊殘損。今審文義，及他處字，擬正。

161　原文「畧」字不清。今審文義，及他處字，擬正。

Tsiu Hei looked on him as though he were nothing, meeting every night, on the pretext of theatre-going, with the objects of her affection.

Throughout the day Sheung Hong was in the shop, and unbeknownst to him, his house's interior was the very semblance of a brothel's, wild bees and wandering butterflies going unceasingly to and fro.[371]

One day, Lin Neung came to visit. The house's double doors, though, were shut fast, and her knocks thereon went unanswered. Having surmised that Tsiu Hei was elsewhere, she suddenly heard the sound of footsteps within. Lin Neung knocked a second time. There was silence. Not knowing what to make of this, she spied through the keyhole. But the keyhole was blocked by a key. Certain there must be someone inside the house, she yelled out reprovingly, "Shrew! You and I have no grievance: why serve me up this dish of closed-door soup?"[372] There was silence still and, to her great alarm, for a long while.

Neighbours, having heard the shouting, had gathered round to watch and listen. Witnessing the situation, and having discerned eight-or-nine-tenths, they began to conjecture in private. Amongst the many venturing suspicions, there were those who said that within there was for certain some affair of an intimate nature, and those who said they feared there might have been some other occurrence.

---

371 狂蜂浪蝶 "wild bees and wandering butterflies" is a rather direct translation of a Chinese expression for "womanizers and philanderers", bees and butterflies having a fondness for flowers, which in Chinese represent women. The word 浪 "wandering" in the expression also has the sense of "loose" or "dissolute", something which is lost in translation.

372 閉門羹 "closed-door soup" is a set phrase, one which has its origin in the practice of a renowned courtesan of the M°. T′ang dynasty, who served a consolatory bowl of soup to those visitors to whom she declined her services.

俏喜視之。值無物耳。每夜必託詞觀劇。以會所歡。日間尚
康在肆中。其室內狂蜂浪蝶。此往彼來。日無停晷。渾如妓
院。而尚康不知也。一日練娘到訪。雙扉緊閉。叩之不應。
意彼他適。忽聞內有步履聲。再叩之。寂然。心甚疑惑。從
鑰隙窺之。內有鑰匙。塞插鑰隙。決其必有人在室內。故疾
聲叫罵之曰。潑辣貨。儂與汝並無嫌怨。爲何以閉門羹待
我。久之。亦寂然。駭甚。斯時街鄰聞叫呼聲。環集觀聽。
睹此狀況。已窺八九。於是竊竊私議。有云內決有暧昧情事
者。有云恐有他變者。紛紛猜擬。

A clansman of Sheung Hong's, who happened to be passing, then said, "Do not make a commotion gentlefolk.[373] I shall prize the doors open, so we may learn the truth of it all." Thereupon he raced to a neighbouring store and borrowed an iron implement, with which he broke open one of the doors. The group, following him, swarmed inside.

Tsiu Hei, who was lying on a bed, rose with a start, and began to rub her star-bright eyes with her hands, affecting the look of one who had woken from deep sleep. Seeing this group assembled before her, she shouted loudly, "What rule of common decency sees people breaking open other's doors in broad daylight and entering the inner sanctums of their houses! How could it be for anything other than to commit robbery?"

"We are not robbers," replied one wily member of the group. "We want only to catch a robber."

"Who's this robber you've seen fit to come here to catch?" asked Tsiu Hei.

"The one we want to catch is not a robber who robs valuables, but a robber who has robbed you mistress,"[374] replied the clansman.

On hearing this Tsiu Hei's face changed colour. But she forced out a rebuke: "Are you all deranged? Why are you spouting these ravings? Leave at once. I shall inform the police and have you arrested should you delay."

---

373 While the term of address that is used in the Chinese (諸君) is generally translated as "gentlemen", it is given here as "gentlefolk". This term of address can be used in Literary Chinese in respect of men and women inclusively and even women specifically, and such usages were current amongst male and female writers at the time, including amongst China's new feminists. The author employs the term in preference to the alternative 諸公, which is also translated as "gentlemen", but is only used in respect of men. The translation "gentlemen" was avoided in the author's previous addresses to readers for the same reason.

時適有尚康之族人經過。乃曰。諸君勿譁。待吾撬門而入。可知其究竟。即奔往鄰店。借一鐵具。破其扉。羣人從之。蜂擁而入。俏喜在臥榻上突起。以兩手揉其星眸。假作熟睡驚覺狀。見羣人畢集。大聲喝曰。青天白日。破人門戶。入人閨閣。成何事體。豈欲作強盜耶。內有狡者曰。余等非強盜。欲捕拿強盜耳。俏喜曰。誰是強盜。容汝到此間捕拿。其族人曰。吾等所欲捕拿者。非盜財之強盜。乃盜嫂[162]之強盜耳。俏喜聞言色變。強罵之曰。汝等瘋耶。何為發此譫語。速去。倘若俄延。即鳴警捕汝。

162 按，《清稗類鈔・音樂類・粵人好歌》：「凡村落人奴之女，嫁日，不敢乘車，女子率自持一傘以自蔽。既嫁，人率稱之為嫂，此言女一嫁不能復為處子也。」

374 The word translated here as "mistress" (嫂) is recorded to have been used in Kwang Tung as a colloquial term of address for wives or concubines who came from a bondmaid background. The standard sense of the word is "one's elder brother's wife". There is no English equivalent for either sense, but "mistress" seemed the most appropriate expression.

Lin Neung, having felt most ill at ease on seeing the state affairs were in, had long since seized a window of opportunity and withdrawn. The group surveyed all around, but there was not a sound or shadow. Suddenly, right in the midst of their surprise and puzzlement, they heard a crash! Something heavy had fallen down from somewhere above. Shocked, the group rushed over to see what it was: It was Song Tak.[375]

They questioned him, but, ashamed, he made no reply. They then strove to land blows upon him. Some wanted to tie him up and hand him over at the police station. But the clansman said, "Such an approach would make for a great impediment to our respectability as Chinese people. It would be more expedient to set him free."

The group spitting in his face, Song Tak scurried away, sheltering his head in his hands. (§41, 4/6/1910)

Song Tak having made his escape, the neighbours ringed about Tsiu Hei, some yelling vitriolic abuse, others reproaching her by way of reason.

"He is a clansman[376] of my husband and the person who brought me to Australia," said a shamefaced Tsiu Hei, fighting to explain herself. "He often comes here to chat, whether my husband is present or not. It is nothing out of the ordinary, nor something to which my husband objects. What concern is it of your good selves that you should make such a commotion over it? This is exactly what is referred to as *blowing a pool of vernal water into furrows.*"[377]

---

375 The same Song Tak who appeared in §31, and accompanied Tsiu Hei over on the boat to Australia.

376 A greater-clan clansman: see footnote 148.

377 This phrase has its origin in a tune poem written by a certain 馮延巳 ᴹ.
Féng Yánsì: 風乍起 吹皺一池春水 "The wind arose asudden, and blew a

練娘見此狀態。情面上甚難過意早已乘間回去。羣人四圍窺
眺。並無影響。正在疑訝。忽聞嘩喇之聲。有一重物。從上
墜下。羣人大驚。趨視之爽德也。羣相詰問。愧無以對。羣
爭毆之。有欲綑交警署者。其族人某曰。若如此辦法。大有
碍於吾華人體面。不如陰縱之去。羣唾其面。彼乃抱頭鼠
竄而遁。(§41, 4/6/1910) 爽德旣遁。街鄰環繞俏喜。有唾罵之
者。有理責之者。俏喜皺顏[163]強辨曰。彼爲吾夫之同宗。又
携妾來澳者。彼不論吾夫在否。常到此坐談。亦尋常事。吾
夫尙不芥蒂。正所謂吹皺一池春水。干卿甚事。而擾
攘若此。

163 「皺」蓋「皺」字之誤也。

pool of vernal water into furrows [i.e. rippled its surface]". The expression
that appears here in the previous sentence, 干卿甚事 "What concern is/was
it of your good self/selves?", was posed to the poem's author by an emperor
of the ᴍᵒ Southern T´ang dynasty in respect of the line in question, and has
become connected with it.

"If he came to chat, then chatting is all he would have been doing," said a neighbour. "What do you have to say about how he came to fall from an upper window while you were lying asleep in bed?"

"He came just now in search of my husband, there being something he had to discuss with him," said Tsiu Hei, after a moment of frozen dismay. "And because the roof had a leak, and because my husband was in the shop, I asked him to go out through the upper window onto the tiles to check, and then to hire a workman to conduct the repair. I was extremely tired, so I lay back on the bed to close my eyes and rest, and happened to fall into a state of black comfort.[378] I then woke with a start on account of a sudden clamour. I should imagine that your commotion also caused him to lose his footing and fall."

"Landlords repair leaks," scoffed the neighbour. "What need was there for someone else to check the roof? He didn't say a word about any such thing when he fell to ground either!"

Tsiu Hei was lost for words.

The neighbours sniggered, and then dispersed in full uproar.

Song Tak and Tsiu Hei, their feelings for each other unbroken, had heretofore oft rekindled their old romance. For the butterfly loves still the remaining perfume of a flower that has been removed to another courtyard, and the swallow seeks regardless his old stronghold in a hall that has changed masters.[379]

---

378 黑甜 "black comfort/black sweetness" is a Chinese expression for (sweet) sleep: see footnote 54.

379 The 燕尋舊壘 "swallow seeking out his old stronghold" is a literary trope that has, perhaps, its ultimate origin in a ᴹᴼ. Tʻang-dynasty poem by the celebrated 劉禹錫 ᴹᴹ. *Liú Yǔxī* entitled 烏衣巷 "Black Clothes' Lane", in which the swallows that once visited the mansions of the powerful in the city of *Nánjīng* are depicted as now visiting their ruins, which have new and less exalted inhabitants.

鄰人曰。彼到坐談。則坐談已耳。何以汝在臥榻而睡。彼又
在樓窗上墜下。汝又何說。俏喜憮然有間曰。彼適間到來。
覓吾夫有事相商。因吾夫在店。我因屋漏。懇他由樓窗上瓦
面檢查。催工修葺。妾倦極。倚榻假寐。不覺偶入黑甜。忽
聞喧噪之聲。故而驚覺。忖彼亦緣汝等擾攘。故失足而墜
耳。鄰人誚之曰。屋漏自有屋主修理。何用別人檢查。況彼
墜地時。並無一語道及此事乎。俏喜語塞。鄰人竊笑。一哄
而散。先是爽德與俏喜兩情未斷。時續舊歡。雖則花移別
院。而蝶尙戀餘香。堂易主人。而燕尤尋舊壘。

Accordingly, Song Tak had watched for every return Sheung Hong made to China. With each regular window of opportunity, he had stepped forward to be *Li donning Chang's hat*,[380] and the dove residing in the magpie's nest.[381] *A wild duck and a gull of leisure as inseparable as layered lacquer, who indulged in mulberry meadow's dewy grass with brazenness as boundless as the sky above.*[382]

On the day in question, Song Tak had tiptoed in as soon as he spied Sheung Hong [leave].

Their lovemaking only just concluded, they had heard a sudden rapping at the door, and alarmed and fearful, had not known what to do. People's voices had then begun to gather, and the door-knocking to grow more impatient. Thinking the game was up, Tsiu Hei had suddenly remembered an upper window leading onto the tiles, which had been devised to act as a fire escape. This she had hurriedly made Song Tak climb through, before covering herself with a quilt and closing her eyes to rest, which she devised to act as her disguise.

Yet on hearing the neighbours break the door and enter, Song Tak's nerve had broken, and his hands and feet had lost their usefulness. His foothold also less than fast, and his body plump and heavy, he had then dropped, flipping in doing so.

The window was fortunately not very high, and he did not meet with serious injury, but his face and limbs were left unbearably sore and swollen.

---

380 張冠李戴 M°. "to be Li donning Chang's hat" or "to put Chang's hat on Li's head" is an idiom that means "to confuse oneself with another, or to confuse one person or thing for another".

381 鳩居鵲巢 "to be a dove residing in the magpie's nest" is an idiom that means "to have taken and to be enjoying that which belongs to another". It has its origin in *The Odes* (召南・鵲巢).

382 This line, which is an antithetical couplet formed from a pair of paired quadrisyllabic phrases, all written in metre, is rich in literary allusion. The essential aspects are the following: 野鶩 "wild duck(s)" and 閒鷗 "gull(s) of leisure" are literary expressions for illicit lovers; 似漆 (an abbreviation of

故爽德每伺尙康囘唐。即踏隙而進。常張冠而李戴。似鵲巢
而鳩居。野鶩閒鷗。情投似漆。桑田露草。胆大如天164。是
日窺伺尙康□165戶。爽德卽躡足而進。正在尤雲滯雨之餘。
忽聞叩扉聲甚急。二人惶駭。手足無措。俄而人聲愈集。叩
戶愈急。俏喜知事已敗露。忽憶樓上有一窻戶。通瓦面爲避
火計者。急使爽德緣窻而上。彼則蒙被假寐。以爲遮飾計。
不料爽德聞鄰人破扉而入。心膽俱顫。手足失其效用。加以
體胖身重。立足不牢。從上166翻身而下。幸而樓不甚高。不
致重傷。而面目四肢。已痛癉不堪矣。

164 膽大如天，言色膽大如天。原文「天」字缺乏上畫。今審文義，及他處
     字，擬正。
165 此字不清。據其文義，似當作「出」。
166 原文「上」字缺底。今審文義，及他處字，擬正。

似膠似漆) "as inseparable as layered lacquer" is a set expression used to
describe the closeness of feelings between friends or lovers; and 桑田露草
"mulberry meadow's dewy grass" means the setting for a sexual assignation.
This last expression might be the author's own coinage: a reworking of the
expression 野田草露 "wild meadow grass's dew", which references a song
within *The Odes* (鄭風・野有蔓草) and has the same sense, through the
introduction of the character 桑 "mulberry", which references another song
within *The Odes* (鄘風・桑中), both songs being concerned with open-air
assignations between lovers.

Not perhaps the perilousness of the horse stable,[383] *but, hah! all the enduring disgrace of the dog hole.*[384] *Had heaven dispensed its retribution on the licentious, or was it merely making, thereby, a little test of their artfulness?* (§42, 25/6/1910)

The affair became the butt of town gossip after its discovery, and the employees in the shop joked and jibed about it amongst themselves. Sheung Hong, too, knew something of its outline. But there was one puzzling thing about it that he could not work out. A thing that gnawed at him and unsettled him deep at heart.

One day, a clansman of his came to visit.

"What news is there on the street?" asked Sheung Hong, as he reclined on his smoking bed.

"Still in a dream are you? The talk of the street, sir," said the clansman crossly, "is nothing other than your domestic affairs."

"What is there that can be said of my domestic affairs?" replied Sheung Hong.

The clansman then proceeded to relate the previous day's sordid goings-on in their entirety, before saying

---

383 On learning that his stable had burnt down, Confucius is reported to have enquired as to whether any people had been injured in the fire, but not to have asked after the state of his horses. This anecdote, which is recorded in 論語 "*The Confucian Analects*", has traditionally been taken as a demonstration of Confucius's concern for human beings over animals. It is also the source of a connection between the stable and human injury, which occasionally features as a literary trope, as would appear to be the case here.

384 The expression 狗竇 "dog hole" is used here, on the one hand, in its colloquial Cantonese and See Yip sense, in which the word 竇 "hole" does not mean hole but rather "nest" or "den". In this first sense, it refers to Tsiu Hei and Song Tak's illicit love nest. On the other hand, 狗竇 "dog hole" retains here what is its Literary Chinese sense of

嘻。雖無馬廏之凶險。而有狗竇之貽羞。天之報施淫人。抑
亦小試其技耳。(§42, 25/6/1910) 自此事發現之後。街談巷議。
藉爲笑柄。店中工伴[167]。互相笑謔。尙康亦稍知其涯畧。但
一箇悶葫蘆。未能打破。中心怒然不安。一日。其族人某到
坐[168]。尙康偃息於烟床上問曰。街上有何新聞。其族人拂然
曰。兄猶在夢中耶。街上所言。盡君家事。尙康曰。吾有何
家事可言。其族人始將前日醜[169]態。和盤托出。復[170]曰。

---

167 「工伴」原誤倒作「伴工」。今正。按，「工伴」，員工也。此詞為奧洲早
　　期之華字報所多用，如言「有工伴私作夜工」，「工伴破門偷竊」是等。
　　或省作「伴」，如言「除夕伊邇，元旦將屆，東報各伴停工一星期」；或
　　以「伴」當量詞用，如言「每伴工人」。

168 此「坐」非單「坐凳」、「坐席」之謂，實乃粵語「登門拜訪」之婉稱
　　也。其粵音為俗音，與「坐收漁利」者相異。

169 原文「醜」字模糊不清。今審文義、別醜字擬正。

170 原文「復」字模糊。今參別復字擬正。

"a hole in a wall that provides for the ingress and egress of dogs". In this second sense, in connection with the concept of disgrace, it forms an allusion to a well-known story: The celebrated thinker, statesman and rhetorician of the sixth century B.C.E. 晏子 ᴹᴼ. Yen Tzŭ made a diplomatic visit, as envoy for his state of 齊 Ch'i, to the rival state of 楚 Ch'u. Desiring to humiliate Ch'i and its representative, who happened to be particularly short of stature, the king of Ch'u had had the gates to his capital closed and an exceptionally low door constructed beside them. When Yen Tzŭ was invited to enter through this door, he is said to have made a statement that had the effect of forcing the opening of the gates: 使狗國者從狗門入 今臣使楚不當從此門入 "He who is an envoy to a country of dogs enters through a door for dogs. As an envoy to the country of Ch'u, I ought not to enter through this door."

"Your failure to take stern charge of her is in fact bringing disgrace upon us Wongs.[385] I should not have taken the liberty of telling you, were it not that I too am a member of your clan."

At this, Sheung Hong cast down the smoking pipe he had been holding, opened wide his somnolent smoker's eyes, and summoned up all the power in his smoke-worn throat, shouting out, "I shall pit myself against this wanton woman with all the life in my veins!" Thereupon he left in high dudgeon for home.

Finding, on reaching there, Tsiu Hei gorgeously attired and appealingly painted, looking as though she was about to head out, Sheung Hong's masculine might surged forth. Rousing his hundredfold smoke-seasoned spirit, stretching out his half-black half-yellow fingers, giving free rein to his half-high half-low smoker's voice,[386] he said abusively, "It's a fine thing you've done."

"You're mad," replied Tsiu Hei. "What is the cause of this departure from your state of normality?"

"Do not try to conceal it," replied Sheung Hong. "I know everything of your wanton behaviour."

On hearing these words, Tsiu Hei knew the game was up.

Immediately she put to effect her tactic of the pre-emptive strike[387] and unleashed her leonine might. Falling on Sheung Hong, she knocked him to the ground. Then, with one hand grabbing at his collar and the other tweaking his ear, she began to bawl and berate.

"Vile plague corpse!"[388]

"In what act of wanton behaviour have I engaged?"

---

385 The speaker refers to the surname "Wong" here by means of a place name (江夏) that has become synonymous with it by reason of an ancient association. Chinese surnames were often given in this fashion, especially in formal or literary contexts, in the same way that "Caledonian" might be used as an alternative to "Scottish" in literary English.

386 Opium-smoking affects the voice.

兄不嚴加約束。實貽吾江夏羞。弟分屬同宗。故敢直言相告
耳。尙康聞言。卽將所持之烟槍擲下。睜圓其似睡非睡之烟
眼。力提其烟喉。大聲呼曰。吾與此淫婦拚命。卽悻悻而
歸。之家。見俏喜艷服靚粧。欲出門狀。於是雄威大震。鼓
其百練之烟氣。伸其半黃半黑之手指。放其半高半低之烟
喉。罵之曰。汝做得好事。俏喜曰。汝瘋耶[171]。何爲失其常
性。尙康曰。汝毋掩飾。汝之淫行[172]。吾已盡知。喜一聞斯
言。知事已敗露。卽施其[173]先發制人之計。大肆其獅威。卽
撲倒尙康身上。以一手握其領。以一手提其耳。大哭大罵
曰。沒天良的瘟尸。吾有何淫行。

171 「耶」原作「卽」。按，第四十一篇之「汝等瘋耶。何爲發此譫語」句，文
　　法、字詞略同。據此可知「卽」蓋爲「耶」之誤。今正。
172 原文「行」字上端略殘。今擬正。
173 原文「其」字上端略殘。今擬正。

387 See footnote 308 for more on the Chinese idiom translated here as
　　"pre-emptive strike".
388 沒天良的 "vile" or "conscienceless" was and still is a common Mandarin
　　epithet; 瘟屍 "plague corpse" was a savage term of abuse in the vernacular,
　　typically applied to men by women.

"Give me the proof of it at once, or you and I die here!"

Sheung Hong was scared pale of face, dumb of speech and shaky of limb.

Tsiu Hei continued bawling and berating, "Old bastard senseless of shame, others give you a green cloth cap[389] and you place it squarely atop your head, with no regard for your own reputation! When their wives are wronged, other men argue on their behalf, conceal on their behalf. Instead, you jump into the cesspit of your own accord, and smear the excrement over yourself, so none can tell whether or not there is a smell when the winds of rumour occasion a commotion. With such a husband, one would be better off single!" Finished, she spat in his face and wrenched at his ear, before taking up the household crockery and throwing it as she bawled, in a reckless act of destruction.

Sheung Hong's masculine might had, by this time, been relegated to a place beyond the highest heaven.[390]

"You might easily fall ill with your temper in such a foul state," he said, his smoker's voice comfortingly lowered. "Having heard something a person said, I came home to put a few questions to you, which was nothing out of the ordinary. What need was there for you to turn the house upside down like this? Would it not be all the more upsetting were your impulsiveness to lead to illness? I have no desire to inquire into the substance of the matters either. Henceforth, I shall take rumours on the street for no more than empty talk. Let us put it down as my mistake that I offended you just now and be done with it."

Tsiu Hei could see that she had defeated her husband. "How good of you!" she said, after spitting once more in his face.

---

389 The wearing of a 綠頭巾 "green cloth cap" is a Chinese metaphor for cuckoldry.

390 In other words, it was nowhere in sight.

速給我憑據來。不然。吾與汝死在箇處。嚇得尙康面靑口
啞。四肢震動。俏喜又哭罵曰。不識羞恥的老龜兒。人家給
汝綠頭巾。汝就端端正正戴在頭上。不顧自己聲名。別人妻
子受冤屈。就替妻子爭辯。替妻子遮瞞。汝反自已跳入糞窖
裏。以糞穢塗在自己身上。隨風攘動。不辨臭香。有夫如
此。不如無有。罵完。唾其面而力捽其耳。復將室內器皿。
隨哭隨擲。肆行毀爛。此時尙康之雄威。已拋向九宵雲外。
卽放沉其烟喉以慰之曰。汝惡性子不大好。何難生病。我聞
別人言語。我回家質問幾句。亦屬尋常。何必如此翻家攪
宅。倘因急迫致疾。更不令人難過。況事之有無。吾不欲深
究。嗣後街上謠言。吾亦付之妄言妄聽之列。適纔[174]冒犯。
算我不是便了。俏喜知已降服其夫。故重唾其面曰。
好心咯。

174 「纔」原作「讒」。字之誤也。今正。

"But I've heard it all before from you men with your honeyed tongues and treacherous hearts. You listen to what others say and then go and cause your wives distress. I have not sufficient small-ness of temper to argue with you, bed bug.[391]" Thereupon she took herself off to lie down. (§43, 16/7/1910)

Sheung Hong tried in every way possible to reassure her, but Tsiu Hei affected a coquettish tantrum, and stubbornly refused to rise from bed.

Unable to vent his anger, Sheung Hong instead redirected it towards certain Chinese women, saying they had lured his wife out on pleasure outings, the outcome of which had invited the asper-sions of licentiousness.[392]

The women, on learning of this, objected. Accordingly, the "women's army" raised a large punitive force. One of its members, the wife of a certain Lui Hei Yiu, was gifted in the art of argument, and proposed to send Sheung Hong a written invitation to her res-idence, for a formal exchange of views.[393]

---

391   Bed bugs are parasitic insects that live in houses, feed on human blood, and were once a widespread problem both in the East and the West. The Chinese word for bed bug that appears here (臭蟲) has the secondary sense of "a pernicious and loathsome individual" and is not overtly connected with beds, i.e. the word "bed" does not form part of the name. However, the insect was indirectly associated with beds and with skin affliction; the author might, therefore, be invoking a similar, though more subtle, connection here in his concubine character Tsiu Hei's usage of it.

392   The author refers to licentiousness here allusively, by means of an expression taken from the title and words of a folk song (牆有茨) in *The Odes* that has traditionally been held to concern inappropriate sexual relations within the palace of the state of 衛 Mᵒ. Wei in the seventh century B.C.E. The expression in question, 牆茨 "mural tribulus" or "mural caltrop" (i.e. the prickly tribulus or caltrop plant growing on a wall), acts as a metaphor in the song for licentious conduct, it being difficult to eradicate and best left alone. For a reasonable translation of the song, see *Ch'iang Yu Tz̆ŭ* within *Book IV. The Odes of Yung* in James Legge's 1876 translation *The Book of Poetry*, copies of which are readily accessible online.

汝等男子口蜜腹劍。儂已聽慣咯。聽別人言語。將妻室難
爲。儂無多聞氣。與汝臭虫爭辯。於是登榻而臥。（§43,
16/7/1910）尙康多方慰解。而俏喜撒嬌撒癡。堅不肯起。尙康
憤無所洩。轉遷怒於某某華婦。謂彼等引誘其妻冶遊。以招
此牆茨之誚。羣婦聞之。不服。於是娘子軍。大興問罪之
師。內有呂禧瑤之妻。善舌辯。提議束招尙康。到其寓宅。
開正式之談判。

---

393 The word translated here as "exchange of views" (談判)—and indeed the
entire expression "a formal exchange of views" (正式之談判)—would appear
to have been modern in the author's day, and is perhaps quite socially and
politically significant. Today the Chinese word in question has more or less
the same senses as the English words *negotiate* and *negotiation*. The
etymology of this word is not given in standard Chinese references, but it
does not appear to be attested to in Chinese writing until near the turn of
the twentieth century. In Australia's Chinese newspapers, it seems to have
appeared around 1905, at first in respect of diplomatic negotiations, and later
in more common contexts, such as with reference to a debate in 1908 at a
committee meeting in Sandringham, Victoria about a possible end to mixed
bathing. The word's component characters suggest a sense connected with
the determination of a matter, or matters, through discussion. Negotiation
does not seem to be quite the author's sense here, nor in many of the
newspaper articles published at the time, in which its usage seems to be
more consistent with the literal sense of its component characters. The
translation given here reflects these and other relevant considerations.

Sheung Hong went proudly off to the appointment, unaware
of what was behind the invitation. Once seated, he was met with
the sight of a clucking group of females[394] with enraged expressions
on their faces, that gave them the appearance of she-ogres.[395]

Lui's wife rose to speak. "Is that you, Mr Sleep Sickness?" she
asked, calling him directly by his nickname.

"Yes," was all Sheung Hong said in answer, for he did not dare
to voice his displeasure. "Might I enquire as to which lady and
rightful wife[396] you are madam?"

"You flatter me," replied Lui's wife. "This little woman[397] is the
wife of Lui Hei Yiu."

"Mrs[398] Lui," replied Sheung Hong. "What have you[399] seen fit
to invite me here to instruct[400] me on? I pray you spare not the
detail."

"We have heard that you, sir, have implicated us without cause
in the matter of your concubine's improper conduct, by saying, of all
things, that we lured her astray," replied Lui's wife, loudly. "We were

---

394 群雌粥粥 "a clucking group of females" is a set idiom, not a phrase coined
by the author. It describes the sound of a group of women by analogy to a
flock of birds.

395 The Chinese word translated here as "ogre" (夜叉) originated as a transliteration of the Sanskrit यक्ष: *yaksha*, with which it is synonymous in the context
of Buddhist scripture. The Buddhist *yaksha* are a broad class of spirits, which
may be benevolent or malevolent in nature, and beautiful or ugly in
appearance. Popular Chinese descriptions of *yaksha* also vary. In a collection
of short stories well known in the author's day, the *yaksha* is depicted as an
ogre-like creature, which, while not necessarily malevolent, is possessed of
superhuman strength, claws, sharp teeth and fiery eyes (見《聊齋誌異》
之〈夜叉國〉篇). In the Chinese novel 水滸傳 the *Water Margin* (also
translated as *All Men are Brothers*, *Outlaws of the Marsh*, and *The Marshes of
Mount Liang*), with which the author and his audience would also have been
familiar, "She-*yaksha*" or "She-ogre" is the nickname of a strong and vicious
female character (母夜叉孫兒娘), first introduced to the reader as an
innkeeper who drugs and butchers passing travellers, and makes

尙康不知底蘊。昂然而往。入坐。則見羣雌粥粥。各具怒
容。如母夜叉狀。呂之妻起言。直呼其混名曰。眼睏[175]病爺
是汝否。此時尙康敢怒而不敢言。祇應之曰唯。敢問娘子是
那位令正夫人。呂妻曰。不敢當。小婦人呂某之妻也。尙康
曰。未士市呂。鄙人蒙汝等柬招。有何敎誨。請道其詳。呂
妻大言曰。聞君因令妾行爲不端。無故牽涉妾等。反謂令妾
爲我等誘獘[176]。妾等

175　此「眼睏」之「睏」字，原文作「困」，並加注曰「從目」。此後作「眼
　　困」，而不加注文。蓋因前注已賅之也。今皆正，亦不復注明。
176　按，「誘獘」與「誘蔽」通。

dumplings from human flesh. Popular descriptions also often draw a
distinction between 母夜叉 "she-ogres" and 夜叉女 "ogresses", the former
term being used for female *yaksha* that are monstrous in appearance, and the
latter for a beautiful and seductive type. It is the former term that appears
here.

396　令正夫人 "lady and rightful wife" was a respectful term of address, which
implied that a married woman was of high station and a wife, not a
concubine.

397　小婦人 "this little woman" was a standard deprecatory term of self-address
for a woman.

398　Sheung Hong does not use a traditional Chinese word here for "Mrs", but
rather a See Yip word that is based on a transliteration of the English word
(未士市), i.e. he addresses Mrs Lui by means of an anglicised title appropriate to what appears to be her Westernised sensibility.

399　"You" is in the plural.

400　In this context, the word 敎誨 "instruct" is merely a more polite way of
saying "tell".

most shocked to learn of this, and have thus invited you here especially to exact your evidence. If you have evidence, [we] shall willingly
face commensurate punishment. If you have no evidence, we will
sue you in court[401] so as to protect our individual reputations."

Dumbstruck,[402] Sheung Hong knew not how to respond.

"Mr Sleep Sickness," said a woman beside her. "You've been
sleepy too long. It's just like the idiom says, you *failed to watch over
the chicks and then blamed the black kite*. You didn't watch over your
concubine-wife or have the authority to keep her in check. You did
as you pleased and let her run amok, and so brought yourself into
disrepute. It stands to reason, therefore, that you should willingly
embrace that disrepute, and not fabricate stories that lay the blame
on others."

"Mr Sleep Sickness," said another women. "You don't ever
wake up. Even if we did have occasional intercourse with your concubine, it was for no more than the sake of neighbourliness between
fellows. How could there have been any other reason? We Chinese
women place importance on integrity and restraint. Surely you do
not think we are all as shameless as your concubine?" This woman's
reproof delivered, the whole group erupted in clamorous agreement, and the room was a hubbub formed from the sounds of jokes
and jibes, vitriolic abuse, and resentfulness given expression.

Sheung Hong was too ashamed and angry to show his face.
Sheltering his head in his hands, he fled. Thereafter, the name
"Sleep Sickness" was much mentioned, and Sheung Hong was all
the less welcome amongst his fellow human beings.

---

401 The word used here for court would appear to be another modern expres-
     sion, one which was used for the Western style of court.
402 The Chinese expression for "dumbstruck" that is used here (目定口呆)
     translates literally as "mouth motionless and eyes gazing transfixedly".

聞之。不勝惶駭。故特招君來。索取証據。如有証據。妾
等[177]甘心抵罪。如無証據。決控汝於裁判所。以保全箇人之
名譽。尙康目定口呆。不知所答。旁有一婦曰。眼睏病爺。
汝一味眼睏。正如諺語所謂。雞雛唔管罵麻鷹。汝無管束妻
妾之權力。任意縱容。得此穢聲。理宜甘心享受。何必誣捏
別人。又一婦曰。眼睏病爺。汝總不知醒。就令我等偶爾與
汝妾過從。不過盡梓里[178]情面。豈有他故。況我等中國婦
女。皆以操節爲重。豈若汝妾之無恥耶。罵完。羣婦鬨和。
笑謔聲。唾罵聲。怨懟聲。一室喧嘩。尙康羞憤無地。抱頭
而遁。自此而後。眼睏病之名大譟。更不齒於人類矣。

177　原文「等」字不清。今據其殘跡與文義擬正。
178　粵語呼同鄉人曰「梓里」。

Having undergone this humiliation, Sheung Hong wanted revenge, but he was without a plan. All he could do, in the hope of venting his anger, was to incite the women's husbands into returning home to beat their wives. But it was to no avail, for the women had resided for a long time in a country of law, and were possessed of some intelligence. All threatened their husbands by saying, "If you should employ China's cruel methods, I will take you before a judge." Their husbands were most fearful, and so, in the end, the plan was not carried out. (§44, 23/7/1910)

With respect to his concubine's affair, Sheung Hong was still an even mix of belief and disbelief. One day, he interrogated his daughter over it, and she proceeded to divulge the facts.[403]

This later became known to Tsiu Hei.

In response, the she-ogre[404] grossly abused her power, cauterising the girl's mouth with a piece of iron she had heated over a fire. Burned and ulcerated about her lips, the pain so extreme that it took her voice, the girl was near death.

On seeing her in this state, incensed neighbours immediately reported the matter to the police, who arrested Tsiu Hei and prosecuted her for the mistreatment of a young child. In consideration of it being her first offence, the judge punished her lightly, imprisoning her for one week.

Later, it was discovered that the girl was not in fact Tsiu Hei's, and because English law did not permit the keeping of

---

403 This instalment appears to be something of an aberration: the storyline is sketchy and makes repeated jumps; and the author introduces a daughter at this point, whose origins he does not explain until some paragraphs in, and even then, rather clumsily.

404 The expression 母夜叉 "she-ogre" was introduced in the previous instalment: see footnote 395 for detail.

尚康經此次挫辱。欲圖報復。無以爲計。祇慫恿各婦之夫。歸家鞭撻其妻。希圖洩憤。無奈各婦人居留法律之國。爲時已久。畧有智識。皆禁嚇其夫曰。如汝等行中國慘酷之手段。決控汝於官。其夫大懼。而計卒不行。(§44, 23/7/1910) 尚康對於其妾之事[179]。猶疑信參半。一日苦詰其女。其女始將實情吐露。後爲俏喜所知。於是母夜叉大肆淫威。即以火烘鐵。烙女之口。唇吻焦爛。女痛極聲嘶。幾致氣絶。鄰人見之。大憤。即報告警兵。警兵拘之於案。控以凌虐幼孩之罪。官念其初次犯案。薄責之。監禁一星期。後查知此女實非其所生。因英例不得養

---

[179] 原文「事」字模糊不清。今參他處字擬正。

slaves or bondmaids, and this was clearly an instance of a child who was actually a bondmaid and only purportedly a daughter, after a judge's ruling, the girl was placed in a children's home.[405] Shortly thereafter, she was taken off by the Salvation Army—the *Saa-low-vay-san Am-mee*.

Prior to these events, a clansman of Sheung Hong's had lost his spouse, and deposited the daughter he had been left, who was wretched and alone, to be raised in Sheung Hong's home, where she had been kept as a slave. Tsiu Hei had scolded, berated, beaten, humiliated and mistreated her in a myriad of ways. She had not withstood the suffering, and her limbs had become so emaciated that she did not look human. Fearing too that this parrot might repeat too much and let news of her romantic engagements slip, Tsiu Hei had more than once cauterised the girl's lips, in an attempt to muzzle her. Truly, it was her great good fortune that this time around the matter had been reported by the police,[406] and that the Salvation Army had rescued the young lotus from hell's furnace.[407]

Authoritarian states distain humaneness. Their governments enslave their people, and their people enslave their fellows. In households of high status and wealth, bonded labourers and servants are tormented at whim. In a single city, cases of bondmaid abuse resulting in death regularly number several tens a day.

---

405 This sentence is equally cumbersome in the newspaper. It is unclear whether this is its original form, or the product of one or more errors during transcription or printing, which might have resulted in the loss of characters that would have made it read more smoothly.

406 "reported *by* the police" is the most natural reading of the original phrase (為警察告發). The preposition contained in it could also be read as "to", resulting in the ostensibly more contextually apt "reported to the police",

奴婢。故陽爲女而陰爲婢者。官判之後。即將此女撥入育嬰
院[180]。旋爲救世軍沙露威臣諳微領去。先是尙康有同宗某喪
偶。遺留一女。伶仃孤苦。寄養尙康家。奴畜之。而俏喜叱
罵挫鞑[181]。凌虐萬端。女不堪其苦。四肢瘦瘠。不類人形。
又恐鸚鵡多言。洩漏春信。故屢以鐵烙其唇。爲鉗口之計。
此番爲警察告發。而救世軍又在火坑裏救出青蓮。誠此女之
大幸也。專制之國。賤視人道。政府奴隸其人民。人民奴隸
其同胞。富貴之家。厮養奴僕。任意磨折。一邑之大。虐婢
致死者。日常數十起。

180　上文「故」字，或與「固」通。雖然，由「後查知」至「育嬰院」，文理
　　略嫌不相順承。未知原如此耶，抑報文有轉寫、排版之訛耶。
181　「鞑」同撻。此處，或因以皮鞭撻之，故作從革之字。

---

but its usage in this sense is limited and would carry the implication that
the report was made for the benefit of the police. It would appear, therefore,
that the author's sense was indeed that the police reported the matter to an
authority, such as the courts.
407 The references here to hell's furnace and a lotus within it are Buddhist.

Alas. Is not everyone someone's child? Does not everyone have
a mother and a father? But, for this world of darkness so far
beyond the light of human reason, how is an army of salvation
numbering in the millions to be found, that will wander the
whole of the big old empire,[408] *and save all such lotuses from*
hell's furnace?

In the course of a few years, Tsiu Hei gave birth to one and
then another daughter. Sheung Hong looked upon them as pearls
in his palm, and held banquets for their first-month birthdays that
were extreme in their sumptuousness. And on their food, drink and
living too, he spent extravagantly.

In no time at all, Tak Yuen's capital had very nearly all been
squandered away. But, interred within his opium den day upon day,
Sheung Hong was like a man long dead, and did not attend to the
shop's affairs. Business[409] consequently plummeted, and Tak Yuen
came close to closing down.

Ching Nam learned of this, and dispatched an urgent letter
from China calling Sheung Hong to account.

Knowing that it would be difficult to keep things going, and
that he was unable to make up the deficiency in funds, Sheung
Hong was in a state of extreme desperation and anxiety. Left with
no alternative, he gathered up everything that remained, and made
his plans for home. (§45, 30/7/1910)

But this is Ching Nam's carpentry shop,[410] *and while I have bled his*
hard-earned capital from it little by little, were I to close it down in a
hurry, what explanation could I give if he questioned me thoroughly
upon my return to China?

---

408 According to a famous essay written in 1900 by 梁啟超 Mᵒ. Liang
 Ch'i-ch'ao (Mᴹ. *Liáng Qǐchāo*), 老大帝國 "the big old empire" was a Japanese
 term for China, that had been taken from an equivalent European term, and
 implied weakness. It was an expression much used by early Chinese
 reformers.

噫。誰非人子。誰無父母。乃黑暗世界。慘無人理若此。焉
得億萬救世軍。徧遊老大帝國。普救此火坑青蓮也耶。不數
年間。倚康連產二女。倚康視若掌珠。彌月筵席。極其豐
盛。而起居飲食。又復浪費無度。無幾時。德元資本。爲其
揮霍殆盡。而倚康日葬於烟窟之中。如陳死人。不理店務。
故德元商業。一落千丈。幾致閉歇。程南聞之。由華馳函詰
責。倚康知難以支持。所虧空之基本金。又無以抵償。焦急
萬狀。不得已席捲其餘燼。以作歸計。(§45, 30/8/1910) 惟此木
店。乃程南所開設。我雖侵蝕其血本。若遽行閉歇。將來歸
國。被他盤詰。何辭以對。

---

409 The word "plummeted" seems the best translation for the figurative Chinese
     expression here used (一落千丈), which has the literal sense of "to fall a
     thousand yards in one drop", though in English it would be more natural to
     speak of "a sharp decline in business" and to reserve the word "plummeted"
     for such simple measurables as values or temperatures.

410 This, either intentionally or by reason of error, is the only passage of interior
     monologue in the novel which is not begun or ended with an expression that
     explicitly identifies it as such, like 自念 "he/she thought to himself/herself"
     or 思至此 "his/her thoughts reaching this point". This said, its first
     character 惟, which is translated here as "but", can also function as a verb
     that means "to think", and read as such, the first phrase could be translated
     as "*This is Ching Nam's carpentry shop*, he thought, *and while...*". However, it
     seems quite improbable, given the context, that the author intended to use
     the character in any other than its conjunctive sense.

*It would be better to find someone to superintend until I am back
there, and then signal for him to lick up what dregs remain and run off,
making for a feat of ear-covered bell theft.*[411] *The move would then be
his, not mine, and Ching Nam would not be able to touch me.*

Accordingly, Sheung Hong directed a clansman of his, Wing
Kwong, to manage the business for him. He then took a Taikoo
steamer[412] back to China with Tsiu Hei, and several months later
dispatched a letter, which prompted Wing Kwong to close down
Tak Yuen and escape to some other place.

Ching Nam, who happened to have been staying in Hong
Kong to purchase stock when Sheung Hong arrived, immediately
went to meet and speak with him. When he enquired about Tak
Yuen, though, Sheung Hong prevaricated, saying only that everything had been passed on to Wing Kwong to manage for the time
being. Ching Nam had long since had news of Sheung Hong's
actions, and so questioned him exhaustively as to what was behind
his answer. Sheung Hong had no explanation.

When the awful news of closure reached him, Ching Nam calculated that, little by little, a total of over 700 pounds of his capital
had disappeared. He decided to go off to ask some questions of
Sheung Hong. But the visit was to no avail, for Sheung Hong
stayed behind a shut door. Ching Nam, seeing that his nature was
bad, did not stoop to argument.

Alas that as different as their faces, are the hearts of men.[413]

---

411   掩耳盜鈴 "to steal a bell with one's ears covered" is a common Chinese
      idiom that means "to deludedly attempt to keep an act of wrongdoing, or
      some other shameful thing, secret from others, when it is in fact obvious to
      them."

412   See footnote 239.

413   人心不同各如其面 "as different as their faces, are the hearts of men [men
      meaning people]" is a Chinese idiom.

不若另覓一人。暫爲支理。待吾返國後。陰使他將所留餘之
殘瀝。餂之而逃。[182] 以爲掩耳盜鈴之計。則其實不在我而在
彼。程南亦無奈我何。於是命其族人榮光代理。他即與俏喜
乘太古之輪船返國。逾數月果馳函唆使榮光將德元閉歇。逃
往別処。及抵港。其時程南適駐港辦貨。即往晤談。詢及德
元。彼言語支吾。但云全盤交與榮光暫理而已。彼之舉動。
而程南早有所聞。故窮詰其底蘊。他無詞以對。及聞閉歇之
惡耗。統計侵蝕貲本七百餘磅。程南欲往詢問於他。奈彼杜
門不出。程南知其無良。亦不屑與較。[183] 噫。人心不同。各
如其面。

182　此處本無讀號。疑當有之。今擬補。
183　此處原有二讀號焉。其一疑衍。今刪其一。

Chan Leung had discerned Sheung Hong's disloyalty early, and had repeatedly urged Ching Nam to guard against him. But Ching Nam, sadly, obstinate in his adherence to mateship,[414] had not been able to bear to sever his ties, and so ultimately suffered the repercussions.

Ma received Sheung Hong when he reached home, but her joy turned at its peak to sadness, and looking on him she was speechless. After a good while, she chided resentfully, "Unfaithful fellow, so even you have not forgotten home? I had thought that, holding your lovely concubine in your arms, you would grow old and die beyond the seas." This said, having provoked a return of her prior sadness and pent-up anger, she began, faintly but deeply, to weep.[415]

Sheung Hong entreated her: "I have just returned. Why must you make such an inauspicious display by crying and weeping like this?"

Ma, on hearing these words, wiped away her tears, and began to laugh and chat as though nothing were amiss.

Seeing Sheung Hong at this time in the senior woman's room,[416] all that was sour, salty, bitter and fiery in Tsiu Hei's breast blended into a single mixture and threatened to erupt. But, considering to herself that she had only just arrived, Tsiu Hei thought better of being too hasty.

---

414 *Mate* and *mateship* are English words that carry strong cultural overtones and are multifariously defined and understood. This is especially the case in Australia, where mateship is held up as an element of the national ethos and its egalitarian and other connotations are vigorously debated. The word mateship, *the condition of being a mate*, is used here in a distinctly older sense, where mate is taken to mean *a man who is or has been a close comrade in adversity*. While its usage differs, the Chinese expression in the source text (患難之交) carries this exact same sense, with the exception that the comrade could be any person regardless of his or her sex. The same Chinese expression appears in §18, also with reference to the relationship between Sheung Hong

尙康之負義。早爲陳亮所窺破。屢勸南預防其人。惜程南泥
於患難之交。不忍割絕。[184] 卒爲其所拖累耳。尙康抵家時馬
氏接見。樂極而悲。相視無言。良久始恨罵曰。負心郎亦不
忘家鄉耶。儂以汝擁抱嬌妾。老死外洋矣。語畢。觸動其疇
昔之悲憤。嗚嗚而泣。尙康勸之曰。我初歸。汝何必如此哭
泣。作此不祥之朕兆。馬氏聞言。果拭淚談笑自若。俏喜此
時。見尙康在大婦房中。其胸中酸的。鹹的。苦的。辣的。
攪作一般。幾欲發作。因自念初次歸來。未敢造次耳。

184 此處原無讀號。疑本當有而誤植乎上文。今擬補。

and Ching Nam. It is translated in that context as "comrades through
adversity", but might equally have been given as "mates". Interestingly, literary
critic Haizhi Luo identifies mateship as an ideal that is present in early
Chinese-language Australian fiction: see his 2017 master's thesis, entitled
"Towards a Modern Diasporic Literary Tradition: The Evolution of
Australian Chinese Language Fiction from 1894 to 1912"(UNSW).

415 The word used here to describe the manner and sound of Ma's crying,
嗚嗚 "faintly but deeply", might very likely have called to the minds of many
readers a well-known passage in Chinese literature, which concerns a bamboo
pipe being played in a boat that is adrift at night on a vast expanse of moonlit
water: 其聲嗚嗚然如怨如慕如泣如訴 "its sound was faint but deep, as
though resentful, as though fond, as though weeping, as though confiding ..."
The original is still known by heart by many Chinese speakers today.

416 As indicated in footnotes 310 and 359, 大婦 "senior woman" is one of many
expressions in Chinese for *lawful wife*.

Kwang Tung custom had required, prior to these events, that when Tsiu Hei entered through the door the senior woman was to be in height of place, her feet supported by a stool, holding in her hands her private apparel,[417] which she was to pass over the top of her concubine's head, in signification of the latter's future obedience to her.[418] Tsiu Hei, though, had been prepared for this in advance, and had yelled out abusively, "Overseas I was as good as properly married to my husband, and cannot be compared to a concubine! What village woman is this that dares to try and humiliate me?" She had then utterly refused to enter.

Ma had been powerless to do anything about this, and when she sighted Tsiu Hei's superb clothes and vampish visage, she was most displeased. But, considering that she was cherished by her own husband, and unable to bear to go against him, Ma restrained her feelings and acquiesced in all matters, to court her good humour. There was, thus, between wife and concubine, no great disagreement. (§46, 20/8/1910)

Thereafter, Tsiu Hei took pride of place in her husband's favour, while Ma, like an idle monk retired from his monastery, occupied a still chamber.

---

417 One or more items of unspecified private clothing, most likely undergarments.

418 This signification reflects a rebus that the author makes clear in the preceding phrase but which is not apparent in translation: 服從於己 "obedience to her" shares the same pronunciation as "clothing, over, to herself". In other words, the wife's act of passing her private clothing from one hand to the other, over the top of "her" new concubine's head, forms a moving image that is a word puzzle with the given significance. Chinese art and culture make much greater and more sophisticated use of rebuses than English, due to the large number of homophones in Chinese. For readers unfamiliar with rebuses, one example in English is the coat of arms of the fifteenth-century bishop of Norwich *Walter Lyhart*, which featured a *hart* *ly*ing in *water*.

先是俏喜入門時。粵東俗例。大婦先以几乘足。高自位置。手持自己所穿之褻服。從其妾之頂上遞過。取其服從於己之意也。俏喜早已預防。疾聲罵曰。儂與吾夫在外洋作正式之婚配。非與媵妾可比。何物村嫗。敢來侮我。竟不肯入。馬氏亦無如之何。及見俏喜衣服華麗。顔容妖冶。甚不滿意。自念彼爲夫所鍾愛。不忍拂逆其夫之心。每事必降心下氣。以承順其色笑。故妻妾之間。無甚齟齬。　(§46, 20/8/1910) 由是俏喜寵擅專房。馬氏如退院閒僧。房幃寂靜。

From time to time, though, Ma had occasional meetings with Sheung Hong. Yet they were like secret trysts, their hidden delight no more than that of a furtive vernal air passing by, when, over the tops of the willows, the moon rose.[419]

And so, Ma having yielded in this way, Tsiu Hei, while peculiarly jealous, [had no window of opportunity in which to move against her.][420]

After several months, however, Tsiu Hei became dissatisfied with their habitation, which she found to be dank and cramped. Life cheek by jowl with their neighbours was, furthermore, not conducive to [her] freedom of movement. Accordingly, having reckoned to herself that the ill-gotten gains in Sheung Hong's coffers still exceeded several thousand taels, and that her own savings would come to over a thousand taels, Tsiu Hei set about persuading Sheung Hong to construct a lodge[421] elsewhere.

Sheung Hong obediently consented, and purchased a piece of land, on which he built a residence, and also constructed a villa, to be the golden house in which he would keep his A-chiao.[422] The whole household then removed there and took up residence.

There Ma would often sigh over the desolateness of their situation, cut off as they were from kith and kin, the few of them residing in isolation, separated from their old neighbourhood by a distance of about five miles. Tsiu Hei looked on it as a land of joy.

---

419 The rising of the moon over willow tops (月上柳梢) is a literary metaphor for the time of a lovers' tryst. It has its origin in a well-known ᴹᴼ. Sung-dynasty tune poem by the celebrated 歐陽修 Ou-yang Hsiu (ᴹᴹ. *Ōuyáng Xiū*), which concerned an assignation after dusk on the night of the new year, and a lonely lover's memories of the same the following new year (生查子·元夕).

420 The square brackets indicate that this phrase was modified in translation to correct for what would appear to be an error in the original. The phrase that appears in the newspaper is the grammatically questionable 無計可乘 "no plan to take", which is a combination of the Chinese expression 無計可施

有時偶與尙康一會。亦如密約幽歡。於柳梢月上[185]時。春風
偷度而已。馬氏如此退讓。俏喜雖奇妒。然亦無計可乘。逾
數月俏喜見居室淰隘怏怏[186]不樂。況且比隣而居。更不利於
自[187]己[188]之行動。默忖尙康囊中不義之財。尙逾數千金。而
自己之蓄積。亦盈千金。於是慫恿尙康。築廬別處。尙康唯
唯應命。乃購地一段。建宅其中。又築一別墅。爲金屋貯嬌
之所。舉家喬遷於此。該處距離其舊鄉。約有五里之遙。戚
黨隔絕。塊然寡居。馬氏時嘆寂寥。而俏喜視若樂土。

185　原文「上」字缺底。今參他處字擬正。
186　後「怏」字，原文作「快」。誤。今正。
187　原文「自」字全闕。今據文義擬補。
188　原文「已」字於文義似未協，應為「己」字之訛也。今擬正。

"no plan to execute" and either 無隙可乘 "no opening to take" or
無機可乘 "no opportunity to take", which are also fixed expressions. For
the purpose of this translation, the second of these expressions, which is
suggested by the last character of the jumbled phrase and seems most
appropriate in the context, has been presumed to be the sense on which
the author would have decided.

421　廬 "lodge" was an alternative name for villa. See also footnote 221, which
concerns the "lodge" built by Ching Nam.

422　An ᴍᵒ. "A-chiao" is a beautiful wife or concubine: see footnote 266.

Tsiu Hei did not have a nature that revelled in the still and quiet. Why then did she take joy in their removal here? Little inkling could anyone have had of her underlying intentions, the truth of which is not easy to relate.

Dwelling within his villa, Sheung Hong was like some hibiscus fairy.[423] With his pretty young thing to hold at left and his old wife to visit at right, he was pleased and contented, and resembled in the greatest respect one who would not change places with a king on high.

After a short while, Ma's tide lost its constancy,[424] and her belly gradually swelled.

Tsiu Hei, who had been keeping a surreptitious eye on Ma, spied her for a bulging nutmeg bloom,[425] and was set thereafter on forcing the expulsion of this embryonic evil.

Fortunately, Ma kept an extremely close guard, such that Tsiu Hei could not find an opening, and in no time at all the sound *waah waah* announced that the old oyster had, surprisingly, brought forth a pearl.

Sheung Hong rushed over to look: it was a boy. He thought to himself, *Were this son to have been born of my lovely concubine, I should harbour gladness beyond compare. Sadly, he was born by mistake of my senior woman.* Nevertheless, he was somewhat comforted at heart to have gained a son late in life.

Ma, by comparison, was in a state of happiness quite beyond normal, and as she caressed her baby, she said "What a surprise that

---

423 Chinese folk lore abounds with different types of flower fairies. Here, though, hibiscus is a reference to 芙蓉膏 "hibiscus paste", meaning opium. See footnote 39.

424 The Chinese word that is used here for tide (潮信) is a literary euphemism for menses.

425 The pregnant-looking partially opened bloom of the nutmeg (所謂含胎花) is a Chinese literary metaphor for a pregnant woman.

俏喜之天性。非能耽於寂寞者。何以樂遷於此。殊不知彼別
有肺腸。實難告語。尙康棲處於別墅之中。如芙蓉仙子。左
抱少艾。右顧老荊。怡然自得。大有南面王不易之慨。居無
何馬氏潮信愆期。腹部漸次膨脹。俏喜窺伺其身體。陰知其
荳蔻含胎。屢欲摧[189]墮其萌蘖。幸而馬氏防維綦嚴。不能得
間。無幾時呱呱一聲。居然老蚌生珠矣。尙康趨往視之男
也。自念此子若爲嬌妾所生。予懷之欣忭。無以比倫。惜其
錯生於大婦。然晚年獲兒。私心亦稍爲慰藉。馬氏更喜逾常
度。乃撫摩其嬰孩曰。不料

[189]「摧」或爲「催」之訛。

the Wong family's ancestral line will continue on! Yet so much heart-in-mouth fear and stomach-knotting worry has gone into creating this one lump of descendent flesh."

But vicious ruthless Tsiu Hei went into a storm of jealousy, and her methods became ever more savage, such that she would not rest until she had removed every root and severed every branch;[426] for a life of sourness had resulted in the utter destruction of her conscience. And the doom that befell Sheung Hong's house was to have its origin in that fact. (§47, 24/9/1910)

Mentally exhausted and depleted of bodily vigour after giving birth, Ma was feeling continuously dizzy. Sheung Hong, on checking a formulary, wrote out the ingredients for a post-partum restorative potion, which he purchased and began to decoct.

Seizing this opportunity, Tsiu Hei affected attentiveness by taking on the decoction of the medicine herself. She then secretly slipped Sheung Hong's hibiscus paste[427] into the pot.

Ma drank. The medicine, however, was bitter in the extreme, and so with eyebrows screwed up and forehead knitted she exclaimed, "This medicine is so exceedingly bitter it is difficult to swallow. I shan't drink it."

Not knowing what was behind this, Sheung Hong responded, "One desirous of a quick recovery should not fear the bitterness of her medicine: *the best medicine is bitter in the mouth.*"[428]

At her side and with a hand supporting her, Tsiu Hei then poured the medicine into Ma's mouth. Having forced herself to swallow it down, Ma laid back, drawing the quilt up over herself. Sheung Hong and Tsiu Hei then went back to their room to take their rest, Tsiu Hei half delighted and half fearful.

---

426 The metaphor of the tree for the family also exists in Chinese, and is being invoked here.

427 芙蓉膏 "hibiscus paste" means opium. See footnote 39.

428 This is the first half of a common Chinese idiom, the second half being "and the best counsel is repugnant to the ear".

黃氏宗祧[190]。尚有延續之時期。然構造此一塊肉。不知幾多
驚心吊胆矣。乃兇殘狼毒之俏喜。醋海生[191]波。手段愈出而
愈辣。不芟絕其根枝不休。酸味一生。天良盡泯。而尚康滅
門之禍。亦由此起矣。（§47, 24/9/1910）適逢馬氏坐蓐後血氣
虧虛。精神憊倦。時覺頭暈。尚康檢查方書。乃手書生化湯
一劑。購而煎之。俏喜乘此機緣。貌作殷勤。親爲煎藥。暗
將尚康所食之芙蓉膏。傾之藥鐺中。馬氏飲之。苦甚。乃攣
眉蹙額曰。此藥殊苦。難以吞咽。儂不飲矣。尚康不知底
蘊。乃曰。良藥苦口利於病。欲病亟瘳。何畏藥苦。俏喜從
旁扶而灌之。馬氏勉強咽下。蒙被而臥。尚康與俏喜同房安
歇。俏喜喜懼參半。

190 原文「祧」字作「姚」。疑訛。今正。
191 原文「生」字缺底。今參他處字擬補。

368 THE POISON OF POLYGAMY

After the clock struck eight the following morning, Ma was still not in evidence, and her infant began to bawl in its bed. Sheung Hong rushed over to look: Ah! She was stiff, and would not move when nudged. In a great panic, Sheung Hong yelled out for Tsiu Hei.

Tsiu Hei rushed to look, and fearing Ma had not yet died, put her hand to her breast to check. She was no longer breathing. Tsiu Hei, who was secretly delighted, then feigned several tearful sounds.

Sheung Hong inspected Ma's corpse, and was most perplexed and alarmed to find that it was black and purple in colour. He conjectured to himself, *There could not be any reason for the restorative broth she drank to have proven fatal. Why then does it look every bit like poisoning?* But struck deep at heart by fear and confusion, he did not dare to inquire further.

Sheung Hong's tears now streamed forth with the grief that emanated from his core; fearing though that he might be seen by Tsiu Hei, he turned his back and wiped them away.

Tsiu Hei, who was afraid the matter might be brought to light, then said to Sheung Hong, "Ma's death was abrupt, and I fear contagion was the cause. To prevent the disease from spreading, [it might be best to] hurry the preparations for her burial."

Accordingly, Sheung Hong gave Ma the simplest of funerals.

The following day,[429] Ma's family learnt of her death, but knowing contagion was the cause, did not venture a visit to mourn and console.

Holding the newly born infant in his arms, Sheung Hong then[430] said to Tsiu Hei, "Within only a few days of his birth, the unfortunate boy has lost his maternal support. I want to find a wet-nurse to suckle him. What do you think?"

---

429 Here, "the following day" refers to the day after the discovery of Ma's death, not the day after her funeral. This deviation from chronological sequence is accomplished quite unambiguously and naturally in the Chinese, which often flows not by chronology but by topic. Overt markers of tense being

翌朝。已逾八打鐘。馬氏猶未見起。床上嬰兒。呱呱而啼。
尚康趨往視之。嘻。殭矣。尚康推之不動。大驚。疾呼俏
喜。俏喜趨視。猶恐其未死。試以手捫其心胸。氣息已絕。
乃竊喜。假意啼哭數聲。尚康細視其屍身。作紫黑色。心甚
疑駭。自忖所飲之生化湯。又無致死之理由。何以酷類中
毒。中心惶惑。不敢究詰。斯時悲從中來。淚如泉湧。恐爲
俏喜所見。乃背立彈拭。俏喜恐事敗露。乃謂尚康曰。馬氏
猝斃。恐中時疫。不若[192]急爲殯殮。防其傳染。於是尚康草
草爲之殯葬。翌日。其母家聞訃。知是時疫。亦不敢到來弔
唁。尚康乃抱此數日之嬰兒。對俏喜曰。 個兒不幸。離胎數
天。便失所恃。吾欲覓一乳媼字之。若何。

192 「不若」原作「若不」。應爲倒文。今正。

---

integral to English grammar, the same ease of flow cannot be achieved in
close translation.

430 The "then" refers to the time immediately following Ma's suggestion of a
hurried burial. As with the previous paragraph, this jump in timeframe is
implicit, clear, and perfectly natural in the Chinese.

"What are you saying?" replied Tsiu Hei. "Your son is my son, and whilst his mother has died, I yet live. Were you to entrust him to someone else to rear, she might not take the utmost care in bringing him up. The boy is the link in your ancestral line: what would you do if misfortune struck?"

"It is not that I do not wish for you to raise him," said Sheung Hong, "merely that I fear you would forgo wet for dry:[431] that you could not bear the strain of parenthood."

"No, no," replied Tsiu Hei. "The strain of parenthood does not intimidate me: the bearing and raising of children is a woman's natural role. I am also his concubine-mother, and should I not tend and nurture him now his mother has died, I fear the laneway scandalmongers will foster rampant gossip, and that opinions of me will soon be formed behind my back."

On hearing this, Sheung Hong breathed a private sigh of admiration for Tsiu Hei's feminine virtuousness, and consequently he did not hire a wet-nurse.

Who would have thought that Tsiu Hei, as ferociously natured as the tiger and dhole,[432] had other plans. For she would not be gratified until she had annihilated both mother and son.

Several days later, having waited until Sheung Hong was soundly asleep, Tsiu Hei poured liquor onto pieces of paper and

---

431 推乾就濕 "forgo dry for wet" is an ancient Chinese idiom (with many
     variant forms), which has the literal sense of a mother forgoing a dry
     sleeping place for a wet one so that the dryness can be enjoyed by her infant,
     and the idiomatic sense of the travails of motherhood in general. The phrase
     used here, however, is not "forgo dry for wet" but "forgo wet for dry". While
     it is not impossible that a printing error was responsible for this reversal, it
     seems more likely that the author modified the idiom quite intentionally, so
     as to indicate veiled ridicule on Sheung Hong's part.

432 The dhole is an Asian canid, which is also known in English as the Asiatic
     wild dog. See footnote 111 for more detail.

俏喜曰。君何言。君之兒。卽妾之兒也。其母雖死。妾尙生
存。若委人撫字。未必能悉心養育。兒爲君之宗祧所繫。設
有不測。將若之何。尙康[193]曰。吾非不願卿撫養。吾恐推濕
就乾。卿不能任此劬勞耳。俏喜曰。否否。生子育兒。乃婦
人之天職。何劬勞之足畏。況妾爲兒之庶母。其母死。妾不
撫育之。吾恐里巷間之造黑白者。飛短流長。行將議妾後
矣。尙康聞言。竊嘆其賢淑。乃不催乳媼。誰料豺虎成性之
俏喜。別有所圖。欲盡殲其母子而後快。逾數天。乃伺尙康
酣睡時。暗以酒灌紙。

193 「尙康」二字原作倒文。今正。

pasted them over the infant's mouth and nose, and in a short time he suffocated to death.[433] (§48, 1/10/1910)

Tsiu Hei then discreetly removed the paper, and made herself out to be in a state of deep sleep.

Dawn broke, and Sheung Hong, having finished his morning smoke, said to himself, "Lying apart from his mother, the ill-fated child has not cried all night. That there is truly a motherless being."

He then called on Tsiu Hei to feed the child some cow's milk,[434] but she did not respond, and not until he had shaken her forcefully did she yawn stretch and rise, berating him, "Knave! I was sleeping soundly. Why this nasty tomfoolery?"

"I was not playing about with you," said Sheung Hong. "I only want to instruct you to give the boy a drink of milk."

Tsiu Hei gave a lackadaisical response and went into the kitchen, saying scornfully under her breath, "Your boy's gone to the Western Paradise,[435] yet still you cherish him so." She then took up a jar of milk, and fiddled about in the child's mouth with a rubber tube for a good while, before calling out to Sheung Hong, "The boy's sleeping deeply and won't wake. You feed him."

Sheung Hong held the boy to his breast and began to stroke him, but his body was ice cold. Greatly shocked, and with tears streaming, Sheung Hong said, "He's died, I don't know when."

"Can that be so?" asked Tsiu Hei, putting on a pretense of fear and alarm.

---

433 This method of murder has a long history in China, and was favoured because it did not leave discernible traces. It involved the application of multiple sheets of a strong type of paper, which was soaked in water or liquor, to a person's face, resulting in the complete occlusion of the airways. The Chinese name for the technique (貼加官) is connected with the fact that the paper was transformed into a cast of the victim's face if allowed to dry before removal, i.e. a death mask.

434 In English it may sound odd that Sheung Hong would be so specific with regard to the type of milk concerned, but this sense of specificity is not present in the Chinese. The reason is one of differences in idiom and

貼其口鼻。須臾悶死。(§48, 1/10/1910) 俏喜潛去其紙。作熟睡
狀。天破曉。尚康吸烟已畢。乃自語曰。苦命兒離母而寢。
終宵不啼。是誠生而無母者。於是呼俏喜以牛乳哺之。不
應。力撼之。始欠伸而起。罵曰。促狹鬼。儂睡方酣。何必
如此惡作劇。尚康曰。我非與汝戲弄。欲命汝以牛乳飲兒
耳。俏喜漫應之。往廚內私嗤之曰。汝兒已往西方極樂世
界。尚如此愛惜耶。乃取牛乳一盅。以膠管撩兒口。良久。
呼尚康曰。兒熟睡不醒。汝哺之。尚康乃抱之於懷。以手撫
之。體已如冰。大驚。淚潛然曰。兒不知何時已死矣。俏喜
裝作惶駭狀。問曰。然耶。

---

semantic scope. In Chinese, for example, it is usual to speak of such things as
milk and eggs in animal-specific terms; whereas, in contrast, it might sound
overly specific to differentiate between such things as sheep and goats, or
rabbits and hares in general speech, but would be normal in English. In
consideration of these differences, the same Chinese expression for cow's
milk is translated simply as "milk" in the following paragraphs.

435 西方極樂世界 the "Western Paradise" or the "Western World of Bliss" is a
Buddhist term and Chinese equivalent to Sanskrit's सुखावती *Sukhāvatī*. See
footnote 42.

"Have a look at him," replied Sheung Hong.

Tsiu Hei used her fingers to push the boy's eyes apart from the rims and to squeeze his nails, and then pretended to cry on finding him unalterably silent and motionless. "How heart-rending that the boy should have lost his mother upon his birth," she said, "and that at such a tender age he should perish, a few days after being left to me to raise. Hurry and send a woman off to lay him in a grave."

Sheung Hong had not inquired closely into the cause of the infant's death, but a decade later[436] the neighbourhood's air was thick with the news that Tsiu Hei had murdered his wife and killed his son.

But how, with Tsiu Hei's secretive and deviously deceptive methods, could what she had done have come to light? *Best it is to do not what thou wouldst have others know not*, said the ancients.

Prior to these events, Tsiu Hei had employed a village woman as a proxy worshiper to entreat the gods and the Buddha,[437] in order that she might run errands for her. Later, Tsiu Hei had made her her confidante, but having come to know secretly of her deeds, the woman had tried to extort several taels from her. With this Tsiu Hei had been unwilling to part, and the two of them had fallen out, the woman, in the end, making the matter known to all and sundry.

When Sheung Hong's clansmen of his uncles' generation[438] learned the news, they called him to account, but Sheung Hong did his utmost to assert its falsity.

Incensed, the villagers had wanted to have the matter made clear to Sheung Hong, but seeing him doing his utmost at shielding and covering, they too let it be.

---

436 Here and below the word "decade" is used in the Chinese sense of ten days.

437 求神拜佛 "to worship and entreat the gods and the Buddha" is a mouthful in English translation, but a simple idiom in Chinese.

438 叔伯(輩) "uncles" is the term used in Chinese for these men, an expression which is inclusive of paternal uncles proper, and paternal cousins, perhaps many times removed, of the same generation.

佾康 曰。汝視之。俏喜故以指撐其眼眶。搦其指甲。寂然不
動。乃假哭曰。兒生背母。留妾撫養。數天而殤。慘怛奚
若。急使嫗往瘞之。佾康亦不細究其致死之由。逾旬。里巷
哄傳俏喜弒嫡殺子之事。嘻。以俏喜狡獪秘詐手叚。所行之
事。何能宣洩。古人云。欲人不知。莫若勿爲。先是俏喜用
一村嫗。爲求神拜佛。以供奔走者。後引以爲腹心。陰知其
事。欲勒數金。俏喜靳不予。兩相齟齬。嫗竟將其事宣布於
外。佾康之伯叔輩聞之。詰責佾康。佾康力白其無。村人大
憤。欲發其覆。見佾康力爲袒庇。亦置之不理。

The news had been broadcast far and wide by a second decade after the death, and Sheung Hong was met with a chorus of abuse whenever he stepped over the threshold of the village.

Reflecting on how his wife and child had died so suddenly and without reason, Sheung Hong could not help but feel a little puzzled. Subsequently, he questioned a village woman,[439] and she told him the facts directly. Enraged, Sheung Hong went home and began to revile Tsiu Hei.

Tsiu Hei, unleashing her she-ogreish might, took a strong grip on Sheung Hong's throat, and berated him, "Fiend of a man! So you want falsely to accuse me of murder, do you? Since you want me to die, I'll strangle you to death first, and we can die together and have done with it, to pay with our lives for the lives of your wife and son! Your wife and son died of illness. You saw it with your own eyes, and you prepared them for burial with your own hands. And yet you want to do me an unrightable wrong over these wild accusations?" Finished, Tsiu Hei gripped his throat all the more tightly, and not until Sheung Hong was ashen faced, and pleading for mercy as he choked, did she release her grip.

Grieved, defeated, and powerless, Sheung Hong lay and drank of tears, often beating his bed in rueful regret as he remembered and mourned his wife and son, and several months hence, he died a despondent death. (§49, 8/10/1910)

After Sheung Hong's death, Tsiu Hei enticed the young ruffians of the area to her villa, and there they congregated and debauched themselves day and night. One of them, a native of Sha Mong Shek Heung,[440] was a notorious local bandit named King,[441] and it was he who was on most intimate terms with Tsiu Hei.

---

439 It is not made clear in the Chinese whether Sheung Hong spoke with one or more village woman.

440 This place name is probably a word play on a real place name, the identity of which has not yet been determined. The word 鄉 c⁰. "heung" at its end means "locality", a somewhat nebulous term that might indicate a 都 "subdistrict" or a village. One definite possibility is that 沙望石 Sha Mong

又逾旬。播揚遐邇。尙康出入。村人眾口交罵。尙康回憶其
母子無端猝斃。未免有些疑惑。乃詰問村嫗。嫗直告。尙康
大怒。歸家責罵俏喜。乃俏喜大肆其母夜叉之威。力扼尙康
之吭。罵曰。黑心漢。欲誣我以殺人之罪耶。汝欲儂死。儂
先扼殺汝。一齊死休。以償汝妻子之命。汝妻子病死。汝眼
見目擊。親爲殯殮。乃欲以莫須有之事。加儂以不白之冤
耶。罵完。扼益力。尙康面色灰死。氣絕求饒。俏喜始釋
手。尙康氣餒心傷。無如之何。臥而飲泣。時復憶妻悼子。
搥床悔恨。遲數月憂鬱而歿。(§49，8/10/1910) 俏喜自尙康死
後[194]。勾引該處惡少。麕聚其別墅中。日夜宣淫。內有一惡
少名景者。沙望石鄉人。爲該処之著名劇盜。與俏喜最相
結契。

194 「死後」原誤倒作「後死」。今正。

Shek is a contraction of 白沙相望石 Pak Sha Seung Mong Shek, i.e. the village of 相望石 Seung Mong Shek (Mᴹ. *Xiāngwàngshí*), in the vicinity of the town of Pak Sha.
441 "King" is a romanisation according to the spelling conventions for Cantonese, in which it is roughly pronounced *geng*.

This situation went on in such a manner for years.

Meanwhile, Ma's adopted son Kam Ngau had come of age, and had taken the daughter of a Mr Lee for his wife. The young couple were cruelly treated by Tsiu Hei, but being impoverished and alone, and without parental support, they could do nothing in the circumstances other than suffer in silence and drink of tears.

One night Ah King[442] brought along a band of good-for-nothings, and as they began to carouse, the villa took on, with their loud voices, jesting and laughter, *chai mui* and tile play,[443] a striking likeness to a brothel.

When his head was hot with wine,[444] Ah King bade Tsiu Hei to instruct Lee that she should come and entertain them while they imbibed.

Tsiu Hei did as bade. Incensed in the extreme, Lee refused her with stern words and a steely countenance.

"What are you saying, Mother-in-law? As your daughter-in-law, I have ever maintained my virtue, and yet you,

---

442 The addition of the "Ah" to the aforementioned given name produces something like an equivalent to the English short form, i.e. it turns a "Samuel" into a "Sam". This is the name by which he would have been known to his fellows. In the Chinese text that follows, this name is generally given as the short form "Ah King", but occasionally it is truncated to the more formal "King". In translation, however, "Ah King" has been used throughout. This approach has been taken in the interests of clarity, and in consideration of the fact that the author's occasional truncations back to the formal form do not appear to serve a rhetorical purpose, but to have been no more than written abbreviations, as is the case with some other names (see footnote 6).

443 The expression 鬥牌 "tile play" could in fact refer to any competitive game involving either dominos, paper cards, or mah-jong tiles. See footnote 233 for more on the game of *chai mui*.

444 The set idiom used here to describe Ah King's state of drunkenness (酒酣耳熱), which coincidentally also appears in §38, translates more literally as "drunkenly merry and with ears hot with wine".

如是者有年。斯時馬氏之養子金牛[195]。年已弱冠。業經娶李氏女爲婦。一對小夫妻。屢爲俏喜所虐待。而無怙無恃。零仃孤苦。勢[196]無可如何。惟有飲泣啞忍而已。一夜亞景率一班無賴。在其別墅中轟飲。喧笑戲謔。豁拳鬥牌。儼若妓院。時亞景酒酣耳熱之餘。使俏喜命李氏往賄觴。俏喜果往呼之。李氏憤極。正色嚴詞却之曰。姑何言。兒以清白之身。作姑之弱媳。姑乃

195 「金牛」二字原作倒文。今正
196 原文「勢」字缺底。今參他處字擬正。

with an utter lack of shame and decency, would seem to take me for a money tree.[445] I should rather die than do as you instruct."

On hearing this, Tsiu Hei was lost for words. Ashamed and angered, she went to Ah King, and said to him, "The obstinate wench firmly refused to come, and instead insulted me, of all people, in vile language. I should be grateful if you would go off yourselves, seize her by the hair, and drag her here. We shall see whether the little wench is still capable of being headstrong then."

Ah King and his party headed off, Tsiu Hei leading the way.

Lifting the curtain, they entered Lee's room. She was crouched by the side of the bed, crying bitterly. At the sight of her, Ah King made a sudden rush forward, and grabbed her up in his arms.

How could Lee, who was young and delicately built, counter this brute force? The shock had at once caused her legs to go soft and her body to shake. Desperate to struggle, she found her hands and feet had lost their usefulness. Repeatedly, she screamed for help, but there was no one living round about to hear.

Lee thought to herself, *All that will be left for me will be to die so as to wash away this humiliation.*

Ah King was ravenous with lust as he held this gorgeous figure in the flower of her youth.[446] Again and again the desire to defile her arose in him, but Tsiu Hei's presence at his side made for an impediment.

---

445 錢樹子 "money tree" or rather "sapling that yields coins" is a colloquial term for prostitute, which had its origin over a thousand years ago in connection with a mother who prostituted her daughter. The author's usage of the expression would appear to indicate an appreciation for this etymology.

446 The sense of "ravenous with lust" is conveyed here by means of an idiom (饞涎径尺) with the literal sense of "a full foot of drool hanging from a ravenous mouth". See §36 for a similar expression, and its footnote 305, for more detail. As with figurative English idioms, such as "bite the dust" or "the devil is in the details", such expressions are not always readily amenable to direct translation.

喪盡廉恥。以兒爲錢樹子耶。兒寧死不敢奉命。俏喜聞之。
語塞。羞憤交併。往謂景曰。妮子執拗。堅不肯来。反以惡
言冒犯老娘。請汝等親往捽[197]髮牽之來。看小妮子尚能強項
否。亞景等果親往。俏喜在前引導。掀簾而入。時李氏伏在
床沿痛哭。亞景一見。驟上前抱之。李氏以青年弱質。焉能
當此強暴。早已嚇得體慄足軟。強欲撐扎[198]。奈手足失其效
用。屢疾聲呼救。奈四面并無居鄰。斯時李氏自念。惟有一
死以洗此辱耳。亞景抱此芳齡艷質。饞涎径尺。屢欲污之。
惟礙於俏喜在側。

197 「捽」原作「卒」，並加注曰「手旁」。其卒字甚模糊。今參他處字，並據
　　注文擬正。
198 按，「撐扎」與「撑扎」通。

He gazed at Lee and, after a good while, made up his mind, thinking to himself, *How can I spit out such a tasty morsel now it is in my mouth?* He was then about to do as he liked and rape her.

Ah! Lee was now in peril! But fortunately Tsiu Hei was there and in the throes of a storm of jealousy. Hurriedly finding a stick of firewood, she clouted him across the back, and scolded him, "I told you to corner and humiliate the wench, not to rape her!"

Ah King quickly released his grip and, hanging his head, apologised for his mistake. Tsiu Hei then led him away to the villa, holding him firmly by the ear.

Hah! How formidable is women's power of attraction that a notorious and powerful bandit should be subdued as though he were a beast of burden being driven. (§50, 15/10/1910)

After Ah King left, Lee leant against the bed and drank of tears. All atremble, furthermore, with the dread of one in precarious danger[447] for fear that he might return, she thought repeatedly of hanging herself.

My husband away, Lee considered, *were I to die now, who would right this unrighted wrong for me? It would be best to await his return, and, after relating the whole story, still not too late to seek death.*

---

447 慄慄危懼 "all atremble with the dread of one in precarious danger" is an ancient expression, still in use, that has its origin in a proclamation (湯誥) attributed to the founder of the Mᵒ. Shang dynasty, who lived in the first half of the second millennium B.C.E. In the proclamation, which is in fact most probably a forgery dating from the fourth century C.E. or earlier, the phrase describes the king's fear that in taking his place as ruler on high he might offend Heaven or Earth, a feeling he likened to that experienced by a person faced with the prospect of plummeting down into an abyss; hence the use of the word *precarious*, which in Chinese, as in English, has an extended sense.

注視李氏。良久。決念曰。如此美味。既入咽矣。安能[199]吐
之。將欲肆意強姦。嘻。危矣哉。李氏。幸而俏喜在傍。醋
風大起。急覓一柴。在背後猛擊之。罵曰。儂使汝窘辱妮
子。誰教汝強姦妮子也。亞景急釋手。垂首謝過。俏喜提其
耳向別墅而去。噫。以一著名之強盜。受制於婦人。如牛馬
之受駕馭。婦女之吸力。亦可畏矣。(§50, 15/10/1910) 李氏自
亞景去後。靠床飲泣。又恐亞景復來。慄慄危懼。屢欲自
經。自思兒夫在外。妾身若死。將來不白之冤。誰代伸雪。
不若待吾夫歸。訴明原委。死猶未晚。

199　原文「能」字缺底。今參他處字擬正。

Kam Ngau was, at this time, employed several tens of miles away at the Yee Loong shop in Pak Hap, and made the trip back home only once a month. The following day, he returned as expected.

Lee choked up with tears at the sight of her husband's face and was unable to speak. But at Kam Ngau's urging, she began at last to tearfully recount the previous night's events from beginning to end.

On hearing the story, Kam Ngau was incensed, and yelled, "I swear to extirpate this wanton creature!"[448] He then made a disgruntled exit, and went off to his old neighbourhood, where he tearfully recounted the story to his clanspeople.[449]

Kam Ngau's clanspeople proceeded to tell him of Tsiu Hei's wife poisoning and child killing, and also warned him, saying, "This wanton woman has a most devious vicious[450] heart. You ought to guard against her." Tsiu Hei's deeds had been entirely unknown to Kam Ngau, because several years ago he was yet of a tender age. On hearing of them now, Kam Ngau, young and full of spirit, was instantly overtaken by irrepressible anger. His hackles raised, his eyes bulging, he clenched his teeth and then angrily declared: "I shall kill this wanton man and wanton woman to avenge my mother!" He then raced home and searched for Tsiu Hei. He did not find her.

---

448 This sentence would appear to be styled on a line within the same ancient text from which the expression treated in footnote 447 derives (所指即為《尚書》〈胤征〉之「殲厥渠魁」句). The text in question is 尚書 "The Writings of Yore", otherwise translated as The Book of Documents, the Shû King &c., which is a classic of the Confucian canon considered to contain the most ancient works of Chinese literature.

449 The old neighbourhood referred to here is presumably Sheung Hong's, i.e. where Sheung Hong and Ma had lived before they relocated in §47. This assumption is reflected in the translations given in the following instalments.

450 The Chinese character used here for "vicious" also means "poisonous" and "poison", and is the same as appears in the novel's title, where its most apparent sense is that of a social poison, i.e. a socially pernicious influence.

翌日。牛果歸。斯時牛在百合怡隆店傭工。離家數十里。經月一歸。李氏見其夫面。嗚咽不能成聲。牛敦促之。良久。始將昨夜之事。泣訴始末。牛聞之。大憤。疾聲罵曰。吾誓殲厥淫虫。罵畢。恨恨而出。往舊鄉泣訴其族人。其族人又將俏喜酖斃殺子之事告之。並戒之曰。此淫婦心甚險毒。汝宜防之。蓋因數年前牛尚幼稚。俏喜所行之事。一切不知也。牛少年氣盛。一聞此事。卽憤不可遏。眦裂髮指。切齒而罵曰。吾定殺此淫夫淫婦。以復母仇。奔馳歸家。覓俏喜。不遇。

Tsiu Hei had anticipated, as soon as Kam Ngau entered through the door, that Lee would undoubtedly tell him of the events of the previous night. She had therefore concealed herself outside the door curtain and listened in silence, and when Kam Ngau had become enraged, she had immediately headed off to search for Ah King, so that they could consider the matter together and plan a plan of approach.

"What have I to fear? That milksop[451] couldn't stomach one bullet from me," Ah King had said. "Being naturally spineless, these words of his would, moreover, have been no more than random raving in the heat of anger. I should reckon he would in fact be incapable of doing anything. Nevertheless, we must get rid of this thorn in our side, and should indeed lay out a scheme for it."

Tsiu Hei had previously deposited some of her garments and accessories at Yee Loong, for fear they might be stolen if kept in the house. About half a month later, she went to Yee Loong and collected these belongings as arranged. She then said to Kam Ngau, "You might escort me back home, for it's now nightfall and I fear that were bandits to have intelligence of me, they might block the road and strip me of my possessions." Kam Ngau acceded to her request.

Alas, he had fallen into a trap. (§51, 22/10/1910)

Outstretched across the route from Pak Hap to [Pak Hang][452] was a large hill. Its name was Centipede Hill.[453] The striking image of [a] one-hundred-legged insect, it wound its way along for several

---

451   豎子, translated here as "milksop", is a belittling term of abuse, which connotes foolishness, weakness and uselessness. Its literal sense is that of "pageboy" or "servant boy".

452   北行 "Pak Hang" would be the name of Wong Sheung Hong's subdistrict or village, and not the only proper name in the novel that the author does not "spell" consistently. It is introduced in §1 as 百行, which shares the same pronunciation in the See Yip language, but employs a different character for the "Pak". (These same characters are similarly interchanged in the name of

當牛初入戶時。俏喜預料李氏決將昨夜之事告訴。故匿簾外
靜聽。當牛怒罵時。他卽往尋亞景會商。籌對待之籌。景
曰。豎子不足咬我一彈。吾何畏。況他秉性柔懦。一時憤
激。偶作此譖語耳。度他亦無能爲力。雖然。此眼中釘。不
可不拔。會當圖之。先是俏喜之衣飾。藏在家中。恐爲盜
劫。故寄貯怡隆。逾半月許。俏喜果到怡隆取衣飾。乃謂牛
曰。時已傍晚。恐爲匪人偵知。攔途搶掠。汝護我囘家。牛
從之。噫。牛中計矣。(§51， 22/10/1910) 　由北合而至北[行]²⁰⁰
鄉。有一大山。橫互²⁰¹其間。此山名百足山。山陽爲[新]²⁰²
甯。山陰爲開平。蜿蜒數

---

200 原文「行」字殘甚。今參他處字擬補。
201 「橫互」之「互」，原誤作「亙」。今正。
202 原文「新」字殘缺。今據文義擬正。

---

the town which is home to the Yee Loong shop, that of 百合 "Pak Hap",
which is given in this part, §27 and §28, as 北合, and in §51 as the
orthographically correct 百合.) See also footnote 2.

453　百足山 "Centipede Hill" is a real hill, and the description given in this part,
both of it and its geographic location, is reasonably accurate. Locals state
that it was fairly free of vegetation up until a few decades ago, when they
stopped cutting brush for fuel and began using gas stoves. Nowadays, it is
covered in thick vegetation and is virtually impassable.

tens of miles, its northerly flanks Hoi Ping, its southerly flanks [Llin Nen]. To make his way home, Kam Ngau had to pass right over its ridge.

Tsiu Hei and Kam Ngau walked up to the crest of the ridge, he in front and she behind. All of a sudden, there was a clap. Looking about him in a frantic instant, Kam Ngau saw several young ruffians with guns rush out from beside a cliff and fire towards him. At their head was Ah King.

Now in a state of great alarm, Kam Ngau flew down the hill. The ruffians, guns booming, gave chase, and right in amongst them, helping in the pursuit, was Tsiu Hei. Seeing them fire repeatedly and fail to strike their mark, Tsiu Hei bent down and picked up a huge rock, which she personally hurled down at Kam Ngau. It too failed to hit him, and by then he had already sped down to the foot of the hill.

At the foot of the hill was a village, which bore the name Chiu Yeung Lee,[454] and Kam Ngau made for its refuge, shouting for help.

Perceiving that all was now futile, Tsiu Hei, Ah King and party slipped away.

Having heard Kam Ngau's calls for help, the villagers gathered together to ask what the matter was. Kam Ngau tearfully recounted the whole story, and inspecting his upper garment, they saw that holes had been punched through in several places. Fortunately the bullets had shot past his sides and missed the skin, though only by reason of his voluminous clothing having billowed out in the wind as he ran.

Seeing him in this state, the villagers were all indignant at the injustice, and wanted to escort him home.

Kam Ngau declined, saying, "They are infamous bandits, and long ago overran and occupied my house. Should I return,

---

454 朝陽里 "Chiu Yeung Lee" is a real village, located at the northeastern end of 百足山 "Centipede Hill". Its name carries the rough sense of "Facing the Southerly Side of the Hill Village".

十里。儼如☐[203]百足之虫焉。牛歸家。必踰嶺而過。牛與俏喜行至嶺巔。牛先行。俏喜後行。突聞轟的一聲。牛遑遽四顧。見有數惡少由崖際突出。持鎗向他轟擊。爲首者乃景也。大駭。飛奔下山。諸惡少尾追之。鎗聲隆隆。俏喜亦雜於諸惡少中。帮同追逐。俏喜見屢擊不中。卽俯拾一巨石。親自磔[204]之。又不中。而牛已奔馳至山麓。山麓有一村。名曰朝陽里。牛奔投之。大呼救援。俏喜與景等。知事無濟。乃潛遁。村人聞牛呼救。團集問訊。牛泣訴始末。視其衣已洞穿數處。幸其衣服寬博。奔走時爲風颺揚。鎗彈旁掠而過。故不及膚耳。村人見之咸抱不平。欲護之歸家。牛不可曰。彼等乃著名劇盜。盤据我室已久。我若歸。

203 原文「一」字半缺。今擬正。
204 按，「磔」為「擲」之同音假借字。蓋「磔」之粵音與「擲」相同。

it is a certainty that they will murder me. It would be much better for you to take me back to the shop."

Accordingly, the villagers took Kam Ngau to Pak Hap.

The townspeople were incensed on hearing the story. Among them were several people of chivalrous character and they joined with the villagers in escorting Kam Ngau to his old neighbourhood, so that he might voice his complaint to the elders there.

On hearing the news, the elders were furious, and unanimously remarked, "What will become of the character of this place if we do not rid it of so savage a wanton man and wanton woman?"

The elders accordingly gave orders to over ten good fighters from amongst the neighbourhood's young men, and they headed off at speed, to run on through the night. (§52, 29/10/1910)

Tsiu Hei, Ah King and party sped back by way of a little path.

Once his breath had steadied, Ah King shook his head and said, "Our inability to get rid of that thorn in our side today is really frustrating."

Angry with him, Tsiu Hei replied, "You profess to be a champion of the green wood[455] and yet you could not kill a milksop. Are you not thoroughly ashamed?"

"Worry not, my dear, the day will come," replied Ah King. "Our guns were unable to hit their target today because that milksop was racing down from a height, twisting and turning as he ran, and there was a strong wind flapping his clothes about. It was on that account alone that we failed. The trap we lay next time will be far tighter. Even were he to be given wings, he would not be able to fly up out of it."

"You are being shamelessly boastful," sneered Tsiu Hei. "If you fail again, I ought to humiliate you with an under-crotch crawl."[456]

---

455 This phrase is a variation on a set of expressions that were once used to describe the bandits of China's wooded hills (若綠林好漢綠林強盜等).

必害我命。不若送我回店。較爲妥善。村人果送他到北合。
市人聞之。大憤。有義俠者數人。協同村人護送他到舊鄉。
投訴鄉中父老。父老聞信。怒髮衝冠。僉曰[205]有如此兇殘之
淫夫淫婦。若不除之。亦復成何風俗。於是督率鄉中子弟。
好身手者十餘人。連夜疾馳而往。(§52, 29/10/1910) 俏喜與亞
景等。由小徑疾回。坌息甫定。景搖首曰。今日不能拔此眼
中釘。正令人悶悵。俏喜恚之曰。君自稱爲綠林之雄。無能
死一豎子。可不愧煞。景曰。卿勿憂。會當[206]有日。今日吾
鎗之未能命中者。緣該豎子由高奔下。曲拆[207]疾馳。又值狂
風拂衣。故此失敗耳。他時再布陷阱。愈爲週密。雖加之以
翼。恐亦難飛上天去。俏喜哂之曰。君大言不慚。如再次失
敗。當以胯下辱君。

205 「僉曰」下似奪一讀號。疑印刷之誤，故譯而正之。
206 此字殘甚。今審其殘跡與文義擬正。
207 「拆」，「折」字之訛也。

---

456 胯下之辱 "an under-crotch crawl" , or more literally "an under-crotch
humiliation", is the humiliating act of crawling through another person's
legs. The expression has its origin in the story of the renowned Chinese
general 韓信 Mᵒ. Han Hsin Mᴹ. *Hán Xìn* (fl. third century B.C.E.), who,
before his rise to prominence, chose, in what is considered to have been an
act of forbearance, to be publicly humiliated in this way in response to a
challenge laid down by a bullying butcher. This well-known story is recorded
in his biography in 史記 *"The History"* (see footnote 365 for more about this
work).

"What can he do?" replied Ah King angrily. "He is no more than a bird in a cage or a fish in a net; whether he lives or is killed is up to me. Let us make a pact that if I cannot fulfill this assignment in three days, I ought to present kneeling before your skirt with a cane on my back."[457]

[Now in the midst of] debating matters, the two of them suddenly heard an eruption of voices. A few moments later, to their great shock, the sounds of slurs and insults, of staffs, cudgels and weapons of war, and of doors being beaten, coalesced to form a single uproar.

Having propped a wooden post up behind the double doors in an attempt at fortifying them, Tsiu Hei found herself [a] kitchen knife, and then shut the door to the bedroom to wait.

Ah King took hold of a rifle, loaded it up with bullets, went out onto the upstairs front balcony, and climbed straight up onto the tiled roof. Electing to shield himself behind the roof's ridge, he surveyed the surroundings. Considering to himself that, being outnumbered, a quick escape would be best, he then took his gun and fired two blasts towards the area behind the house: the villagers could not run out of the way quick enough. Ah King took his window of opportunity and jumped down, turning afterwards to shoot off several more blasts.

The villagers, having not dared to tail him, knew that Ah King was [long gone].

When the sky was bright, the group broke open the doors and swarmed inside. They then saw that the bedroom door was closed, and broke it open too.

Tsiu Hei, holding the kitchen knife in her hand, shouted loudly, "What sort of robbers are you who in broad daylight dare to plunder people's homes?"

---

457 See footnote 365.

景憤然曰。彼直籠中之鳥。網中之魚耳。生殺由我。彼何能
爲。請以三日約如不能報命。當負荊裙下。二人 方 [208] 辯論
間。忽聞人聲鼎沸。俄而搗戶聲。呰罵聲。兵刀棍棒聲。嚷
成一片。二人大驚。俏喜即用木樁支撐兩扉。爲固拒計。覓
廚刀 □ [209] 柄。復閉寢室門以俟。亞景挾一快 [210] 鎗。實以子
彈。由前樓出晾臺。直上 [211] 瓦面。擇屋脊以障身。四圍偵
望。自思眾寡不敵。不如速 [212] 逃。乃以鎗向屋後連轟二聲。
鄉人奔避不迭。乘間跳下。復回首轟擊數響。鄉人亦不敢尾
追。知景去已 遠 [213]。時天已大明。乃破扉蜂擁而入。羣見寢
門已閉。復破寢門。俏喜手執廚刀大聲喝曰。何處強盜。於
青天白日之下。敢刮掠人家耶。

---

208 原文「方」字半缺。今參他處字擬正。
209 此字全缺。據其文義，似當作「一」或「二」。
210 「快」原作「恔」。誤。今正。
211 原文「上」字缺底。今審文義，及他處字，擬正。
212 原文「速」字缺底。今參他處字擬正。
213 原文「遠」字模糊不清。今參別篇遠字擬正。

"What sort of wanton woman are you," replied an old man,[458] "who in broad daylight dares to murder a wife and kill a son?"

At that moment, several brave and tactically minded individuals amongst those present moved forward and snatched Tsiu Hei's kitchen knife. Her hands and feet were then tied with hempen rope, and she was packed into a pig basket and carried to the old neighbourhood's ancestral hall.[459] Therein, villagers old and young, male and female, walled around her staring, an unceasing sound of invective flowing from their mouths.

In time, the gong was rung for a collective discussion.

An old man proclaimed the grounds for her guilt, and asked as to what method of punishment might be employed. There were those who said to take her to the authorities, and those who said to apply domestic law,[460] and the talk went on incessantly.

An elderly farmer then said loudly and abusively, "All the Manchu Ch'ing's officials know is how to take bribes and exact heavy taxes.[461] They pay no heed to civil matters. It would be better and more straightforward to apply domestic law." All assembled having voiced their approval, they then began discussing the method of execution. Some wanted to shoot her dead with a gun, and some said it would be best to hang her.

---

458 The word 老者 "elder", meaning *old person*, is translated here as "old man", so as to distinguish it from the unconnected word 父老 that is translated in this and the previous part as "elder" and means specifically *old men who are leaders or senior figures in their community*. Technically, the word used here could equally denote an old woman, but this seems unlikely in the context.

459 祖祠 "ancestral halls" were important buildings dedicated to the veneration of the deceased members of a family or clan, whose names were inscribed on individual plaques or a common name board that sat on an altar housed within, before which offerings were made and other rites performed. Ancestral halls also functioned as centres of community life, and sometimes doubled as schoolhouses.

一老者曰。何物淫婦。於青天白日之下。敢害嫡殺子耶。時
有胆畧者數人。即上前奪其廚刀。以蔴繩縶其手足。裝
以豚笠。扛囘舊鄉祖祠內。村中老的少的男的女的。圍觀如
堵墻。詛罵之聲。不絕於口。尋即鳴鑼集議。有老者宣佈
其罪由。問處治之方法。有云送官者。有云處以家法者。刺
刺不休。老年農人大聲罵曰。滿淸官吏。祇知厚斂受賄。不
理民事。不若處以家法。較爲簡捷。衆皆贊成。隨議處死之
法。有欲用鎗擊死者。有云不如縊之。

---

460 The unofficial laws or rules that governed the family or clan. These rules
     were accorded a degree of legal status by the official law of the state, but the
     exact way in which the two interacted is now not fully understood. See pages
     62 and 63 of *Chinamen at Home* (published 1900) for a little sketch on the
     application of these unofficial laws, and on the village elders who applied
     them. The book's Wesleyan missionary author Thomas Gunn Selby lived for
     many years in the Cantonese-speaking region which neighboured the novel's
     See Yip region, and his views, in this respect at least, would appear to be
     consistent with those regularly expressed in Australia's Chinese-language
     newspapers at the time. This book is available online: https://archive.org/
     stream/chinamenathome00selbiala
461 See footnote 90 for a brief outline of the ᴍᵒ. Manchu Ch'ing dynasty.

The elderly peasant spoke again, "The family has been unfortunate to have had this accursed woman enter it. Shooting and hanging would likewise pollute our lands. Better and singularly satisfying it would be to cast her into a murky current."[462] Once again, all voiced their approval.

When the group had lifted her up and were about to start walking, Tsiu Hei said pathetically, "My guilt, I accept. My crimes make for a long litany.[463] How could I hope for life when my death is not enough to make amends? Yet I hope you elders might give me the slightest bit of face[464] and remove this pig basket, that I might make my way on foot."

In compliance, the villagers removed the pig basket. They then set off with long poles held out to surround her.

---

462 The reason this approach would be "singularly satisfying" is that it would make for poetic justice. This poetic justice has its basis in word play: The Chinese word 濁 "murky/turbid" has the secondary senses of "morally turbid", "impure", "immoral" and "sullied", and the word 流 "current/stream" has the secondary sense of "a class of persons" (most likely an extension of its literal sense of stream, through likening humanity to a river with different branches). The expression 濁流 "murky/turbid current" thus carries the secondary sense of "immoral people", and the action of casting Tsiu Hei into a murky current the sense of returning her to where she belongs. The analogy is not a novel one. It appears, for example, in a well-known passage from the tenth-century work known to latter ages as 舊五代史 "*The Old History of the Five Eras*" (generally translated as the *Old History of the Five Dynasties*): 此輩自謂清流 宜投於黃河 永為濁流 "It would be fitting to cast these fellows, who claim to be of the *virtuous class* [secondary sense: 'clear/pellucid stream'], into the Yellow River, that ever after they should be of the *sullied class* [secondary meaning: 'the murky/turbid stream']."

463 This phrase is an adaption of an idiom, which is based on a line within the founder of the 周 Mᵒ. Chou dynasty's condemnation of the previous Shang dynasty (泰誓) that is recorded in 尚書 "*The Writings of Yore*": 商罪貫盈 "The crimes of the Shang make for a long litany", or more literally, "Shang's crimes would be sufficient to fill a money string" (which suggests that money strings were once particularly long). The condemnation, like some other parts of *The Writings of Yore*, is considered to be apocryphal; it may, however, be the product of the amalgamation of similarly ancient writings.

464 The word *face* is used here in the Chinese sense of the appearance of dignity.

老年農民復曰。家族不幸。出此不祥之婦。擊死與縊死。皆
污吾境土。不若投之濁流。尤爲痛快。衆又贊成。羣扛之欲
行。俏喜慘然曰。妾知罪矣。妾之罪貫滿盈。一死不足以蔽
辜。奚望生爲。望諸父老稍予薄臉。去此豚笠。妾卽步行而
往。鄉人果去其豚笠。持長竿攤之而去。

About two miles from the village was a certain Peck-pot Temple, beside which was a bottomlessly deep pool.[465] Tsiu Hei walked to its edge, jumped of her own accord, and with a single kerplunk! went down into it. Up she floated and down she sank several times over. The villagers then pushed her under with their poles, and consigned her forever to haunt the rippled waters.[466]

Kam Ngau,[467] fearful of the threat posed by Ah King's brazenness, evaded him by fleeing to the Southern Seas,[468] and it is said no word of him was ever heard thereafter.[469]

(The End.)
(§53, 10/12/1910)

---

465   "Peck-pot Temple" is a literal translation of this temple's name. A 刁斗 "peck pot" is an ancient military cooking pot with a capacity of one Chinese peck (a unit of volume once roughly equivalent to two litres), which was used for the secondary purpose of sounding the night watches. Today the word is used in Chinese to connote military presence (e.g. in the phrase 刁斗森嚴). Whether "Peck-pot Temple" is the name of an actual temple or not is unclear. There is, however, a village named 吊斗廟村 "Hanging-bucket-temple Village" about ten kilometers (as the crow flies) south of 白沙鎮 the town of Pak Sha, and, reportedly, it was once home to a temple of that name, which had a deep pool beside it (the temple is said to have been demolished and the pool filled in). 吊斗廟 "Hanging-bucket Temple" and 刁斗廟 "Peck-pot Temple" are pronounced identically in the See Yip language. This may therefore have been the temple to which the author was referring. Whether it was originally called 吊斗廟 "Hanging-bucket Temple" and the author's use of the homophonous 刁斗廟 "Peck-pot Temple" was merely a see-through attempt at disguise is unclear. In the modern era, the Chinese characters that form village names have sometimes been forgotten and fixed anew; it is therefore also conceivable that 刁斗廟 "Peck-pot Temple" was the original name, and 吊斗廟村 "Hanging-bucket Temple" is a modern corruption.

離村二里許。有一刁斗廟。廟側有一潭。深而無底。俏喜行
至其旁骨董²¹⁴一聲。彼自跳下。浮沉數次。鄉人以長竿撐
之。已爲凌波仙子矣。亞牛畏亞景之兇燄。避之於南洋。後
亦杳無音耗云。(已完)(§53, 10/12/1910)

214 原文「董」字模糊不清。今參別處董字擬正。

466 A more literal translation of this sentence's final phrase might be "she was
an immortal that treads lightly upon the rippled waters". This, however,
would fail to convey the darker dimensions of a Chinese expression that has
a history of use in connection with the spirits of people who have perished
by drowning (凌波仙子), and the association between immortality and the
less pleasant connotation of *eternal consignment*.

467 In the original text, the author gives the short form of Kam Ngau's name
here, "Ah Ngau", possibly so as to form a rhetorical match with "Ah King".
This name has been changed back to Kam Ngau in the translation for the
sake of clarity.

468 南洋 "the Southern Seas" is used here in its extended metonymic and rather
nebulous sense of "the lands of the southern ocean," by which is meant
Southeast Asia, and, in the author and his characters' day, Australia too.

469 Kam Ngau presumably took his wife Lee with him. The author, however,
neglects to mention her fate.

Acknowledgements

I should like to acknowledge and express my sincere gratitude to the numerous people and organisations whose varied contributions, which I shall attempt to summarise below, have made this publication possible.

Historian Michael Williams, who not only conceived of and instigated the project, but has acted as its co-ordinator, one of my unofficial reviewers, and a contributor to the publication's historical content, and who has selflessly given a great deal of his time in order to see the project through to successful completion. He has been an excellent collaborator—sensible, reliable, encouraging, and focused on the big picture—and his steady yet not over-controlling hand on the tiller has been a source of great comfort to me from start to finish.

Mei-fen Kuo, historian and contributor to the book's front and end matter, who rediscovered the novel and brought its existence to light, and has assisted with historical research and project coordination throughout, despite her busy schedule.

Historian and curator Sophie Couchman, who provided much assistance during the early stages of the project, and who helped in the securement of a grant, without which the project might never have gone ahead.

Australian sinologist and historian John Fitzgerald, who has provided me with much advice and encouragement, and hours of selfless assistance.

Professor of Chinese Studies at the University of Melbourne Anne McLaren, who generously agreed to look over the novel and my draft translations of its initial instalments, and provided a positive and helpful assessment, which reshaped my views on matters of relevance to my translator's introduction.

The Chinese Australian Historical Society (CAHS) for its promotion of the project and provision of resources from an early stage.

Public Record Office Victoria—perhaps better known as PROV or the Victorian Public Records Office—whose Local History Grant funded the project, and represented a reassuring vote of confidence in it.

Former Senator Tsebin Tchen, who, in his capacity as Director of History Projects for The Kuo Min Tang Society of Melbourne (Melbourne KMT), aided the project in the securement of the above-mentioned grant. Thanks are also due to the Melbourne KMT's executive committee, which voted in favour of rendering unconditional support to an academic endeavour.

Sydney University Press (SUP), for recognising the novel's worth, and having the breadth of mind to take on a bilingual publication that, with its fictional and nonfictional content, defies neat classification. Thanks are due to all members of SUP's staff who have helped in bringing the book into existence, but in particular to my editor Denise O'Dea, for her patience, professionalism and dedication. Freelance designer Duncan Blachford, who produced the excellent cover design, also merits special mention.

Cartographer Peter Johnson, for his expert preparation of the very instructive maps that conclude this volume, and for being so good as to accommodate the work within his busy schedule.

My official academic peer reviewers, who gave of their own time to read and carefully assess my translator's introduction, as well as the academic peer reviewers of the book's historical content, all of whose words of praise and right-spirited criticism and helpful comments are deeply appreciated.

My unofficial reviewer Tamar Lewit, history of ideas lecturer and expert on the Roman world, for her meticulous and thoughtful reading of my translation and introduction, detailed comments, exuberant enthusiasm, wisdom and encouragement.

My unofficial reviewer Haizhi Luo (羅海智), literary critic, for his close reading of the translation and original Chinese text, and many helpful comments. I am also grateful for his official review of my Chinese footnotes, and willingness to give of his time freely in the midst of a doctorate to correspond with me on matters which are beyond the ken of most native Chinese speakers of my acquaintance.

My unofficial reviewer Elris Mendoza-Finch, English and art-history teacher, and my mother, for instilling in me from a young age an appreciation for the power and beauty of the written word, and for her many helpful comments on the manuscript, and advice.

My unofficial reviewer Malcolm Oakes, Senior Counsel and fellow aficionado of Chinese-Australian history, who like each of my unofficial reviewers gave freely of his time to read the translated novel and provided unique and useful feedback.

Kow Mei Kao (辜美高), former Professor of Chinese literature at the National University of Singapore, and expert on early overseas Chinese-language newspaper fiction, for his invaluable comments on genres and the novel's literary structure, and his enthusiasm.

Selia Tan (譚金花), Associate Professor in architecture and diaspora-district studies at Wuyi University, and expert on the architecture and history of the See Yip region, for her interest in the novel and for imparting much valuable local knowledge. Thanks are due too to her able assistant Zoe Huang (黃淑瑜) for her help in facilitating my and Michael Williams's tour of the See Yip region in December 2016.

The author's family, for their willingness to share their family history with us and the public, and their wholehearted support for the project.

Des Cowley and others at the State Library of Victoria, for facilitating access to the original copies of the *Chinese Times*, and for outstandingly obliging service.

Sarah Pickering, graphic designer, and Hilary Finch, artist, both of whom provided wonderful advice on design. And Jenny and Jessica Little for their advice on proposed cover designs.

Mei-Su Chen (陳美夙) for her pertinent observations from the perspective of an educated Mandarin speaker and reader.

Khuong Lai, information-technology whiz, for his generous assistance in moments of crisis.

林國奇 and 陳麗群 or Mr and Mrs Lam for their advice on the Teochew language.

Annemarie Levin for her advice on the Danish language.

Denis O'Riordan, veteran genealogical researcher, for advice which assisted in my historical researches.

Kazuya Kawasetsu (川節和哉) for his assistance in Japanese-language communications.

Colleagues, family—including my cousin Roger Vickery—friends and acquaintances for their support, interest and encouragement.

Most importantly, my wife Vivian Chan, who has for over three years worked tirelessly in the background, in order that I might be able to devote my time to the work of translation and the myriad tasks that attended the journey to publication. The project has consumed most of the precious hours left to us outside of our busy working lives. That it reached fruition can be credited in large part to her faith in my abilities, love and unfailing support.

Penultimately, in full cognizance and wilful transgression of the conventional proscription on the acknowledgment of quadrupeds,

I should like to register my debt of gratitude to the late Belle Finch, Pyrenean Mountain Dog, for her wisdom, care, and willingness to lend a sympathetic ear.

Last but not least, my teachers, in childhood and adulthood, from antiquity to the present, upon whom all my mistakes and deficiencies are no reflection.

Incidental to that final acknowledgement, I should like to invite readers to alert *The Poison of Polygamy* team to the presence of any errors, and to share their thoughts and knowledge on matters of relevance. Contact can be made by means of the following email address: thepoisonofpolygamy@gmail.com

The Translator,
April 2019.

Appendix I: Character Names and Connotations

Surnames, which come first in Chinese, are underlined.

黃尚康 <u>Wong</u> Sheung Hong (*wong˩ serng˧ hong˥*), protagonist and antihero: This character's given name belongs to the more subtle and subjective class of character names. The association seems to be with the first character 尚 *sheung*'s verbal sense of "to value/to attach importance to" and the second character 康 *hong*'s classical sense of "comfort", which yield the overall sense of "one who values comfort". Wong is a very common surname, translatable as "Brown" or "Yellow".

馬氏 <u>Ma</u> (*mar˧*), Wong Sheung Hong's virtuous wife: Ma is a common surname, which means "horse". In Chinese, the horse is a well-established allegorical symbol of the 臣 "subject". This fits with the traditional comparison of a wife and her husband to a subject and his prince, on which the author clearly draws within the novel.

吳壽世 <u>Ng</u> Shau Sai (*ng˩* as in "singing", *sow˧* ow as in how, *sigh-ee˧*), traditional physician: The given name 壽世 Shau Sai means "to bring longevity to the world", but the surname 吳 Ng is pronounced, in Cantonese and the See Yip language, like the word

---

A Note on Pronunciation

Approximations of the the names' pronunciations in modern standard Cantonese are given in parentheses:

- The Rs are not intended to be sounded (English speakers with non-rhotic accents may ignore this point).

- The horizontal bars in the tone letters ˥ ˦ ˧ ˨ ˩ indicate the pitch of pronunciation relative to the range of one's natural speaking voice: a high bar indicates a high pitch; a skewed bar indicates a pitch change from the pitch at left to the pitch at right. In Cantonese, tones make the difference between one word and another. (Essentially, the Cantonese tone is just English intonation playing a different role. A circumspect English "Yes?" and crossly repeated "Yes" could be marked ˦ and ˨ respectively.)

唔 "not", and thus the full name takes on the satirical sense of "does not bring longevity to the world".

黃賓南 **Wong Pan Nam** (*wong˨ bun˥ narm˨*), scholar and sojourner: This character's given name can be read to mean "one who spends time as a guest in the South", which is an obvious reference to his stay in Australia.

黃鵬程南 **Wong Pang Ching Nam** (*wong˨ pung˨ ts-heng˨ narm˨*), Wong Pan Nam's heroic cousin and Wong Sheung Hong's loyal mate:

- What is perhaps most important about this heroic character is the discovery that the author's father seems to have been the inspiration for him. The author's father appears to have been named 黃鵬德 "Wong Pang Ack", but to have gone by the name Wong Pang in English (sometimes given as the short form Wong Ah Pang), the Chinese characters of which are identical to those of Ching Nam's surname and given name. See the historical introduction for further discussion and detail on the real Wong Pang, and Appendix III for the names of businesses owned by the novel's Wong Pang that appear to be transparent references to businesses owned by the real Wong Pang.

- The character's given name, 鵬 Pang, is the name of a mythical bird thousands of miles in length, which is generally translated as the Chinese roc, and features in the eponymous work of the ancient Chinese philosopher 莊子 Chuang Tzǔ. The roc in *Chuang Tzǔ* symbolises a great being with lofty aspirations that flies south from the sea at the northern end of the world to the ocean at its south, and is contrasted with lesser more terrestrial creatures, which are not only physically smaller and shorter lived but inhabit smaller worlds, both physically and spiritually.

- The courtesy name 程南 Ching Nam (see the end of this appendix for an explanation of courtesy names) literally means "journey south", and hence ties in with the story of the Chinese roc. The connection between that ancient allegory and the "Southern Ocean" is also relevant, because the expression "Southern Ocean" (both the common term 南洋 and the archaic form 南溟/南冥 that appears in *Chuang Tzǔ*) was used in the author's day in the extended metonymic sense of "the lands of the southern ocean", in reference to Southeast Asia and Australia collectively.

- The second Chinese character of Wong Ching Nam's courtesy name, 南 Nam, is shared with his cousin Wong Pan Nam. It was common for members of the same generation within a family or clan to share a character in their names. 南 Nam would therefore appear to be these cousins' family or clan generation name.

佐治 **George**, "heroic" white hunter: This name was a standard Chinese transliteration (phonetic rendering) of the English name George, and has therefore been given in its original form in translation. For speakers of Cantonese and the See Yip language, it was and still is an archetypal English name. I.e. the hunter is a Tom, Dick, or Harry.

陳亮 <u>Chan</u> Leung (*chun˩ lerng˩*), miner and market gardener: Chan is a common surname, and Leung is a given name with a number of positive connotations, such as brightness, enlightenment, sincerity and fidelity. Chan Leung also happens to have been the name of a famous Sung-dynasty intellectual, who argued for such things as modernisation, militarisation and nationalist resistance against a foreign foe. He was a thinker who appealed to members of Japan's Meiji Restoration and Australia's late-Qing reformist movement. It seems probable that the author knew who he was, and therefore possible that he was the inspiration for this character's name. The real Chan Leung took his given name Leung, which can also be written "Liang", later in life after a man he idolised, the great strategist and statesman of China's Three Kingdoms period the steadfast 諸葛亮 M°. Chu-ko Liang (M^M. *Zhūgě Liàng*). It is possible that the author was also—or exclusively—referencing Chu-ko Liang in his choice of the given name Leung.

俏喜 **Tsiu Hei** (*tsee-oo˧ hay˩*), concubine: The first character, 俏 Tsiu, means "pretty of face". The second, 喜 Hei, is a stative verb (a type of word similar to an adjective) that means "to be in a state in which joy is given expression". It can therefore be translated as "happy", "merry" and "pleased". As a noun, it might be given as "felicity". It also has the sense of a 喜事 felicitous event, especially with reference to marriage. And it can function as a verb with the sense of "to be fond of" or "to induce fondness or felicity". For the Chinese reader, these additive associations are not necessarily as superficially pleasant as they might seem; for example, the first character's sense of prettiness of face brings a well-known utterance of Confucius's to mind: 巧言令色鮮矣仁 "Rarely are those fine of face and clever of speech full of the milk of human kindness."

爽德 **Song Tak** (*song⌐ duck⌐*), philanderer: This given name connotes dissoluteness, its second character 德 Tak meaning "virtue" and its first, 爽 Song, indicating "loss", "looseness" or "deviation". The author may have coined the name himself, or have taken it from a line in a classical text, there being at least two classical texts in which the characters appear together with the sense of "loss of virtue": the 國語 Discourses of the States and 尚書 *"The Writings of Yore"*.

練娘 **Lin Neung** (*lin⌐ nerng⌐*), canny bridal chaperone: This name implies that the character is a 練達人情之婦女 "woman who is world-wise", i.e. one who has a strong understanding of human nature, acquired through thorough experience.

周遂卿 <u>**Chau**</u> **Sui Hing** (*tsow⌐* "ow" as in how, *so-oo⌐* "oo" as in loom, *heng⌐*), educated and righteous opponent of polygamy: In Cantonese and the See Yip language, this character's name is pronounced identically to the phrase 周遂興 "Chau subsequently flourished". The sense to which the author was alluding would therefore appear to be that once dynastic founder (the) Duke (of) Chou had framed the rites of marriage, the Chou dynasty (Chau in Cantonese) flourished, i.e. 周公製禮有周遂興. Refer to footnote 366 for further explanation, with respect to another reference within the novel to the legend of (the) Duke (of) Chou's framing of the rites of marriage.

黃榮光 **Wong Wing Kwong** (*wong*꜖ 　*weng*꜖ 　*gwong*꜒), Wong Sheung Hong's proxy: This character's given name is formed from the Chinese word "glory" with its characters 光 *kwong* and 榮 *wing* in reverse order. This is the equivalent of spelling a word backwards in English, and would appear to constitute an intentional pun on the inglorious role which he plays.

黃金牛 **Wong Kam Ngau** (*wong*꜖ 　*gum*꜒ 　*ng-ow*꜖: "ng" as in singing, "ow" as in cow), Wong Sheung Hong's adopted son: 金牛 "Kam Ngau" translates directly as "Metal/Gold(en) Ox". The author might have been implying with this name that the boy was born in the Chinese year of the metal/golden ox (the second of the sexagenary cycle), which in the period in question would have been the one that started in early 1865 and ended in early 1866.

李氏 **Lee** (the modern standard pronunciation is *lay*꜖), Wong Kam Ngau's wife: Lee is a common surname, and means "plum". Just as steadfast and flexible people might be referred to in English as "oaks" and "reeds", so too can certain plant names be used in Chinese to denote people with defining qualities. The plum is one example, and the connotations which appear relevant here are those of virtue and beauty.

GIVEN AND COURTESY NAMES

In traditional Chinese culture, there are taboos around the 名 given names of adults (both men and women). Another class of name called a (表)字—which is most often translated as "courtesy name", "style name" or "style"—is used in place of the given name when the taboo is being observed. There is generally a direct semantic or literary relationship between the courtesy name and the given name. They might, for example, be synonymous or antonymous, or the courtesy name might serve to clarify the intended meaning of the given name. A full exposition is not possible here, but the following real examples may help illustrate some of the types of connections: (1) Given name 全 "full" and courtesy name 景完 "great completeness". (2) Female given name 蕙 "cymbidium orchid with multiple blooms per stem": courtesy name 若蘭 "thou (first character) + cymbidium orchid with single bloom per stem (second character)", secondary sense: "like cymbidium orchid with single bloom per stem". This is an example of a common form of courtesy name in which a character semantically related to the given name is combined with a pronoun or term of address (such as 君, 子, 公, 臣, 伯 or 之). (3) Given name 蠆 "scorpion"; courtesy name 子尾 "thou/sir + tail". (4) Given name 鼎 "cauldron"; courtesy name 子九 "thou/sir + nine". The relationship played on is that nine enormous cauldrons, which were a symbol of political power, are said to have been cast in the 夏 M°. Hsia (Mᴹ. *Xià*)[1] dynasty to symbolise rule over the nine administrative regions (州) into which China was then divided. (5) Given name 念孫 "consider grandchildren": antonymous courtesy name 懷祖 "think with affection of ancestors". Ching Nam's given and courtesy names are a typical example, and the connection between them would not have been lost on the author's intended audience. Nowadays, however, courtesy names have been largely dispensed with, and even the concept of them is poorly understood, with the result that people, including academics, may sometimes mistake given names for courtesy names or fail to recognise when the two belong to the same individual. The issue is complicated by the fact that the connection between them is often formed through classical literary or historical allusion, and may therefore escape the notice of modern speakers unfamiliar with Chinese history and classical literature.

---

1 See Appendix II for the key to the symbols used with romanisations.

Appendix II: The Romanisations Used in the Translation and the Footnotes

Chinese characters are pronounced differently in different languages and dialects. Therefore, when a Chinese character is transliterated into English, a choice must be made as to which pronunciation to give it. A choice must also be made as to which spelling to use. This publication does not adopt the standard approach of giving all romanisations according to one or another romanisation system for northern Mandarin, but rather injects a dose of the spice of life by representing a number of Chinese languages in its romanisations, and employing both old and modern romanisation systems. The intent is not to confound readers or introduce inconsistency, but to better reflect the style of the novel and the heterogeneousness of the language family or "superlanguage" that is Chinese.

IN THE TRANSLATION

The approach taken is to use spellings dating from the time of the novel that reflect older standard-Cantonese pronunciation, except:

- Where there is a recorded spelling for the native pronunciation of the name concerned, which dates from the time of the novel or earlier (e.g. 新寧 Llin Nen).
- Where there is a romanisation that was already widely established in English at the time the novel was written (e.g. 廣東 Kwang Tung, 香港 Hong Kong). In cases where there were several established romanisations in common use, I have generally opted for what appeared to be the one most preferred in Australia.
- Where the name concerned is from Chinese literature or history, in which case the Wade-Giles romanisation, which reflects the pronunciation in northern Mandarin, is used (e.g. 陳仲子 Ch´ên Chung Tzŭ).

The primary aims of this approach are:

- To avoid the use of anachronistic spellings, such as ones based on Mandarin Pinyin romanisation, which, while in many ways superior to the older Wade-Giles romanisation, would look out of place in an early twentieth-century novel.
- To avoid speculative romanisations where contemporaneous native pronunciations are not definitely known.
- To accord due respect to native See Yip pronunciations, by using romanisations that reflect them, or, where such romanisations do not exist or cannot be ascertained, by using Cantonese romanisations, which are the closest practical alternative.
- To use, in the case of names from Chinese literature, a similar style of spelling to that of most nineteenth- and early twentieth-century English translations.

In accordance with the general preference outside of linguistic contexts, tone numbers are not given for the Wade-Giles romanisations, e.g. "Ch´ên Chung Tzŭ" is given as such, not as "Ch´ên² Chung⁴ Tzŭ³".

Transliterations are not used where there exist alternative English names or anglicisations that were established at the time the novel was written (e.g. Mencius, Confucius, Canton).

IN THE FOOTNOTES

In addition to the older romanisations used in the text of the translation for Cantonese, the See Yip language and Mandarin, the footnotes employ the modern Pinyin romanisation system for Mandarin and Yale romanisation system for Cantonese. The following abbreviations serve to indicate which style of romanisation is being used:

C°. An **older** style of romanisation reflective of **Cantonese** pronunciation that is still in common use in Hong Kong.

C^M. The **modern** Yale romanisation system for **Cantonese**.

S. A romanisation reflective of old or modern **See Yip** pronunciation.

M°. The **old** Wade-Giles romanisation system for northern **Mandarin**, without tone numbers.

M^M. The **modern** Pinyin romanisation system for northern **Mandarin**.

O. Romanisations based on **other** Chinese languages, and non-standard romanisations.

These abbreviations are:

- not repeated in a footnote when the romanisation style remains unchanged;
- not to be taken to count as a change to a footnote's romanisation style when they appear in parentheses, e.g. the romanisation that follows "石崇 M°. *Shih Ch'ung* (M^M. Shí Chóng)" should be taken to be in the M°. style unless otherwise specified;

- only used to introduce the first instance of any particular romanisation within a footnote;
- used before text in quotation marks for the romanisations that appear within them;
- not used with the novel's character and business names;
- not used with established romanisations, e.g. Taiping Rebellion, Sheung Wan, Kwang Tung.

The choice of romanisation depends on the context, but in general:

- Mandarin Pinyin is provided for modern place names, because it is the romanisation scheme most often used on modern maps and will therefore facilitate referral.
- Wade-Giles Mandarin romanisation is used for names from Chinese history and literature, and the names of dynasties, an approach which accords with the use of Wade-Giles romanisation in the translation.

Appendix III: Business Names

See Appendix I for guidance on the pronunciations shown in parentheses.

CHINA

怡隆 Yee Loong (*ee↘ loong↘*), Pak Hap, See Yip, Kwang Tung, China, Parts 28 and 51.

HONG KONG

均祥興 Kwan Cheung Hing (*gwun˥ ts-herng↘ heng˥*), Hong Kong, Part 24.

廣榮金山莊 The Kwong Wing Goldfield Agency (*gwong˧ weng↘*), Sheung Wan, Hong Kong, Part 9.

MELBOURNE

新瑞勝 San Sui Shing (*sun˥ so-oo˧* "oo" as in loom *seng˧*), Melbourne, Australia, Part 29. This business name would appear to be a play on the real business name 新遂盛, which is pronounced almost identically in Cantonese and the See Yip language (the

only difference being the tone of the final character, which is pronounced *seng˩* in Cantonese). The real business was known in
English as "Slin Suey Sheng", "Sin Suey Sheng" and "Sun Suey
Shing", the first of which clearly reflects See Yip pronunciation.
It was located at 86 Little Bourke Street East (which became 191
Little Bourke Street after a renumbering in 1888), and owned or
part-owned by the author's father, whom historical research
reveals to be the inspiration for the novel's hero Ching Nam: see
the first dot point on Ching Nam in Appendix I and the historical introduction. (A business of the same name was later located
a few doors down at 181 Little Bourke Street. Its connection with
the former is yet to be established.)

新同源 San Tung Yuen (*sun˩ toong˩ yoon˩*), Melbourne, Australia,
Part 22.

新源勝 San Yuen Shing (*sun˩ yoon˩ seng˩*), Little Bourke Street,
Melbourne, Australia, Part 29. This business name would appear to
be a play on the real business name 新源盛, which is pronounced
almost identically in Cantonese and the See Yip language (the difference is the same as for San Sui Shing). The real business was
known in English as "Sun Goon Shing", a romanisation reflective
of See Yip pronunciation. It was located at 73 Little Bourke Street
East (which became 198 Little Bourke Street after the 1888 renumbering), and part-owned by the author's father.

德元 Tak Yuen (*duck˩ yoon˩*), Melbourne, Australia, Parts 29, 35,
45 & 46. This business name would appear to be a play on the real
business name 德源, which is pronounced identically. The real
business seems to have been a furniture polishing operation
known in English as "Ack Goon", a romanisation reflective of See
Yip pronunciation. It was located at 125 Little Bourke Street East
(which became 118 Little Bourke Street after the 1888

renumbering), Melbourne, and relocated in 1883 to the rear of 51–55 Little Bourke East (which became 282–288 Little Bourke Street after the 1888 renumbering), after meeting with financial troubles in 1882.

The locations of the real Slin Suey Sheng, Sun Goon Shing and Ack Goon are marked on the map of Melbourne's Chinese precinct.

Appendix IV: The Newspaper Business and Chinese Australians

Mei-fen Kuo

The birth of Chinese-language journalism and literature in Australia can be traced to the late nineteenth century, some four or five decades after Chinese immigrants first arrived in significant numbers as indentured labourers in the 1840s. This flourishing of Chinese-Australian newspapers began as Chinese communities diminished on the goldfields but emerged as significant players in market gardening, fruit and vegetable stores, carpentry and general import-export businesses, supporting an increasingly urban and politically engaged Chinese-Australian population in the growing economies of Sydney and Melbourne.

In the wake of the gold rush and mining boom of the mid-nineteenth century, the largely male Chinese population of Australia declined from 38,077 in 1891, to 33,165 in 1901, and to 25,772 in 1911.[1] However, as the Australian colonies grew and developed in the last two decades of the nineteenth century, the concentration of Chinese in its major cities, especially in Sydney and Melbourne, increased between two and threefold,

---

1   See *Official Year Book of New South Wales*, 1921 (Sydney: Government Printer, 1922), p. 122.

as people, both Chinese and non-Chinese, moved from rural to urban areas. Sydney's commercial development and social transformation in the 1890s saw Chinese immigrants seeking forms of enterprise better suited to the new environment, including market gardening, storekeeping, and furniture making and this contributed to a large and growing readership among the increasingly numerous Chinese market gardeners and storekeepers.

By the end of the nineteenth century, Chinese newspapers had been circulating in Hong Kong and Canton for several decades and Chinese-Australians would have been familiar with them as conveyers of news and shipping details. In the 1890s, Chinese-Australian journalists and merchants joined Chinese publishers in Hong Kong, Southeast Asia, North America and Honolulu to establish local Australian newspapers to join the network of Chinese-language newspapers across the Chinese diaspora.

The earliest Chinese-language newspaper in Australia had in fact been established on the Victorian goldfields in the 1850s. This was the bilingual Chinese *Advertiser* (later the *English and Chinese Advertiser*; its Chinese titles were 唐人新文紙 *Tangren Xinwenzhi*, 番唐人新文紙 *Fan-Tangren Xinwenzhi* and 英唐招帖 *Ying-Tang Zhaotie*). However, its content was largely confined to advertisements, and it was short-lived.[2] The first Chinese-language newspaper with a national Australian circulation, the *Chinese Australian Herald* 廣益華報 *Guangyi Huabao* (1894–1923) was launched in Sydney in 1894. The second, the *Tung Wah News* 東華時報 *Donghua Xinbao* (1898–1902), commenced publication

---

2   The *Chinese Advertiser* was published weekly by Robert Bell in Ballarat from 1856 to 1858(?). It had a circulation of 400 and its primary aim was to carry advertisements and inform the Chinese community in the goldfields about government regulations.

in 1898, also in Sydney, and from 1902 continued as the *Tung Wah Times* 東華報 *Donghuabao* (1902–36).

The Poison of Polygamy was serialised for publication in the first Chinese newspaper to appear in Melbourne, the *Chinese Times* (愛國報 *Aiguobao*, 1902–1905, later the 警東新報 *Jingdong Xinbao*, 1905–14, 平報 *Pingbao*, 1917, and 民報 *Minbao*, 1919–22), which was first published in 1902 before moving to Sydney in 1920 where it continued until 1949. Sydney was also home to the *Chinese Republic* News (民國報 *Minguobao* 1914–37) and the *Chinese World News* (公報 *Gongbao* 1922–5?), and the *Chinese Australian Herald* (廣益華報 1894–1923).[3] It is important to note that the Chinese press was the only foreign-language press in Sydney to publish without interruption over three decades from the 1890s to the 1920s.[4]

Judging from the growth of a large and vibrant local Chinese-language newspaper industry at the time, we can infer the existence of a relatively large readership pool and a high rate of literacy among Chinese Australians.[5] And colonial records confirm this. In 1891, before the first of these Chinese-language newspapers was published in Sydney, the New South Wales colonial government carried out a population census which indicated a high level of Chinese-language literacy among Sydney Chinese: while only 9% could read English, of the 9,259 Chinese residents

---

3   There was, in addition, a short-lived publication that appeared in 1923, the *Chinese Weekly Press*. See Archives of the Chinese Consul-General of the Kuo Min Tang Society of Melbourne, no. 522-0229. Another proposal to publish a Chinese-language newspaper in Sydney in 1927 was unsuccessful. See '3 Chinese newspaper workers for establishing a new Chinese newspaper in Sydney', National Archives of Australia, SP42/1, C1927/11114.

4   Mei-fen Kuo, *Making Chinese Australia: Urban Elites, Newspapers and the Formation of Chinese Australian Identity*, 1892–1912 (Clayton, Victoria: Monash University Publishing, 2013).

5   Kuo, *Making Chinese Australia*, p. 53.

surveyed, 65% were able to read and write Chinese. In comparison, among the Chinese population of Hawaii, at the time the largest Chinese community in the Pacific region, only 2% and 40% respectively were literate in English and Chinese at around the same time.[6]

Given the overall size of the population, however, circulation of individual Chinese newspaper titles was not large. Records show that in 1897 the *Chinese Australian Herald* had a respectable circulation of 800 copies per issue, distributed through Chinese storekeepers around Australia and New Zealand.[7] By 1900 the *Chinese Australian Herald*'s circulation had expanded further to New Caledonia, Samoa, Fiji, Tahiti, Rarotonga, China, Java and the Philippines.[8] From 1906 onwards, the *Tung Wah Times* is said to have even circulated in North America and Mexico,[9] attracting advertising revenue from across the Pacific in California.[10] In 1925, the average circulation of another Chinese newspaper, Sydney's *Chinese Republic News* was stated to be 5,000 copies per week.[11]

The flow of news, commentaries and stories in the Chinese-language press allowed publishers and readers to engage in regular conversations across transnational networks stretching from Australia to New Zealand, North America, and Southeast Asia. These newspapers published items on community, local and

---

6   Kuo, *Making Chinese Australia*, p. 53.

7   State Records Authority of New South Wales (hereafter SRNSW), Colonial Secretary's correspondence, 5/6363, letter from the editor of the *Chinese Australian Herald*, 15 July 1897 (97/10712).

8   *Chinese Australian Herald*, 27 January 1900. Records of readers of the *Chinese Times* in Sydney also indicate that it circulated in the Pacific islands. See archives of the Chinese Nationalist Party of Australasia in Sydney, no. 523-01-296 and 523-01-299.

9   *Tung Wah Times*, 23 June 1906, p. 3 and 14 July 1906, p. 6.

10 *Tung Wah Times*, 22 September 1906, p. 6.

11 "Chinese Republican [Republic] News—Exemption for staff", National Archives of Australia, A433, 1947/2/6297/PART2.

Figure 13: The masthead of the *Chinese Times*. (State Library of Victoria)

international affairs, along with market information, photographs, shipping timetables, advertisements, public debates, travel dairies, poems, fiction and folk literature. It is also important to note that political differences dividing radical revolutionaries from more conservative constitutional reformers also found expression in partisan debates between Chinese newspapers in the early decades of the twentieth century.[12] These debates mattered not only for the communities that engaged in them but also for China itself, where the ideas and innovations of Chinese overseas were taken very seriously in political and social circles. The Manchu Qing government opposed domestic reformers and revolutionaries alike, banning their organisations, suppressing their publications, and sending their leaders into exile, where they harassed them from London to San Francisco. The Chinese diaspora, in turn, were a valuable resource for exiled reformers and revolutionaries wanting to change China. In this setting, Chinese-language newspapers published overseas, including those published in Australia, were valued not just for the forums they provided for political debate or discussion

12 On vibrant political debates among these newspapers see Kuo, *Making Chinese Australia*, Chapter 7.

of social reform at their sites of publication, but also for bringing these debates and ideas for reform back into China.

It was into this environment that the future author of *The Poison of Polygamy*, with its subtitle *A Social Novel*, arrived in Australia and worked as an editor of a re-launched Melbourne *Chinese Times*. To understand why Wong Shee Ping chose to write a novel at all, something of the history of Chinese fiction is required. The genre of the social novel first appeared in the fiction magazine *Xin Xiaoshuo* (新小說 *New Fiction*), launched by conservative reformer Liang Qichao 梁啟超 in 1902 during his political exile in Yokohama, Japan. *New Fiction* introduced different genres of fiction to its readership, ranging unevenly across political, historical, scientific, diplomatic, social, and detective novels, among others.[13] According to Liang, in order to educate the people of a nation and reshape their moral behaviour "we must have new fiction". Liang's literary nationalism influenced a literary movement known as the "revolution in fiction" (小說革命).[14] *The Poison of Polygamy* can be seen as a part of this literary movement.[15]

Liang Qichao himself had visited Australia between October 1900 and April 1901. Although only 28 years of age at the time, his thoughts and ideas had already reached a new generation of intellectuals through his published writings. His hosts among the Chinese merchants in Sydney had launched the *Tung Wah News* in 1898 as an official newspaper of the reformist Chinese Empire Reform Association (*Bǎohuánghuì*

---

13   Pingyuan Chen, *Xiaoshuoshi: Lilun yu shijian* (小說史:理論與實踐, "The History of Fiction: Theory and Practice"), (Beijing: Beijing University Press, 2010), pp. 1–22. The Translator's Introduction discusses this topic from a different angle.

14   This slogan was presented in 1902 by Liang Qichao in his *Lun Xiaoshuo yu Qunzhi zhi Guanxi* (論小說與群治之關係, "A Discussion of the Relation between the Fiction and Politics by the People"). See Liang Qichao, *Yinbingshi Heji* (飲冰室合集 "The Collected Works of Liang Qichao") vol. 4 (Beijing: Zhonghua shu ju, 2015), p. 6.

15   Xiaobing Tang, *Chinese Modern: The Heroic and the Quotidian* (Durham, N.C.: Duke University Press, 2000), p. 13.

保皇會), an organisation that aimed to support and propagate the movement for reform (not revolution) in government. A Christian editor of the *Tung Wah News*, Thomas Chang Luke 鄭祿 (Zheng Lu), accompanied Liang on his tour of Melbourne. There Chang established Melbourne's first Chinese newspaper, the *Chinese Times*. His paper was especially concerned with the promotion of Chinese-Australian patriotism toward China and this led him to adopt a Chinese title for his paper which translates as *The Patriot* (*Aiguobao* 愛國報). Chang was a member of the Chinese Christian Union and found support for his newspaper among Melbourne's Chinese merchants.[16] Early in his editorship, Chang tried to attract a wider readership in Melbourne but found that the provincialism and native-place identity of Melbourne's Chinese communities hindered their ability to embrace a Chinese national identity or a reformist agenda on the scale promoted among Chinese merchants and labourers in Sydney.

Over time Chang's Melbourne *Chinese Times* strayed from its reformist position and began to introduce readers to a number of revolutionary publications from mainland China and other diaspora communities. Between January and April 1904 the newspaper published a popular revolutionary pamphlet, The Revolutionary Army (*Gemingjun* 革命軍), which was penned by radical nationalist Zou Rong (鄒容 1885–1905). Written in a lucid style, this important pamphlet expounded revolutionary and anti-Manchu ideas in China and Southeast Asia, and also made reference to the suffering of overseas Chinese, including Chinese in Australia, allegedly resulting from the weakness of the Manchu government in defending Chinese overseas.

To attract more readers to its increasingly revolutionary position, the *Chinese Times* launched a reading-club project and revised the style of language used in its columns. In 1904, Chang Luke introduced the

---

16   *Weekly News*, 25 April 1903, p. 2.

reading club, stocked with revolutionary periodicals and books,[17] and the *Chinese Times* also held public lectures on patriotism for an initial group of about twenty to thirty sympathisers, a number which grew over time.[18] The *Chinese Times* developed a more colloquial written style to attract readers to its revolutionary cause. It published drag-on-boat songs (*longzhouge* 龍舟歌),[19] a rustic form of folk song, traditionally sung by men, which were used to promote republican anti-Manchu sentiment among lower-class Chinese, much as Chinese revolutionaries were doing in China around the same time. With these initiatives, Chang actively transformed his newspaper into a vehicle for popular moral and political education, and for cultivating identification with China and a sense of national responsibility towards that country among Chinese communities in Melbourne.

In addition to publishing popular revolutionary pamphlets and folk songs, and establishing a reading club, the *Chinese Times* also established new civic organisations. In 1904 it founded the New Citizen Enlightenment Association 新民啟智會, which had a membership of between 500 and 600 members by 1905.[20] This Melbourne organisation was the earliest Chinese association with revolutionary sympathies to be founded in Australia, but the level of support for anti-Manchu nationalism was insufficient to maintain the *Chinese Times* as a viable newspaper and Chang Luke was forced to sell in 1905. The paper was then relaunched, under a new Chinese name, with the support of a Chinese nationalist alliance that included former editors of the *Chinese Times*, members of Christian churches, and employee unions in Melbourne. After

---

17   *Chinese Times*, 25 May 1904, p. 3.
18   *Chinese Times*, 12 October 1904, p. 2.
19   *Chinese Times*, 18 May 1904, p. 2.
20   Zhiming Chen, *Zhongguo Guomindang Aozhou dangwu fazhan shikuang* (中國國民黨澳洲黨務發展實況, "Historical Outline of the Development of Kuo Min Tang Party Affairs in Australasia") (Sydney: Australasian Branch of Chinese Nationalist Party, 1935), p. 163.

Chang's later departure, Lew Goot Chee and Wong Yau Kung, also known as Wong Shee Ping, from China became managers and writers for the re-launched newspaper.[21] Lew Goot Chee was appointed general editor, while the other journalist and our author, Wong Shee Ping, began as a compositor but soon rose to editorial work and became sole editor on Lew Goot Chee's departure in mid-1914.[22] Under the new direction of Lew Goot Chee and Wong Shee Ping, the *Chinese Times* expanded its literary supplements and shifted to a populist, colloquial style suited to its mission of popular education. Under Wong Shee Ping's influence, the paper adopted a folk-oriented style, and published a range of humorous satires. The aim was to distinguish his paper from the rival reformist faction and attract more readers to learn about the ideas of the Chinese revolutionaries.[23] Despite this colloquial push *The Poison of Polygamy* itself, as has been noted, was written in the older form of Literary Chinese.[24]

The focus on women that is to be found in *The Poison of Polygamy* has also been noted. During the early part of the 20th century virtually all Chinese-Australian newspapers adopted the position that marriage should be free, that men and women should be equal,[25] and that in families the needs of wives and children should be given first consideration.[26] They also covered the activities and speeches made by "new Chinese women" around the world. The *Chinese Times* for example began to advertise progressive women's books and magazines bearing titles such as "Legends of National Heroines", and to offer a magazine published under the banner

---

21 *Tung Wah Times*, 10 January, 1920, p. 2 & Yong, The New Gold Mountain, p. 129.
22 For more details on the author see Wong Shee Ping biographical note.
23 *Chinese Times*, 25 September, 9–10 and 18 December 1909, p. 9.
24 See the Translator's Introduction.
25 For example, *Chinese Australian Herald*, 3 Feb 1906, pp. 2–3; Tung Wah Times, 27 July 1907, p. 7.
26 *Chinese Australian Herald*, 12 Jan 1907; Tung Wah Times, 27 July 1907, p. 7.

"Women's Education News" for loan to readers.[27] Also starting in 1904, the *Tung Wah Times* advertised the sale of books and magazines on "women's topics" such as women scientists who brought about social reform and promoted public hygiene.[28] Through discussion of women's roles and women's rights, Australia's Chinese-language newspapers gradually helped redefine the family as a social arena in which a woman enjoyed a degree of flexibility to assert her individual rights, and was regarded as the equal of her male partner. Wong Shee Ping no doubt intended *The Poison of Polygamy* as a tool to further such ideas.

Since its first publication in serial form between 1909 and 1910, *The Poison of Polygamy* has not been republished or until recently even considered as part of Australian literary history. This is partly due to the fact that the significance and development of Chinese-Australian newspapers was little appreciated until the 1970s and not well understood even then. In their pioneering study of the foreign-language press in Australia, Miriam Gilson and Jerzy Zubrzycki excluded the Chinese press from their sample because they considered its history as markedly distinct from that of European-language newspapers.[29] The lack of attention paid to Chinese journalism reflected a general lack of interest in the historiography toward the Chinese immigrants in Australia before the 1980s.[30]

---

27   *Chinese Times*, 25 May 1904, p. 4.
28   *Tung Wah Times*, 22 October 1904, supplement.
29   Miriam Gilson and Jerzy Zubrzycki, *The Foreign-Language Press in Australia, 1848–1964* (Canberra: Australian National University Press, 1967), p. vi.
30   On the historiography of Chinese immigrants in Australia see J. W. Cushman, "A 'colonial casualty': The Chinese Community in Australian Historiography", *Asian Studies Association of Australia Review* 7, no. 3 (1984): pp. 100–102; Keir Reeves and T. Khoo, "Dragon Tails: Re-interpreting Chinese Australian History", *Australian Historical Studies* 42, no. 1 (2001): pp. 3–8. Also, John Fitzgerald, *Big White Lie: Chinese Australians in White Australia* (Sydney: UNSW Press, 2007), p. 23.

In the 1970s, C.F. Yong made extensive use of Chinese-language newspapers in his pioneering study on Chinese Australian history, *New Gold Mountain*.[31] Poon Yuk Lan offers another reading of Chinese-language newspapers in a later study of the Chinese community.[32] Both Yong and Poon claim that the appearance of the Chinese press served to harden racial boundaries separating Chinese and European Australians. They tended to downplay the role of newspapers in pursuing legitimate community objectives or advocating for the rights their editors felt were due to community members as Australian residents and British subjects.

In recent decades, the advent of diaspora perspectives in transnational history has offered further insights into the role of Chinese-language newspapers as social agents for community building locally and internationally.[33] The growth of the Chinese press in the years leading up to Federation and the early years of the Commonwealth of Australia was not simply a reaction to racism. In this respect, newspapers can enhance our understanding of Chinese-Australian history—mundanely through the historical

---

31 Yong, *The New Gold Mountain*.

32 Poon Yuk Lan, "The Two-Way Mirror: Contemporary Issues as Seen through the Eyes of the Chinese Language Press, 1901–1911" (BA Honours thesis, University of Sydney, 1986).

33 Fitzgerald, *Big White Lie* (2007); Kate Bagnall, "Rewriting the History of Chinese Families in Nineteenth-century Australia", *Australian Historical Studies* 42, no. 1, March 2011, pp. 62–77; Kuo, *Making Chinese Australia*: (2013); 楊永安, Yang, Yong'an, *Changyexingxi: Aodaliya Huarenshi 1860–1940* (長夜星稀澳大利亞華人史, "Lonely Star on Lonesome Nights: A History of the Chinese Australians 1860–1940") (Xianggang: Shangwu yinshuguan, 2014); and Michael Williams, *Returning Home with Glory: Chinese Villagers around the Pacific*, 1849 to 1949 (Hong Kong: Hong Kong University Press, 2018). All of these scholars have used Chinese newspapers as sources, but it was not until Kuo's *Making Chinese Australia*, where *The Poison of Polygamy* itself came to light once again, that the full significance of this history was fully demonstrated.

archives they supply, more profoundly through the windows they offer on community formation and on awareness of the political, social and economic issues of the day. Australia's local Chinese-language press offers a rich resource for exploring all aspects of the life of Australia's early Chinese communities.[34] In this setting, the publication of *The Poison of Polygamy* looms as an outstanding but not altogether unusual illustration of the cultural and social sophistication of Chinese-Australian communities around the time of Federation in Australia, and of their growing anti-Manchu nationalism coupled with a desire to modernise China on all levels.

---

34   A good beginning to this is Haizhi Luo, "Towards a Modern Diasporic Literary Tradition: The Evolution of Australian Chinese Language Fiction from 1894 to 1912" (Masters thesis, University of New South Wales, 2017).

Appendix V: Place Names

THE CHINESE DIASPORA DISTRICT OF SEE YIP

四邑 See Yip is the name of a region that lies to the southwest of Canton. The underlying sense of the name is "the four cities" or "the four districts". (The place name Tripoli and its underlying sense of "the three cities" makes for a good comparison.) The four districts from which the region is constituted and its name derived are: (1) the northerly district of 開平 c°. Hoi Ping, (2) the southerly district of 新寧 s. Llin Nen c°. Sun Ning (which was renamed 臺山 s. Hoi San c°. Toi Shan ᴹᴹ. *Táishān* in 1914), (3) the easterly district of 新會 c°. Sun Wui ᴹᴹ. *Xīnhuì*, and (4) the westerly district of 恩平 c°. Yan Ping ᴹᴹ. *Ēnpíng*. Only the first two, Hoi Ping and Llin Nen, which occupy the region's geographical centre, feature in the novel.

It should be noted that, while the geographical limits of the See Yip region were defined by the outer borders of a grouping of four administrative districts, the region itself never had an official existence as an administrative unit. Essentially, it was and still is a geographical region, distinguished by a distinct language and culture to which it is home. The See Yip region is the place from which most of the Australian colony of Victoria's Chinese residents hailed. (That quintessentially Antipodean snack the *dim sim* accordingly derives its name from the See Yip language.)

The district of 新寧 **Llin Nen** was the last of See Yip's four districts to come into existence. The name translates literally as "Newpeace" or "Newcalm", reflecting its history as a mountainous backwater that was established as a district in the Ming dynasty with the intent of quelling the bandits that inhabited its hinterland and the pirates that plagued the sea to its south. It has since risen to economic prominence and usurped in the eyes of many the position that See Yip's oldest district of Sun Wui, from which it was originally excised, formerly held as the See Yip region's premiere city. The economic contribution made by the many citizens who went overseas during the nineteenth century assisted the district in its rise.

During the timeframe of the novel, Llin Nen consisted of six 都 "subdistricts". The northern three were collectively referred to as the 上三都 "upper three", the southern as the 下三都 "lower three". The expressions 上新寧 "Upper Llin Nen" and 下新寧 "Lower Llin Nen" were also used.

Upper Llin Nen consisted of the little 文章都 c°. Man Cheung and 平康都 Ping Hong subdistricts in the north and northwest tips respectively, and the larger 德行都 Tak Hang subdistrict, which covered the administrative capital and most of the north, and in the novel is home to the protagonist's village and villa, and the town of 白沙 Pak Sha.

Lower Llin Nen consisted of 潮居都 Chiu Kui subdistrict in the southeast, 矬峒都 Tso Tung subdistrict in the central south, and 海宴都 Hoi An subdistrict in the southwest.[1]

Administratively, the district of Llin Nen fell within 廣州府 the prefecture of Canton.

---

1   Much of the information in this appendix is based on Qing-dynasty district chorographies, which are freely available online. (E.g. 清道光三年開平縣志: https://ctext.org/library.pl?if=gb&res=90009; and 清道光十九年新寧縣志: https://archive.org/stream/sunning-county-chorography-1839-edition/)

Approximate Pronunciations (see Appendix I for guidance) and
Alternative Spellings

四邑　See Yip (this spelling reflects the local pronunciation see⊣, or thee⊣ "th" as in "thin", *yip*˥; the modern Cantonese pronunciation is say⊣ *yup*˥; the old Cantonese pronunciation is sir⊣ *yup*˥, usually spelled "Sze Yup"), A.K.A. M^M. *Sìyì*.

新寧　Llin Nen (this spelling reflects the local pronunciation *thin*⊣ *nen*⊣; the Cantonese pronunciation is *sun*˥ *neng*˩), A.K.A. M^M. *Xīnníng*, o. Sinning, c°. Sun Ning, and 寧邑 Ning Yup s. Nen Yip, meaning "Ning City".

開平　Hoi Ping (*hoy*˥ *peng*˩), s. Hoy Hen, M^M. *Kāipíng*.

荻海　Tik Hoi (*deck*⊣ without English's puff of air after the "ck" *hoy*˩), M^M. *Díhǎi*.

長沙　Cheung Sha (*cherng*˩ *sar*˥), M^M. *Chángshā*.

白沙　Pak Sha (*bark*⊣ without English's puff of air after the "ck" *sar*˥), M^M. *Báishā*.

百合　Pak Hap (*bark*⊣ without English's puff of air after the "ck" *hup*⊣; note that this "Pak" is pronounced with a different tone from the "Pak" in Pak Sha), M^M. *Bǎihé*.

朝陽里　Chiu Yeung Lee (*tsee-oo*˩ *yerng*˩ *lay*˩), M^M. *Cháoyánglǐ*.

上環　Sheung Wan (*serng*⊣ *warn*˩), M^M. *Shànghuán*.

開平 c°. **Hoi Ping** is the district from which the novel's Wong Ching Nam and Wong Pan Nam hailed. Today the district, while still largely rural, is officially a "city", and the name Hoi Ping is also ambiguously applied to the actual city that has been its administrative capital since 1952.

Hoi Ping's modern administrative capital is known colloquially as 三埠 c°. Sam Fau, which translates as "Three Towns", with reference to its three parts. Sam Fau straddles the confluence of the 潭江 M^M. *Tánjiāng*, its largest tributary the 蒼江 *Cāngjiāng*, and a third river, the 荻江 *Jiāojiāng*, which flows from the city of 臺山 *Táishān*. The island of 長沙 *Chángshā* cᵒ. Cheung Sha (literally "Long Sand") forms its oldest part, having reportedly been established in 1368 C.E. The next oldest part is 荻海 ᴹᴹ. *Díhǎi* cᵒ. Tik Hoi, reportedly established in 1851. Both Cheung Sha and Tik Hoi feature in Part 8. The city's third part, 新昌 ᴹᴹ. *Xīnchāng* cᵒ. San Cheung, is recorded to have been established in 1881, after the time referred to in Part 8. Tik Hoi and San Cheung, which were on the southern side of the *Tánjjiāng* river, were part of Llin Nen until 1949, when they were absorbed into Hoi Ping. The island of Cheung Sha, however, was part of Hoi Ping.

Like Llin Nen, the district of Hoi Ping was divided into 都 "subdistricts", of which there were five during the timeframe of the novel. The most northerly of these, 長靜都 cᵒ. Cheung Ching subdistrict, was home to Hoi Ping's erstwhile capital of 蒼城 ᴹᴹ. *Cāngchéng* cᵒ. Chong Shing.

Administratively, the district of Hoi Ping fell within 肇慶府 the prefecture of the city of Shiu Hing. (The cities of Shiu Hing and Canton were the eyes of 廣東省 Kwang Tung province—Shiu Hing its administrative centre, and Canton its commercial centre. It was for this reason that the early Jesuit missionaries Matteo Ricci (利瑪竇) and Michele Ruggieri (羅明堅) visited these cities when they came to China. In fact, it was during their sojourn in Shiu Hing that they created the first European-style map of the world in Chinese, and the first bilingual dictionary between a European language and Chinese—a Portuguese-Chinese dictionary.)[2]

白沙 **Pak Sha** (ᴹᴹ. *Báishā*) seems to have been the closest town to protagonist Wong Sheung Hong's village. The traditional physician

---

2   Angelo Cattaneo, "World Cartography in the Jesuit Mission in China: Cosmography, Theology, Pedagogy", in Artur K. Wardega (ed.), *Education for New Times: Revisiting Pedagogical Models in the Jesuit Tradition* (Macau: Macau Ricci Institute, 2014), pp. 71–86; Roderich Ptak, "The Sino-European Map (*Shanhai yudi quantu*) Encyclopaedia Sancai tuhui", in *The Perception of Maritime Space in Traditional Chinese Sources*, ed. Angela Schottenhammer and Roderich Ptak (Wiesbaden: Harrassowitz Verlag, 2006), pp. 191–211; J. Needham and

who treats his mother is based in the Pak Sha marketplace, which is also the location of Sheung Hong's opium den. Pak Sha is still a busy market town today (and part of M^M. *Táishān*).

The town of 百合 **Pak Hap** (M^M. *Bǎihé*) is the location of the Yee Loong shop that Ching Nam, Sheung Hong and their business partner Tam jointly own (cf. Parts §27 and 28). Pak Hap is on the western bank of the 潭江 *Tánjiāng* (the same river that later flows through the city of Sam Fau). Looking across to the other bank is the prospect of 百足山 "Centipede Hill" looming in the distance. The village of Chiu Yeung Lee, the town of Pak Sha, and Sheung Hong's village are on the other side. Centipede Hill features prominently at the end of the novel. Pak Hap fell within Hoi Ping's 平康都 Ping Hong subdistrict, which was immediately to the south of the aforementioned 長靜都 c°. Cheung Ching subdistrict.

朝陽里 Chiu Yeung Lee, which belonged to the same Hoi Ping subdistrict as Pak Hap, is the village at the foot of Centipede Hill which features at the end of the novel. It is still a village today.

The present-day 吊斗廟村 M^M. *Diàodǒumiàocūn* "Hanging-bucket-temple Village" near 赤水鎮 the town of *Chìshuǐ* may be the location of the "Peck-pot Temple" that features in the novel's final instalment.

THE AUSTRALIAN COLONY OF VICTORIA

Bendigo and **Ballarat** (the old Chinese names for these towns that are used in the novel are 品地高 and 孖嘮辣, or 孖辣 for short) are rural cities in what is now the state of Victoria that both began as goldfields. They had substantial populations of Chinese miners, and many residents today claim descent from them. Bendigo in

Wang Ling, "Mathematics and the Sciences of the Heavens and the Earth", *Science and Civilization in China*, Volume 3 (Cambridge: Cambridge University Press, 1959), p. 583; Michele Ruggieri and Matteo Ricci, *Dicionário Português-Chinês*, ed. John W. Witek (Lisbon: Biblioteca Nacional Portugal, 2001).

particular has an historic Easter Parade that has long featured a Chinese Dragon; the town is also host to the Golden Dragon Museum, and a Joss House that is a remnant of a goldrush-era Chinese settlement.

Melbourne (美利伴, 美利畔 and 美利彬 in the novel, though the meaningful transliteration 美利濱 eventually became the favoured form, until it was replaced by the current meaningless and ahistorical Mandarin transliteration) also flourished as a result of the gold rushes and had a substantial Chinese precinct that thrives today in much the same location as features in the novel. Emerald Hill, where the See Yup Temple that features in the novel still stands, was just outside of Melbourne when it was first established, but is now the inner suburb of South Melbourne (see Figure 6).

PLACES EN ROUTE BETWEEN SEE YIP AND VICTORIA

Sheung Wan, Hong Kong, is the location of the Kwong Wing Goldfield Agency that features in Part 9. Hong Kong also features in Parts 6, 7, 8, 21, 24, 28 and 46.

Singapore and **Port Darwin** (石叻 and 潑打運) also feature in Part 9. Port Darwin was established in the 1860s but was not a stopping place for steamers until after the Victorian goldrush period and closer to the author's own time. It had a large Chinese precinct; in fact in the late 1800s the majority of the population was Chinese. The town itself was known as Palmerston until officially changed to Darwin in 1911.

Guichen Bay (Robe) (古慎尾) in the colony of South Australia was the starting point for the trek into the neighbouring colony of Victoria, which was made to avoid Victoria's discriminatory £10 poll tax levied on Chinese arrivals. This trek has recently been commemorated in re-enactments. Sheung Hong's ship arrives in Guichen Bay (*gooch-en*) in Part 9.

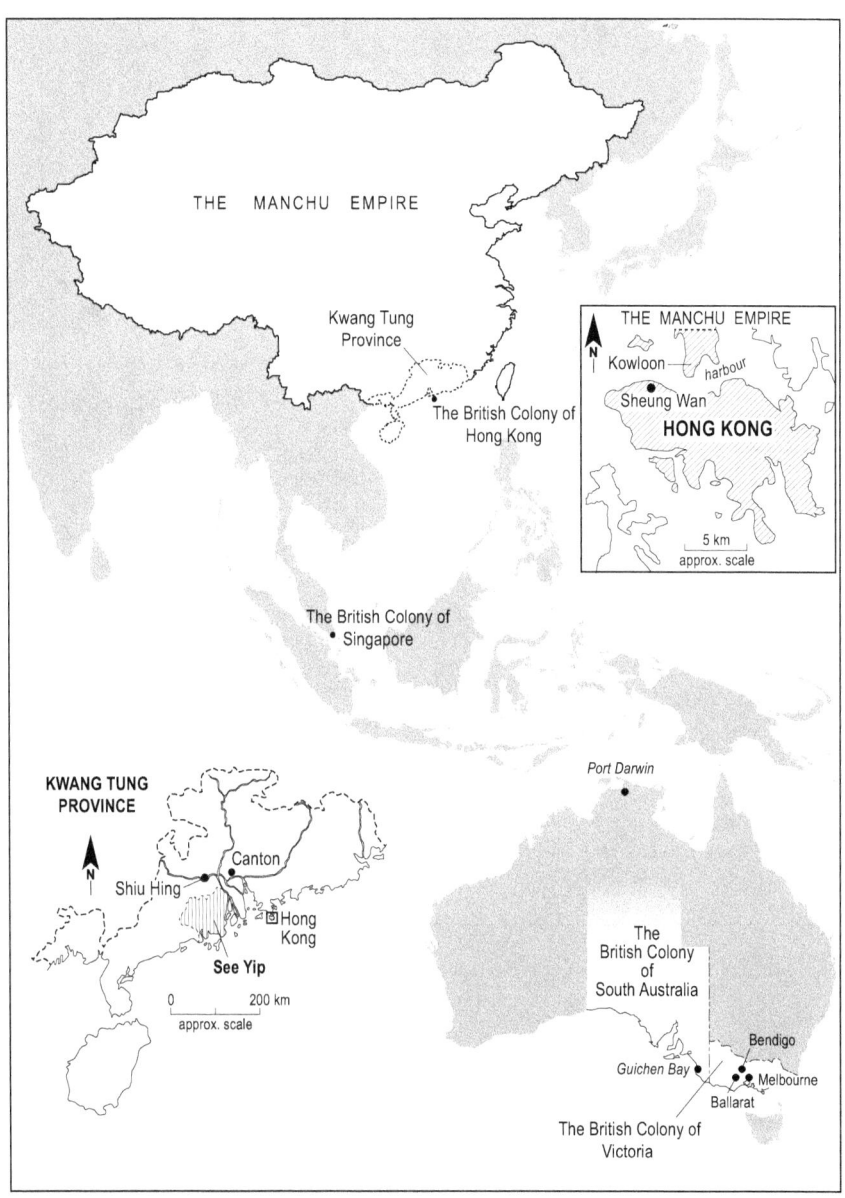

Map 1: Empires (the latter half of the 19th century).

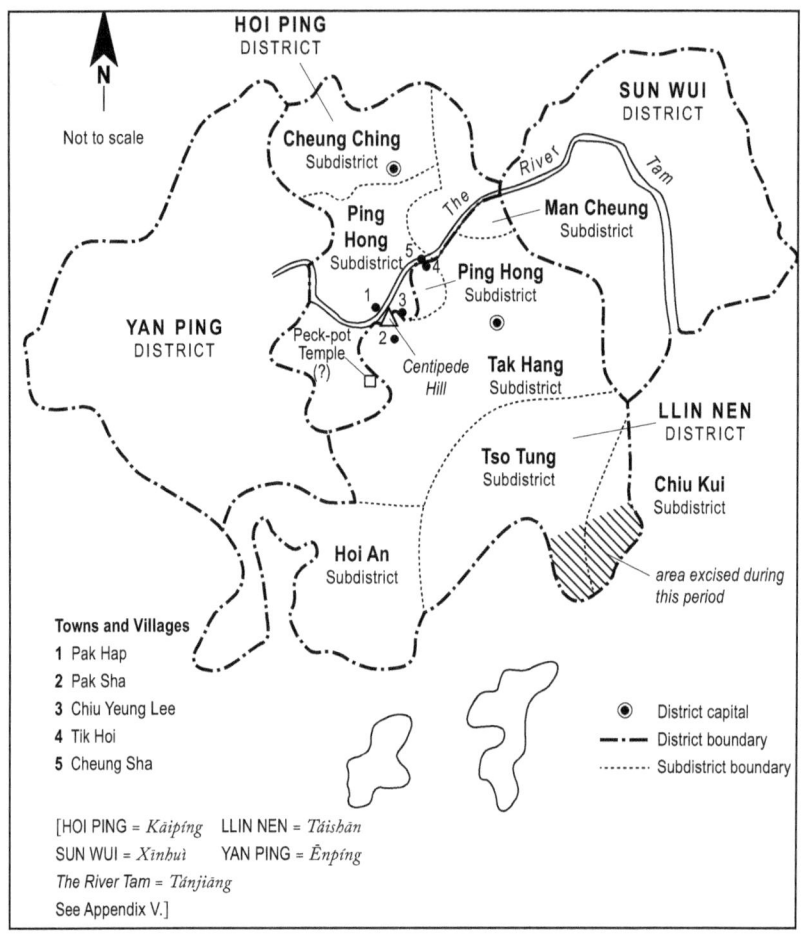

Map II: The See Yip Region in the timeframe of the novel.

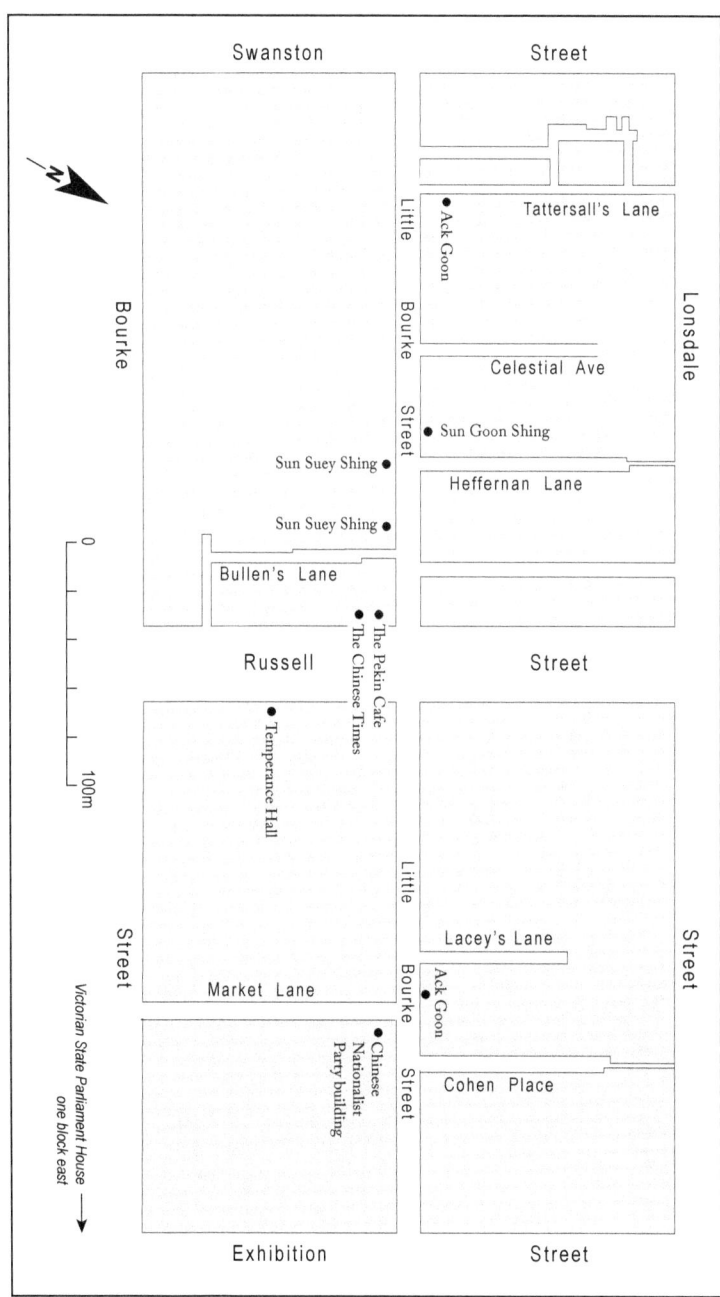

Map III: Melbourne's Chinese precinct.

About the Contributors

Ely Finch is a consultant translator and linguist who lives in Melbourne. He specialises in historical documents and inscriptions written in Literary (Classical) Chinese, Cantonese, and other southern Chinese languages. His works to date include private and published translations of poetry, letters, goldrush-era newspapers, account books, inscriptions and literature.

Mei-fen Kuo is a scholar of Chinese Australians from a diasporic perspective. Her *Making Chinese Australia: Urban Elites, Newspapers and the Formation of Chinese Australian Identity, 1892–1912* was shortlisted for the W.K. Hancock Prize and, with Judith Brett, she authored *Unlocking the History of the Australasian Kuo Min Tang, 1911–2013*. She was an ARC DECRA Fellow at the University of Queensland and is currently a visiting scholar at National Chengchi University under the MOFA Taiwan Fellowship.

Michael Williams graduated from Hong Kong University, is a scholar of Chinese-Australian history and a founding member of the Chinese-Australian Historical Society. Author of *Returning Home with Glory*, Michael has taught at Beijing Foreign Studies and Peking Universities and is currently an Adjunct Fellow at

Western Sydney University. His current research includes the Dictation Test, early Chinese Opera in Australia and a history of the Chinese in Australia.